CROWBONES

CROWBONES

THE WORLD OF THE OTHERS

ANNE BISHOP

ACE
NEW YORK

ACE
Published by Berkley
An imprint of Penguin Random House LLC
penguinrandomhouse.com

Library of Congress Cataloging-in-Publication Data

Names: Bishop, Anne, author.
Title: Crowbones : the world of the others / Anne Bishop.
Description: First Edition. | New York : Ace, [2022] | Series: The world of the others
Identifiers: LCCN 2021034756 (print) | LCCN 2021034757 (ebook) |
ISBN 9780593337332 (hardcover) | ISBN 9780593337356 (ebook) |
Subjects: GSAFD: Fantasy fiction. | Mystery fiction.
Classification: LCC PS3552.I7594 C76 2022 (print) |
LCC PS3552.I7594 (ebook) | DDC 813/.54--dc23
LC record available at https://lccn.loc.gov/2021034756
LC ebook record available at https://lccn.loc.gov/2021034757

Printed in the United States of America
1st Printing

Book design by Laura K. Corless
Title page art: Feather background © Sergey Nivens / Shutterstock.com

For Jennifer Crow

THE FINGER/FEATHER LAKES

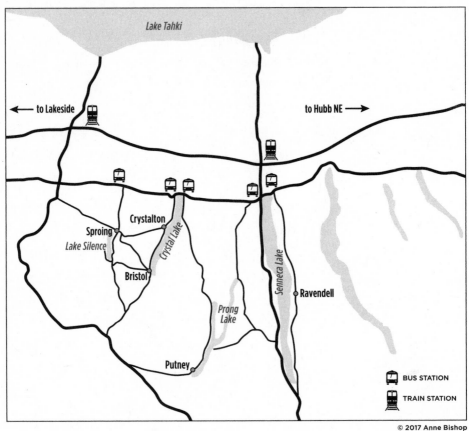

Note: The geographically challenged author created this map and did her best to match the main roads to the story but makes no promises about accuracy.

Don't matter if you caw,
Don't matter if you shout.
Crowbones will gitcha
If you don't watch out!

—CROWGARD RHYME

CROWBONES

CHAPTER 1

Vicki

Leading up to Sunday, Grau 30

It wasn't my fault.

Okay, it sort of *was* my fault because I should have realized that the Crowgard who worked for me would be wildly excited about a human celebration called Trickster Night and want to participate firsthand—first-wing?—in such an event. I also should have realized they would tell the rest of the Crows and other forms of *terra indigene* who lived in The Jumble about a human custom of dressing up and putting on masks to try to look scary. In the weeks prior to that actual night, Aggie, Jozi, and Eddie Crowgard pestered every human who visited The Jumble about how to "Trickster properly"—choice of costumes, choice of treats, what to say and what to do.

Wayne Grimshaw, Sproing's chief of police, was sparse with details whenever he dropped by to check up on me. Julian Farrow, who owned Lettuce Reed, the village's bookstore, was cautious with his explanations. Paige and Dominique Xavier, on the other hand, gleefully told the Crows about their childhood adventures and what they wore when they knocked on neighbors' doors and shouted, "Trick or treat!"

After receiving one of Grimshaw's patented grim looks, which turned his blue-gray eyes a steely gray, Paige and Dominique quickly emphasized that playing tricks was *not* the point of the evening.

"It won't be that bad," I had muttered to Ineke Xavier one afternoon as we waited by her car for Paige and Dominique to finish "explaining" a few more details about Trickster Night to my Crowgard employees. "My bookings for the lake cabins and the suites in the main house are all adult guests. No children."

"Have you bought enough bags of candy to hand out?" Ineke asked, sounding mildly curious.

"Mildly curious" coming from a woman who had a tattoo on one thigh that included the words "I Bury Trouble" was not to be mistaken for actual mild curiosity.

"Who is going to come out to The Jumble for a piece of hard candy?" I asked.

"Pops Davies mentioned that you hadn't come by the general store to pick up the bags of candy he'd set aside for you. Small chocolate bars."

I blinked. "Chocolate? Really?" Ever since the Great Predation—a terrifying time last year when the Elders and Elementals swept over the world and seriously thinned the human population as retaliation for the Humans First and Last movement starting a war and killing shifter forms of *terra indigene*—some things weren't as readily available as they used to be, and that included small bars of chocolate. I could put out some of the chocolate for my guests and keep a stash for myself for the times when I needed a reward for getting through a difficult day.

I made a mental note to call Pops and let him know I was interested in the chocolate so he wouldn't sell it to someone else.

"You're fully booked for the days before and after Trickster Night?" Ineke asked, still sounding mildly curious and calling me back from my distraction-by-chocolate.

"Yes." I had been fully booked for weeks, so I hadn't thought there was anything unusual about these reservations since we were just coming to the end of our peak tourist season and still required a three-day-minimum reservation—but I was catching on that maybe, just maybe, I had done something to earn the look Grimshaw had given me last night when he came over to play pool with Ilya Sanguinati, who was a very yummy-looking vampire and my attorney.

"So am I," Ineke said. "It's unusual to have people specifically booking a three-day stay midweek to make sure they are here for Trickster Night." She took pity on me. "The Jumble's residents are going to have the most *amazing* costumes."

"They don't need costumes. Most of them . . ."

I finally got it. Aggie, Jozi, and Eddie could pass for human unless they got excited and started sprouting black feathers. Robert "Call Me Cougar" Panthera and Conan Beargard could pass for human if you ignored Conan's excess body hair and the fact that the boys still had trouble with their teeth. They were getting those sorted out as they spent more time around humans, but the teeth were still an unnerving mix of human and large predator. As for the rest of The Jumble's *terra indigene* residents . . .

The between form isn't fully an individual's animal form and it isn't fully human, and it sure isn't whatever they look like in their true form, which is a form no human gets to see unless the human is the main course for that night's dinner. Maybe not even then, because the one time I asked Ilya why the Others' true forms were such a big deal, he said very, *very* quietly, "You don't want to know, and you should not ask anyone else."

I took the hint and never mentioned it again.

The days prior to Trickster Night, I juggled looking after my current guests, getting ready for my soon-to-arrive guests, and approving the "costumes" of The Jumble's full-time residents. After I persuaded Aggie, Jozi, and Eddie that a between form that mixed *too* much Crow with their human forms would be bad for business, they agreed to keep their shifting to a human-size Crow head and a few feathers on their hands, which would be startling enough but wouldn't freak out the guests. I hoped. It also meant they couldn't talk to the guests or convey any messages about what the guests might want, but I could live with that for one evening. As for the rest of the Others who wanted to mingle with the humans in order to study them during this celebration . . .

Female Fox with foxy ears, foxy tail showing through a slit in her capris, and foxy front paws with elongated digits that were necessary to hold her treat sack. Cute.

Male Bobcat who looked the way he usually did when he took guests on a donkey-cart tour of The Jumble—in other words, he looked more

Bobcat than human but could converse with humans. More or less. His "costume" consisted of a short cape that might have come from the large cardboard lost-and-found box I had tucked away in one of the first-floor rooms I wasn't currently using. I was certain some guests left things behind on purpose—a book, a sweater, a hairbrush—so that the Others could use them. And some things were left behind because the guest was in too much of a hurry to leave to check the closet or drawers.

Interestingly enough, it was the guests who were rude, too demanding, or "handsy" with Aggie, Jozi, or me who were motivated to leave in a hurry. I never asked who did the motivating, since there were scarier forms of *terra indigene* living around Lake Silence than a Panther, a black Bear, and the Sanguinati, and I really didn't want to know for sure that *they* were studying my guests in the same way some of my guests studied the more . . . benign? . . . forms of Others.

Back to the costumes. There were other blends of human and animal that . . . Okay, the individual was going for scary, and that included Cougar and Conan, which forced me to explain that there were degrees of scary, and if they didn't want to pour a thick layer of sand—or kitty litter—in front of the door to soak up all the pee from terrified children and adults, they needed to adjust their Trickster Night look to something that wasn't *too* scary.

I sat through, including the boys, six individuals "adjusting" their look until I gave them thumbs-up, no-pee approval. Then I took the key to the liquor cabinet that held Grimshaw and Julian's private stash of sipping whiskey, chose the bottle that was open without looking at the label, and poured myself a hefty dose of courage, which got me through the rest of that day.

Check-in time is two p.m., and I was fully booked. Not that I had many available rooms. At this time of year, I didn't offer the "primitive" cabins. Out of the twelve cabins that were in The Jumble, three cabins located near the lake had been renovated and had updated electricity and indoor plumbing. Two were available for guests, since the three Crowgard who worked for me occupied the third cabin. I also had two suites with private bathrooms in the main house. Sleeping arrangements for the two renovated cabins were two single beds in one and a double bed in the other. The suites in the main building had a double bed and a sofa bed in each. The sofa beds were a recent purchase I'd made for the guests who did bring a child or other relative to The Jumble, but it also worked for a variety of sleeping arrangements.

All of my Trickster Night guests arrived on Grau 30 shortly before check-in and spent the time making small talk while I got the registrations sorted out. All adults, which I'd expected. Fred and Wilma Cornley, an almost-newlywed couple, had reserved one of the suites in the main house. The other suite was reserved by Ben Malacki and David Shuman, who were professors at one of the universities in the Finger Lakes. I figured they would flip a coin to see who slept on the sofa bed and who got the double bed. Jenna McKay had the cabin with single beds because she'd originally booked a reservation for two people, but her friend had canceled at the last minute. When Jenna heard that Ian and Michael Stern, cousins who had ended up with the last cabin, were going to flip a coin to see who got the double bed and who would sleep on the air mattress and sleeping bag they'd packed as a "just in case" option, she offered to switch cabins with them so that they could have the two single beds. That worked well for everyone, and assisted by my Crowgard employees, three of my guests headed for their homes away from home in high spirits.

Who slept where wasn't any of my business as long as guests didn't create a mess or draw too much attention to themselves. But I had that part covered by the sign on the reception desk that read: IF YOUR BEHAVIOR ATTRACTS ATTENTION, YOU HAVE TO EXPLAIN THAT BEHAVIOR TO SOMEONE WHO MIGHT EAT YOU. GOOD LUCK.

It wasn't subtle, so most guests got the point, and no one had been eaten since that unpleasantness this past summer when my ex-husband and his cronies had tried to force me out of The Jumble in order to turn it into a posh resort.

I escorted the Cornleys and the two professors up to their suites, giving them a rundown of possible activities they could enjoy during their stay, emphasizing tomorrow night's festivities since I assumed those were why they were here and also pointing out that the TV was already reserved for the evening. Since this was the only TV available to guests, it was a not-so-subtle way of saying *Make out your will before you attempt to change the channel.*

This being cop and crime night, I had ordered enough pizza and salads from the Pizza Shack in Sproing to feed my employees and guests. As the proprietor, I'm supposed to be available for guests, but Conan and Cougar made it clear to everyone that no one who wanted to keep all their digits disturbed me or the rest of the staff during the cop and crime shows.

Surprisingly, all the guests stayed to watch the shows with us, even the almost newlyweds. The men chowed down on pizza—wisely not touching the one called the Carnivore Special after Conan and Cougar growled at them—and fielded questions about human behavior both in the show and in the commercials. Jenna and Wilma ate mostly salad, which they almost dumped on themselves when Aggie jumped up and started yelling at one of the cops in the show when he paid *no* attention to the crow in the trees, who, according to Aggie, was trying to warn him that the sneaky human had *just* passed that way and was waiting to spring a trap.

That created a lively discussion during commercials about whether the cop, who didn't speak crow *or* Crow, could have realized he was being warned. And then everyone wondered if the crow had been just a bird that happened to be in a tree when that scene was shot or if it was *supposed* to be one of the Crowgard.

That led to questions of how to write to the show and suggest that they hire a Crow to assist the cops in the show in the same way the Crowgard assisted the police who protected Sproing.

My guests were fascinated by this claim of assistance. I ate my pizza and thanked all the gods that Grimshaw hadn't decided to drop by to play a game of pool and snag a couple of slices of pizza. I knew the look *I* would get if my guests started asking how the Others assisted the police in their apprehension of wrongdoers. Telling the truth—that wrongdoers were often eaten if the police didn't get to them first—would not help Sproing's tourist trade. Or my bottom line.

Grimshaw didn't watch the cop and crime shows, although he often dropped by because cop and crime night was also pizza night. Julian Farrow didn't watch those shows either, because he'd been a cop until the Incident that ended his career and he never knew if something in the shows would stir up post-traumatic memories. So whenever Grimshaw or Julian did turn up on that night, it was for pizza and pool. That's what they said, but David Osgood, the rookie police officer who worked for

Grimshaw, had told Paige Xavier, who had told me, that Chief Grimshaw had made a passing comment about me being a trouble magnet, which was the real reason he stopped by a couple of times a week. Keeping his finger on the pulse, so to speak.

I preferred to think it was just a Grimshaw sort of justification for coming to The Jumble. Ilya Sanguinati had turned one of my downstairs rooms into something that looked like a pool hall just to give Grimshaw a private place to play pool. It could be used by my guests too, but when the Reserved sign was on the door, it was Grimshaw either playing on his own or playing with Julian and/or Ilya. A bit like an exclusive club—and we'd all learned how much trouble *those* could be, but the three males liked being able to discuss things in an informal setting. Keeping their fingers on the village's pulse—and their eyes on the trouble magnet, a label I thought was unfair since all I'd done that first time was call the police to report a dead man after I stopped Aggie from heating up one of his eyeballs for lunch.

And all I'd done a few weeks ago was mention Trickster Night, so everything that happened afterward really wasn't my fault.

CHAPTER 2

Grimshaw

Windsday, Grau 31

Even as a child, Wayne Grimshaw hadn't seen the point of Trickster Night. Why dress up in some kind of costume in order to walk down a couple of neighborhood streets and knock on people's doors in order to receive a questionable mix of candy that was, for the most part, something you didn't want to eat anyway?

Of course, when he *had* to participate because his parents wanted him to do an activity with other children, he'd dressed as some kind of cop. A frontier lawman. An old-time city detective who wore a suit and a bowler hat. The last time his parents encouraged him to knock on people's doors, he went out as an undercover cop, and his costume was a pair of jeans, a white T-shirt, a secondhand leather jacket, and a lot of attitude.

His career choice wasn't a surprise to anyone who had known him when he was young. His choosing highway patrol wasn't a surprise either. He was ideally suited to being a lone officer who traveled the roads through the wild country to assist people who'd had some kind of accident or needed another kind of help—or to apprehend idiots who thought they could taunt the Others and drive away, *if* the highway patrol officer managed to arrest said idiot *before* said idiot had been caught by one of the larger, more dangerous forms of *terra indigene*, then ripped into chunks and generously dispersed as handy meals for the smaller carnivores.

The surprise was finding himself the chief of police of the two-man police station in the village of Sproing, a small human community near Lake Silence, the westernmost of the Finger Lakes. Or Feather Lakes, depending on which species was identifying the bodies of water. His presence in Sproing had started out as a temporary assignment a few months ago, when he'd responded to the call Vicki DeVine had made to the Bristol Police Station reporting a dead body. That body had been the first of many as a secret group of men had tried to take The Jumble away from Vicki. Her ex-husband had thought she would be a pushover, not realizing that her new friends included several Crowgard, a Panther, a Bear, the Sanguinati who were her attorney and CPA, and a couple of Elementals, including Silence's Lady of the Lake.

The loner he'd always been had found himself teaming up with Julian Farrow, a friend from his academy days; Ineke Xavier, the intimidating owner of the village's boardinghouse; and a variety of *terra indigene* in order to protect Vicki DeVine and, by extension, the entire village. The end result of *that* was the offer to become Sproing's chief of police.

So there he was, standing on the main street of a village whose population had swelled to almost four hundred residents—a significant jump from the three hundred people who had been in Sproing the first day he'd walked into the police station—wondering about a custom that encouraged children to go out at dusk, dressed in ways that might make it difficult for anyone to know, without examining teeth, if the children were humans dressed to look strangely furry, or furry youngsters enjoying a day when not being able to pass for human might be an advantage.

He had three choices for village information: the Xaviers at the boardinghouse; Helen Hearse, who ran Come and Get It, the village's diner; and Julian Farrow, the owner of Lettuce Reed, an establishment that was equal parts bookstore and the village's revolving library of used paperbacks.

Deciding he had a better chance with Julian of getting information and walking away in a reasonable amount of time, Grimshaw zipped up his jacket and crossed the street, steeling himself for an encounter with the Sproingers, the small critters that looked a bit like happy, bouncy rats but were a lethally venomous form of *terra indigene*. They were Sproing's major tourist attraction, hopping around the village, cadging chunks of carrot or pumpkin from the shop owners while people from all around the Northeast Region of Thaisia came to Sproing for the chance to get their pictures taken with the happy-faced hoppy things before purchasing an I ♥ Sproingers T-shirt.

On the continent of Thaisia, Sproingers were exclusive to the land around Sproing and Lake Silence.

Thank the gods for small favors.

Julian Farrow stood outside Lettuce Reed with a bowl of carrot chunks he was handing out as treats.

When they'd gone through the academy together, instructors sometimes called them Day and Night because they were opposites in looks. Even then, Grimshaw was a large man with dark blond hair and blue-gray eyes, while Julian had a lean build and finely sculpted face, gray eyes, and dark hair. In many ways, they were still opposites. Grimshaw still wore his hair short, while Julian's hair was long enough to look shaggy or bedroom disheveled or whatever adjectives women liked to apply to such things. There was a thin scar beneath Julian's left cheekbone—a souvenir of the attack that had ended Farrow's career as a cop.

Julian carried other scars too, and not all of them were visible to the eye.

Like the children Grimshaw noticed going from store to store, the Sproingers approached the businesses in small groups. A quick tally of the critters he could see put the count at around fifty, which was half the Sproinger population. He didn't want to consider where the other half was.

He stood at the edge of the sidewalk and continued scanning the street while Julian dealt with two boys who wore furry-looking hats and mittens, a length of clothesline pinned to their jeans, and hopped after the Sproingers.

"I have carrots," Julian told the boys. "Helen at Come and Get It is giving out brownie squares."

The Sproinger wannabes hopped toward the diner and a better treat.

Shaking his head, Grimshaw joined Julian.

"Carrot?" Julian held out the bowl.

Grimshaw hesitated, then took a chunk. "Why not?"

"You were almost called to break up some fisticuffs at Pops Davies's store today when two female tourists laid claim to the last bunch of carrots in the hopes of some up-close-and-personal contact with the Sproingers. Fortunately, Officer Osgood arrived before the first punch was thrown and pointed out that, since both women were staying at the boarding-house, they could split the cost of the carrots and any candy they wanted to contribute to the goody bowl the Xaviers were using to lure costumed residents to their door."

Grimshaw sighed. "I have one officer to help me patrol three potential trouble spots." The Jumble was one; the boardinghouse was another. He considered the village of Sproing in its entirety to be the third.

"Two officers, two spots," Julian corrected. "I heard Ineke walked into the dining room this morning wearing her 'costume,' which was a long leather coat over a smoking-hot top and a pair of shorts that were just this side of legal."

"Gave her guests a good look at her tattoos?"

"Uh-huh."

He nodded. Ineke had a smoking revolver on her left thigh. On the right thigh was a big-eyed caricature of Ineke that had a miniature board-inghouse tucked in her multicolored hair and a necklace made of tomb-stones. Beneath the caricature were the words "I Bury Trouble."

There was nothing *Other* about the Xaviers. They *were* human. They were just potently Female in a way that was a bit scary. Sometimes a lot scary.

He wondered what it said about David Osgood that the rookie was casually dating Paige Xavier. At least Osgood thought it was casual. Per-sonally, Grimshaw thought fish probably looked the same way when they were well and truly hooked. The only question was whether Paige be-lieved in catch and release or if she didn't bait the hook at all unless she intended to keep what she caught.

He hadn't heard any gossip about Dominique, the third Xavier, but that could be because he hadn't asked the right person.

"So, the kids are doing this little trick or treat on Main Street this afternoon to show off their costumes before sticking to their own streets?" Grimshaw asked, watching four youngsters slowly approach Lettuce Reed. The two boys and one of the girls were teenagers, although not all the same age. The other girl looked like she belonged to the under-ten crowd. The girls wore calf-length black dresses; the boys wore black suits with pale gray shirts. They *could* have been young humans in costume, except they all had dark hair, dark eyes, and olive skin, and that said Sanguinati.

"Wayne . . ." Julian glanced at the four youngsters, then looked at the second-story windows of the police station. Paulo Diamante, the village's lone human attorney, occupied one office on the second floor. The occupants of the other office, the office that had no name on the door, had a great deal of influence in and around Sproing and Lake Silence—not to mention owning several of the commercial buildings and the bank.

Ilya Sanguinati met Julian's eyes for several seconds before stepping back from the window.

"You all having a look around?" Grimshaw asked, keeping his voice friendly.

"Yes. Sir," the younger teenage boy replied. "We are . . . strolling."

Definitely not a word the boy used every day, and the stilted speech gave the impression he'd had limited contact with humans.

"And observing," the older teenage boy added.

More confidence in that one—and something under that confidence made Grimshaw's cop radar hum for a moment before the feeling faded. Could be nothing more than one boy coming across as more mature because he was a few years older than the other one. But it could be something else.

Or he could just be feeling crabby because he wasn't looking forward to dealing with Trickster Night in Sproing.

The four youngsters came to attention as Ilya Sanguinati crossed the street and joined them. It was subtle, but it told Grimshaw that these youngsters were used to obeying their leaders. Or the dominant family member?

"The bookstore is open if you'd like to take a look around," Julian said.

The youngsters looked at Julian, then at Ilya.

"You may look until Boris arrives with the car," Ilya said.

Julian stepped aside.

The teenage girl's shy smile didn't match the assessing look she gave Julian before she lowered her eyes and walked demurely into the store.

Grimshaw thought, *Gods save us all from girls that age, regardless of their species.* Then he wondered if that mix of shy and assessing wasn't just because of her age. He knew how the Sanguinati hunted. Was he looking at a teenage girl becoming aware of her attraction to men—or was he looking at a predator who used sex as bait?

And how could he pose that question to Ilya Sanguinati without offending the leader of Silence Lodge?

"Family come to visit?" Julian asked.

"You could say that," Ilya replied. Then he hesitated, and Grimshaw realized this was one of those moments when he would learn how much trust he and Julian had earned with the Sanguinati.

"The shadow of Sanguinati at Silence Lodge is not currently raising any young of its own," Ilya continued. "Under such circumstances, youngsters from other shadows might be fostered for a time in order to further their education and gain experience that is not available in their home territory."

"Like interacting with humans the adult Sanguinati consider safe?" Julian guessed.

"Exactly. Such opportunities are unusual for the young, and Silence Lodge, like the Lakeside Courtyard, has been deemed such a place. It is an honor to be considered in this way."

Grimshaw had the impression that Ilya didn't feel the least bit honored. "If you let the girls acquire any knowledge from Paige Xavier, you are on your own dealing with the consequences."

Ilya looked startled. Julian choked on a laugh.

"I was thinking of introducing them to Victoria," Ilya said after a moment.

Oh gods. Look what happened when Vicki and one juvenile Crow became friends. The thought must have shown on his face, because Ilya suddenly avoided meeting his eyes.

"Ah, there is Boris." Ilya sounded relieved—and looked a wee bit pale.

As if summoned, the Sanguinati youngsters filed out of Lettuce Reed.

"Sir?" the younger girl piped up. "Is it permissible to purchase books?"

The adults, human and vampire, hesitated. Probably because none of them knew which "sir" was supposed to answer the question.

"Yes," Ilya said. "But not now. Mr. Farrow is closing early for Trickster Night. We will return tomorrow."

They crossed the street as Boris, Ilya's driver, opened the back door of the black luxury sedan.

One by one, the human-looking youngsters changed into a column of smoke and flowed into the back of the sedan. When four columns were inside the car, Boris closed the door. Ilya got in front on the passenger side, and Boris settled behind the wheel.

"Adults in front, children in back," Julian said. "Not so different from humans."

Grimshaw saw plenty of differences, and he wasn't looking forward to talking to Ilya about not allowing the youngsters to snack on the tourists— or do anything else. After all, one of the reasons the Sanguinati helped keep Sproing afloat was to have a supply of transient meals. And since the adult Sanguinati could give lessons in romantic seduction, most of their prey didn't connect a love bite with an extraction of blood.

It said a lot about Ineke Xavier and Helen Hearse that they served plenty of iron-rich foods at their establishments to counteract the languid-ness that was a natural part of the rest and relaxation experienced by some of Sproing's tourists.

They'd given him that explanation at different times and in slightly different ways when he'd observed the change in some hyperactive tour-ists. But only Ineke had pointed out that the languid women had a par-ticular smile the next day—a smile she hoped that he, as a man who had enjoyed female company at some point in his life, recognized.

He had changed the subject and never brought it up again. At least, not where any Xavier could hear him.

"I'd send Osgood over tomorrow so you wouldn't be alone with the Sanguinati girls, but he's already in over his head," he said.

"I know how to be careful. With women, anyway."

He let that comment hang in the air and said casually, "You going to The Jumble this evening?"

Julian nodded. "I was invited to the party Vicki is holding for her guests, and I gather all the residents are going to participate in the treat part of Trickster Night. I heard that the academics who are staying at the Mill Creek Cabins are also invited in order to observe the Others, but their invitation came with a BYOF-and-B addendum."

"Bring your own . . . ?"

"Food and booze."

"Makes sense." Grimshaw waited a beat. "How many pizzas are you contributing?"

Julian laughed. "Four."

He nodded. "Sounds about right."

"You too?"

"Osgood can man the phones at the station this evening. I figure being at The Jumble is the best chance of seeing who is living around Lake Silence and might cross paths with humans. And I'm officially escorting the academics back to the Mill Creek Cabins since they'll be driving after dark."

Sproing was a human community, but it wasn't human controlled. That meant there were no boundaries between humans and the wild country. There was no longer a curfew, but no one with any sense stayed out too long after dark.

"I'll see you at The Jumble," Grimshaw said.

When he was halfway across the street, Julian said, "Are you going to wear a costume?"

His reply was an unmistakable hand gesture that earned a gasp from a couple of women he'd seen around for the past few weeks. New residents? Well, when he took this job, he didn't promise to work on his public relations skills. At least, not with the human population. Still . . .

"Ladies." He gave them a nod and walked into the police station.

The station looked outdated, but it was clean, had everything he and Osgood needed, and had enough room for one more officer now that they had shoehorned in a third desk and a desktop computer for police business—assuming anyone else wanted to work in a place like Sproing. So far, he and Osgood had been able to handle the calls, especially since residents realized that anything fanged, furry, and curious might show up to "assist."

Hopefully fisticuffs over the last bunch of carrots or bag of candy would be the worst he'd have to deal with, especially if he kept an eye on Vicki DeVine tonight. She meant well, and he couldn't dispute that The Jumble being a working concern again had improved the economy of the entire village, but she was also the reason he knew a whole lot more about the *terra indigene* residents around Lake Silence than most of the humans in the area. It wasn't knowledge that gave a man a good night's sleep.

On the other hand, he firmly believed that ignorance was bullshit, not bliss. Given a choice, he'd rather lose some sleep and have a chance to wake up the next morning.

CHAPTER 3

Them

Windsday, Grau 31

His adversary was here! In *Sproing*!

They had an agreement not to work in the same place at the same time because the results of one research project might give authorities some concern, but two projects, given the nature of their research, were bound to draw too much attention to themselves. He'd been planning this for weeks, preparing the ground, so to speak, and bringing in all the pieces for the project. Carefully. So carefully, because this was far more dangerous than research that dealt with just humans.

The *terra indigene* were not without weaknesses, not without flaws of personality, and he had a knack for finding those weaknesses and exploiting those flaws, regardless of species. Sometimes it was as simple as telling someone over and over that their malignant thoughts were good and true, and they were justified in inflicting evil upon others of their own kind as well as anyone else. Sometimes, bringing about the desired result took a little more convincing.

Everything was ready. There was no other place suitable for this particular experiment, so he didn't have a choice. He had to go ahead with his plans for this evening—and he would deal with any potential interference in an appropriate manner.

Adversary. No. That sounded like someone of equal strength and skill, and that wasn't true. This rivalry had been going on for years, and he had never been bested. Never.

And he wouldn't be bested now.

CHAPTER 4

Vicki

Windsday, Grau 31

On Trickster Night, the children arrived around dusk. I learned later that cars lined both sides of Lake Street, and a man with yellow-and-blue-tipped red hair, riding a brown horse with a storm gray mane and tail, had directed traffic. It had taken only a couple of impatient honkers suddenly facing a fire tornado instead of a horse and rider to encourage everyone to be very polite and patient.

So Aiden, the local Fire Elemental, and Twister, who looked like a chubby pony when he wasn't being an Elemental's steed or tornadic devastation, directed traffic while a couple of enterprising parents with larger vehicles ferried children up the gravel access road to The Jumble's main house to receive the treats being handed out by Cougar and Conan.

Grimshaw remained outside near the front door, watching everyone and scanning the darkness that seemed to swallow the light shining from all the windows, as well as the lights on either side of the door. Julian stayed inside, helping me with my guests and the academics staying at the Mill Creek Cabins as they navigated the twists and turns of making small talk with beings who saw no reason for such communication.

I thought we were doing quite well until Foxy Female grabbed a treat out of the bowl Cougar was taking to the door, then shifted her head to full Foxgard in order to crunch down on a bit o' mouse.

Funny thing. Even after she shifted her head back to mostly human, the men who had been flirting with her had shown reluctance to get better acquainted. Might have been her breath at that point. Or the tiny end of the mouse tail that was caught between two teeth.

I, on the other hand, had rushed to the door just in time to hear Cougar say, "Heads or tails?" before offering the bowl to a male child of indeterminate species.

"No!" I yelped.

Grimshaw snapped to attention.

"Why not?" Cougar asked. "We have plenty."

The boys—or someone—had been busy collecting treats. Conan held the bowl with the hard candy, thank the gods. Cougar's bowl held neatly halved mice and chipmunks that were missing the gooiest innards.

Cougar assured me that he and Conan could tell the difference between human and *terra indigene* young, but I wondered how many phone calls Grimshaw would take tonight from hysterical parents of human male children when they dumped the treat bag on the dining room table and found The Jumble's unique contribution to Trickster Night.

I took over treat distribution—hard candy only. We were down to the last handful of children when a girl walked up to the door from one direction and two boys about the same age headed toward me. All of them were dressed in black, but two of them looked like they were in costume and the other one looked like . . . what she was.

"We're vampires," said a boy with a cape and red lips that had to have come from raiding his mother's makeup bag.

"So am I," the girl said.

"Yeah? Let's see your fangs." The boy was genuinely interested enough that he thrust his treat bag in my direction without checking to see what he might be getting.

Ilya's voice came out of the darkness. "It is impolite to show fang in public."

Unless you're going to bite someone.

I knew that wasn't quite true, since Ilya showed a hint of fang when he was amused—or threatening someone—but I imagine he didn't want

Sanguinati youngsters to be thought of as some kind of entertainment. *Gimme a nickel and I'll show you fang.*

The young vampires, both real and wannabes, retreated. The car ferrying human children went down the access road.

Three more Sanguinati approached. Teenagers. The girl was gorgeous and seemed a little shy, which struck me as the perfect bait for the kind of man who thought shy meant being unable to say no. One boy had pleasant looks, while the other had the sort of looks that made me think he would be able to challenge Ilya for the title of Mr. Yummy in a few years.

Only the pleasant-looking boy had a treat bag. Before I could distribute the hard candy, Julian stepped up beside me and dropped four small chocolate bars in the bag. He looked at the teens and said softly, "Share."

They thanked him and stepped away from the door as Ilya approached.

"Would you and Natasha like to join us?" I asked. Natasha Sanguinati was my CPA. Recently she had accepted Ilya as her mate, which wasn't common knowledge among the human population because the Sanguinati—or any form of *terra indigene*—weren't inclined to answer questions about their species.

Julian said there was a word for people who got too nosy about vampire mating rituals: "chum."

Having met the Elders who live in Lake Silence, I knew he wasn't trying to be funny.

Ilya hesitated a moment and turned his head, as if conferring with someone. Then he looked at me and smiled, carefully not showing fang. "Thank you. We'd like the chance to mingle. We'll take the youngsters back to Silence Lodge and return."

Since I didn't hear a car, I assumed the Sanguinati had shifted to their smoke form and crossed the lake to reach The Jumble and would return to Silence Lodge the same way.

I'd started to close the door, more than ready to take a head count of my guests before getting something to eat, when four teenage boys swaggered up the access road and came into the light.

They were human. I knew they were human. But they looked at me the same way my ex-husband's friends had looked at women—and that made them the most bestial creatures to enter The Jumble that night.

CHAPTER 5

Grimshaw

Windsday, Grau 31

When his mobile phone started buzzing, Grimshaw stepped away from the door, far enough for some privacy and still close enough to have a chance to reach safety if any of The Jumble's more dangerous residents were out there in the dark observing this human ritual. "Grimshaw."

"Sir?" Osgood said. "We just received an unusual message."

Not what he wanted to hear on Trickster Night. "And?" When there was no response, he wondered if he'd lost the connection. "Osgood? You there?"

"Yes, sir."

"The message?"

"Jack-o'-lantern. Bones. Black feathers. Rattlesnake tail." A shaky breath. "Coffin."

Crap. "Who called that in?"

"Captain Burke. From Lakeside. He said the message came from a girl in the Courtyard."

Gods above and below. "Girl in the Courtyard" meant the blood prophet. And *that* meant this wasn't a Trickster Night prank. "Did Burke say anything else?"

"He said a question was asked four times. The answer for Talulah Falls, Great Island, and Lakeside was the first four images. Lake Silence was the only one that had the coffin."

"Call Ineke Xavier. Tell her to keep an eye on her guests. And watch your back."

"Yes, sir."

He ended the call and returned to the front door, reaching it at the same time as four teenage boys swaggered up to leer at Vicki DeVine in a way that was meant to frighten any woman with sense. Since aggressive men tended to send Vicki into severe anxiety attacks, he gave a quick prayer of thanks to Mikhos, the guardian spirit of police, firefighters, and medical personnel, that Ilya Sanguinati hadn't returned yet.

"You're a little old for this, aren't you?" he asked, working to balance the voice he wanted to use with a tone and volume that wouldn't cause Vicki to collapse.

"Aren't *you*?" the one who had a fake hatchet buried in his head replied.

So. Not local boys if they didn't know who he was. They might have rented one of the campers on the edge of the village in order to be in Sproing for Trickster Night. With that attitude, they wouldn't have lasted long enough at Ineke's to unpack, let alone put on costumes that made them look like they were extras in a horror movie.

A second boy looked at Vicki in a way that made Grimshaw want to haul the fool to the station and check if he had any arrests for assaulting women.

Grimshaw took a step closer to Vicki, letting his size provide a shield—and knew it wasn't going to be enough. Four young males full of themselves—and probably full of something else. Drugs? Might be. They must have left their car near the end of the access road. Long way to walk in the dark, especially around here.

Hatchet Head smiled. "You're in the way."

Which was the point. "You boys run along now."

"Not until we get our treat. You don't want us to start playing tricks, do you?"

Behind him, Grimshaw heard Vicki whispering, "Be brave, be brave, be brave." He wanted to tell her this wasn't the time to be brave. This was a time to lock the doors and call the cops before . . .

"Monkey man," a female voice sang out of the dark.

"Moooonkey man," a second female voice sang.

Grimshaw shuddered. He'd hoped never to hear those voices again.

"Come play tricks with us, monkey mans," a third female voice sang.

Now there was movement behind him, and suddenly Vicki was gone and Conan and Cougar were at his back, filling up the doorway.

"Wayne, come inside," Julian said quietly. "There's nothing you can do. Those fools are standing in the wild country."

"I could arrest them and let them spend the night in a cell," he replied.

"Arrest us?" the third boy sneered. "For what?"

"For being a pain in my ass. Since I'm the chief of police around here and this is Trickster Night, that's enough of a reason." *And it will keep you alive.*

He felt something press against his shoulder, felt whiskers tickle his cheek before a low, angry sound resonated through his back and into his chest. And he heard Julian whisper, "Don't look."

The teenage fools were looking right at whatever pushed against him—and he watched four swaggering pricks turn into squealing children, losing control of their bladders seconds before they ran down the access road.

A satisfied growl.

Then Vicki, her voice vibrating with suppressed panic, said, "Cougar? That's a too-scary face for our party."

Cougar pushed past Grimshaw, disappearing beyond the lit areas.

Conan huffed out a breath that could have knocked down a small child. "Need to get rid of that smell, or everything in The Jumble will be coming by to mark territory and warn off the intruders."

Grimshaw shuddered at the thought of the Elders who lived on this land marking territory just beyond Vicki's front door—especially when the main house was full of strangers tonight.

Very quiet strangers.

He turned and studied the partygoers. Humans on one side of the big entrance hall, *terra indigene* on the other side. Vicki standing in between with Julian's arm around her for support. And everyone looking at him.

He looked at Julian, who shook his head.

Julian Farrow was an Intuit, a kind of human who sensed things. They didn't see visions of the future like the *cassandra sangue* did, but they had feelings about people or places. Julian was a living barometer for the health of a place. He sensed when something was going wrong.

Grimshaw didn't know if that head shake meant there was nothing he could do or it was already too late to do anything.

Ilya and Natasha approached from the back of the building. They must have come in through the screened back porch and kitchen.

Ilya, too, looked at him and shook his head.

If he couldn't find the bodies, would he find any identification and be able to provide the next of kin with a Deceased, Location Unknown form?

Almost got through this night without anyone dying. I guess the blood prophet was right about the image of a coffin for us.

Accepting what he couldn't change, Grimshaw stepped inside and closed the door.

Everyone nibbled on food and drank too much. Understandable under the circumstances, and not a problem for the folks staying at The Jumble, but not so good when it came to getting the four academics back to the Mill Creek Cabins.

When Julian joined him, Grimshaw immediately scanned the room for Vicki.

"She's in the kitchen with the Crows, putting more nibbles on plates," Julian said.

"She's okay?"

"Nervy, but she's holding it together."

"You going to stay over?"

Julian hesitated, knowing what Grimshaw was asking. Then he finally said, "Vicki isn't ready for that kind of guest."

Vicki had her own efficiency apartment in the main house, a perk of being the owner/caretaker of The Jumble. Grimshaw knew Julian didn't always go back to the Mill Creek cabin he rented at Silence Lodge, but apparently he was making use of an available room when he stayed over. Not surprising that this romance was like a tortoise race, since both parties had traumatic pasts.

"I'm sober enough to drive," Julian continued, "so I can drive the mini-van two of the academics arrived in, and Ilya says Boris will be over soon and he can drive the other car—if the men don't end up staying here and sleeping on sofas or in chairs."

"How many do you figure will vote for a sleepover?"

"Most of them. Having the universities rent some of the Mill Creek Cabins in order to mingle with the Others is a new venture. I have a feeling the people aren't going to want to see whatever you might find on your way out of The Jumble."

"Is that a feeling or a *feeling*?"

"Let's call it an ex-cop's intuition, since you know as well as I do that not all four of those boys got away."

"Yeah." And there wasn't a damn thing he could have done about that. Sometimes that was a hard truth to live with.

CHAPTER 6

Vicki

Windsday, Grau 31

Aggie, Jozi, and Eddie shifted back to looking fully human, which helped all the guests relax. Or it was an alcohol-induced relaxation. Julian had poured me a stiff glass of relaxation after those four boys ran away, so I was able to pretend aggressive men didn't scare me. I think everyone believed that I wasn't worried that those boys would come back when there were fewer people about. Everyone except Julian, of course. And Grimshaw. And Ilya.

Julian didn't offer any of the words that sounded kindly meant but were never kind because the words indicated surprise that any leering or lusting would be aimed at someone who looked like me—a short, pudgy thirty-year-old woman whose curly brown hair usually gave the impression it had been styled by sticking a fork in an electrical outlet. Julian doesn't see me that way, which I don't understand but am working to accept since he's a good friend. I think he would like to be more than a friend, and sometimes I think I'd like him to be more than a friend, but every time I wonder what it would be like to kiss him—or be kissed by him—I suddenly hear my ex-husband's voice telling me to use some mouthwash because who would want to kiss someone whose breath smelled like *that*? Since I always brushed my teeth at bedtime and Yorick never did, I never understood why it was *my* breath that smelled bad. It took a long time to realize those remarks were another way to control my feelings and leave me vulnerable to other manipulation, but those memories still got in the way of my exploring anything more than friendship with Julian.

Having had enough socializing, Fred and Wilma Cornley, the almost newlyweds, took a plate of pizza and other treats up to their room. Two of the Owlgard and two Hawks showed up with an almost-human-looking Cougar to help finish off the snacks in the heads-or-tails bowl. Jenna McKay made arrangements with Bobcat to do our donkey-cart tour of The Jumble tomorrow. Ilya and Natasha were holding glasses of red wine—I hoped— and listening to a couple of men talk about . . . Well, I wasn't sure if they were trying to impress the Sanguinati with their academic credentials or were trying to persuade Ilya to invest in something, but I hustled over to Grimshaw intending to ask him to break up that conversation before one or both men ended up with an extreme case of anemia.

Thump. Thump. Thump.

And that's when someone thumped on the front door.

Ilya and Natasha turned in that direction. So did Julian and Grimshaw. And I headed for the door.

And Aggie and Jozi rushed to the door, gleefully shouting, "Another trickster!"

No one at the door. No one within the reach of the lights.

A rattling sound came out of the dark, and I heard Grimshaw say, "Crap!" as he rushed toward the door.

Rattle, rattle, rattle. Then something stepped out of the dark.

I caught a glimpse of ragged feathers and a skin-over-bone crow's head with black eye sockets.

Aggie and Jozi sucked in a breath.

A feathery hand pointed at them and a harsh voice said, "Gonna gitcha."

Aggie and Jozi screamed and knocked me into Grimshaw as they bolted toward the kitchen. Grimshaw shoved me into Julian's arms as he and Ilya ran out the door. But the thing I'd seen was already gone.

"Gods above and below," one of the academics said. "I never thought I would see . . ."

He looked excited and sick, which was unnerving, but I needed to find Aggie and Jozi. And Eddie, since he seemed to have disappeared too.

Julian and I found Aggie and Jozi hiding under the kitchen table. Aggie had a skillet. Jozi had a rolling pin. They were shaking and whimpering.

I crawled under the table with them, my size for once being an advantage. "It was a scary costume," I offered.

Jozi shook her head. "Coming to get us."

"Who is coming to get you?" Julian asked quietly, crouching beside the table in order to see us.

Aggie looked at him, her dark eyes filled with terror—and resignation. Then she whispered, "Crowbones."

CHAPTER 7

Grimshaw

Windsday, Grau 31

G rimshaw took two steps into the dark before Ilya grabbed his arm to stop him.

"I'll look around," Ilya said.

"It's my job."

"It's not your territory. Jurisdiction. Is that the proper word?"

Damn lawyer. You know all the proper words as well as I do. "This place is flexible when it comes to jurisdiction."

"Then let's say I have a better chance of looking around and surviving than you do," Ilya said.

Grimshaw hesitated. If the leader of the Sanguinati around Lake Silence said *better chance*, that was reason enough to be cautious. "Do you know what that was?" he asked quietly. "Why the Crows freaked out like that?"

"No," Ilya replied. "I'll look around; then we'll both go inside and talk to Victoria. The Crowgard are more likely to tell her what frightened them than tell either of us."

Ilya shifted to his smoke form—another sign that the vampire felt cautious about whatever else might be out there—and headed away from the access road. Headed in the direction where, a few months ago, a corrupt detective had been grabbed by an angry Elder and twisted in a way that still gave the cops and the local medical examiner nightmares.

Grimshaw stood where he was, scanning the edge between human lights and wild-country dark and listening for movement, whispers. Anything. Everything. He hadn't heard any screams from the teenage boys, no sound of a car crashing as they tried to escape. Then again, the Elders were fast when they attacked.

Smoke drifted toward him. He braced, hoping it was Ilya and knowing he had no way to counter an attack from anything in that form.

Ilya shifted to his human form and stepped into the light. "Do you have any evidence bags in your vehicle?"

"Sure," Grimshaw said, turning toward his cruiser. "I keep a few for—"

"Something that can hold wet evidence?"

He stopped. Turned back to study the vampire. "How wet?"

Ilya didn't answer.

Crap. "I keep a body bag with my crime scene kit. We can use that, but I'll have to help you carry it."

Ilya hesitated. Then he nodded. "Very well. You should bring that big flashlight you usually keep in your car."

"For illumination or protection?"

Ilya didn't answer.

The evening was going pear-shaped in a hurry.

Grimshaw retrieved the flashlight and body bag. After a moment's thought, he grabbed the small camera he also kept in the car. It wasn't as good as the cameras used by the Crime Investigation Unit in Bristol, but whatever photos he could get of the evidence in situ tonight would have to do. He didn't need Ilya to tell him that if he waited for CIU, there wouldn't be anything for any of them to photograph in the morning.

He slipped the camera strap over his head, tucked the body bag under one arm, gave Ilya the flashlight, and said, "Lead the way."

They were close to the trees but still on clear ground. In daylight, they would be in sight of anyone looking out a window on that side of the main house. Grimshaw gave thanks that all the children who had come to The Jumble tonight had been spared whatever he was about to face.

He smelled blood.

Ilya's hand was steady, but Grimshaw still took in the scene in flashes.

A bottle of bleach on the ground. A decorative hollow gourd lying next to an arm that had been severed at the elbow. And a lump of something black and feathered.

"I need to take some pictures," Grimshaw said quietly, setting the body bag near his feet. He pointed to the bleach and then aimed the camera. "Lighting isn't the best, but I doubt we'll have another chance."

He took several shots of each piece of the tableau. Even with the light shining on it, he couldn't make sense of the lump of feathers—and he wasn't eager to find out what might be underneath it.

Tucking the camera between his shirt and jacket, Grimshaw opened the body bag to transport the evidence.

Rattle, rattle, rattle.

A sound like a rattlesnake's tail, but worse. Somehow worse. And nearby.

Grimshaw looked at Ilya and tipped his head toward the building. The Sanguinati had a chance of getting away from whatever was out there, and all of Sproing's residents needed a *terra indigene* leader who had a tolerance for humans.

"Chief Grimshaw," Ilya said in a normal tone of voice, "now that we have photographed the items, the next step in investigating is to transport the evidence to the police station for analysis. Is that not true?"

"That is true," Grimshaw agreed, understanding that he was explaining their actions to whatever watched them. "We will use these items to identify the person who played a cruel trick on the Crowgard tonight. Then the person can be properly charged and arrested for a crime."

"Just like in the cop and crime shows that Victoria, Aggie, Jozi, and Eddie enjoy watching."

"Yeah, like that."

Ilya picked up the unopened bottle of bleach and placed it at one end of the body bag. The severed arm and gourd were placed in the middle. Wishing he'd brought gloves and accepting that his clothes were going to get soiled with something, Grimshaw lifted the bundle of soggy feathers.

Something inside the bundle of feathers. Something hard and round, but this wasn't the time or place to investigate.

Stuffing the bundle into the bottom end, he zipped up the bag. Keeping tension on the ends of the bag, he and Ilya lifted it, trying to prevent everything from sliding into the middle and destroying any evidence he might be able to glean once he got back to the station.

Rattle, rattle, rattle.

Just his imagination, or was there anger in that sound?

Every step was taken with the expectation of an attack. Even after they reached his cruiser and placed the evidence in the trunk, Grimshaw felt his skin crawl. The attack on this prankster had been so fierce and so fast—and so silent. Except for that rattling sound coming out of the dark.

"You can't go inside like that," Ilya said, looking at Grimshaw's bloody hands and the cuffs of his shirt and jacket. "Natasha is bringing out some towels and water."

He looked at his bloody hands. Gods above and below, what was in that bundle? "Thanks. Can you talk to Aggie and Jozi?"

Ilya nodded. "With Victoria. Do you want Julian Farrow to accompany you to the station?"

He did, but Julian wasn't a cop anymore, and he needed someone at The Jumble who would sound the alarm if there was more trouble. "No need. I'll talk to him in the morning."

When Natasha stepped outside, they walked up to meet her. Grimshaw cleaned up as best he could.

"I'll escort Victoria's guests to their cabins," Ilya said.

"*We* will escort Victoria's guests." Natasha smiled, showing a hint of fang that no man could mistake for anything but a spousal warning.

Ilya didn't look happy, but he said, "Yes. *We* will escort the guests."

"Will you be okay returning to Silence Lodge?" Grimshaw asked. "You don't know what's out there."

"I'll find out what I can from the Crows before we leave," Ilya replied.

Meaning the Sanguinati really *didn't* know what was out there, and that wasn't good. "I'll be back in the morning."

He drove slowly, scanning the land on either side of the gravel access road. He didn't expect to see any of the *terra indigene*, but he breathed a sigh of relief that he didn't find a car that had been flipped or crushed or bent around a tree. He didn't see any debris or body parts. Maybe those idiot teenage boys had gotten away.

As he turned onto Lake Street and headed north toward Sproing, he also didn't see Aiden. Apparently Fire had completed his stint of directing traffic.

Grimshaw pulled into his parking space in front of the station. A month ago, there hadn't been any officially reserved parking spaces on Main Street. People took any available spot. But after he'd returned from answering a call one afternoon and had trouble finding a parking space near the station, someone who wasn't him or the Sanguinati had decided that the three spaces in front of the station were now reserved for police vehicles and Ilya's black luxury sedan and had painted ~~POELEESE~~ PO-LICE across the spaces.

It had taken only a couple of cars having *BAD HUMAN!* clawed into the hoods to teach the residents of Sproing the value of letting the police have those spaces.

"Assess, then decide," he said quietly. It wasn't that late in the evening, and he couldn't leave the evidence in his trunk overnight. Best get on with it, then, as long as things had stayed quiet in the village.

He went into the station and nodded to Osgood, who was on the phone.

"No, ma'am," Osgood said politely, "you can't make out an official complaint against the diner for running out of brownie squares and offering peanut butter cookies to youngsters coming in for a treat."

Standing on the other side of the desk, Grimshaw couldn't make out the words, but he heard the tone loud and clear—and he recognized the voice. Mrs. Ellen C. Wilson was one of Sproing's newer residents. She seemed determined to let everyone know that living in a village the size of Sproing was beneath her. She complained about everything and reported poor quality at least twice a week in an effort to be given a steep discount at a store or receive something for free from any business serving food. And somehow, despite the growing dislike for her throughout the village, she usually managed to get what she wanted.

Personally, he thought it was because her voice grated in a way that reminded him of a horror movie he'd seen as a kid where sentient worms burrowed into people's brains and took control, causing people to go on murdering rampages.

He'd love to see the back of her. He'd happily drive her and her son,

Theodore, to the train station and see them heading anywhere. And he was afraid that, one of these days, she would offend someone who wasn't human and most of her wouldn't be seen again.

"We don't have time for this." He held out his hand.

Osgood hesitated, then gave him the receiver.

"Mrs. Wilson? This is Chief Grimshaw." He listened to her diatribe for a full minute before he interrupted. "Since I saw your boy stuff a handful of those peanut butter cookies into his mouth earlier this afternoon, you and I both know any tummy ache he has right now was caused by overindulgence rather than him being sensitive to certain foods, and I'm telling you now that, at his age, he should know if there is something he shouldn't eat. The people working at the diner aren't going to act as surrogate parents while you go flitting from store to store, spreading ill will, but if you want to pursue this, here's what you do. You have Doc Wallace give your boy a thorough physical and run whatever tests are available to check for food sensitivities. I, in the meantime, will inform the food businesses in the village that they should not serve your son unless he can give them a note from you specifying what food he is allowed to purchase. And if you think for one moment you're going to use whiny complaints to slide out of paying for those tests or the doctor's bill, you should know that the Sanguinati can also test blood for all kinds of things. They just take an extra pint or two as their fee."

He hung up and looked at Osgood, whose brown eyes were wide with shock and whose brown skin was looking paler by the minute.

"The Sanguinati can test blood?" Osgood asked.

"They react to substances in the blood." Grimshaw shrugged. "Any trouble in the village? Besides Ellen Wilson?"

Osgood shook his head. "The younger kids cleared out early. Even the home parties are done by now. No calls about any adult parties getting out of hand."

"Anything about the people in the camper park? No trouble there?"

"No, sir." Osgood waited a beat. "Were you expecting some trouble?"

If those teenagers were on the road, they were someone else's problem by now, but he'd like to be sure. "In the morning, you go over to the camper park and knock on every door. I want to know who's renting the campers and how long they plan to stay. If anyone doesn't answer the door, you roust the park's owner and find out who he has listed on the rental agreements."

"You looking for someone in particular?"

"Four boys. Teens. They were looking to cause some trouble at The Jumble this evening. If they are renting one of the campers, I want to know if all four of them made it back. Right now, I want you to call Doc Wallace and tell him I'm picking him up in ten minutes. Then call Sheridan Ames and tell her we need her facility to examine some crime scene evidence, and Doc Wallace and I will be there shortly."

Sheridan Ames and her brother Samuel ran the village's funeral home. It was the only place to access the equipment to examine a body without driving to the mortuary in Crystalton or Bristol.

"You have a body at The Jumble?"

"Part of one."

"Gods," Osgood breathed. "Do you know what did it?"

This past summer, Osgood was one of the four police officers who had been left at The Jumble when Vicki DeVine had been brought to the station to answer questions about a dead body. He had been the only survivor when the other men ignored the boundaries the Others had heard Vicki establish.

"No," Grimshaw said. "I don't."

CHAPTER 8

Ilya and Aggie

Windsday, Grau 31

F ind out who is still here and who has returned to their own dens,>
Ilya said, using the *terra indigene* form of communication, when he
and Natasha stepped into the main house and closed the door. <And tell
Boris that the youngsters should stay inside the lodge tonight.>

<I already did that,> Natasha replied. <Are you going to continue
thinking that being mated to you has deprived me of the ability to use my
brain?>

He wrapped a hand around her wrist, stopping her as he watched one
of the academics bearing down on them. He could almost taste the man's
excitement. What he didn't understand was the reason for it.

<I'm . . . concerned. The Sanguinati are in charge of the land around
Lake Silence as well as the village of Sproing. Different forms of *terra
indigene* have their territories within that land, especially around the lake
itself.>

<The north end of the lake is exclusively *terra indigene* who have as
little contact with us as they do with the humans.>

<Yes. But the Elders and other forms who live there are known to us.
At least the feel of them is familiar. This was . . . different. Unknown. I

think it's *terra indigene*, but it didn't acknowledge my authority. Didn't acknowledge me at all.>

<An Elder?>

<Maybe.>

<You really are concerned.>

<Yes.>

<For me?>

<For all of us.> *But now, especially you.*

Natasha gave Ilya a full-fanged smile that stopped the academic two steps before he reached them. <Then you deal with the excited human, and I will deal with our kind.>

She glided away, leaving him to deal with the excited academic.

"Did you see it? Did you see?"

"Who are you?" Ilya asked. "We weren't introduced earlier."

"What? Oh. Professor Rodney Roash. I'm writing a book about urban legends, folklore, and myths, human and Other. I was hoping to interview some of the *terra indigene* about their myths and folktales to try to establish how such things come into being, but I never thought to see . . ." He reached for Ilya's arm.

Ilya showed fang and snarled a warning. Not very proper for an attorney who was usually so good at mimicking human behavior, but he didn't want to be touched and he didn't want to be mistaken for human tonight.

Professor Roash took a step back but didn't give up. "I'd like to interview those Crows about what they saw that frightened them so much. And *why* it frightened them."

"Not tonight," Ilya said. "If I think there is anything that would be of interest to you, I will tell you."

"But . . ."

"If you persist in being a pest, I will shove you out the door and let you find out for yourself what is out there in the dark."

Roash's expression was one of offended dignity. "Being enthusiastic about one's field of study is not being a pest."

"Do humans have a word for someone who exploits another being's fear?" Ilya asked.

A flicker of something in the man's eyes. Had this human been *waiting* for something to happen? And did it happen as he'd intended?

Something to discuss with Grimshaw in the morning.

"You're staying at the Mill Creek Cabins?" Ilya asked.

"Yes, but I think I'll remain here tonight. Several of my colleagues are planning to do the same."

That flicker in the eyes.

"No," Ilya said. "A driver will be along soon, and we'll take you and your colleagues back to the Mill Creek Cabins."

"You can't decide that."

He showed a hint of fang. "Oh, but I can."

He walked away before he gave in to the urge to shift to his smoke form and drain the fool enough to make sure no trouble would come from that direction. Getting drunk from consuming alcohol-infused blood wouldn't be prudent tonight.

An academic interested in urban legends, folklore, and myths. Nothing strange about someone like that coming to The Jumble to observe Trickster Night. But Ilya couldn't shake the feeling that the man knew more about what had happened tonight than he and Grimshaw did.

And that made him wonder if Roash would be surprised by anything Grimshaw was transporting in the body bag.

A ggie held the skillet in one feathered hand and held on to Miss Vicki with the other. There were feathers on her face, feathers in her hair. Feathers, feathers, everywhere.

Jozi hadn't been able to hold the human form and had shifted completely to Crow, needing Julian's help to get untangled from her work outfit.

Aggie wanted to shift too, wanted to feel safer in her own shape, but she had to tell Ilya what she saw, had to make Miss Vicki understand the danger.

Conan had sniffed out Eddie, who was hiding on the screened porch, paralyzed with fear and unable to speak in any language.

Ilya arrived in the kitchen and crouched beside the table, like Julian.

"Tell me what is out there," Ilya said.

"Caw." An almost human throat, but no human sounds.

Don't matter if you caw, don't matter if you shout.

"Aggie told me earlier it is someone called Crowbones," Miss Vicki said. She looked at Aggie, gave her hand a gentle squeeze. "Isn't that right?"

Crowbones will gitcha if you don't watch out!

Aggie nodded.

"Some kind of *terra indigene*?" Ilya asked. "An Elder perhaps?"

She shrugged.

"Does this Crowbones carry a gourd?"

"A gourd full of bones," she whispered, finally able to say human words. "Bones of the taken."

"And a cape made of the feathers of the taken?" Ilya asked.

Aggie shook her head. "Feathers of the fallen. Feathers of Crows killed by humans or other Crows. Bones are taken from Crows who do bad things. That's how you know they were bad Crows." Shaking, she dropped the skillet and tore at the buttons on her blouse. Unable to free herself, she grabbed Miss Vicki with both hands. "Hunting here. Gonna git us. Can't . . . escape. Be . . . careful. Might get you too."

With a cry that turned into a *caw*, Aggie shifted to her Crowgard form, then struggled to get free of her clothes. She perched on Miss Vicki's thigh, shaking and shaking.

Gonna gitcha!

Why? *Why?* What had she and the other Crowgard living in The Jumble done to draw Crowbones to Lake Silence?

Ilya confirmed that Conan Beargard was still on the porch, keeping an eye on Eddie as well as making sure nothing came toward them from the beach or backyard.

Leaving an agitated Cougar, who had shifted to his Cat form, to guard Victoria and the two Crows who were still under the kitchen table, Ilya led Julian Farrow to the poolroom. He shooed out a couple of guests who had ignored the Reserved sign on the door, then turned to Julian, who leaned against the pool table.

"A hollow gourd and a cape made of feathers?" Julian asked.

"Chief Grimshaw and I found those items when we investigated." He didn't mention the bleach—or the severed arm.

"Meaning you went wandering out in the dark?"

"You would have done the same." Ilya waited for a denial but wasn't surprised when he didn't get one.

"Whatever you found might be what Jozi and Aggie saw," Julian said carefully, "but not what Eddie saw."

"The individual could have reached The Jumble by boat, could have come up from the beach. Eddie, standing in the screened porch, would have seen a figure moving past." Ilya didn't believe it, but it was a valid scenario.

"Maybe for what Jozi and Aggie saw, but not what Eddie saw," Julian repeated.

"Has the feel of The Jumble changed?"

Julian hesitated. "I think you, Wayne, and I should meet at the bookstore tomorrow and play a game of Murder. You'll have to get the altered game board from Wayne; he confiscated it and all the game pieces."

Not good. Julian Farrow had sensed the trouble last summer by playing Murder on a game board that had been altered to represent The Jumble. If he was suggesting this as a way to feel the pulse of the land and beings around Lake Silence . . .

"You can't tell from The Jumble itself?"

Julian shook his head. "Maybe because there are too many strangers here right now. I didn't have a feeling of anything being wrong, but something terrified the Crowgard, and we have to figure out what it is."

"Agreed." He had four young Sanguinati staying at Silence Lodge. Was it a coincidence that this unknown threat showed up around the same time as he had this additional responsibility?

Another hesitation, which made Ilya wonder how much information Julian Farrow was keeping to himself. The man had been a reliable source of information about the village and villagers until he'd developed an emotional attachment to Victoria DeVine. Farrow was still a reliable source for most things.

"You should give your associates in Lakeside a call as soon as you can," Julian finally said. "A couple of times this evening, Grimshaw started to tell me about a message he'd received, but we didn't have a chance to have a private word before things got exciting."

Yes, the evening had certainly gotten exciting.

"Will you call Chief Grimshaw to arrange a time for this meeting tomorrow?" Ilya asked.

Julian nodded.

They left the poolroom. Ilya checked on Victoria one more time, then rounded up the four academics who weren't official guests at The Jumble. Professor Roash wasn't happy about being required to leave; the other three men, after being encouraged to take a pizza box full of leftovers with them—and after being reminded that the chief of police lived in one of the cabins—were more than ready to return to their own lodgings to continue the festivities and discussions.

Boris drove the minivan that belonged to Roash, and Ilya drove the car belonging to Peter Lynchfield. They made sure the men were all safely inside their own cabins. Then Ilya shifted to a mostly smoke form and swiftly went over to Grimshaw's cabin, keeping close to the ground and then close to the porch floor in case any of the academics looked out a window or stepped outside and wondered what he was doing. After a moment's debate, he left the keys to the minivan and car next to the front door since he didn't see any obvious place to hide them.

There was a third vehicle parked at the cabin next to Grimshaw's, but Edward Janse had scampered into his cabin and locked the door. The human struck him as timid, at least in comparison with the other three men. Ilya couldn't picture Janse trying to drive off before daylight, so he didn't insist on having the keys to that car.

<Ilya!> Boris warned.

Ilya flowed off the porch and across the small, enclosed front yard. Flowed under the wooden gate. Then he shifted back to human form to face Fire and Air.

"Would humans call that theft?" Air asked, sounding curious.

"I don't want these humans to leave until Chief Grimshaw and I have a chance to meet tomorrow morning and discuss some things. Confiscating keys to their vehicles is a simple way to make sure they don't."

"They might have more than one set of keys."

"That had occurred to me."

Fire looked at Air. Then he looked at Ilya and smiled. "We will assist."

"Your help would be appreciated." It was the only safe thing to say.

Even for other *terra indigene*, receiving help—or any attention—from Elementals was not without its risks, but like some of the Elders, they found The Jumble, as it was run by Victoria, to be a variety show of entertainment. They participated when it suited them, and he wondered why it suited them now.

And he wondered what the Elementals knew about the *terra indigene* visitor that had been watching him and Grimshaw collect the bits and pieces of a foolish prankster. If something *had* come to The Jumble to hunt, would the other Elders object? Or was this unfamiliar form something even the Elders who resided around Lake Silence would avoid?

Shifting back to smoke form, Ilya and Boris returned to Silence Lodge. Natasha had left a message that she was going to stay with Victoria tonight and keep an eye on things. That meant she wouldn't be traveling across the lake, in the dark, alone.

He suspected that decision had more to do with his emotional adjustments to having a mate than any real need for one of the Sanguinati to remain at The Jumble, but he was grateful that she had allowed him that comfort tonight.

He was even more grateful after he placed a call to the Sanguinati in Lakeside and talked to Vlad.

Jack-o'-lantern. Bones. Black feathers. Rattlesnake tail. Coffin.

The warning wouldn't have changed anything, even if he'd known about it earlier, but he wondered what else might be headed their way.

CHAPTER 9

Julian

Windsday, Grau 31

Has the feel of The Jumble changed?

Since Vicki was still under the table, and her employees were either traumatized or protecting the traumatized, Julian checked on the human guests. The almost newlyweds had the Do Not Disturb sign on their door, so Julian didn't anticipate seeing them until breakfast. Jenna McKay was in the library, browsing through Vicki's selection of books.

"Alan Wolfgard," Jenna muttered as she studied a book cover. "I wonder if he's . . . ?"

"He is," Julian said, walking toward her. He looked at the title. "I have a couple copies of that one at the bookstore, if you decide you want to finish reading the story."

Jenna smiled. "That's the place with the funny name. What time do you open?"

"Later than usual tomorrow. I have to assist the police in their inquiries."

"I don't check out until Firesday morning. I could go to the village for lunch tomorrow and visit the bookstore after that." She grinned at Julian. "I'm doing the donkey-cart tour in the morning."

"I haven't done the tour, but I've heard it's an adventure."

Jenna selected two books from the shelves and moved her hands up and down as if weight could indicate content. "I can't decide which to take back to the cabin. Scary or romance?"

"Take both," he suggested. "When it comes to books, better to have too many than not enough."

"I like the way you think."

Unable to decide if she was flirting with him or if she was just an enthusiastic booklover, Julian was about to make a reasonable excuse to escape when Natasha walked into the library.

"Since Ilya is dealing with the guests at the Mill Creek Cabins, Conan is escorting Victoria's male guests to their cabin," Natasha said. "If the female is ready to leave, they can all go together."

Jenna grabbed a couple more books, grinned at Julian, and said, "Sampling before a bookstore spree."

Since the books she'd chosen were by Intuit or *terra indigene* authors and not likely books she would find in human-controlled cities, he had a feeling "spree" might be an accurate word.

Once the cabin guests were on their way, Julian took the Reserved sign off the poolroom door and left Ben Malacki and David Shuman to resume their interrupted game. Then he fetched an old issue of *Sproing Weekly*, helped Vicki crawl out from under the kitchen table, and covered the floor with the paper while Vicki filled a bowl with water so the Crows would have something to drink.

When Conan returned, he brought Eddie into the kitchen and settled him under the table with Aggie and Jozi before returning to the porch, shifting into Bear form, and going to sleep in front of the porch door.

Julian went around the main house with Vicki, locking doors, turning out lights, and making sure everyone inside was as secure and safe as they could be.

Vicki hesitated, clearly uncertain about what to do with him. Her apartment didn't have a guest room or a couch long enough for a man to sleep on, and her guest suites were booked. His thoughts leaned toward romance and had for a while, and he thought she entertained similar thoughts at least some of the time, but decisions like this left her skittish.

He solved her internal struggle by saying, "If you don't mind, I'll watch some TV and then sack out on the couch down here."

Her smiled wobbled with relief, but he couldn't say if it was relief because he was staying or because he wasn't pushing. "Okay. Sure. Help yourself to the food. There's plenty."

"I will stay with Victoria tonight," Natasha said as she joined them. "We will enjoy . . . girl talk."

For a moment he wondered what a newly mated vampire and a human woman with serious trust issues would talk about—and then decided he did not want to know. But he might, out of male solidarity, warn Ilya when he saw him tomorrow.

Julian opened a bottle of beer and warmed up a couple of slices of pizza in the wave-cooker. Then he went into the TV room, found a channel that was showing a marathon of old horror movies for Trickster Night, and felt the house settle around him.

He sensed no change in The Jumble, despite the evening's frights—and whatever Ilya and Wayne had found in the dark. If there was some kind of malevolence infecting Sproing and Lake Silence, it hadn't been here long enough to change the feel of the place. With luck, it would move on or the police would uncover it and deal with it.

Julian focused on the movie and refused to think of what might happen if the police, and the rest of the humans around here, weren't lucky.

CHAPTER 10

Grimshaw

Windsday, Grau 31

Grimshaw helped Samuel Ames lift the body bag from the gurney onto the table in the mortuary's preparation room. He opened the bag, put on some gloves, then pulled out the bottle of bleach and set it aside. He'd take it to the station and dust it for prints. He didn't think it would help him identify the individual, but he would follow procedure.

"Why the bleach?" Samuel asked. "Did someone really think there would be time to clean away evidence before the Others gave chase?"

"I don't know," Grimshaw replied. It was a good question because it indicated a serious lack of knowledge about the *terra indigene* and how they would respond to someone playing a trick—especially at The Jumble.

Doc Wallace, who was Sproing's medical examiner as well as the junior partner in the village's only medical practice, handed Grimshaw the gourd and removed the severed arm from the bag.

Grimshaw shook the gourd. Hearing the rattle, he tipped the gourd over one hand.

Pebbles that you could find in any creek bed. No helpful clue there.

Then the three men looked at the soggy mass of black feathers.

By rights, he should call the CIU team in Bristol to come up and examine the evidence. In the morning, he *would* call Captain Hargreaves, who was his old boss and the man who had assigned him to deal with the trouble in Sproing over the summer, but tonight he was going to be his own CIU team.

The feathers were sewn in patches onto some kind of netting shaped like a cape. His own skill began and ended with sewing buttons on a shirt and mending a small rip in a seam, but this struck him as shoddy workmanship rather than something ragged from wear. And some of the feathers, brown in color, definitely didn't come from a crow—or a Crow.

As he lifted one side of the cape, he felt the round, hard something in the center of the mass. Slowly, methodically, the men uncovered what the feathers and netting had hidden.

Samuel Ames and Doc Wallace sucked in a breath. Grimshaw looked at the broken beak and the grotesque head that was caved in on one side and said, "Papier-mâché. It's a mask."

At the same time, Doc Wallace said, "Plague doctor."

Samuel frowned. "What?"

"A few centuries ago, there was a devastating plague in the lands we know as Cel-Romano. The doctors who tried to treat the victims of the plague wore these masks that had a long beak, probably as an attempt to protect themselves from breathing in the disease. I'm guessing this is supposed to be a Crowgard skull and beak, but it reminds me of the plague doctor." Doc gave them a faint smile. "It's a popular Trickster Night costume among medical students, which is why I thought of it."

The mask was split and crushed in places, but Doc Wallace still removed it as carefully as if it were living tissue.

Then they stared at the partially crushed head that had been under the mask, and Grimshaw breathed out the word "Crap."

CHAPTER 11

Them

Windsday, Grau 31

Not wanting to get knocked over or smacked in the face by a wild gesture, Richard Cardosa sat in a chair and watched his colleague's feverish pacing around the cabin.

"Did you see anything?" Roash demanded. "Did you see it?"

Cardosa shook his head. "I was too far away from the door."

"All that fear in the Crowgard, just from something seen for a moment combined with a sound in the dark and a couple of words. I *have* to interview those Crows and find out what they saw. This is big, Richard. This is breakthrough research."

It wasn't even close to being breakthrough research. At least, not on Roash's end of the project.

Gonna gitcha.

Well, they had certainly done that.

Cardosa listened and listened and patiently listened to Roash's speculation and conjecture about something that couldn't be verified from the available data.

And he wondered what Roash would say about the bleach.

CHAPTER 12

Windsday, Grau 31

His brain didn't work right anymore. Even so, as he approached the body that was hidden by darkness but still too close to the house, he knew he had to be careful. If the Sanguinati found him too soon, all his effort would be for nothing. He couldn't let that happen.

His brain . . . blinked . . . as it sometimes did these days. One moment he was alone, and the next . . .

A long black cape covered a slender female body. One of her hands held a gourd. The other held a short-handled scythe.

She stared at him without any pity for what he had become. Then she shook the gourd. *Rattle, rattle, rattle.*

A warning? Like the things she had left behind?

He raised a hand and pointed toward the spot where a Sanguinati and a human had removed the warning. "They . . . work together. Help. Protect. Good." He struggled for words, but he wasn't sure it mattered. She was primal, feral. An Elder. A Hunter.

Dangerous.

Was she here to find him? Or was she hunting someone else?

Maybe, if he told her why he had come to The Jumble, she wouldn't interfere.

A pouch with a cross-body strap carried everything he'd had with him when he'd eluded his keepers in order to reach this place. He opened the pouch and removed a folded sheet of paper. Unfolding it, he showed her the drawing, then pointed toward the main house. "Reader . . . lives here. I come . . . to keep watch. To . . . warn. Protect her."

He wondered if she understood. He wondered if she cared about anything beyond the hunt.

He carefully folded the paper and put it back in the pouch.

She held out the gourd and gave it a little shake. Not a threat.

"Warning?" He took the gourd and shook it. *Rattle, rattle, rattle.* Yes. This sound would warn.

He pointed to what was left of the body. "Worked . . . alone?"

She shook her head.

"Worked . . . with others?"

A nod.

"Police . . . need to find."

She tilted her head, a silent question.

"In village. I know . . . place."

She attached the scythe to her belt. Then she stared at him for a long time before she removed the cape of black feathers and put it around him, securing the clasp made of woven pieces of leather.

He felt protected—connected—in a way he hadn't felt in a long time.

After swiftly hollowing out the torso, she picked up the body with one hand—and he led her to the place in the human village where the police would find it.

CHAPTER 13

Vicki

Thaisday, Novembros 1

I must have fallen asleep, because my alarm woke me up.

I grumbled my way out of bed, opened the drapes, and stared blearily out the window. Apparently the sun was also not a morning person today, which made me feel a little better. I was aligned with nature. Go, me.

The hot shower didn't help my body much, but it got my brain churning over everything that happened last night.

What *did* happen last night? Either, by sheer coincidence, someone came up with a costume that happened to match the Crowgard's idea of the bogeyman, or someone had heard this Crowbones story and thought it would be fun to scare the feathers off some of the Crows. Which was more than mean; it was all kinds of dangerous.

Deciding I couldn't think about dangerous stuff before coffee, I got dressed in jeans, a long-sleeve pullover, and a loose-weave brown sweater with cap sleeves. The sweater, combined with my curly brown hair, made me look like an electrified sausage, but it was practical and warm enough for a morning of chores and cleanup.

The guests weren't up by the time I went downstairs, but Julian must have been awake and working for a while, because a pot of coffee was already made, the kitchen table had been wiped down, and the little bowls I used for condiments were set out in rows, waiting for curls of butter or scoops of berry jam from the jars I purchased from the Milfords, who sold fresh fruit as well as homemade jams and jellies.

Like Ineke Xavier, I tried to buy from local suppliers, including the Milfords, whose orchards adjoined The Jumble. Unlike Ineke, who was a good cook, I didn't inflict my limited cooking skills on my guests, but I did supply the means for the guests to make toast to go with a bowl of seasonal fruit, along with cheese, yogurt, and pastries. There were usually eggs that could be scrambled or made into an omelet. And on the mornings after a special occasion, or cop and crime night, there was my personal breakfast favorite—leftover pizza.

I weaved to the coffeepot and poured myself a mug of brain-starter.

"Good morning," Julian said. He pointed to the bread on the counter. "Toast?"

I raised the mug and said, "Cheers."

Looking amused, he put slices of bread in the toaster. "How late were you up with your girl talk?"

Girl talk. Natasha not quite explaining vampire mating rituals, although I do remember her saying Ilya was a very skilled kisser. And me not quite explaining trust issues and how fear of bad breath even after brushing your teeth got in the way of finding out if you liked how a friend kissed—and being anxious about what might happen if, after a kiss, you discovered you didn't have *that* kind of chemistry but still wanted to be friends.

I think we decided that Sanguinati courting rituals went on longer than human courting rituals and were more complex before a pair made the final commitment, but things were easier once the individuals reached the actual mating. I *think*. Since I don't remember Natasha leaving my apartment, I can't say if we reached any other conclusions. Or any conclusions.

"Natasha?" I said.

Julian put a piece of toast on a plate and handed it to me. "She's around somewhere. She's catching a ride to the village with me." He dropped a piece of toast on his own plate and spread butter and berry jam over it. "Aggie, Jozi, and Eddie left with Conan. They're still in Crow form, so I'm not sure they'll be working today. Safety in numbers—and the ability to fly away from danger—seems to be the Crowgard thinking this morning. Conan said there is some concern about a friend of theirs—Clara Crowgard. There's been some argy-bargy between your employees and Clara—Conan wasn't sure about what—and she's been going off on her own. But after last night . . . Well, friends are still friends."

The Crows didn't have an argument. They had some argy-bargy.

Julian came up with such interesting words.

"I hope the idiot who made that costume is pleased with himself," I grumbled as I slathered butter and jam on my piece of toast, then took a big bite. Somewhere between bites I realized Julian's silence wasn't a way to ignore or disapprove of what I'd said. "Julian?"

"Be careful out there," he said quietly. "Know where your guests are going today."

When I sucked in air, I realized I had stopped breathing. "Should I warn Ineke?"

"I already called her."

Oh, gosh golly. Julian was seriously spooked. "It was a person in a costume." I wanted to believe it, wanted him to agree.

He hesitated. "Maybe."

"But it's daylight." I glanced at the kitchen windows that looked out over the screened porch. "Sort of. The spookies should be tucked under their blankies for a good day's sleep."

That got a tiny laugh out of him. Then he sobered. "Let someone know where you are whenever you leave the main house. Okay?"

That's when Natasha walked into the kitchen and said, "Conan and Bobcat wanted you to know that they found a partially eaten donkey close to the main house."

CHAPTER 14

Grimshaw

Thaisday, Novembros 1

By the clock, it was morning, and the gloomy start to the day fit his mood even before Grimshaw spotted the bundle someone had dumped in the middle parking space, reserved for the police station. Pulling across all three spaces, he turned on his flashing lights, grabbed the flashlight he'd left on the passenger seat, and got out of the cruiser. Walking around the front of the cruiser, he took careful steps in the first open space until he reached the bundle.

He touched the gold medal under his shirt, said a quick prayer to Mikhos, then turned on the flashlight to get a good look at what had been left where the police would find it.

Blood-soaked jeans. Bloody shoes. The ripped shirt was the worst because he could see the hollowed-out torso and part of the rib cage stripped to the bone.

Gods above and below.

He unlocked the police station, called the Bristol station, and informed the dispatcher that he needed Detective Kipp and his CIU team in Sproing as soon as possible. Kipp headed one of the two CIU teams that worked out of Bristol and had been the lead investigator who had come to The Jumble that summer. The man wouldn't thank him for the specific request, but Grimshaw figured a team that had some experience working around Lake Silence had a better chance of staying alive.

He also called Captain Hargreaves, catching his former boss as the man was walking out the door to go to work, and repeated his request for assistance from Kipp and his CIU team.

After he hung up, a thought occurred to him. Chilled him. Taking a pair of crime scene gloves out of his desk, he went outside and studied the bundle. Last night he'd had a head without a body. This morning he had a body without a head.

If this wasn't a taunt or a threat . . .

Trying to disturb as little as possible, he eased a wallet out of a back pocket of the jeans. When he opened the wallet, he sucked in a breath.

Just a kid, he thought as he looked at a student photo ID belonging to Adam Fewks. *Just a damn fool college boy.*

He stripped off one blood-smeared glove, removed the ID, then laid the wallet beside the remains before he slipped the ID into his shirt pocket. Having stripped off the other glove, he dropped the gloves in the empty parking space, to be collected with whatever debris the CIU team would create.

He fetched the two manila envelopes from the passenger seat of his cruiser and brought them into the station—two sets of the photos he'd taken last night at The Jumble and Ames Funeral Home. One set would go to Bristol with Kipp. The other would stay here.

He opened one envelope and pulled out one of the prints of the head. Then he set Fewks's photo ID next to the headshot—and swore with quiet savagery before slipping the ID back into his shirt pocket and going outside to stand guard until Kipp arrived.

Just a ballsy college boy who, like every boy that age, believed he could survive anything and everything, and a prank would have no consequences.

Then he thought about the academics from various universities and colleges around the Finger Lakes who had gathered at The Jumble last night and were staying at the Mill Creek Cabins. And he thought about the Elementals who were guarding the gravel road, preventing anyone from driving away. And he thought about the car keys he'd found next to his cabin's front door when he got home last night.

And he thought about how he and Ilya had talked about police procedure while something Ilya didn't recognize had watched them from the
dark.

Not a taunt or a threat. Someone had left *evidence* where he would
find it.

Grimshaw recognized Julian's car and gave his friend a nod as the car
slowed, then turned into the narrow driveway that led to the parking area
behind Lettuce Reed. A minute later, Julian and Natasha Sanguinati were
standing next to him.

"Gods," Julian said softly.

"Maybe we can rig a tarp or block the space with cars until the CIU
team arrives," Grimshaw said. "We've got too many tourists in town, and
we need to keep people from seeing this."

"Ah," Natasha said at the same time Grimshaw spotted the black luxury sedan heading toward them.

Then a sudden gust of wind lifted Natasha's hair—and a dense fog
obscured the parking space. Just that space.

"Air says you owe Fog a carrot," Natasha said before she stepped away
from them to meet Ilya as he got out of the car.

"I have a couple of carrots at the bookstore," Julian said. "I'll be back
in a minute."

Julian returned with a small bowl of carrot chunks. Seconds after that,
a chubby, misty gray pony with clompy feet stood next to Grimshaw, clearly
expecting his payment. Grimshaw fed him the carrot chunks, thanked
Fog for his assistance, and watched the pony wander down Main Street,
covering other parking spaces—and wondered how the pony had learned
to fog between the lines.

Grimshaw looked at Ilya and tipped his head before walking into the
station. When Ilya followed, Grimshaw went to the supply room, opened
a drawer in a filing cabinet, and returned with the game board and all the
extra pieces of the altered Murder game.

"When Osgood comes in, I'll go over to the store," he said, handing
the game to Ilya. "I'd like to be there before you start playing, but there's
no reason not to start setting up."

He hesitated, sure that the village's human government wouldn't be
happy about his including the Sanguinati in the investigation of a crime.

But this crime was connected with humans as well as the *terra indigene*, and he needed all the help he could get.

Besides, his paycheck might come out of the village's budget, but Ilya was the person who had hired him.

"I printed out all the photos I took last night. When Doc Wallace and I unwrapped that bundle of feathers, we found a head."

Ilya stiffened. "One of the *terra indigene*?"

He removed Fewks's photo ID from his pocket and held it out. "Not one of your people. He's one of mine."

CHAPTER 15

Vicki

Thaisday, Novembros 1

S oon after Julian and Natasha drove off to meet Grimshaw and Ilya in Sproing, I heard the outer porch door open. Thinking it was the guests in the lake cabins coming for breakfast, I didn't look up from making butter curls and berry balls before I said, "Come on in. The coffee is fresh and hot, and there's . . ."

In hindsight, it was more than foolish to invite anyone in without knowing *whom* I was inviting in, although I hadn't met anything in The Jumble that *needed* an invitation to enter a building. Having locked doors and windows—or walls or a roof—wasn't much of a deterrent to something big enough that it could huff and puff and blow your house down.

I looked up and stared at four Sanguinati youngsters, all neatly dressed in black.

"Good morning," the gorgeous teenage girl said. "I am Kira. This is Lara."

The younger girl gave me a full-fanged smile and seemed delighted to be standing in my kitchen.

I really hoped she wasn't hungry.

"I am Viktor," the next generation's Mr. Yummy said. "And this is Karol."

Karol was the other Sanguinati male I'd seen last night. He seemed to be in that age bracket of young teen who wanted to look and act mature, especially around the gorgeous girl, but also wanted to run off and explore every room in the main house. I had a pretty good idea how the Cornleys would react if they suddenly found a teenage boy standing next to their bed asking questions about their morning aerobics.

"Does Ilya know you're here?" I asked. "Or Natasha?"

None of them had a poker face.

"They didn't say we *couldn't* come and visit," Kira said.

A chill ran down my spine as I thought about the partially eaten donkey that had been found too close to the main house, and the weirdness that had spooked the Crows last night. The Crowgard were noticeably absent this morning, but the Hawks were outside keeping an eye on things—including my potentially delicious guests.

I heard laughter and voices, male and female, heading toward the house. Jenna McKay was doing the donkey-cart tour with Bobcat this morning—assuming there was another donkey in The Jumble's small herd that was tame enough to pull the cart. Conan was confident that the guests would be safe, but Cougar would follow them. Just in case.

Immediate problem first. "How did you reach The Jumble?"

"We crossed the lake in our smoke form," Lara said, sounding pleased with herself.

"Does *anyone* know you've come to visit?"

Really, there wasn't a poker face in the bunch.

"You want us to leave?" Kira asked, clearly disappointed by my unenthusiastic reception.

"No." I blew out a breath. Besides being my attorney and CPA, Ilya and Natasha were friends and had done a great deal to help me maintain my claim on The Jumble during the trouble this past summer. Now they needed me to step up to this particular line. "It may be different among the Sanguinati, but when human youngsters leave their house to visit friends, they tell an adult where they are going and who they are going to see. Otherwise, adults worry."

What was that saying about asking for forgiveness rather than permission? I had a feeling the young Sanguinati were operating on that principle.

"An important tip," I said as the outer porch door opened. "You should never stand between a human and the coffeepot first thing in the morning."

Three adult humans opened the kitchen door and stared at four Sanguinati youngsters before the Sanguinati stepped out of the way with a politely murmured good morning.

"Help yourself to breakfast," I said, waving toward the partially prepared offerings. I looked at Viktor, who appeared to be the oldest teenager. He gave me an amused smile and nodded to indicate message received.

No snacking on the guests.

I hurried to my office, figuring this needed to be a private conversation. I unlocked the office door, stepped inside, then called Silence Lodge.

"What?" The male Sanguinati who answered the phone snarled at me, and I flinched. It was an ingrained response to male aggression that I was working to overcome. At least I hadn't slid into a full-blown anxiety attack, so that was progress.

Reminding myself that he wasn't mad at *me*—yet—and that he was on the other side of the lake, I braced one hand on my desk. "This is Vicki. They're here and they're fine."

A beat of silence. Then . . .

Maybe the Sanguinati don't have their own swearwords. Or maybe they've decided that human swearwords are more . . . fulfilling. Either way, it was like listening to someone play building blocks with short, pithy words while my anxiety kicked in and rose toward meltdown.

Then the male voice disappeared and a female voice that sounded slightly calmer said, "Ms. DeVine? Our fosterlings are with you?"

I let out a shaky breath. "They came over for a visit and forgot to leave a note for the grown-ups."

"One moment, please."

While I waited for whatever she was doing on her end, it occurred to me that the youngsters could have used *terra indigene* communication to tell the adults at Silence Lodge about their destination. They could have *received* communication telling them to come home.

Of course, if you don't answer, no one can prove you heard.

"Ms. DeVine? If it would not inconvenience you, could the youngsters stay with you this morning?"

"I'm not sure what they'll find of interest to do over here, but they can stay." A thought occurred to me. "One of my guests is doing the donkey-cart tour of The Jumble this morning. Could they do that too?"

Another pause, probably for discussion. Either the adults at Silence Lodge didn't remember their youth or they *did* remember their youth and that was why they were all panicking now.

"The older ones could do that if they choose," she said, addressing me again. "The younger female needs . . . firmer authority . . . and should not be on her own for long."

Firmer authority would be me? Were they joking?

Apparently not, since she thanked me and hung up.

Back in the kitchen, breakfast was going on in full swing, with Jenna McKay showing Lara and Kira how to use the small melon scoop to make jam balls for individual servings, while Michael and Ian Stern chatted with Viktor and Karol about Trickster Night. The men's eyes strayed toward Kira, who really was gorgeous, but they kept their distance from the girls, which indicated they had a healthy survival instinct.

Someone had scrambled some eggs for general consumption. Someone had located the leftover pizza and warmed up a couple of pieces in the wave-cooker before slicing them into smaller pieces.

Everyone stopped talking when I entered the kitchen.

"You have permission to stay and visit," I told the Sanguinati. I waved a hand to indicate Kira, Viktor, and Karol. "You three may join the donkey-cart tour if you would like to do that."

"But we want—" Lara began.

"To stay and help Miss Victoria," Kira finished.

She exchanged a glance with Viktor. Something about that look struck me as conspiratorial and gave my anxiety a twitch. Since I couldn't figure out what two teenage Sanguinati would conspire about that involved me, I put that anxiety down to leftover emotion caused by the snarling vampire on the phone.

"Yes," Viktor said. "We are here to visit Miss Victoria today."

Okeydokey.

I was making the third pot of coffee and wondering where I was going to put all the little bowls of jam balls—because everyone had to have a turn at making at least one ball—when more of my guests wandered into the kitchen, looking for food.

The Cornleys, who had been watching the tricksters arrive in their "costumes," looked at the Sanguinati and had the sudden understanding that not all the costumes had been costumes. And the Sanguinati, probably picking up accelerated breathing and heartbeat and whatever other signals prey gives off before being eaten, suddenly looked like the young predators they were. A stillness in all four of them. A focused look in the dark eyes.

Ian Stern clapped his hands loudly and said, "Is there any toast?"

The tableau broken, Kira turned away from the Cornleys and said, "I can make it. I have seen how the toaster machine works." She looked at Michael and Ian. "Two pieces?"

They nodded. Suddenly everyone was in motion, except the Cornleys, who were impersonating frozen bunnies. I guess they hadn't expected to get an up-close-and-personal look at the Others—or have the Others look at them. Which made me wonder if they'd understood the nature of The Jumble or had just seen it as a place where they could go for a rustic getaway.

I sidled over to them and suggested they go into the dining room, which was a quiet spot in the morning, and I would bring them something to eat.

As I put together a tray for my skittish guests, Jenna McKay showed Viktor how to make scrambled eggs. Once they were cooked, she plated some of the eggs for herself, then gave another plate to the youngsters so they could all have a taste. Lara and Karol clearly didn't like the eggs but knew enough not to spit out the food. Viktor's and Kira's expressions were carefully neutral.

Then Bobcat walked into the kitchen and spotted what was left of the Sanguinati's share of scrambled eggs.

"Use a spoon, please," I said in time to stop him from using a digity paw to scoop butter curls out of the bowl. After he'd spooned up a couple of jam balls as well, I handed him a fork.

Watching him add butter and jam to each bite of scrambled eggs, Lara found a fork and followed his example, exclaiming happily over the changed taste. If Bobcat had been hungry, he probably would have snarled her away from his plate. I figured he was already full from eating dead donkey and this was his sweet after the meal—and something he was willing to share.

I didn't have room on the tray for mugs and the coffeepot, but I didn't have to make a second trip to the dining room because Michael Stern said, "Let me give you a hand with that," and grabbed the coffeepot and two mugs.

I set out the food for the Cornleys, and Michael poured the coffee.

He stopped me on the way back to the kitchen, and as soon as his hand lightly touched my arm, my brain got ready to panic even though his touch wasn't the least bit threatening.

"Julian Farrow is a friend of yours?" Michael asked.

Feeling wary, I nodded.

"You know he gets feelings about things?"

"We all get feelings about things." My response was instinctive, protective, a way to hide what I knew about Julian. I wished I was the one holding the coffeepot, in case I needed to whack my guest.

"My cousin and I get feelings," Michael said, watching me. "We have that in common with Julian."

I realized he was wary too. He was offering a secret in a place that wasn't home.

"Oh. *Those* feelings." I hadn't realized Michael and Ian Stern were Intuits, but to avoid persecution, Intuits usually hid their ability to sense things about their surroundings. "It must have been a strange night for you."

He let out a soft, surprised laugh. "It was fascinating. And terrifying."

"And . . . ?" I prodded, since it seemed he had more to say. I decided it was best to cut through cryptic talking since he had the coffeepot and someone was going to come looking for it soon. "What should I tell Julian?"

"Duplicity. We felt it last night, but not this morning."

He was telling me someone was deceitful, or had been last night, but it wasn't one of my guests. Which meant it was either someone staying at the Mill Creek Cabins or one of the tricksters who had come to The Jumble last night.

Or it was one of the Others? *Something* out there had caused Aggie, Jozi, and Eddie to retreat into their feathered form.

"And the girl. Kira. Tell Julian . . . honey trap. Not quite true in the usual sense, but true nonetheless."

I wondered if Kira was being labeled—and blamed for men's naughty thoughts—because she was gorgeous, but Michael seemed genuinely concerned.

"I'll tell him." I took a step toward the kitchen. He moved with me.

"I like your place. It feels welcoming—in a strange, adventurous sort of way." He smiled.

"Wasn't that what you were looking for? A bit of adventure?"

"We were. Are you open year-round?"

"Yes, but just the two suites in the main house and the two upgraded cabins. There are some . . . very rustic . . . cabins available for human guests in the summer."

"Would those cabins be considered highly adventurous?"

I thought about the residents in some of those cabins. "Oh yes."

When we returned to the kitchen, Aggie was at the sink, her uniform sleeves rolled up as she explained dish washing to Kira.

"How are you?" I asked her.

Terror still filled her dark eyes. "Eddie saw . . . last night. Crowbones is here."

"Well, Chief Grimshaw will figure out who played that nasty trick."

"No, he won't. Chief Grimshaw is human. He can't . . ." She turned away from me and ferociously scrubbed an already clean plate.

I turned to my Intuit guests. "If you want to see some of The Jumble today, you can join the donkey-cart tour." I was told the cart could hold four people. Nobody actually said the donkey could *pull* the cart if it had four people.

I'd let Bobcat figure that out.

"Best not to walk the trails alone today?" Michael asked.

"Best not," I agreed.

"Karol and I could walk down to the beach with your guests," Viktor offered. "It's open ground from the house to the sand. Or the dock." He looked at the men. "The dock at The Jumble has become a significant place in the stories about Lake Silence."

"Umm . . . ," I said.

"Ilya says it is permissible to recount those events as long as we don't embellish."

I would have one or two things to say to my attorney about recounting. "Go ahead. Show them the dock and recount."

Viktor grinned at me, revealing a hint of fang. That startled the men, but they must have realized they weren't in any danger, because they followed Viktor and Karol out the door.

I looked around. "Where is Lara?" Had I lost the vampire that required firmer authority?

"Jozi is showing her the library," Kira said. "Ilya was going to take us to Lettuce Reed to choose books, but I don't think that will happen today. Jozi said you had books Lara might like to read. That is permitted?" She looked anxious, which increased my doubts about Michael Stern's feeling about the girl—and helped me believe that my interpretation of the look I'd seen Kira give Viktor earlier was mistaken.

"Yes, that is permitted," I said. "I think she'll like the Wolf Team books." All the *terra indigene* enjoyed the stories about a group of adolescents with special skills who helped beings in trouble. I turned back to Aggie. "What is Eddie doing?"

"He is dusting the wooden floors," Aggie said. "He was going to use the vacuum cleaner, but that is too noisy."

"Because it would disturb the guests?"

Aggie gave me a look that chilled me. "Because you wouldn't be able to hear someone coming up behind you."

CHAPTER 16

Grimshaw

Thaisday, Novembros 1

While Grimshaw waited for Detective Samuel Kipp and his CIU team to arrive from Bristol, Osgood drove up to the station, found an unfogged parking space, and joined his chief.

"I checked the campers first thing," Osgood said.

"They must have been thrilled to see you before the sun," Grimshaw remarked.

"I wanted to get on top of things in case we had a situation." He looked at the densely fogged space in front of the police station.

"We have a situation," Grimshaw confirmed. "As soon as Detective Kipp arrives, we'll need to figure out how to blow this fog off the crime scene."

The hairs on the back of his neck rose as he heard a soft female laugh coming from somewhere nearby.

I guess Air is still keeping watch.

"Did you find out anything when you were knocking on doors?" Grimshaw asked.

Osgood nodded. "Four teenage boys from Putney of all places had rented one of the campers, wanting to spend Trickster Night in Sproing."

Putney. A whole lot of trouble had come out of that human town a few months ago. "You get their names and home addresses?"

"Yes, sir, but . . . After they returned to the camper, one of them—Tom Saulner is his name—went back out and didn't return last night. His friends just thought he'd gotten lucky, you know?"

It was possible, since there *were* a few teenage girls in the village. Not likely, but possible. Except he thought about all that attitude—and the dangerous vibes—those boys had been projecting when they'd come up to The Jumble, and the way they had looked at Vicki. And he thought about what had invited those boys to come and play.

He shuddered. "You get a description?"

"They claimed they couldn't remember hair or eye color or what he'd been wearing, but his 'costume' had consisted of a hatchet buried in his skull."

"I saw that boy last night at The Jumble. You call the EMTs and Doc Wallace. Ask if anyone reported a girl being assaulted last night."

"You think . . ." Osgood's brown eyes turned stone hard.

"Just ticking the boxes, Officer." Grimshaw sighed. "I have a meeting with Julian Farrow and Ilya Sanguinati. I'm going to mute my mobile phone, but I'll be across the street if you need me. This discussion shouldn't take long."

"Yes, sir."

Grimshaw crossed the street and went around to the back of Lettuce Reed since the front door still had the Closed sign.

He had a college boy who had paid a dear price for a prank. Now he had this other boy, Saulner, who was missing and might never be found. He had Elementals detaining the academics staying at the Mill Creek Cabins and "assisting" him in shielding the evidence left at the police station from the residents and tourists. And the gods only knew what Julian would be able to tell him after they played Murder.

Could the day get any better?

CHAPTER 17

Ilya

Thaisday, Novembros 1

The Sanguinati fosterlings were intelligent and inquisitive and had the boldness of young who knew they were, on one level, apex predators. They had also recognized that Victoria DeVine was harmless, at least in the ways they could understand at their age, and curiosity had overwhelmed sense when they decided to cross the lake and visit The Jumble.

He was relieved they had been found unharmed.

As soon as he returned to Silence Lodge he was going to wring their necks for creating this panic among the adults. The Sanguinati did not breed as often as other shifters, so children were cherished and protected. To lose all four of their fosterlings, even for an hour . . .

"This is good practice," Natasha said. "For when we have our own offspring."

"Ours will be well behaved," he growled as he helped her set up the Murder game in the bookstore's break room.

She gave him a smile that said, *With you as their father?* Out loud she said, "Perhaps Chief Grimshaw and Julian Farrow can teach the older fosterlings how to play pool."

"Perhaps."

Julian returned to the break room with Grimshaw, who said, "Is there any way to make this a quick game?"

"I have given this some thought, and I do not believe we need to play the game as a game," Natasha said. "From what I heard about the first Murder game, it was the combination of people and objects that triggered the reaction in Mr. Farrow that was, in fact, the warning that Victoria was in danger."

Ilya eyed his mate. Natasha hadn't actually been *invited* to this meeting, but it seemed she had taken charge.

"What do you suggest?" he asked.

"If Mr. Farrow would stand on that side of the table?" She pointed to the side of the game that had the blue paper representing the lake. When Julian moved into position, she began arranging the small figures. "Most of Victoria's guests were in the large entrance hall that serves as the reception area in order to see the tricksters coming to the door, or they were in the rooms that had a view of the front of the main house."

Natasha placed a bear and a golden cat at the front door, with teeny Victoria behind them. Teeny Julian was near the kitchen, and teeny Grimshaw was outside, beside the door. Several other human figures were placed in and around the hall and adjoining rooms, positioned to look as if they were conversing with one another.

Julian Farrow stuffed his hands in his pockets and said nothing.

Looking over the available pieces, Natasha positioned a black bird that was meant to be a Crow next to teeny Victoria.

Ilya watched Julian Farrow shift his feet, as if he wanted, *needed*, to move.

Natasha reached into a paper bag she had brought in from somewhere and placed two more teeny figures on the board. One was a woman with dark hair wearing a black dress, and the other . . .

Ilya narrowed his eyes. "Teeny Ilya is wearing a cape?"

Natasha smiled at him. "How else will the other teenies know he is Sanguinati?"

She was teasing him. Before their mating, he had been the leader of Silence Lodge, the one who was obeyed. Now she was teasing him.

He liked it.

But Julian Farrow began to pace, his eyes never leaving the game board.

Natasha moved the teeny female vampire next to teeny Victoria and the Crow.

Julian Farrow paced.

Natasha reached into the paper bag and removed something that she kept hidden in her hand. She set it on the game board just beyond the front door.

Julian Farrow grabbed teeny Victoria, the female vampire, and the Crow and leaped away from the table, his face a sickly white and his breath sounding like he'd just run all the way up one of the Addirondak Mountains.

"Well," Ilya said as they all stared at the skull of a crow that Natasha had placed on the board, "I guess that confirms that there is an unknown predator in The Jumble that poses, or will pose, a threat to Victoria."

"But not until a particular combination of females is together," Natasha said.

Like now, with the fosterlings and the Crows and Victoria all together in The Jumble's main house? he thought.

"Crap." Grimshaw breathed out the word. Then he pulled out his mobile phone and checked for messages. "Detective Kipp needs to see me ASAP." He looked at Ilya.

<Go help Chief Grimshaw,> Natasha said. <I will assist Mr. Farrow.>

"Julian?" Grimshaw stared at his friend. "Will you be all right?"

"Yeah," Julian said, wiping one hand across his mouth. "You go."

Ilya followed Grimshaw out of the bookstore. "Natasha will look after him."

"I don't like any of this," Grimshaw said as they crossed the street.

"That makes two of us."

"Kipp?" Grimshaw nodded to the brown-skinned man who was the CIU team's leader. "What have you got?"

Kipp gave them both a long look. "Was this some kind of ritual killing?"

"Why?"

Kipp crouched and pointed. "Because of that."

Kipp moved out of the way. Grimshaw and Ilya crouched to have a look.

Swinging from a black thread tied to one of the exposed ribs were the feet and lower legs of a crow.

CHAPTER 18

Vicki

Thaisday, Novembros 1

Once everyone had been fed and sufficiently caffeinated and had wandered off to do whatever they were going to do, I stayed in the kitchen and tried to call Julian to deliver Michael Stern's message.

The bookstore's phone rang and rang and then went to voice mail. Julian's mobile phone went to voice mail.

The bookstore wouldn't be open yet, but I was surprised that Julian was ignoring both phones. Then I worried because he was meeting Chief Grimshaw and Ilya Sanguinati to discuss whatever they hadn't mentioned to me about last night's scary excitement.

Which was totally unfair because I *should* be informed if they knew something about the scary excitement. After all, it was *my* guests who could end up being eaten, because scary things did not live on dead donkey alone.

Then again, there was such a thing as too much information.

Ignoring the little inner voice that kept asking if I *really* wanted to know what the men knew, I called Ilya's office—and got voice mail. I called his mobile phone—and got voice mail.

"If there was an emergency, we'd all be in deep doo-doo while you all did your manly talking," I muttered. Unless they weren't answering their phones because they were already dealing with deep doo-doo.

I hung up the wall phone in the kitchen and almost jumped out of my shoes when the darn thing rang right under my hand.

"The Jumble. Vicki speaking." I sounded slightly squeaky, but still professional.

"Vicki?"

"Ineke?" She did *not* sound professional, which made my stomach take an unexpected roller-coaster ride, because anything that spooked Ineke Xavier could not be good.

"Is Chief Grimshaw there with you? No one's answering the phone at the station, and I think his mobile phone is turned off. I wondered if he was playing a game of pool before work."

Oh, golly. Really deep doo-doo, since she knew as well as I did that Grimshaw wasn't a play-before-work kind of man. "Julian went to meet him and Ilya, but I haven't been able to reach either of them."

A beat of silence. Then Ineke said, "Would you give the chief a call? He'll pick up the phone if it's you."

I'd call that optimism over reality. Then again, if the designated trouble magnet calls the chief of police, you have to figure there is trouble.

And then I wondered why Ineke hadn't called Officer Osgood. He still lived at the boardinghouse and wouldn't dare ignore a phone call from her. But Ineke was my friend, so I said, "Sure. What do you want me to tell him?"

She told me.

Eventually I realized I was sitting on the kitchen floor listening to a dial tone.

Eventually I stood up and placed a call to Grimshaw's mobile phone, hoping I'd get lucky and get his voice mail, because he was *not* going to be a happy camper.

No such luck.

CHAPTER 19

Grimshaw

Thaisday, Novembros 1

M r. Sanguinati and I collected a head and a severed forearm," Grimshaw told Detective Kipp. "The body parts are at Ames Funeral Home, along with other evidence I collected last night. The student photo ID I found this morning in the victim's wallet matches the head. That's enough for me to say the head and these remains belong to Adam Fewks, and he was the individual who was at The Jumble last night dressed up as the Crowgard bogeyman."

"Do you think we'll find the rest of the body?" Kipp looked at Grimshaw, then at Ilya.

"You mean the organs? Unlikely," Ilya replied.

They were lucky to have this much—something they all knew and wouldn't say out loud.

Grimshaw's mobile phone buzzed. Pulling it out of his pocket, he looked at the caller ID, then pushed the Talk button. "Ms. DeVine?"

"Hey, Chief. How's it going?"

She sounded odd. Was she drunk at this time of the morning or reacting to some kind of anxiety medication? "Something I can do for you?"

"Yep. I was given a message for Julian. 'Duplicity. And honey trap.'"

"'Duplicity and honey trap'?"

"Yep. That's the message from one of the guests staying in a lake cabin. Julian will understand."

"Okay." When all he heard was breathing, he said, "Anything else?"

"Ineke couldn't reach you, so she asked me to give you a message because she figured you would answer the phone if the trouble magnet called, which I think is an unfair appellation since all I did the last time was make the phone call. Which, actually, is all I'm doing this time too. She's hoping it's just a prank."

"Okay." He was certain now that nothing was okay, including Vicki DeVine. "What is the message?"

Deep breath in, deep breath out. In. Out.

Finally she told him.

Maybe it *was* an unfair appellation, and he was certain she didn't mean to be, but damn it, the woman really was a trouble magnet.

He disconnected and looked at Ilya and Kipp. "We've got another crime scene, at the Xavier boardinghouse. I'll check it out first and make sure it's not a hoax. Officer Osgood will stay here and assist Detective Kipp and his team." He looked around but didn't see the rookie.

"Touch of food poisoning," Kipp said quietly. "Happens to all of us."

In other words, Osgood saw what was under the fog and lost his breakfast. Grimshaw couldn't blame him. The rookie had already seen too much of what the Others could and would do to a human body.

He looked at Ilya. "I'd appreciate it if you came with me."

Ilya studied him before saying, "Very well."

He'd moved his cruiser to make room for the crime scene vehicles, so he and Ilya walked down the block to reach his ride. They were heading to the boardinghouse before Ilya said, "I'm assuming Ms. Xavier found some remains? Is there a specific reason you wanted me to come with you?"

Grimshaw nodded. "She doesn't think the remains are human."

Grimshaw stared at the body that had been partially buried in one of the large compost bins tucked at the back of the boardinghouse's yard. Ineke had already told him what she could. No sounds of a fight or any kind of trouble last night or early this morning. Her guests were all accounted for. She'd noticed that Maxwell, her border collie, had wanted to come back inside as soon as he'd done his business instead of making his morning inspection of the property, but she hadn't realized anything was *wrong* until she'd come out after breakfast to dump the kitchen scraps and Maxwell had become so hysterical in his efforts to herd her away from the bins that she'd had to take him back to the house and shut him inside.

When she'd returned and opened the other bin to give it an "aeration fluff and stir," she found the body.

He could see why she'd thought it was a Trickster Night prank. Not only had the body been savaged; it had been caught in a shape so deformed it defied description—as if the male Crow had been trying to shift in order to flee and had died in this nightmarish, mangled body that was neither human nor Crowgard.

"Do you recognize him?" he asked Ilya.

The Sanguinati shook his head. "You're going to have to ask the Crows who work for Victoria or live in The Jumble."

"I'll get one of Kipp's men to come here and take photos, although . . . That face." Would anyone be able to identify this Crow from that face?

A sharp whine. A bark that held a pitch Grimshaw would have labeled fear in a human.

He turned and studied Maxwell, who had escaped from the house and had followed them to the bins. The dog was a diligent herder of the people-sheep who were Ineke's guests. Since Grimshaw had boarded here when he first came to Sproing and Osgood still did, Maxwell counted the police among the people-sheep he had to herd away from trouble.

Whatever Maxwell had smelled or found on the property before Ineke discovered the body was the reason the border collie was now hysterical about having one of his sheep near danger—and yet the dog wasn't willing to come close to the compost bin. Like there was an invisible fence made of fear that the dog couldn't cross.

Grimshaw studied Maxwell, then studied the ground. Not having anything else at hand, he used the heel of his shoe to create a divot in the lawn.

"The dog is afraid," Ilya said.

"Yeah. And that's the line he won't cross. I'll have the CIU team take a careful look around. Maybe they'll spot something." A thought made his stomach swoop and roll. "I'd like your permission to disturb the crime scene."

"Why do you need permission?"

"The body is *terra indigene*, and I could end up compromising evidence, but I'd like to see the rest of the body—and I don't think I'll be able to arrest whoever did this."

Ilya sucked in a breath. "Perhaps it is better if I compromise the evidence." He picked up the tool that Ineke had dropped and carefully uncovered an arm that had a hand that was partially feathered and half its proper size. Then he uncovered the lower part of the body—or what remained.

"Crap," Grimshaw said softly. The *terra indigene* shifters could change their size and shape *fast*. But this Crow was not only a warped blend of human and Crow; its body was a sickening mix of differently sized parts—more confirmation that the attack had happened so fast, the Crow hadn't had the few seconds it needed to shift.

"Even if it was the right size, the bones in a human hand are small, are they not?" Ilya asked, looking at the feathered hand that had been sliced open.

"Yeah," Grimshaw said. "They're small, and it's a good bet some of the bones in that hand are missing." Tired of hearing Maxwell's barks of desperation, he stepped to the other side of the divot—the boundary beyond which something terrible had touched the Xavier property.

Ilya joined him, although Grimshaw noticed that the dog had quieted as soon as he crossed the invisible line and hadn't been upset about the Sanguinati staying near the compost bin. Apparently vampires didn't qualify as herdable people-sheep.

He called Kipp to tell him they had another crime scene. Then he blew out a breath and looked at Ilya. "We need to talk to those academics staying in the cabins, especially that professor who is so interested in folklore and urban legends. He might know a thing or two about the Crowgard bogeyman. And we need to see if any of them recognize the college boy who pretended to be the bogeyman last night."

"You think there is a connection between that human and this Crow?"

"You know as well as I do there's a connection, because I'm sure this Crow's missing lower legs and feet are tied to what's left of Adam Fewks's rib cage."

CHAPTER 20

Vicki

Thaisday, Novembros 1

When I'd knocked on the door of the Cornleys' suite, I found them packing for an early checkout.

Forgot about an appointment first thing tomorrow morning. Pressing business. Weather reports forecast snow next month, so they really should start heading home now.

Unless they had fibbed when they signed the register, they lived in a town that was only a few hours away from Sproing. Snow shouldn't be an issue for a while yet—unless someone had ticked off Winter. I'd been told she was one of the scarier Elementals, especially when she was riding a steed named Blizzard.

I listened to the fibs about why they were leaving and wondered if I should make up some brochures that reflected The Jumble a little more accurately: *Come to The Jumble for a relaxing—or possibly scary—adventure. Take a spin on the Eat or Be Eaten wheel of chance.*

I told them I would be able to check them out in an hour, and went on to the other suite to see if anyone wanted fresh towels. Since the used towels had been dumped on the bathroom floor, I swapped them for fresh and eyed the rest of the suite. Ben Malacki and David Shuman sure wouldn't win the neatest-guest award, but they also weren't running out the door.

On the other hand, I wasn't sure where they were.

"Miss Vicki?" Eddie stood in the doorway. He was dressed in his uniform of white shirt, black trousers, and black vest. He looked wan, but the only indication of stress that I could see were the feathers sticking out of his hair. "Chief Grimshaw wants you on the phone in your office. He has something to tell Aggie and he wants you to listen too."

"The wastebaskets need to be emptied," I said. "Can you do that?"

He nodded, so I went to my office by way of the laundry room and dropped off the towels before bracing myself for another chat with Grimshaw, who didn't waste time on unnecessary words.

"I'll be by later to talk to you and your employees, especially the Crowgard," Grimshaw said. "For now, I'd like everyone to do a quick check on friends and see if anyone has left the Lake Silence area for any reason."

I heard Aggie, who was on the kitchen extension, suck in a breath. "You found a body."

A beat of silence. "We did."

"Were the eyeballs squooshy?"

"No."

Missing eyeballs didn't squoosh, but I wasn't going to say that, and I hoped the thought didn't occur to Aggie since Grimshaw wanted a roll call. The Crows and I had watched enough cop and crime shows to know what that meant.

"Did you give Julian the message?" I asked.

"Not yet, but I will," he replied. "And I'll be wanting to talk to the person who gave you that message."

"I'll tell him. If you want to talk to all the guests, you'll have to hurry. The Cornleys are doing an early checkout."

"No, they're not. You're going to park your car across the access road to make sure nobody leaves before I get there."

"But . . . Chief."

"Aiden is already helping the academics staying at the Mill Creek Cabins understand why they need to assist the police in this inquiry. Should I ask him to send a friend to The Jumble to provide the same kind of assistance?"

Hey, I know a threat when I hear one, and I really didn't want to know whom Fire considered a friend. Aiden and I were friendly, but we weren't friends. Humans just weren't important to the Elementals' view of the world. "I'll block the access road as soon as I hang up. I promise."

"Ilya Sanguinati and I will be up to talk to your guests as soon as we can." He hung up.

"You can hang up now, Aggie." I waited until I heard the click, then called the bookstore.

"Lettuce Reed."

It wasn't Julian's voice, but I recognized it. "Natasha? Is Julian there?"

"One moment." It was more than a moment, and when I heard his voice, I wondered what he'd been doing. "Bad day?"

"You could say that." He tried to rally and couldn't quite get there.

I repeated the message about duplicity being at The Jumble last night but not this morning. And I told him about Kira somehow being connected with a honey trap.

"Okay, thanks," he said. "I have to go." He hesitated. "Vicki? Be careful, all right?"

"Sure."

"Really. Be careful."

It wasn't a no-confidence vote like it might have been from someone else. This was Julian trying, not too successfully, to hide that he was scared. "Could I talk to Natasha again?"

"We used the Murder board for clues about what is happening," Natasha said. "Mr. Farrow is still recovering. I will stay with him and liaise with the Bristol police."

"Can a CPA do that?" I wondered what they would want to ask her.

"Right now, I represent Silence Lodge while Ilya is assisting Chief Grimshaw."

I was busy doing my own kind of addition. "There's something besides the body Ineke found."

"Yes. That is why you need to be careful. All of you. Please tell the Sanguinati youngsters that they are to stay with you until we fetch them. They are not to leave on their own."

We talked about her bringing the next handful of books about the Wolf Team when she returned to fetch the youngsters. The Wolf Team always bested the baddies, and right now we all needed to feel that we could win.

I hung up, took my car keys out of the middle desk drawer, and went out to block the access road before the Cornleys had a chance to scamper off.

I was so not going to get a glowing review from them.

CHAPTER 21

Grimshaw

Thaisday, Novembros 1

Because something about the academics staying in the Mill Creek Cabins made his cop instincts itch, Grimshaw chose to interview the people staying at The Jumble first. He also wanted to hear the Crowgard's version of the Crowbones legend before he heard the human version.

He didn't recognize the naked earth native who unhooked the chain that ran across the access road, but he knew it was a Coyote in a between form that blended human and Coyote well enough not to be too disturbing.

"I don't believe he . . . associates . . . with humans except to attend Victoria's story times," Ilya said quietly as they watched the Coyote drag the chain to one side of the road.

Vicki DeVine was the Reader, an important position in any *terra indigene* settlement because it gave all the residents access to stories, both human and Other, that had been written down. Each form of *terra indigene* had its own teaching stories and oral tales, but it wasn't that long ago that stories written by Others were first published and could be read by anyone.

Grimshaw lowered his window and gave the Coyote a friendly smile. "Thanks. Anything Mr. Sanguinati and I should know before we go up to the main house?"

The Coyote cocked his head and took his time pondering the question—or attempting to adjust his vocal cords to accommodate human speech.

"The mated pair are screeching at the Reader," Coyote said. "Cougar doesn't like it. The young fanged shadows are talking to humans. Some of the shadows are pleased. Some are . . ." He made an angry sound.

"We'll take care of it." As he drove up the access road, Grimshaw looked in the rearview mirror and saw the blindingly quick shift from partly human to all Coyote seconds before he heard the yipping howl.

Then he heard answering howls—and not all of those howls came from another Coyote.

"Are we riding to the rescue?" Ilya asked dryly.

"Yes, but who are we rescuing?" He didn't expect an answer, and he didn't get one.

Vicki had picked a good spot to park her car. Not only did it block the road, but the trees on either side guaranteed there wasn't a chance of anyone squeezing a vehicle around it. He parked the cruiser, and then he and Ilya hurried up to the main house.

Vicki looked shaky, but Grimshaw figured she wasn't going to have an anxiety attack brought on by being yelled at, simply because she was too busy holding on to Cougar to keep him from mauling the guests. It was a dumb-ass thing to do, but he'd let Ilya explain why it wasn't a good idea to grab a big angry kitty.

Wilma Cornley was screeching about wanting to leave. Her husband, Fred, was waving his arms and threatening to sue. Vicki was trying to tell them the police would be there soon to talk to them.

Grimshaw let out a piercing whistle, then boomed, "Shut up, all of you!"

"What the . . . ?" said a male voice from another room. But no one came out to investigate.

"Since you're so eager to leave, I'll interview you first," Grimshaw said. "Ms. DeVine? May I use your dining room?"

"Sure," Vicki said. She looked at the husband and might have said something conciliatory—or offered to forgive the rest of the bill so he wouldn't go through with his threat to sue—but Ilya calmly opened his thin, obscenely expensive briefcase, took out a business card, and handed it to the husband.

"I am Ms. DeVine's attorney," he said. "If you want to threaten a lawsuit against Ms. DeVine because the police needed to speak to you and there was some concern that you might not wait to be interviewed— implying that you had something to hide—have your attorney call me, and I will explain *everything* to him."

Fred Cornley looked at the name on the business card and paled so quickly Grimshaw was surprised he didn't faint.

"Of course we'll assist the police in whatever way we can," Fred stammered. "It's just . . . This weekend has been upsetting, you know?"

"I do," Ilya replied. He turned to Grimshaw. "Why don't I interview the gentleman while you get *all the details* about what the lady was doing between the hours of nine p.m. and seven a.m.? Would that not cover the window of opportunity for the incidents?"

You bastard, Grimshaw thought with grudging admiration. Anyone with eyes could figure out what those two had been doing for most of the time after leaving the party and going up to their suite. He might be willing to accept general descriptions of the activities, but Ilya was going to wring every excruciating detail out of the man as payback for yelling at Vicki and stirring up The Jumble's employees.

Grimshaw led Wilma Cornley into the dining room and pointed to the chair farthest from the door.

"Now," he said. "Let's be clear about a few things. So far this morning, I've dealt with two mutilated bodies, and I'm looking for a teenage boy who is missing and might be in serious trouble. I'm all out of patience. I'm going to ask questions; you're going to answer. If you get mouthy or if I suspect you're telling even the smallest white lie, I *will* require every last detail of what you did last night and early this morning, and those details will go in my official report. If you cooperate, I can show some discretion."

Her lower lip quivered, but she was smart enough not to try the big-sad-eyes routine on him.

He sat down, took out his little notebook and a pen, and said, "Why did you come to The Jumble for Trickster Night?"

CHAPTER 22

Ilya

Thaisday, Novembros 1

Ilya listened and wondered if human females actually enjoyed some of these mating activities as much as this male seemed to think. Eventually he stopped trying to hide his distaste and asked about Fred Cornley's employment—where he worked, who he knew, what connections he had to any of the other guests. If he knew anything about spooky Crowgard folklore or had talked about such with other guests.

"We'd heard this place was a quiet getaway. Discreet because, well, the service is nothing to write home about." Cornley tried huffy attitude. "We didn't expect *this*."

"And didn't anticipate having your name show up in an official police report?" Ilya asked mildly. "It would be awkward for you if your mate found out what you've been doing for the past couple of days, would it not?"

"I don't know what you're talking about."

Ilya caught the whiff of fear that confirmed a guess. "Ms. DeVine gives people the benefit of the doubt. The Sanguinati do not." That wasn't quite true. Victoria had serious trust issues, especially when it came to men. Discovering that The Jumble had been used for illicit mating would be difficult for her since her ex-husband had been unfaithful many times.

"Be assured that if any of us hear so much as an unkind whisper about Ms. DeVine or The Jumble, your name—your *real* name—will appear in more than just a police report." He smiled, showing a hint of fang. "I see no reason why you can't leave—unless Chief Grimshaw uncovers a connection between you and the human's death that occurred here last night."

"Death? What kind of death?"

"The gruesome kind."

Having finished with Fred Cornley, Ilya found the guest register and read the information the humans had provided, then decided to check on the Sanguinati youngsters.

Lara was in the library with a human female and one of the males who was staying in the lake cabins.

"Mr. Stern is an author," Lara said excitedly.

"I don't write anything as exciting as the Wolf Team books," Stern said.

Something about the way the man met his eyes made Ilya wonder if Stern might be more interesting than he'd anticipated. Stern had listed Ravendell as his place of residence. Since he wasn't one of the Simple Life folk, that meant he was probably Intuit.

"Mr. Stern writes thrillers under his own name and also writes under a pseudonym," Jenna McKay said. "We've been trying to guess the genre of his other work. So far, Michael hasn't admitted to writing any of the books on the shelves here."

"Ilya?" Lara smiled at him but hesitated. The way she hugged the Wolf Team book, he had a good idea what she wanted to ask.

"I don't believe the bookstore will be open today. However, if Natasha is still in the village, I will ask her about purchasing some books from Mr. Farrow."

"Are you taking orders?" Jenna McKay asked.

He wasn't a clerk; he was the leader of Silence Lodge. Then he realized he owed these humans some consideration because their presence in the library wasn't just about selecting a book to read; they'd been keeping an eye on Lara and engaging her in a discussion about books—a safe and carefully chosen topic.

"I'll see what I can do," he said.

"Mr. Sanguinati?" Stern said. "If I could have a word?"

"In a few minutes."

Ilya stepped out of the library and closed the door. Then he removed his mobile phone from his briefcase and called Natasha, who handed him to Julian.

"Vicki already asked for more of the Wolf Team books for The Jumble's library, and Natasha purchased a full set of the books for Silence Lodge," Julian said. "I have some of Michael Stern's books. Do you want Margaret Shaw as well?"

"Why would I want this Shaw female?"

"Michael's pseudonym. He writes romances with a touch of the strange. Enchanted objects or haunted houses."

"He is an Intuit?" Ilya didn't wait for Julian to confirm what he'd already guessed, since it wasn't likely that Julian *would* confirm that about a fellow Intuit. "Would he participate in a prank for research?"

"No." A hesitation. "I have family in Ravendell. Michael, Ian, and I knew each other when we were young. Anything Michael passively observes would be research for his books, but he wouldn't have participated in what happened last night."

Ilya doubted that whoever had planned that prank had intended for someone to die. "How does The Jumble feel?"

"Unsettled but not threatening." Another hesitation. "But not without threat."

If he understood the words, the unknown hunter wasn't currently *in* The Jumble but was close enough to touch the boundaries and could attack again at any time.

"I realize it is inconvenient for you not to open your store today, but purchasing books would be a distraction for Victoria's guests since it may be a while yet before Chief Grimshaw allows them to leave."

"I'll pack up a couple of boxes of books for Vicki's guests to peruse; then Ms. Sanguinati and I will head to The Jumble," Julian said.

"Very well." Ilya disconnected, slipped the phone back in his briefcase, and headed for the TV room to check on the other three youngsters.

He paused in the doorway, studying the arrangement of people in the room.

Ben Malacki and David Shuman, the academics who were staying in the main house's second suite, were sitting in chairs. Viktor and Karol were perched on the arms of the couch, poised to attack. Kira was sitting on the couch with Ian Stern, the other male who was staying in the lake cabins. One of his arms rested on the back of the couch, and his body was turned toward Kira. Not . . . suggestive. Cautious. Wary. Protective.

Ilya studied Kira, who looked intimidated by the presence of two of the human males and in need of rescuing. With two other Sanguinati in the room, that look struck him as wrong, as false.

Was Ian Stern being manipulated into believing that Kira needed protecting? If that was the case, Stern was the one in need of protection.

"How many Sanguinati live around Lake Silence?" Malacki asked.

"Enough of us," Viktor replied.

"Is it a family clan? Like, an extended family supporting a dominant pair?"

"Enough to do what?" Shuman asked.

"That's a question that should be directed to one of the adults, don't you think?" Ian Stern said quietly. "Attempting to extract information from young people is unseemly."

"I agree," Ilya said, stepping into the room.

Malacki gave Ilya a smile that was in no way sincere. "Well, it's not often we get to converse with the Sanguinati."

"I have had many conversations with humans. They don't sound like police interrogations, even when the people are asking questions to find some common ground." Ilya set his briefcase next to the sofa, then turned to the youngsters. "Mr. Farrow is bringing books that you may purchase. Why don't you ask Victoria where he can set up his stock and assist her in getting things ready?"

Karol, Kira, and Viktor hurried toward the door. Then Kira stopped and looked back. "We enjoyed conversing with *you*, Mr. Stern."

A look in Viktor's eyes as he closed the door.

Ilya wondered if Malacki and Shuman understood they had been condemned by seven words and a look.

The alarm he saw in Stern's eyes before the Intuit looked away told him that one human understood what had happened in that room.

Nothing fatal. Thanks to Stern's presence and interference, Malacki and Shuman hadn't crossed a line to that extent. But word would go out to all the Sanguinati who lived in the Northeast Region, with emphasis to any and all who lived around the college where these men taught.

They would be watched. Perhaps even hunted. Supplying the Sanguinati with a meal would be educational and increase their understanding
of one kind of *terra indigene*.

Ilya removed a pad of paper and a pen from his briefcase. He smiled,
showing a hint of fang. "Since you enjoy questions and answers so much,
you can talk to me. I have questions, gentlemen. I hope, for your sake, that
you have satisfactory answers."

CHAPTER 23

Vicki

Thaisday, Novembros 1

Grimshaw and I moved cars and watched the Cornleys scamper off. Something about the way the husband looked at Grimshaw, then at me, before driving away gave me a funny feeling.

I don't want to be the morality police, and I'm hopeful that someday I'll wrestle my trust and man issues into submission enough to entertain the possibility of being a consenting adult, but . . . "They're not married, are they?"

A beat of silence. "Not to each other."

I sighed. "I guess that explains why they looked so happy to be together."

"Don't," Grimshaw said.

"I didn't—"

"You're thinking your dickhead ex-husband looked that happy when he went off for a romantic weekend with someone else, leaving you home to do the laundry and pay the bills, and maybe you really weren't interesting enough or sexy enough for him to want to take you on a weekend adventure." He looked at me. "Am I close?"

Right on the nose. "No comment."

He kept looking at me, which wasn't comfortable because Grimshaw was a large man with a gun and all those other nifty cop accessories.

"You're nervy about some things, and having met your ex, I can see why, but you've got more sand than Yorick Dane will ever understand or appreciate. Maybe you should look for someone who can accept the nerves and the trust issues and also appreciates that sand."

I stared at him. Was he suggesting . . . ? No. Did he . . . ? Gods, no. I did like the man most of the time, but . . . Not Grimshaw.

Besides, when I was badly injured this past summer, I received a transfusion of Grimshaw blood. So anything of a romantic nature between us would be kind of, sort of, almost like kissing my brother. If I had a brother.

"Good pep talk, Chief." I punched the air. Don't know why, except it was safer than punching Grimshaw.

"Well, I'm glad of that, because now it's time to gather your Crowgard employees so that we can all have a talk about crime."

A car drove up the access road. "Oh, look! There's Julian and Natasha!"

Grimshaw closed a hand over my arm and tugged me to the side of the road to let Julian drive up to the main house and park near the door.

"Come on." He tugged me toward the house. "The sooner we're done, the sooner you can join everyone else in checking out the books Julian brought to sell."

"More than the Wolf Team books I requested? How many books? Can I just see . . . ?"

"Show your sand, Vicki."

"I'd probably get arrested for doing that," I muttered.

The darn man not only laughed; he scooted me right past those boxes of temptation, not even letting me get a glimpse of the top layer of book covers as Julian hauled one box out of his trunk and Natasha picked up the other box with an ease that told me who I was going to ask for help the next time I couldn't open a jar of pickles.

Apparently Grimshaw thought if he released me I'd make a dash for the library, where the Sanguinati youngsters and I had set up a long folding table as Julian's auxiliary bookstore. Making a dash to another room for just a minute or ten to look at books wasn't the same as evading the long arm of the law, but Grimshaw chose not to test that idea and didn't release his hold on me until we reached the dining room, which I newly renamed the interrogation room.

Ilya was already there with Aggie, Jozi, and Eddie. He pulled out a chair for me. Aggie and Jozi immediately moved their chairs to tightly bracket mine while Eddie stood behind me.

Grimshaw and Ilya sat opposite us.

"Are all your friends accounted for?" Grimshaw asked the Crows.

"Yes," Aggie replied. Then she hesitated, leaned in to look at Jozi. "Well . . . Maybe Clara?"

"What about Clara?" Ilya asked when it seemed like Aggie wasn't going to say anything else.

"She was a friend," Eddie said. "But her feathers got ruffled when she wasn't chosen to work at The Jumble, so she wasn't spending much time with us anymore."

Chosen? Who had done the choosing? I had acquired *terra indigene* employees because *they* had decided I needed them, but I didn't remember being approached by a Crow named Clara.

"Two Crowgard males came to Lake Silence recently," Jozi said. "I'm not sure where they were from originally. They haven't come into The Jumble, but Clara met them one day just beyond the boundary, near the farm track, and has been spending time with them ever since."

The farm track ran between The Jumble and the Milfords' orchards. It was also the place where Aggie found the dead man with the squooshy eyeball, and that was the reason I had called the police and had ended up in all kinds of trouble.

"They didn't want to meet *us* because we work for Miss Vicki and have been contaminated by humans," Eddie said.

I think Eddie made air quotes when saying the last few words, but he was behind me, so I couldn't be sure.

"Have you been contaminated?" Ilya's voice was silky in a quiet, terrifying sort of way that made me glad he was my attorney and on my side.

I still made a mental note not to annoy him anytime soon. I made another mental note to ask if he understood air quotes.

Maybe I should ask Natasha about that instead.

"No!" Aggie said fiercely. "*We* don't think so, but *they* didn't want Clara to have anything to do with us."

"But they wanted to know everything she could tell them about The Jumble and Miss Vicki," Jozi added. She leaned her head against my shoulder and sighed—such a sad sound. "She thought they were smart and dedicated to . . . something secret. They wouldn't tell her what it was until they could be certain she would be loyal to the cause."

This wasn't surprising since it sounded like Clara had told the Crows here all kinds of things about her new friends. If I wanted to keep some scheme or cause a secret, I sure wouldn't tell someone like Clara, who, it seemed, didn't understand the concept of keeping a secret from other Crows, even if they were no longer friends.

"She didn't want me to go with her when she went to meet them, didn't want them to know we were still sort of friends," Jozi continued. "But I followed her one time to find out why Clara wasn't acting like Clara anymore, and I saw them, heard her say their names before they noticed me and shushed her. They looked angry and mean, and I got scared, so I flew away fast."

"Who are they?" Ilya asked.

"Civil and Serious," Aggie said.

"Their names are Civil and Serious Crowgard?" Grimshaw asked.

The Crows nodded.

I'd noticed that all the Crows interacting with humans in The Jumble had chosen first names that fit in with human names. But Civil and Serious? That said these two Crows *wanted* to call attention to themselves and stand out as different from humans as well as other Crowgard.

"We got worried when Clara stopped coming back to The Jumble," Eddie said, "so I flew around looking for her and saw Civil and Serious talking to humans, and I got angry because it was all right for *them* to deal with humans who were acting sneaky but it wasn't all right for us to help Miss Vicki and learn about humans properly?"

"Would you recognize these humans?" Ilya asked.

Eddie shrugged. "Maybe the younger one. Couldn't see the other human's face."

"Where is Clara now?" Grimshaw asked.

"She's around," Jozi said, but I heard uncertainty.

"You've spoken to her?" Grimshaw leaned forward. "Have you seen her?"

They hesitated, then shook their heads.

Feeling chilled, I looked at Ilya. "Is Boris at Silence Lodge?"

Ilya nodded. "Do you need a driver?"

"No." *Breathe, Vicki.* "I think the Crowgard should send a message to all the *terra indigene* around Lake Silence that Clara is to report to the Sanguinati at Silence Lodge immediately. No delays, no excuses. If she doesn't show up at the Lodge within an hour, the Sanguinati will come looking for her."

"If the Crows broadcast a message like that, the Sanguinati will not be the only form of *terra indigene* that goes looking," Ilya warned.

I looked at the leader of Silence Lodge and Sproing's chief of police, two strong males who believed that I had sand. I said, "I know."

CHAPTER 24

Thaisday, Novembros 1

Her face revealed nothing, but in her very stillness, he could sense her sorrow—and her growing, cataclysmic rage.

He had learned some things about her. She was hunting a contamination. Something sly and insidious had touched Crowgard, had touched Sanguinati, turning them against their own kind in ways the leaders of those *terra indigene* forms couldn't detect until it was far too late. She had found and eliminated minions, the ones who were contaminated beyond any undoing, but she hadn't found the source. She would get close, and the source, a cunning predator in its own right, would slip away—and she would have to wait for the signs of contamination to surface again before she continued her hunt.

Opening the small pouch on her belt, she removed a spool of black thread, bit three lengths of thread off the spool, and used them to secure three feathers in her long black hair. As she returned the spool to her pouch, a light breeze made the feathers in her hair dance.

He looked around, ready to shake the gourd in warning.

No need to warn. No point in warning.

Four Elementals—Earth, Air, Fire, and Water—stood nearby, watching her. Watching them.

Maybe information was exchanged between the Elementals and her. Maybe the look in her eyes was all they needed. He didn't know, couldn't say.

As one, the Elementals tipped their heads to acknowledge her. Then they looked at him, at the gourd in his hand and the feathered cape around his shoulders—and they disappeared.

"Easy place . . . for police . . . to find," he said, looking at the Crow.

She nodded, then headed off to look for other signs of the source of contamination.

For a moment, he wondered if he should give the Sanguinati here some warning. Except . . . They would send him away, and he had a purpose here. At least for a little while.

His brain . . . blinked . . . and he looked around, panic rising, not sure where he was or why he was there.

Then he saw her waiting for him—and he remembered. Again.

And he followed.

CHAPTER 25

Grimshaw

Thaisday, Novembros 1

Grimshaw gave everyone a five-minute breathing break. Before Vicki could untangle herself from the stressed-out Crows, who had feathers popping out everywhere, he strode to the library, where a long folding table had been set up for Julian's auxiliary bookstore. He wanted to ask Julian about the duplicity-and-honey-trap message, but mainly he wanted to block the doorway before Vicki and the Crows could engage in book delirium as a way to quiet anxiety. If they reached the books, he'd never get them focused on the information he needed from them.

"If your store is called Lettuce Reed, what are you going to call this? Mini Munch?"

"Stop being helpful, Michael," Julian said.

A bit of a bite to Julian's reply, but also . . . an old understanding?

Grimshaw remembered the man's face from last night's party but hadn't been introduced. Then again, he hadn't done much socializing last night, between the prophecy sent via the Lakeside police; Tom Saulner—aka Hatchet Head—and the other teenage boys giving Vicki's anxiety a kick; and the very dead body of Adam Fewks, the faux Crowgard bogeyman. "Need to talk to both of you."

"Are you going to come in or just block the doorway?" Julian asked.

"Block the doorway."

Julian gave him a sharp look. So did the other man.

Julian made the introductions when they joined him in the doorway. "Michael, this is Wayne Grimshaw, Sproing's chief of police. Wayne, this is Michael Stern and Margaret Shaw, depending on which genre you're reading. If the name is familiar, it's probably because you've read one of his books and not because you've seen the name on a police report."

"Good to know." He studied Michael Stern. "Where are you from?"

Stern hesitated. "Ravendell. It's a town on Senneca Lake."

Grimshaw nodded. "You sent the message about duplicity and honey trap?"

Another hesitation.

"You can trust him," Julian said, looking at Stern. "He understands about our kind."

"Just sensing emotions that didn't weigh up right," Stern finally said quietly. "Everyone's emotions were a bit skewed last night. Socializing with the *terra indigene* wasn't quite what my cousin and I expected. It was . . . wow." He lowered his voice even more. "Did Ms. DeVine really leap off the end of the dock and meet the lake's Elders when she tried to swim to Silence Lodge to escape from a man with a gun? The young Sanguinati who told me and Ian the story said he wasn't embellishing, but . . ."

"Met the Elders, knows the Lady of the Lake *and* Fire, and has a pony named Whirlpool show up in the kitchen once in a while looking for a carrot," Julian said dryly. "And that's not touching on the employees and other residents of The Jumble, or the fact that her attorney and her CPA have fangs."

Stern blinked, then swallowed hard.

"Can we focus on my investigation?" Grimshaw asked.

"Sorry," Julian said. "What do you need?"

"Duplicity. Honey trap."

"The feeling of duplicity was here last night but not after the party broke up," Stern said. "Or, to be exact, felt superficial after the party broke up. Honey trap?" He shrugged. "Could be cultural differences and we were reading more into it than was intended. Just . . . the Sanguinati girl is a bit of a flirt with a mean undercurrent, which surprised Ian and me since she comes across as shy and demure—at least when the Sanguinati adults are around. She's a contradiction that makes us uneasy. But that could just be what Sanguinati girls are like at that age."

Grimshaw caught Julian's look. Yeah. He'd have to talk to Ilya about that later. Right now . . . "You didn't get a feel for the almost newlyweds who weren't married to each other?"

Julian swore softly.

"That's what I meant by 'superficial.' A small deceit in comparison," Stern replied. He looked at them. "That's a problem?"

"For Vicki it is," Julian said. "Does she know?"

Grimshaw nodded. "I need to talk to you later, after I finish with Vicki and the Crows." He started to turn away, then added, "Mini Munch. I think you should keep the name."

Not waiting to hear Julian's reply, he rounded up Vicki and the Crows before they managed to reach the library. Ignoring their grumbles, he herded them back to the dining room.

Ilya resumed his seat and said quietly, "Boris will let me know if Clara Crowgard shows up."

Grimshaw took his seat and considered how to continue. Vicki and her employees did better with providing information when real police work could be referenced from the cop and crime shows they watched each week. He also figured he'd have the best chance of getting information from them if he started with the least scary and worked up to the most terrifying. He just hoped he'd guessed the correct order.

He took Adam Fewks's student ID out of his shirt pocket and set it on the table. "Have you ever seen this man?"

"Is this where we say we haven't even though we didn't look at the picture and the police have to ask again?" Jozi asked Vicki.

"Those people don't want to be helpful," Vicki replied. "We *do* want to be helpful, so we'll all take a careful look at the picture."

They all leaned toward the student ID and stared.

Grimshaw counted off the seconds.

"I'm not sure," Vicki said. "I might have seen him coming out of Pops Davies's store the other day, but there wasn't any reason to pay attention to him. I just remember seeing a young man who wasn't familiar come out of Pops's store at the same time I came out of the post office."

He'd have to ask Pops if Fewks bought the bleach at the general store.

Aggie and Jozi gave him sorrowful looks and apologized for not recognizing the human.

Eddie said, "I recognize him. He was the younger human talking to Civil and Serious Crowgard."

Score, Grimshaw thought. "Do you remember anything about the other human?"

Eddie shook his head. "I didn't see his face. We're good at remembering faces."

"Yes, you are." He thought for a moment. "There are other ways police can describe a human and narrow down a suspect list. Tall or short. Skinny or heavy. Hair color. What clothes he was wearing."

"Clothes change," Aggie said. "You can't depend on recognizing an unfriendly human by the clothes."

"That's true, but we can ask if other people saw a human wearing that particular outfit, and someone might have heard a name or where he's staying." He waited while the Crows conferred among themselves and Vicki frowned at the table.

He looked at Ilya, who had been too quiet. "Your thoughts?"

Ilya didn't reply before Eddie said, "A muddy green coat with the collar turned up. Hands in the coat's pockets, so I couldn't see if he wore any shinies. Brown . . . cap."

"Muddy green is the color?" Ilya asked. "Not mud on a green coat?"

"Color." Eddie sounded certain.

"It was a chilly night," Vicki said slowly. "The humans who came to the party all wore coats. I piled up the outerwear on the dining room chairs so it would be out of the way but still accessible."

"You saw that coat?" Grimshaw asked. "The other person talking to the Crows might have been an adult who was at the party?"

Vicki nodded. "I saw more than one coat of that particular color green. I thought the coat must be practical, because the color wasn't appealing. A muddy green, like Eddie said. But other people were being helpful and carrying coats into the room, so I don't know which coat belonged to which person."

"It still gives us something to work with." And narrowed their suspect pool to the people renting the Mill Creek Cabins and the guests at The Jumble. It was possible it had been an earth native who had hidden face and hands because they didn't look sufficiently human, but he didn't think a Crow would mistake one of the *terra indigene* for a human, regardless of form.

Grimshaw rested his forearms on the table. He wasn't sure what was going on with Ilya, who was unnaturally still. "Now we're getting to the scary part. Tell us about Crowbones."

Feathers popped out everywhere.

"Maybe there is a Crowgard storyteller who could tell you?" Vicki suggested.

"No," Aggie said, clinging to Vicki's hand. "I can tell. I can."

Grimshaw waited while Aggie, who looked like a human teenager, gathered herself—and wondered how much time it took for a Crow to reach that equivalent stage of maturity. Months? Years? He knew *terra indigene* aged differently than the animals whose form they had absorbed, so he had no idea what her chronological age might be.

"Crowbones wears a cape made out of the feathers of the fallen and carries a gourd filled with the bones of the taken," Aggie said. "If you hear the *rattle, rattle* of the gourd, it's a warning that Crowbones is coming to get you because you've been a bad Crow. Or you're an enemy of the Crowgard."

"Has anyone seen this being? Any idea what Crowbones looks like?"

Aggie's mouth twisted in a smile. "Plenty have seen. None have lived."

"Are feet used as a token of some kind?"

That was too much for Jozi, who shifted to her Crow form and hid under her clothes.

"Warning," Eddie said, trembling. He looked at Aggie. "And . . . ?"

"Signature?" Vicki suggested when Aggie just shivered and sprouted more feathers.

"Connection," Aggie whispered.

That's what he'd been afraid of. Between Fewks being seen with Civil and Serious and this physical connection between the two mutilated bodies . . . Whatever was out there was *telling* him and the Sanguinati that the body in the compost bin and the remains that had been left outside the police station were connected.

Ilya finally stirred and reached into his briefcase. "This is a crime scene photo. It will frighten you. Chief Grimshaw needs you to be brave long enough to look at the photo and tell him if you know this Crow."

"A Crow?" Aggie's voice was whispered terror. "You found one of us?"

"Be brave long enough, and then there will be no more questions today."

Grimshaw looked at Ilya but didn't point out it wasn't the Sanguinati's place to decide if there would or wouldn't be more questions. Of course, Ilya was the unofficial—or perhaps the official—attorney for the *terra indigene* around Lake Silence and could, therefore, make that call.

Ilya laid one photo on the table.

"Gods above and below," Vicki breathed. "Was that . . ." She looked at Grimshaw and mouthed, *at Ineke's?*

He nodded.

"That was one of the Crows talking to the humans," Eddie finally said. "I don't know if it's Civil or Serious."

He bolted out of the dining room.

Ilya put the photo back in his briefcase. Grimshaw slipped Fewks's student ID into his own shirt pocket.

Vicki pushed back from the table. "I'll . . . We'll . . ." She gathered up Jozi and the bundle of clothes and staggered out of the room, Aggie still clinging to one of her arms.

Grimshaw pulled out his mobile phone. Ilya laid a hand on his arm before he could make a call.

"I've told Natasha that Victoria is having . . . difficulty . . . right now. She'll alert Mr. Farrow." Ilya gave him an assessing look. "Unless you were calling someone else?"

"No."

"Feathers of the fallen. Bones of the taken. There is a distinction. Last night Aggie mentioned that the fallen are the innocent, and the taken are the ones who prey on the innocent."

Grimshaw thought for a moment. "And feet left with a body tells everyone there is a connection between two deaths? Is this a Crowgard vigilante meting out a savage brand of justice?"

"Perhaps."

"But no description of Crowbones. So why did Adam Fewks make up a mask that looked so skeletal? Because it was Trickster Night? Or because someone else had more information about this piece of Crowgard folklore?"

"Right now, fallen or taken is the question that needs to be answered," Ilya said quietly. "Clara Crowgard has been found."

CHAPTER 26

Vicki and Aggie

Thaisday, Novembros 1

By the time I settled Jozi on the porch with Eddie, who was wearing trousers and nothing else in order to accommodate feathers and Crowy feet, and reached the library with Aggie, I wasn't sure if I felt disappointed or relieved that my guests hadn't depleted the stock that Julian had brought. Ben Malacki and David Shuman, my academic guests, had a condescending "it's not lit'rature, so I can't bother with it" look on their faces, which seemed strange since they claimed to be interested in knowing about the Others, and you wouldn't find some of these books anywhere but in a *terra indigene* Courtyard or a bookstore like Julian's. However, Jenna McKay more than made up for the academic fart-faces by looking through the selection of books with undiluted glee. I'd seen that same glee on Lara's face when I passed the social room where the Sanguinati fosterlings were looking over the hoard of Wolf Team books Natasha had brought for them.

"Until yesterday, I hadn't *heard* of authors like Alan Wolfgard, let alone read them," Jenna said excitedly.

Julian smiled. "I brought copies of Wolfgard's books as well as books by other authors that I don't think you'll find in human-controlled towns." He handed me a book. "I don't think you've read him yet."

"Michael Stern?" I stared at my guest, who had casually placed himself on the other side of the table. "You're *this* Michael Stern?"

"You don't have any of Michael's thrillers here since you usually pick up gently used books," Julian said. "But I know you've read a couple of the romances he writes as Margaret Shaw."

I channeled the bit of Grimshaw's personality that I'd acquired during the blood transfusion last summer. Everyone told me that personality isn't transferred with the donated blood, but sometimes channeling some Grimshaw is useful, so I choose to ignore science and facts—at least about that.

"Ship's captain." I gave Michael a narrow-eyed stare. "Female stowaway. Danger on the high seas." I'd had a very strange dream while reading that book, and the golden-haired pirate captain on the cover—whose face in the dream had morphed into other faces—could have been Grimshaw's less trustworthy brother.

"Uh . . . yeah." Michael looked a little wary.

Then Julian smiled in a way that included everyone in the room. "I'm sure Michael wouldn't mind signing any of his books that you purchase today."

Poor Michael. Jenna McKay, Natasha, and I fixed our sights on a cornered author.

I wondered if deer had the same look when cornered by a pack of wolves.

Julian pulled out a chair and asked—politely—if Michael needed a pen.

Based on the look Michael gave Julian, I think he wanted something more stabby than a mere pen, but he sat while the book-buying frenzy took place. Julian taped slips of paper with our names to the table so that we could stack our selections.

Ian Stern wandered over to check out authors and titles, and he and Natasha compared notes about which genres they enjoyed. Turned out Ian wasn't as keen on the bloodthirsty stories as my CPA. Go figure.

Malacki and Shuman finally came over to purchase a token book, which, really, was all that was left. Aggie was guarding the Wolf Team books I'd purchased for The Jumble's residents, and Natasha, Jenna McKay, and I had claimed just about everything else.

Ian handed a book to Malacki and said, "A *terra indigene* author. I think you'll find the story . . . educational." He gave both men a smile that held some kind of warning.

Julian pulled a cash box out of one of the boxes he'd brought and tallied the sales. Michael dutifully signed all the copies of his books, including the Margaret Shaw romances I already owned. Natasha smiled at Malacki and Shuman in a way I'm sure would give them erotic dreams . . . that would turn into terrifying nightmares of fangs and bloody feasts.

The book binge was so satisfying, it was another hour before I realized that Grimshaw and Ilya had left at some point to go to do cop stuff.

Aggie stayed in the library and shelved the new Wolf Team books in their proper order. They wouldn't stay that way. Human guests would take the books off the shelves and put them back any old way, but she checked the shelves each morning and put the books in their proper places.

Normally, she liked to have this little bit of alone time with the books, but today being alone didn't feel so good. Bad things had happened in The Jumble a few months ago, but this was different. Something . . . old . . . had come here to hunt. To kill. Something even the Sanguinati didn't want to challenge.

Something that even the Elders around Lake Silence hadn't interfered with. That was a warning all by itself. The Crowgard wouldn't get any help from the rest of the *terra indigene*, but Miss Vicki would help Aggie and her kin figure out who had done the bad thing that had brought Crowbones here—and then they would find a way to deal with it.

CHAPTER 27

Ilya

Thaisday, Novembros 1

Ilya crouched beside the body of Clara Crowgard while Grimshaw made a slow circuit around the area, looking for evidence that might have been dropped at the scene.

"It's a savage kill," he said as Grimshaw joined him.

"But not like the other Crow," Grimshaw replied. "My guess is we have two killers, not one. And that's not good. We need to figure out who's targeting the Crowgard."

"Besides the bogeyman?"

"Yeah. Assuming there is an actual bogeyman."

"You have doubts?"

Grimshaw blew out a breath. "No. I wish I did." After a pause, he added, "I can ask Detective Kipp to send his team over here to collect whatever evidence they can."

A sincere offer, but would it be seen as human help or interference? Until he knew if Lake Silence's residents had been targeted or if this was just another hunting ground, he needed to be careful about how much help he accepted from humans. Grimshaw lived here and was involved in keeping the peace between humans and the *terra indigene*. Working with him was no different than the Lakeside Courtyard working with select police officers in that city. But Detective Kipp, who was with the Bristol police, might be a step too far.

"I appreciate the offer, but it isn't necessary." Ilya watched the Coyote slowly approaching them. "I think he can tell us everything we need to know."

They moved away from the body, making room for the Coyote to give Clara's remains a thorough sniff. The male moved in widening circles similar to Grimshaw's circuit.

When the Coyote shifted to the blended form of Coyotegard and human, Ilya recognized him as the one who had moved the chain from across The Jumble's access road earlier that morning.

"Well?" Ilya asked.

"The only human scent belongs to the police human," the Coyote said, giving Grimshaw a nod. "Then there is Sanguinati—and there is Crow." He hesitated but didn't say anything more.

Ilya nodded. "Thank you for assisting us."

"This is investigating? Like in the human stories?"

"Like in the stories," he agreed.

"Would a particular Crow smell different to you than other Crows?" Grimshaw asked. "To me it looks like a human weapon or tool was used to kill Clara. I'm thinking whoever did this walked here to meet her—or had clothing stashed somewhere nearby, which was why this place was chosen. If that individual doesn't know how investigations work . . ." He left the sentence hanging.

The Coyote smiled, showing teeth that were as species jumbled as Conan's and Cougar's, confirming that the Coyote didn't have much interaction with humans. "I will follow the trail to the hiding place—if there was a hiding place."

A reminder that the shifters might not bother with clothing when dealing with one another.

"Be careful," Ilya warned.

The Coyote looked up when one of the Hawkgard began circling overhead.

"We will," the Coyote assured them. He hesitated again, then pointed to Clara's arm, which had partially shifted before she died. "There—only there—is another scent." He leaned toward Ilya and lowered his voice.

"You should be careful too." Then he shifted to his Coyote form and trot-
ted away.

Ilya crouched again and studied the feathered arm. He pointed.
"Three feathers are missing."

"Feathers of the fallen?" Grimshaw asked. "Collected if Crow kills
Crow?"

"Maybe. At least, collected from a Crow that hadn't betrayed its own
kind in some way." Ilya rose. "We need more information, and I don't
think the Crowgard around Lake Silence can provide it."

"I'm going to ask Julian for the names of the Intuit villages around the
Finger Lakes. I'll contact the police in those villages and see if they've had
any murders similar to ours or have heard of anything in neighboring villages. Crowgard bogeyman or vigilante, there will be more bodies. If we
find them, we might be able to figure out why Crowbones is here before
someone else dies."

"And I will ask the Sanguinati. Someone might have heard a rumor
about Crowgard dying in the wild country."

"The Coyote." Grimshaw hesitated. "He was specific about identifying
my scent, but he didn't say the only Sanguinati scent around the body was
yours."

"I noticed that." And it troubled him.

Grimshaw removed his hat and scrubbed his fingers through his short
dark-blond hair. "You going to leave her out here?" He looked past Ilya
and sucked in a breath.

Ilya watched the two Sanguinati in smoke form rushing toward them.
"My people will take Clara to Silence Lodge and hold her there until the
Crowgard can decide what should be done."

"In that case, we'd better find out what the folks staying in the Mill
Creek Cabins have to say for themselves."

CHAPTER 28

Grimshaw

Thaisday, Novembros 1

It was afternoon when Grimshaw and Ilya arrived at the Mill Creek Cabins to talk to the men staying there. Since three of the academics looked like they wanted to say plenty of things, Grimshaw wondered why they weren't voicing complaints about being detained. Then Aiden handed him a lump of melted metal that had been the keys to two of the vehicles.

"Where is he?" Grimshaw asked, meaning the professor who was staying in the cabin next to his.

"Edward Janse asked permission to see the water mill and walk along the creek path," Aiden replied. "He couldn't run away by walking in that direction, so I gave him permission."

"Is it safe for him to be walking on his own?"

Aiden shrugged, then looked toward the creek. "He has returned, so it was safe enough."

Grimshaw watched the man Fire had identified as Edward Janse moving toward them at a swift walk. Something off. Something odd. When Janse reached the cabin where he waited, he noticed the man was pale—and he noticed Janse was sweating, despite not wearing a coat.

"I heard . . ." Janse shuddered. "There's something out there."

Aiden laughed—a sure sign that nobody human would want to meet up with whatever was out there.

Since the Sanguinati owned the cabins and had rented three of them on short-term leases to various colleges in the Finger Lakes region, Ilya's response was more diplomatic than Fire's. "It is the wild country. Many beings are out there."

Grimshaw would have bet a month's pay that Janse was an Intuit, and whatever he had sensed hadn't been the "friendlier" Others who usually studied the humans who came to study them.

He took Adam Fewks's student ID out of his shirt pocket and held it out. "Have you seen this man?"

Janse looked at him, then at the ID. "Maybe in the village yesterday or the day before? There were several young men around that age wandering Main Street." He lowered his voice. "They were disturbing—unnatural aggression covered by boisterous behavior."

That fit the four teenagers who had come to The Jumble on Trickster Night.

Janse might have lowered his voice, but not enough, because one of the other men muttered, "Pansy."

As Grimshaw turned to the other three men, Ilya said, "Chief Grimshaw, I'm sure you remember Professor Rodney Roash, who expressed such interest in Crowbones last night. His colleague is Richard Cardosa, and the man who is so eager to share his questionable opinions about other humans is Peter Lynchfield."

Ilya had already confirmed with the Sanguinati who took care of rental properties which colleges had rented which cabins. Fewks had attended the college where Roash taught. That was a connection—especially since Roash had been so insistent about interviewing the Crows last night after the Crowgard bogeyman's appearance.

Grimshaw focused on Roash and held out Fewks's student ID. "You know him." It wasn't a question.

"No." Roash shook his head. "I don't recognize him."

Richard Cardosa frowned at the student ID. "Are you sure, Rodney? Isn't Adam Fewks one of the students who takes your Folklore and Urban Legends class? I remember hearing him make some noise about a special project."

He didn't have time for lies, so Grimshaw opened the manila envelope he'd taken out of the cruiser, pulled out the photo of the severed head, and said, "How about now, Professor? Recognize your student now?"

Three men stared at the photo. Janse, who was standing behind Grimshaw and couldn't see the image, said, "Could we go inside now? We should—"

"*Monkey man,*" a female voice sang out from somewhere nearby.

"*Moooonkey man,*" a second voice sang.

"*Don't matter if you caw,*" a third voice sang.

"*Don't matter if you shout.*" A fourth voice.

"*Crowbones will gitcha if you don't . . . watch . . . out!*" The fifth voice.

Grimshaw shuddered.

Ilya opened the gate in the short wall that enclosed the cabin's front yard and said, "The front yard is considered neutral ground under most circumstances. Let's continue the discussion there."

"Wouldn't it be better to be inside?" Janse asked.

Aiden sat on the wall, swung his feet up, and wrapped his arms lightly around his legs. "Better for you if everyone can hear what is said."

And you wouldn't want them, whoever and whatever they are, inside the cabin with you, Grimshaw thought as he herded the men into the small yard.

"There's no reason for everyone—" Roash began.

"Yes, there is," Grimshaw said, overriding him. "You've put these men in jeopardy, so they're entitled to know how this scheme of yours was supposed to work. Right now I've got a dead college boy and two dead Crows, and everything points to your research project being the trigger that set off this chain of killings. Now, you can tell me what the plan was, or I can force you to look at the photos of the rest of the body parts we recovered."

Silence.

"Are you playing bad cop, Chief Grimshaw?" Aiden asked.

"I'm the pissed-off cop who's working up to a righteous mad if I don't get answers now and end up getting a call about another body," Grimshaw snapped. Not diplomatic. Not even smart, considering Fire had asked the question.

"Ah," Aiden said.

"Now, look here—" Roash blustered.

"Moooonkey man."

Grimshaw had never seen someone still breathing look so much like a corpse. "Would you prefer explaining it to them?"

"All right, yes, it was a research project," Roash said. "Adam Fewks is—was—a student in my Folklore and Urban Legends class. I had found an old book about early human settlements in the Northeast Region of Thaisia. It had a woodcut illustration of a creature called Crowbones—a skeletal figure about the size of a man, with a crow's head and feet but the rest of the body looked humanlike, wearing a ragged cape made out of feathers. It held a gourd in one hand and a scythe in the other." He wiped the sweat off his forehead with a shaking hand. "There was almost no information about the creature, just that a death rattle was heard when it was nearby. I figured the gourd was hollowed out and filled with stones or beans or something to make it rattle."

"So you had this student dress up in a cape and put on a papier-mâché head, and knock on The Jumble's door during Trickster Night to scare the feathers off the Crowgard who work for Vicki DeVine?"

"It was *research*. I wasn't even sure if Crowbones was from human or *terra indigene* folklore. The more we understand—"

"Stop there," Grimshaw said. "You've dug the hole deep enough."

"What was the bleach for?" Ilya asked.

"Bleach?" Roash frowned. "What bleach?"

Maybe Fewks thought he would have time to wipe down the props? If that wasn't part of Roash's plan, it wasn't likely that he and Ilya would ever get an answer. He still had to ask Pops Davies if he'd sold a bottle of bleach to a college boy.

Before Grimshaw could decide if Roash really didn't know about the bleach or was a habitual liar, his mobile phone buzzed. There wasn't any room in the small yard to move out of hearing, but he turned his back on the other men before answering the call. "Grimshaw."

"Chief?"

He heard nerves stuffed under training and reminded himself that Osgood was barely out of the academy and had already seen more than most veteran cops had seen in their entire careers. "Did you find Tom Saulner?" The missing teen might be an aggressive ass, but there was something Janse had said about that aggression that bothered him.

"No, sir." A long pause while Officer Osgood sucked in air. "There was a vehicular incident on the road heading east, not far beyond the village limits."

In other words, in the wild country.

"A Fred and Wilma Cornley were heading home after spending a couple of nights at The Jumble when ice fog suddenly formed across the road and rapidly became thicker," Osgood continued.

"Did they hit something with their car?" Grimshaw asked. *Or someone?*

"Not exactly."

"Then what exactly?" He and Osgood were going to have a talk about giving succinct reports.

"Their car is now stuck in a glacier."

Grimshaw rubbed a hand over his face, as if that would help his hearing. "Say that again."

"There's a small—well, smallish—glacier filling the road leading out of Sproing, and the Cornleys' car is stuck inside it. Mostly inside it—one of the back windows was still visible when I got to the scene, and the fire department and I were able to extract the Cornleys from the car before the ice . . . swallowed the vehicle."

Gods above and below. "Any way to get around the ice?"

"A couple of the firefighters did a walk around and said the ice is about two village blocks across and three blocks deep and half a block high. No vehicles are going to get in or out of the village from that direction." A pause. "What should I do, Chief?"

"Take the Cornleys to Doc Wallace and have him check them out, make sure they don't have frostbite or whatever. Then escort them to the station and take their statements."

"Yes, sir." Another pause. "Chief? Could you check the road heading west?"

Grimshaw felt a chill run down his spine. "Yeah. I'll do that."

When he ended the call, he glanced at Aiden, then focused on Ilya. "Seems there's a problem on the road heading east. Could you ask your driver to check the road heading west for obstacles?"

"Of course," Ilya replied. "Is he looking for something in particular?"

"He'll know it when he sees it." Grimshaw considered his options, then added, "I'd like you to come with me."

"What about us?" Richard Cardosa demanded. "We're supposed to leave today. I have classes to teach tomorrow."

"I'll let you know when you can leave," Grimshaw said. "In the meantime, stay in your cabins." *And hope they don't burn.*

He didn't think Aiden would burn down a structure that belonged to the Sanguinati on a whim, but you never could tell with the Elementals.

"Boris is leaving Silence Lodge now," Ilya said when they were in the cruiser and heading back toward Sproing before Grimshaw turned at the crossroads and drove north. "May I know where we're going?"

"There are two roads out of this area. One runs east–west and the other runs north–south. We're checking out the north road. I don't expect we'll need to go far before we confirm that the road is blocked."

"With what?"

"Well, the road heading east is blocked by a glacier. The Cornleys' car is trapped inside it, so Osgood is bringing them to the station."

Ilya stared at him. "I wasn't aware of that."

"Didn't think you were. But what started as a prank or *research* has brought a shit storm down on top of us, and . . ." He slowed the cruiser and stopped well behind a handful of cars that were going nowhere. Then he pulled the cruiser across both lanes before he and Ilya got out to study the earth mound that blocked the north road.

He wasn't sure what disturbed him more—that the Others were able to excavate that much dirt from either side of the road and pile it into a hill that quickly . . . or the smiley face made out of boulders that was pressed into this side of the mound.

Ilya's mobile phone rang. He reached into the cruiser and pulled it out of his briefcase. "Boris?" He listened for a minute, then ended the call.

"The road heading west is blocked?" Grimshaw asked.

"Yes. Earth mound."

He blew out a breath. "We'd better see what's blocking the south road before figuring out what to do."

"There is nothing to figure out," Ilya said quietly when they were back in the cruiser and heading south. "We have to survive. That is what we have to do."

CHAPTER 29

Them

Thaisday, Novembros 1

She had learned long ago how to pitch her voice in such a way that it corroded another person's willpower, making them malleable. And the beauty of it was that the people she molded into such lovely monstrosities never realized what was happening. She was just an annoyance, an irritant other people were convinced didn't do any actual harm.

If only the fools in this village knew what she had already achieved.

There was only one person who was immune to her peculiar talent, because he had the same skill. That made him a rival—or worse, a potential enemy. And he was *here*. He shouldn't be. They *never* overlapped their experiments. On the occasions when they met to compare notes over dinner, they met on neutral ground.

This wasn't neutral ground. This was *hers* and he *knew it*.

All those fancy-pants men from the colleges would be packing up and going home by tomorrow, except . . .

Something was wrong. Very wrong.

She'd noticed Pops Davies readying a couple of orders when she walked into the general store. Nothing odd about that, except . . .

On impulse, she grabbed two packages of toilet paper off the shelves,

prepared to complain that he wasn't carrying the brand she preferred—
something she'd asked him to do several times already.

"Only one package per household," Pops said, putting the other package behind the counter.

"But I need two," she whined, pitching her voice in a way that should have drilled a hole right through the damn man's brain. "Theodore is having tummy troubles, and it's so *messy*."

She saw him waver. He *should* have given in.

Pops shook his head. "You and Theodore will have to cope. Only one package per household."

He watched her until she walked out the door, which denied her a chance to slip anything interesting into her purse or coat pockets.

No matter. She would send in one of her lovelies. They knew she always had special treats for them.

CHAPTER 30

Vicki

Thaisday, Novembros 1

The Jumble. Vicki speaking."

"It's Pops. Listen, I've set aside a box of supplies for you. Things I figure you wouldn't want to do without. Ineke's coming over to pick up the box I set aside for her. You should come soon. And pull up behind the store."

"What's going on?" It seemed like a sensible question, but I actually heard Pops gulp before he answered.

"Barricades across all the roads," he said. "Looks like the village is cut off from . . . everywhere. And no one is *going* anywhere. As soon as enough people figure out they can't get to Crystalton or Bristol, there's going to be a run at the store for whatever supplies I have in stock." Another gulp. "And you've got guests."

Who were supposed to check out tomorrow morning. "You don't think the roads will be clear by tomorrow?"

"You should talk to Chief Grimshaw. Come soon for the supplies." Pops hung up.

The good news? I didn't end up sitting on the floor this time. The bad news? Pops Davies's general store was the *only* store in Sproing that carried food as well as a wide variety of other goods. Most folks went to

Crystalton or Bristol to do a big grocery haul every couple of weeks and then picked up a bit of this or that at Pops's when they needed it. But if nobody could get anywhere, everyone who hadn't already stocked up for winter would panic. Including me. I didn't have employees last winter and didn't know how much food they might expect me to provide, to say nothing about having guests. And I hadn't stocked my pantry with the view of feeding an extra five people three meals each day for several days, and I didn't know what I'd do with the guests who were supposed to arrive tomorrow afternoon—*if* they managed to get here at all.

Get supplies now. Panic later.

I collected my purse and car keys, asked Natasha to keep an eye on things while I ran to the store—and then whispered that she should contact Ilya ASAP. She didn't ask why, which made me wonder if she already knew what was going on and hadn't told me or if this would be her mate's first lesson in the importance of communication.

I hurried out and caught Julian as he finished loading up empty boxes. He looked pale, distracted.

"Have you heard from Grimshaw?" I asked.

He eyed me, and frowned as he focused on the purse and car keys. "Where are you going?"

"To the general store. Pops has some items on hold for me."

"Something changed while I was inside," he said quietly. "It feels . . . different . . . out here. Unsettled."

"The roads out of the village have been barricaded. I'm going to the store for supplies before everyone else figures it out."

"I'll drive you to the village."

"Then you'll have to come back here."

He looked so pale, the scar on his left cheek seemed to disappear. "Vicki . . . don't go anywhere alone."

So not what I wanted to hear.

We didn't attempt small talk on the drive to Sproing. Julian was hyperalert, watching the road and the sides of the road. I watched on my side, not sure what I was watching for or if I could do more than scream before whatever it was pounced on us.

Julian drove behind Pops's store, loaded the box Pops had already made up for me, then filled up a couple of his empty boxes with canned soups and fruits as well as toothpaste and paper products. I did a quick walk around the store, choosing a few more food items along with two jigsaw puzzles, a few coloring books, and a couple of boxes of colored pencils and crayons. I figured giving my guests safe activities might distract them from realizing they were trapped—at least for a few minutes at a time.

Ineke came in as Pops was boxing up my additional items.

"Good idea," she said after looking at my additions. "Won't be much longer before the news gets out, but it's a bit like snow. People aren't going to get antsy until they realize they really can't leave. Most folks are going to expect the roads to be open by morning, so they'll enjoy simple entertainments this evening."

"I just talked to Wayne," Julian said quietly, tucking his mobile phone in his jacket pocket. "Roads won't be open anytime soon, but Ilya Sanguinati will be meeting with Mayor Roundtree and Chief Grimshaw in the morning and hopes to offer some insight into the situation then."

"Who's supplying Mr. Sanguinati with these insights?" Ineke asked.

Julian just looked at her. "Don't ask."

Silence.

"Is this another predation?" Pops finally asked.

"I don't know," Julian replied. "But we all need to be careful. And if any of you see anyone behaving oddly, tell Chief Grimshaw or Officer Osgood. There has to be more to this than some jackass dressing up in a costume on Trickster Night and scaring the Crows."

When we were back in the car, I suggested placing a large order at the Pizza Shack.

Julian smiled. "Already did that. One of the TV stations is running another horror movie marathon this evening, so you're doing an extra pizza night this week for your guests."

"That's my story?"

I wasn't a fan of horror movies. They scared me. I could *read* horror stories; I just couldn't watch them. Neither could the Crows, although they did find the rent bodies of the victims a lot more interesting than I did. That was why, when we did watch a horror movie, we insisted that Conan stay in his furry form, so that the four of us could hide behind him and peer at the screen over his back.

"That's your story," Julian agreed. "I also ordered a pizza for each of the Mill Creek Cabins and have a box of canned goods the men can split between them."

"How long do you think this—whatever this is—is going to last?"

Julian pulled into a spot in front of the Pizza Shack. Then he turned off the car and looked at me. "Until it's done."

CHAPTER 31

Grimshaw

Firesday, Novembros 2

Bertram Roundtree had been elected mayor before last year's Great Predation and before the villagers realized just how much of their village the Sanguinati controlled. Since being mayor of a village the size of Sproing was a part-time job with a token salary, Grimshaw figured Roundtree wasn't any better or worse than anyone else the residents could have elected. But now that Roundtree was dealing with the Sanguinati directly—and by extension, the even more dangerous forms of *terra indigene*—the mayor was way out of his league.

What bothered Grimshaw more than a mayor whose actions might get them all killed was seeing Ilya Sanguinati walk into the police station looking like he'd been dragged over a mile of bad road, which made the cop wonder if the Sanguinati's leader was facing trouble that was above his pay grade.

If that was the case, the humans were well and truly screwed.

Osgood returned from his inquiries at Pops's general store, the look on his face all the confirmation Grimshaw needed that there was panic building among the residents and especially among the trapped tourists. Moving casually while he waited for the last two people he'd requested for this meeting, he pushed buttons on the phones so that all the lines were busy, then muted his mobile phone.

As soon as Ineke Xavier and Julian Farrow walked into the station, Grimshaw turned the lock on the door.

"If we're inviting local businesses to attend this meeting . . . ," Roundtree began.

"They aren't here because they own local businesses," Grimshaw said, not bothering to explain why those two people were there. "Mr. Sanguinati?"

"Contacting police stations in the Northeast should be a priority, to find out what towns or villages have had similar killings," Ilya said.

"But the problem is here!" Roundtree protested.

"Yes," Ilya agreed. "The . . . contamination . . . has been tracked to Sproing and isolated here—and the hunt will end here."

Contamination. Hunt. Gods above and below.

"The prank?" Julian asked. "That would limit the suspect list to Vicki's guests and the academics at the Mill Creek Cabins."

"The Jumble!" Roundtree held up a finger as if making a point. "I should have known. All the trouble started—"

Ilya hissed, showing his fangs.

Roundtree darted behind Osgood.

"Victoria DeVine holds an esteemed position in that *terra indigene* settlement," Ilya said. "You will not criticize her or try to shift the blame onto her in any way. Not if you want to remain the mayor—and remain among the living."

Roundtree sounded like a teakettle on the boil. "Are you *threatening* me? In front of *witnesses*?"

"I'm warning you," Ilya snarled.

"Why isn't Vicki here?" Ineke asked. "Considering The Jumble's pivotal role between the Others and the village, she should be here."

"I'll discuss this with Victoria privately," Ilya replied.

"So, we're looking at eleven suspects?" Grimshaw asked. "Vicki's seven guests and the four men in the cabins?"

"And Ms. Xavier's guests, and the people renting the campers at the edge of the village—and the nearly one hundred people who have moved into Sproing in the past few months," Ilya said.

Crap. So more than a quarter of the village was on their suspect list?

"Until the contamination is found—and eliminated—the roads will remain closed," Ilya continued.

"I'll contact the police in Crystalton and Bristol and ask them to set up roadblocks at the nearest crossroads," Grimshaw said. "Some of those big rigs that carry goods won't have any way to turn around if they reach one of those barricades."

Well, he was pretty sure a pony named Twister would be happy to play spin the semi, but being that he was the chief of police, that wasn't something he wanted to encourage.

Ilya nodded. "Smaller trucks carrying necessary supplies will be allowed to approach the barricades. Humans will be permitted to walk around the barricades with packs or horses or handcarts to fetch the supplies. Any human who tries to flee or who assists a human who is trying to flee . . . Well, they're in the wild country, and the Elders will be watching."

"Anyone who flees won't survive," Julian said, looking at the mayor to make sure the man understood that the Others had a different definition of "meals to go."

Ilya nodded again. "Until the contamination is found—and eliminated—no one is allowed to leave Sproing or the surrounding area." He looked at Roundtree. "You can tell the humans that the village is under quarantine until further notice."

"Quarantined for what?" Roundtree squeaked.

"I'll leave that up to you." Ilya unlocked the door and opened it, then gave the mayor a pointed look. "Human stupidity?"

Roundtree rushed out of the station, hesitated, then rushed to the government building next door.

Ilya closed and locked the station door.

"You gave him the official line," Grimshaw said. "Are you going to tell us the rest?"

"Very few humans have any dealings with the Elders, and even fewer of those humans survive," Ilya replied. "So you don't appreciate that, even among the Elders, there is a hierarchy. They are all dangerous, but some are . . . more. When Elders become aware of a problem that might endanger the *terra indigene* or the wild country, they call on a particular kind of Elder to come and investigate."

"So that none of *them* are sullied by human thinking or actions?" Julian wasn't asking a question so much as confirming a guess.

"That is certainly part of it," Ilya agreed. "They call on a powerful hunter, a savage hunter, and that Elder comes to that place to find and eliminate the contamination."

"And the problem has been tracked to Sproing?" Grimshaw guessed, feeling chilled.

Ilya looked at him and nodded. "And the hunter who is here is a primal, ferocious Elder called Crowbones."

CHAPTER 32

Vicki

Firesday, Novembros 2

Professional innkeepers are not the morality police and should not whine about guests since they need the income that comes from every guest.

I told myself that three times before I whined at Grimshaw and Ilya, *"Why* do I have to let the Cornleys come back and stay? Couldn't Ineke and I play swap the guests?"

"No," Ilya said.

An implacable something in his voice warned me that he wasn't going to change his mind or explain the whys or wherefores of that decision. Which made me wonder if he was the one who had made that decision.

I glanced at Natasha, who seemed equally puzzled by her mate's tone.

"However," Ilya continued, sounding more like himself, "I have explained to the faux newlyweds that they will be courteous to you and the staff at all times, they will keep their room tidy, and they will assist with chores in the common rooms. If they give you any trouble, Conan or Cougar will give them a swat, and the likely result of *that* will be that one or both of them will end up with a broken neck, so they should provide the police with the name and location of their next of kin while they still can."

Okay, so maybe Ilya was a wee bit stressed-out from the realization that everyone in Sproing was playing fish in a barrel, and the Sanguinati were among the fish this time, and he had four fosterlings under his care whom he couldn't send away to someplace safe—which was another one of those things he wasn't explaining to anyone wearing a "Hi! I'm a Human!" button.

"Did the Cornleys provide information on their next of kin?" What would I have said if I'd received a call like that about Yorick before I became the ex–Mrs. Dane?

"Not exactly." Ilya paid a lot of attention to adjusting an already perfect shirt cuff. "Two of the Sanguinati from Silence Lodge found a way into the car Mr. Cornley was driving and examined the car's registration card, making special note of the name and address of the person who owned the vehicle—a name and address that didn't match anything Fred Cornley provided to you."

This is why I'm grateful that Ilya is my attorney. He has a mean streak beneath those polished manners. Not to mention fangs. "You called the person listed on the registration?"

"I did," Grimshaw said. "Official police inquiry regarding a vehicle that wasn't registered to either Fred or Wilma Cornley, the people who were in the vehicle at the time of the incident. I asked the woman who answered the phone if the vehicle was borrowed by a friend or had been reported stolen recently."

Three of us waited, breathless for the answer.

Well, I was breathless. Natasha looked curious, and I had the impression that Grimshaw rose a little in Ilya's estimation because our chief of police had a mean streak equal to his own.

Grimshaw shrugged. "The response wasn't articulated in any way I could put in a report, but I did manage to tell the woman that the village was under quarantine and no one would be leaving for at least a day or two."

"Sufficient time to move liquid assets," Natasha said. Then she gave us all a mischievous smile.

I really wish I'd known Natasha and Ilya when I was getting my divorce. They took bloodsucking to a whole different level.

"Fine," I said, feeling more cheerful. "I'll put up with the Cornleys."

"Thank you." Ilya exchanged a look with Natasha. "And now we would like to ask for a personal favor."

Ben Malacki and David Shuman weren't in Ilya's good books for some reason, and I didn't like the way they eyed Kira when she showed up to be my new helper and learn some of the ins and outs of running a place that provided rustic accommodations for humans who wanted to plunk themselves in the middle of a *terra indigene* settlement.

I'd sent Kira and Aggie to freshen up the Cornleys' room in advance of their return. Jozi and Eddie were taking care of housekeeping chores in the cabins. I didn't know where Conan and Cougar were, so I was on my own at the reception desk when Officer Osgood dropped off the Cornleys and then skedaddled.

I didn't ask where they had spent the night. Fred Cornley looked ready to pop a blood vessel or three, and Wilma no longer looked like she thought her "precious sausage"—she really said that out loud the other day, in front of other people—was all that precious. But unless she wanted to sleep on the floor in one of the common rooms, she was stuck with Fred for the next few days.

Then again, I was stuck with both of them, so my sympathy for both of them was down to a half thimbleful.

Kira returned to report that their room was ready, and Aggie escorted them up to the suite, mostly to confirm that they didn't go anywhere else.

The phone rang in my office, and I hustled to catch the call before it went to voice mail. The caller didn't identify himself, but I recognized him as the panicked Sanguinati I'd talked to the other day. He calmly informed me that they—he was vague about who "they" were—had managed to open the trunk of the glacier-wrapped car and extract the Cornleys' luggage. Boris would pick up the luggage and bring it to The Jumble.

I thanked him for the information and hurried back to the reception desk. I wasn't sure which twitched my anxiety more—Ben Malacki leaning on the desk and smiling at Kira in a way that made me want to fetch some soap and give him a scrubbing or David Shuman looking at her as if she was a specimen he could break open and study.

Or Kira, who seemed to be playing to their predatory instincts for reasons of her own.

Then she looked at me as if needing help, and I wondered why there were moments when I entertained a negative opinion of her.

"Need help with something?" I said as I joined Kira behind the desk. "Should I give Conan or Cougar a shout?"

"How long is this quarantine going to be in place?" Shuman asked.

"Don't know. I'm sure the authorities are working as fast as they can to get things resolved." I looked toward the front door. "It's crisp out but sunny. Maybe you'd enjoy a walk. There are plenty of paths through The Jumble."

"How many of your guests come back from taking a walk?" Malacki asked.

"Most of them." I paused as if thinking. "Almost all of them." Another pause. "It depends."

Malacki stepped away from the desk. "Okay if we play pool?"

"Sure."

Kira and I watched them walk to the room Ilya had transformed into a private pool hall as an added incentive for Grimshaw to take the job of chief of police.

I took a deep breath and found a little bit of my sand. "I don't think anyone will misbehave, but did Ilya tell you what to do if one of the guests tries to . . . persuade . . . you to do something you don't want to do?"

Kira nodded. "He told me to go for the jugular."

Okeydokey.

CHAPTER 33

Ilya

Firesday, Novembros 2

Sex in the human form wasn't the same as mating to produce offspring when a Sanguinati female was in season, but with Natasha, there was a pleasure to the act that Ilya hadn't found when participating with human females as a way to feed. There was pleasure in holding her afterward to strengthen the bond between them.

And there was comfort to not being alone while he struggled with troubling thoughts.

"Does anything about Kira's behavior bother you?" he asked, thinking about the feeling Michael and Ian Stern had conveyed to Grimshaw about the girl.

"You're asking about the way she teases Karol?" Natasha countered.

Was he asking about that? "Tell me."

"He is infatuated in a way that humans indulgently call puppy love. He is eager for her attention, flattered when he receives it, and downcast when Kira shows a preference for Viktor's company."

"Kira and Viktor are close in age. Karol is younger and not as mature."

"Yes, but he doesn't want to be paired with Lara and seen as a child, so being ignored by Kira and Viktor stings," Natasha said. "Others in our shadow have heard her set Karol a ridiculous task and then give him high praise if he performs it. She is careful around me—and around you too, I think—but I've begun to wonder why she was chosen for this fostering."

"Why these four youngsters?" Ilya asked softly. "We were supposed to foster Lara and Karol for a season or two. Why did we end up with Kira and Viktor as well?"

"There must have been a reason for the change," Natasha said. "And all the youngsters had the necessary permissions from the leaders of their home shadows."

"Did they? Papers can be forged."

Natasha propped herself on one elbow and looked at him. "That would be so . . . human."

"Yes. Isn't a human connection exactly what we're looking for?" The concern Grimshaw had conveyed to him had been about Kira. Nothing had been said about Viktor, the other unexpected arrival. If Grandfather Erebus had a reason for sending the two older fosterlings to Silence Lodge, he had chosen not to share that reason. Maybe because the leader of all the Sanguinati in Thaisia had decided that Ilya's experience before becoming the leader of Silence Lodge might be needed? If that was the case . . .

"Is Lakeside hosting as many fosterlings?" Natasha asked.

"I don't know. But the Lakeside shadow has many more Sanguinati who can keep watch over the young."

Natasha lay down and settled comfortably on his shoulder. "You're worried one of the fosterlings is connected with the contamination."

"They are here. So is Crowbones. It's hard not to wonder—and worry."

"If there is a connection, you will find it," Natasha said.

Will I find it in time? Ilya wondered.

It was a question that might not have an answer—until it was too late.

CHAPTER 34

Them

Watersday, Novembros 3

Trapped in this damn village!

What had Fewks done after his little performance to get himself killed and get the Others so agitated that they had locked down the entire area? Couldn't have been the performance itself. That was so *minor*. Something else must be going on. Something that wasn't under his control.

Maybe it wasn't *his* project. Maybe his rival had stirred up the trouble. He thought he'd spotted a couple of her monstrosities roaming the village when he'd first arrived. He didn't recognize them—and he doubted they would recognize him, thank the gods—but he knew the signs of his rival's tampering and training.

Too many pieces in motion, too many ways this could go wrong now and threaten *him* if someone managed to ask the right questions of the wrong person. He should have left Sproing the moment he realized his rival was conducting her latest experiment here, but she could have picked *anywhere* for her study, while The Jumble really was the only place for him to carry out *this* particular project. She *knew* that and still risked exposing years of careful studies in how to shape nebulous thoughts into sharp beliefs, along with the studies into how to train a group of people into adopting specific behaviors.

Years of study might be erased unless enough pressure could be brought to bear on the right people in order to clear one road out of this place. Until then, he had to be careful not to provoke his rival into taking impulsive action. He had to blend into the background and let the other academics take the lead.

He was good at that.

CHAPTER 35

Grimshaw

Watersday, Novembros 3

Grimshaw ambushed Ilya on the staircase that led up to the Sangui-nati's office above the police station. He waited for the vampire to come down a few more steps before he leaned against the wall, a deceptively casual pose.

"If you could have, you would have gotten those kids away from Sproing," he said in a conversational tone. "I have to figure that someone higher up the chain of command said no to that request but wouldn't tell you why. I also have to figure that you don't feel comfortable about the security you have in place around Silence Lodge. So you split up the kids, keeping the youngest with your own people and having the three teens doing 'internships' at human businesses."

Ilya came down another step. "Perhaps I wanted some businesses to have a means of reaching me and mine quickly if there was trouble and the human ways of communication were severed. Perhaps the presence of Crowbones makes me feel vulnerable in a way I never have before." He stared at the glass door at the bottom of the stairs. "Perhaps the arrival of the fosterlings coinciding with the arrival of this Hunter is the reason the youngsters can't leave."

He'd wondered about that as he'd brooded by himself last night.

"Teenagers can certainly kill people. Even children can kill by accident or on purpose. But I don't believe any of your youngsters did what was done to Adam Fewks's body or killed either Crow. Which means one or more of your fosterlings might be a target or might be the bait that can flush out the contamination that landed Crowbones on our doorstep, and separating them gives you the best chance of keeping some of them alive." *Especially if one of them is a killer who would endanger other young Sanguinati.*

"What would you have done?" Ilya asked quietly.

"I don't know that I would have done anything different," Grimshaw replied. "But putting Kira with Vicki?"

"The Jumble has layers of defenses."

He didn't point out that Adam Fewks had been killed with breathtaking speed within sight of The Jumble's main house—and he didn't point out that at least one enemy might be inside with Vicki and Kira. Ilya already knew that. But Grimshaw wasn't sure the vampire had considered the unintended consequences of pairing a young Sanguinati female with Vicki DeVine. It wasn't Vicki herself; it was the attraction she seemed to have for the more reclusive *terra indigene* around Lake Silence. "All right. Let me see what sort of busywork I can assign to my intern."

"And I should not keep Mayor Roundtree waiting much longer." Ilya smiled, showing a hint of fang. "I believe he has opinions about the current situation."

May all the gods help the village's mayor if he tried to turn this into political fodder.

Grimshaw and Ilya walked out together, then went in opposite directions.

When Grimshaw walked into the station, he found Officer Osgood and Viktor huddled around the desktop computer.

"Hey, Chief." Osgood looked a little flushed, which Grimshaw took as a sign that the rookie wondered if he'd overstepped some boundary.

Better flushed than pale, Grimshaw thought as he approached the desk that held the computer.

"We've ignored e-mail for a couple of days, so I thought Viktor could go through the e-mails and delete the junk," Osgood said.

Grimshaw studied Viktor, who studied him in turn. "You know how to work e-mail?"

"Yes, sir."

"You know how to separate important from junk?"

"Do you need your penis enhanced?"

"No."

"Then that is junk e-mail."

Smart-ass. But sharp. And aware. And already a predator. "Fine. You sort the e-mail and delete the junk. I'm going to make a circuit around Main Street. Osgood, you have the phones. Don't head out for anything but an emergency until I get back."

"Yes, sir."

Grimshaw zipped up his jacket, walked out of the station, and turned right. As people had moved into Sproing over the past few months, some of them had taken over empty storefronts on Main Street to start up new businesses. Or so he'd been told. Most of the new ventures didn't have signs in the store windows to indicate what they would be. One of them had long folding tables piled with cheap or used goods. A storefront flea market?

The owner hadn't bothered to wash the windows or put up any kind of sign but seemed to be open for business, more or less.

Some of the abandoned houses in Sproing had been looted after the Great Predation. Since Grimshaw didn't claim to be a trusting man, he wanted to know if any of the items taken from those houses were showing up on those tables. He'd give Paige and Dominique Xavier money out of petty cash and have them take a good look at the merchandise being offered. They had a skill for distinguishing quality items from dross.

As he continued down the street, Grimshaw stopped when he saw Gershwin Jones, the owner of Grace Notes, Sproing's only music store. A flamboyant dresser whose deep voice held the lyrical rhythm of the Eastern Storm Islands, Jones was an Intuit whose ability to sense things around him was more focused than Julian Farrow's talent. Except during times of acute danger, Julian responded to the underlying health of a place; Gershwin was more like an early warning siren when a tornado was about to touch down.

"How's the music?" Grimshaw asked, using the code that had developed naturally between them.

"Somber but not a dirge," Gershwin replied.

"If you hear the first note of a dirge, you let me know."

Gershwin looked up the street. Five Sproingers were gathered in front of Lettuce Reed. The door opened and Karol Sanguinati crouched to hold a wooden tray of the carrot chunks that were the critters' treat.

"The day they don't show up on Main Street to make their rounds?" Gershwin said, raising his chin to indicate the Sproingers. "That's the first note of the dirge, full on."

Grimshaw nodded and continued on his own rounds. Residents who had been there over the summer gave him a nod but didn't approach because they knew the routine. Osgood was approachable and willing to listen to gossip; the chief wasn't approached unless you had a real emergency. But Grimshaw dropped by Come and Get It at some point every day and casually told Helen Hearse anything he felt Sproing's citizens should know—and Helen would pass that information on to everyone who came into the diner.

It was early, but he picked up sandwiches for lunch, choosing rare roast beef for Viktor since he wasn't sure what the young Sanguinati usually ate that would be on a human menu.

"Best way to get the roads back open is to assist the police in their investigation," he said as Helen packed the meals into one of the diner's delivery boxes. "And folks should be on the lookout for a teenage boy named Tom Saulner whose friends haven't seen him since he parted company with them on Trickster Night."

"Could he have gotten a ride out of town that night?" Helen asked.

"Possible. He could also be holed up somewhere. We still have plenty of empty houses someone could use for romantic assignations." He waited until Helen finished snickering over his choice of words. "But I haven't received any reports of a missing teenage girl, so I don't think that's the reason he hasn't returned to his friends."

"Could be another boy that's missing," Helen pointed out.

"Could be," he agreed. "Even if parents think their son is out tomcatting somewhere, if someone hasn't come home when expected, regardless of age, I want to know about it. What's out there isn't playing around, and I'd rather not be looking for bodies—or what's left of them."

Helen tucked some paper napkins into the box. "I'll pass the word."

Leaving the diner, Grimshaw walked up the street, stopped in front of one of Lettuce Reed's windows, and looked at the selection of books on display.

A lot of names ending in "gard." It looked like Julian had pulled stock from the back of the store, where people in the know went to browse for books written by Intuits and Others.

Julian stepped outside a minute later.

Grimshaw casually pointed at the display. "Enticing the tourists or warning the residents?"

"A little of both," Julian replied. "I'm taking a look at any books I have in inventory that deal with folklore or urban legends. I'm also taking a look in my personal library."

Like most of the buildings on Main Street, the bookstore had two stories. Unless the previous owner did something truly weird with the space, the second floor of the building was big enough to be a three-bedroom apartment. Since Julian preferred to live in one of the Mill Creek Cabins and hadn't rented the upstairs space to anyone, Grimshaw didn't know what the Intuit had up there—and until Julian chose to tell him, he figured it was better for both of them if he didn't know.

"So far I haven't found any information about Crowbones," Julian continued. "I'm reaching out to other booksellers, on behalf of a customer, to see if anyone has an early edition of a book of folklore that might fit what Professor Roash claims to have seen." He hesitated. "Ian Stern has connections to an Intuit college and could reach out to colleagues without raising suspicion. Michael, as an author, could be researching a new story. Enlisting their help might be a way of gaining information without tripping any alarms."

Julian had a point, especially since they didn't know the extent of the trouble they were in.

"I'll think about it. I can't rule them out as suspects any more than I can rule out any of the other guests who were at The Jumble on Trickster Night, but I'll think about it."

Grimshaw crossed the street. As soon as he walked into the station, Viktor said, "Sir? I have some urgent messages for you."

Setting the box of food on his desk, he went to see what the young Sanguinati considered urgent. Captain Douglas Burke had sent a current list of names and contact information for all the police captains in the

Finger Lakes area. Asterisks after names indicated the men Burke considered trustworthy.

He felt a shiver of relief to see an asterisk after Captain Walter Hargreaves's name. He hadn't worked with Hargreaves long before being sent to Sproing, but he trusted the man and needed the cooperation of the Bristol police force. And he knew there was some connection between Burke and Hargreaves.

Another list came from Greg O'Sullivan, an agent in the governor's Investigative Task Force who was working out of Lakeside. That list contained the names and contact information of the agents in the ITF.

"Good work," he told Viktor. "Print those out for me." Then he reviewed the calls that had come in to the station, prioritized the calls, and distributed the food.

As he sat at his desk to write a carefully worded message that would be sent to the men on those two lists, the word "urgent" kept bothering him. Why would Viktor say those e-mails were urgent? Important? Absolutely. But "urgent" indicated a need for immediate action. Was that the excitement of youth talking, or did Viktor need him to act within a timetable and was he pushing the information that would produce the desired result?

Or was Grimshaw just too damn suspicious of everyone right now?

Then again, *someone* who had come to the area recently was a target. Or bait. Or both. And for Wayne Grimshaw, that meant there was no such thing as being *too* suspicious.

CHAPTER 36

Julian

Watersday, Novembros 3

Grateful his new stock had arrived before the roads closed, Julian grabbed the handcart and reached the front of the store as Karol Sanguinati picked up the phone. He'd wondered about how Ilya had chosen which youngster for which "internship," but it didn't take long for him to understand the decisions. Karol didn't have Viktor's quiet confidence or maturity and had some trouble with impulse control, so the bookstore, where impulsive actions would have fewer consequences, was a better place for him to work than the police station.

"Lettuce Reed," Karol said. "How may I help you?"

Julian watched the Sanguinati's expression change from bafflement to wariness to something that bordered on fear.

"I'll find out," Karol said. "Hold, please." He put his hand over the mouthpiece and looked at Julian. "Someone wants to know if the story place is going to be open this evening."

"We're closing at five p.m. for the next few days," Julian replied. Then the words hit him. *Story place.*

He leaped for the island counter and grabbed for the phone—and noticed how Karol partially shifted to the Sanguinati's smoke form in response to his sudden move.

Karol extended his arm to hand Julian the phone and maintain some distance between them.

Julian took a deep breath to steady himself. "This is Julian."

"The story place is closing early?"

He recognized the voice. The Five came into the bookstore once a week at dusk to do a used-book swap. They were the ones who had named the store. He didn't know where they lived around Lake Silence or what they were in their usual form. He suspected they were some kind of Elder—and he knew they were not benign when they were encountered anywhere outside of his store.

Until that moment, they had never used a telephone to communicate with him, and that set off his internal alarms. Anytime Elders did something unexpected, humans were at risk.

"I am closing the story place early for a few days to assist Ilya Sanguinati while he investigates some trouble around Sproing and Lake Silence." Julian prayed to the Lady of Lost Souls that he wasn't putting Ilya in danger, but just the thought of the Five coming to the bookstore while everyone was stirred up and afraid gave him chills.

"We are also assisting the Hunter."

The Hunter. He could hear the capital *H*.

Given who they were, the Hunter was *not* Ilya. Which meant the Five were helping Crowbones.

His mind raced, trying to figure out a compromise where the Five could exchange their books without coming to the bookstore.

There was one way to do it.

Gods above and below, am I about to gamble with other people's lives?

Julian snapped his fingers and pointed to the pad and pen on the counter. Karol pushed it within reach, still watchful but back to looking fully human.

"I could bring a box of books to The Jumble that you could look at after dusk. Just like doing an exchange here at Lettuce Reed. Do you know how to find the main house at The Jumble?"

"We know the place."

Of course they did. Their voices sang out of the dark as warning and threat.

"I will call Vicki and ask if she can put out the books for you to look at, in case I'm not there when you arrive. The telephone you are using has a number. If you tell me what that number is, I can call you back to confirm the books will be there."

He held his breath. They had understood enough about phones to call the store, but that didn't mean they knew the number of the phone they were using.

Where did they get the phone they were using?

A different voice recited the numbers. Julian wrote them down. "I'll talk to Vicki right now and call you back in a few minutes."

A final whispered instruction spoken in a tone that had never been directly aimed at him before.

Julian hung up, surprised to see his hand shaking.

Karol set a glass of water near the phone and stepped back.

"Thanks," Julian said, grateful for the water and wishing for something stronger.

"Are you in trouble?" Karol asked.

"No. I just need to call Vicki and make arrangements to have the store's auxiliary location set up before dusk." He felt a bead of cold sweat roll down his spine. "Why don't you open the boxes of new books and put a couple of each title on the counter for me to look at? Then you can pack up the new books I select while I put together a box of used books that I think will be of interest. After that, we'll arrange to get the boxes to The Jumble."

"You're afraid."

Julian wondered what to say to this young predator who would tuck away everything he said. "They've come into my store every week since I opened Lettuce Reed, and they have never harmed me. But that doesn't mean they aren't dangerous."

"That is true of all *terra indigene*," Karol said.

"Yes," Julian agreed. "It is."

He called Vicki, mixing apologies and explanation—and emphasizing the one instruction that would prevent her guests from being slaughtered. He called his special customers and confirmed that there would be books available in The Jumble's library room to exchange or purchase.

Then he walked across the street and handed Grimshaw the slip of paper with the phone number on it—and hoped that number had belonged to a college boy they already knew was dead rather than to a fresh corpse.

CHAPTER 37

Ilya

Watersday, Novembros 3

W e can't have our roads closed by blocks of ice and mounds of dirt,"
Mayor Roundtree said, his face flushed. "It's bad for bidness."

"What business? The established businesses in the village are mildly
inconvenienced, but no more than that." Ilya sounded calm, but his mind
raced because he had the impression the established businesses weren't the
ones calling the mayor to complain about road closures. That meant newcomers.

The Sanguinati who handled property owned by Silence Lodge would
have told him if they had leased any storefronts to Sproing's new residents
and what kind of business would be going into each space. Which meant
none of those new enterprises were in buildings owned by the Sanguinati.
Coincidence? Or something less benign?

"What do you mean, what bidness? We've got tourists *trapped* here!
You think that's going to help our village grow? That we can expand and
prosper? You think people are going to come here to live if you all close
the roads whenever you get a bug up your butt?"

The being that was prowling the land around Lake Silence and actively hunting for a contamination was a lot more than a bug—and certainly wasn't anything humans should dismiss as unimportant.

Grandstanding. Denying the truth in the face of reality. It wasn't *completely* out of character, because Roundtree, as humans put it, changed his opinion more often than he changed his underwear. But even for Roundtree, that question about expansion was . . . odd.

Studying the mayor, Ilya wondered how much of what was said at this private meeting would be repeated at a public meeting or show up in Sproing's weekly newspaper. He could almost write the headline: *Mayor Stands Up to Sanguinati Leader About Road Closures and Declares the Others Are Bad for Bidness.*

There were advantages to working behind the scenes, but that was no longer an option. After Silence Lodge took open control of the village's only bank, dealing with the village government became inevitable, and a task that fell to him as the Sanguinati leader because the Sanguinati were the dominant form of *terra indigene* around here—at least where dealing with humans was concerned.

It wasn't his job to know everything about every human in the village or the surrounding farms. The Sanguinati were supposed to monitor human behavior to protect the *terra indigene*'s interests—and that included maintaining the boundaries between land the humans could use and what belonged to the Others. Was Roundtree's talk of expansion a prelude to an attempted land grab? Or was this perilous change in attitude somehow connected with the contamination? If it was, *how* had Roundtree been contaminated?

"Growth," Ilya said quietly. "Expansion. Prosperity. That sounds like a reelection platform rather than practical reality. The village cannot expand beyond the boundaries that already exist. It cannot alter the use of farmland and replace pastures and crops with houses or businesses. There is still some room for growth in terms of population. Sproing has gained about a hundred people in a very short period of time. Not all of those people are adults, and not every adult has a separate dwelling, so there are still some residences available for people who want to relocate to the village—and work in the village."

Ilya smiled, showing a hint of fang, and watched Roundtree pull into himself. "I've heard some storefronts have been rented," he continued, "but no one has seen any indication of businesses making use of those spaces. It has been my observation that humans are not casual about earning a living, since they need money for things like food and shelter. Now

I'm wondering why the people renting those storefronts aren't making an effort to get their businesses up and running."

"Some of our new citizens might work elsewhere—which is another reason having those roads closed is making the village look bad," Roundtree said, flustered.

That confirmed his suspicion of one reason the mayor was fielding calls about closed roads and lobbing a complaint at him.

"Hmm. Perhaps. But if people are working elsewhere, why did they leave the town where they are employed? Even commuting from Crystalton or Bristol every day isn't practical. Are the new residents living here on the weekends in order to do a kind of double-dipping by claiming a share of rationed goods in both locations?" Ilya paused, not because he needed to think but because he wanted Roundtree to pay attention. "Every adult who came to Sproing recently and took over an abandoned dwelling or leased an apartment would have come to the village hall to provide your government with their name, new address, and their contact information. You would need to know that to add them to the tax roll since they would be making use of the available water and government services like garbage pickup. Human forms also usually have a space to fill out for occupation."

"That's optional," Roundtree said quickly.

"Not anymore." Ilya stood. "Before I discuss anything with the Elders about opening the roads, you are going to supply me and Chief Grimshaw with information about the people who have taken up residence in Sproing since this summer. You should have most of that information available already. I also want to know where they lived prior to their move to Sproing and where they are working. If they are opening a new business here, I want to know what kind of business. And I want to know who signed the leases on the storefronts that are supposed to have new occupants. I'll give you seventy-two hours to get that information to me. If you can't—or won't—do this, I'll send someone who can."

Roundtree shot out of his chair. "You think you can order the police to go knocking on doors and harass our citizens just because they want to live here?"

Ilya smiled. "Oh, no, Mayor Roundtree. If *I* have to get the information, I won't be sending the police."

CHAPTER 38

Vicki

Watersday, Novembros 3

After Boris Sanguinati arrived with two boxes of books and the Corn- leys' luggage, Michael and Ian Stern helped me set up the long fold- ing tables that would become Lettuce Reed's auxiliary bookstore, which Michael had dubbed Mini Munch.

I made two tabletop signs: USED BOOKS and NEW BOOKS. New books had to be purchased. Used books could be swapped, equal exchange. I wasn't sure what Julian expected me to do if his special customers wanted to purchase a new book. He hadn't covered that possibility.

Well, I would hand over the book. That's what I would do. And leave Julian a note to keep his ledgers balanced.

Michael and Ian made a display of the new books on the second table while I handled the used books on the table closest to the library's door.

"Can we purchase any of these books?" Ian asked as he read the cover copy on a couple of the new books.

"The special customers get first pick, but Julian didn't say the rest of you couldn't browse after they left," I replied.

Michael rearranged a couple of titles to more prominently display his newest book. "So, these special customers usually show up at Julian's bookstore at dusk and select some books. But they're coming here instead."

I think there was supposed to be a question in there somewhere about *why* the special customers were coming to The Jumble, but Michael didn't actually ask, so I didn't feel compelled to answer. "Yes."

"And we're supposed to stay out of sight while they're here."

"Yes."

"Why?" Ian asked. "We've seen—and talked to—other kinds of *terra indigene*. Wouldn't talking about something we both enjoy be a positive experience?"

"Maybe at another time, but they were quite insistent that they didn't want to interact with any of my guests." Just me. The Jumble's acknowledged Reader.

"Maybe if they had a chance to see us?"

I wondered why Ian was pursuing this when I'd already said they all had to stay away from this part of the main house. I hoped it was professional curiosity and not something that could be interpreted as sinister intentions. "They've already seen you. All of you. And they told Julian flat out that none of you were allowed to see them. I'm sorry. I know you're curious, but . . ."

"Julian is nervous about this, isn't he?" Michael said. "Not just cautious about the change in location, but truly nervous about offering these particular *terra indigene* this alternate arrangement so that they can get their books."

I nodded.

"So we're not talking about shifters like Crows or Coyotes or Foxes."

I shook my head. "I'm pretty sure we aren't talking about anyone like that."

Michael and Ian exchanged a look.

"Before your customers are expected to arrive, I think your guests should make up a couple of platters of leftovers and stay in the TV room with one of your . . . larger . . . employees keeping an eye on things," Ian finally said. "Temptation to ignore a request is easier to resist when someone is watching."

"We'll take care of the food and will make sure Jenna McKay is here in the main house before dusk," Michael said. "You focus on . . . this."

I didn't have time to wonder what the two Intuits were sensing. The afternoon was slipping away, and I had to explain to my surly guests why they were going to be confined to the TV room to watch whatever might be on at that hour while something interesting was going on in another part of the house.

CHAPTER 39

Grimshaw

Watersday, Novembros 3

C hief?" Osgood pushed the Hold button on the phone. "It's Mr. San-guinati for you."

Ignoring Viktor's wary look—the expression of a teenager wondering if he'd done something wrong and this was about him—Grimshaw took the call.

"I need to see you in my office," Ilya said. "Now."

Hearing controlled anger in the Sanguinati's voice, Grimshaw figured the meeting with the mayor had not gone well. And he wondered if he should call the EMTs to see if Roundtree was suddenly suffering from acute anemia—or something worse.

"Mr. Farrow will be joining us," Ilya added.

"I'll be up in a minute." He hung up, then looked at Osgood. "Anything I need to know about?"

"A complaint from Ellen C. Wilson about Pops Davies not serving customers whose account is overdue and whose last check bounced. He's now requiring cash, which, apparently, is insulting to someone of her status."

"She doesn't have any status outside of being the village pest." The woman seemed to have enough money when it suited her, but he didn't think she did any work—unless her job was to harangue shop owners to see how long it would take them to ban a customer.

"Pops has made a countercomplaint about Mrs. Wilson's son, Theodore, stuffing a few things in his pockets and bolting out the door while Mrs. Wilson badgered Pops," Osgood continued. "And a couple of other people complained about Pops limiting some items and keeping some things behind the counter."

"Did you get the names and addresses of the people who made those complaints?" Grimshaw asked.

"Yes, sir."

"Anyone we know besides Mrs. Wilson?"

Osgood shook his head. "Newcomers."

The rookie made it sound like he'd lived in Sproing all his life when, in truth, he'd been transferred here during the troubles that past summer and was still living at the boardinghouse—and didn't seem to be in any hurry to find his own place.

"Go over to the general store. If Pops wants to make a formal complaint about the shoplifting, you take his statement, and we'll deal with it." Grimshaw paused. "And see what he has to say about any other newcomers." He remembered something else. "Did you ask Pops about selling bleach to Adam Fewks?"

Osgood nodded. "The name didn't mean anything, but he recognized the picture from the student ID and confirmed that was the boy who purchased a bottle of bleach on Trickster afternoon. He thought it was an odd purchase for a boy that age, but he saw no reason to question it."

That crossed another item off the list. They didn't know what Fewks had thought he could do with the bleach in the moments before the *terra indigene* came hunting for him, but at least they had confirmed where he'd bought it in the village.

Grimshaw walked over to the desk with the computer.

"Am I in trouble?" Viktor asked.

"Can't see how," he replied. "Have you sent those e-mails out?"

"I sent the message to the ITF agents."

"Hold off on the messages to the police until I find out what's scratching at Ilya."

Grimshaw stepped out of the station and almost collided with Mayor Roundtree.

"You have *got* to *do* something about . . . *them*," Roundtree said, poking a finger at Grimshaw.

"No, I don't," Grimshaw replied. "My job is to handle human-against-human crimes and to stop any fools from antagonizing the Others to the point of starting another purge."

Roundtree's face turned an alarming shade of red. "You think you'll get reelected with that attitude?"

"I wasn't elected; I was hired. If Ilya Sanguinati decides I'm not doing my job, he'll fire me. He's the only one who can. Now, if you'll excuse me, Mayor, I'm going upstairs to find out what you said that pissed him off. And then, if you want, I'll come to your office to hear your version of that meeting."

"My version? *My version?* Who do you think you are?"

"I'm the chief of police, and you are one word away from being arrested for causing a public disturbance."

Grimshaw waited while Roundtree did a passable imitation of a landed fish. Then he walked around the other man and went upstairs.

Well and truly pissed off, Grimshaw thought when he entered Ilya's part of the office.

Ilya handed him a sheet of paper with "From the Mayor's Office" as the heading. Must be the letter Roundtree's office submitted for the next issue of the *Sproing Weekly*.

After reading Roundtree's latest thoughts, Grimshaw understood why Ilya was angry. The letter was one long whining complaint about roads being closed and the *terra indigene*'s high-handed control of the village, which made law-abiding citizens too fearful to live and work in Sproing. Grimshaw figured Ilya would have filed that away for future reference when dealing with Roundtree and remain unruffled. But the Sanguinati's leader wouldn't shrug off the paragraph strongly hinting that Sproing's troubles were mostly due to the current ownership of The Jumble.

"If Roundtree makes a move against Victoria, we will kill him," Ilya said.

If that was Ilya's conversation opener, every human in and around Sproing was in trouble.

Julian appeared in the doorway of Ilya's office. "The village is starting to feel unhealthy. Cracked. And something is seeping in through those cracks."

Crap. "Why here?" Grimshaw laid the letter facedown on Ilya's desk. Then he looked at the other two men. "Why now?"

"Why is Roundtree trying to get people stirred up when last winter he was all about cooperating and everyone working together to get through the hard times?" Julian countered.

"Last winter he wasn't dealing with us," Ilya said. "Last winter he could pretend, or even believe, that everything that wasn't human was Out There, not sitting in an office in the building next to the village government."

And last winter, something the Others called a contamination hadn't appeared in Sproing. Grimshaw took a seat, stretched his legs, and crossed them at the ankles—a deliberately relaxed position, even if he didn't feel the least bit relaxed. "So, what did you and the mayor wrangle about?" he asked Ilya.

"Reopening the roads, among other things," Ilya replied.

"Well, everyone wants the roads open, so that's not a surprise," Grimshaw said. "And I imagine Roundtree would like to pin the blame for this current trouble on someone who lives outside the village limits."

Ilya gave him a sharp look. That letter had made it clear enough where Roundtree wanted to place the blame. Then the vampire flicked a look at Julian, confirming Grimshaw's suspicion that the Sanguinati knew more about Julian Farrow's past than he did—and didn't want to aim Farrow toward Roundtree.

"It may have been a mistake to rent some of the cabins to colleges in the Finger Lakes without stipulating approval of the individuals who want to make use of that arrangement," Ilya said. "Especially since we reduced the time on the leases to four months to accommodate the number of professionals who wanted a chance to have contact with the *terra indigene*."

"You can't preapprove Vicki's guests or Ineke's, and they're more transient than professors coming to observe the *terra indigene* in order to write papers for academic journals," Julian pointed out.

"The influx of new residents is now a concern," Ilya said. "It didn't seem within Silence Lodge's duties to preapprove them either. Now it seems that knowing where those humans came from is vital to the village's survival. Do you agree, Chief Grimshaw? Is the difference between new and settled residents the crack Mr. Farrow is sensing?"

"Could be," Grimshaw agreed. "We certainly have a few people stirring up trouble within the human community. And those still-empty storefronts are becoming an itch I can't scratch." He looked at Ilya.

"None of the buildings that supposedly have new occupants belong to the Sanguinati," Ilya said.

"Any chance of someone picking the locks, so to speak, and taking a look around the inside of those buildings?" Julian asked.

A flicker of amusement in Ilya's dark eyes. "Mr. Farrow. Are you suggesting, in front of the chief of police, that the Sanguinati break a human law?"

"As long as you don't set off a smoke alarm or write your name in the dust, how is the chief of police supposed to know?" Grimshaw asked dryly.

"I would prefer that human methods of gaining information about the occupants be employed first," Ilya replied, his voice equally dry.

Not angry anymore, Grimshaw thought, watching Ilya. *Still pissed off, sure, but there's not that smoldering anger that could turn into a flash fire of violence.*

Julian cleared his throat. "You should both know that some of my customers are going to The Jumble this evening to do their weekly book exchange."

Grimshaw felt his heart beating. "Which customers?"

A hesitation before Julian looked at Ilya. "The Five who come at dusk."

Ilya hissed, showing his fangs.

"*Those* five?" Grimshaw asked quietly. "Why?"

"A compromise—and a gamble," Julian said. "I thought it would be safer for everyone if the Five didn't come into the village right now. Conan and Cougar will make sure none of Vicki's guests cause trouble. The Five only want to deal with the Reader."

Silence.

Grimshaw focused on breathing and tried not to think about those voices in the dark. *Moooonkey man.*

"Vicki can handle it," Julian said. "Gods, she survived the Elders who live in the lake, so she can supervise the exchange of used books."

Was Julian trying to convince them or himself? Grimshaw wondered. Then he said, "Vicki will be fine. They're female, aren't they? Other females don't trigger her anxiety attacks, so as long as the guests can be corralled for the time your customers are browsing, everyone will be fine."

The men agreed on a plan. Julian would close early as he had intended to do and head over to The Jumble to be on hand if Vicki needed assistance. He would take Karol and Viktor with him and make sure they were safely tucked in with Vicki's employees before the Five showed up. Grimshaw would talk to some of the owners of existing businesses and see what he could find out about the newcomers. Since Ilya had sent Boris home because he'd planned to be at his office most of the day, Grimshaw agreed to drop Ilya at The Jumble before heading home.

He doubted any of them would get any rest, let alone sleep, that night. There was no way to tell where trouble would strike next, but he figured between the three of them and Osgood, one of them wouldn't be too far away from the next body.

CHAPTER 40

Aiden

Watersday, Novembros 3

Those humans with their books and their big words and their thinly veiled contempt for anything that wasn't like them were up to something sneaky.

Not all of them, no. Edward Janse, the male who had been identified as an Intuit, was polite and trying to interact with the *terra indigene* while staying within the neutral ground of his cabin's front yard. Unfortunately, whatever bit of special Intuits had when dealing with humans didn't seem to work when dealing with the Others.

Aiden spent an hour watching Janse set out chunks of pizza crust on the short wall that enclosed his cabin's front yard. He'd had plenty of interest from a variety of creatures, but it became obvious that he couldn't tell a crow from a Crow and he simply talked to every bird of that shape that flew over to snag a bit of food.

<Should we tell them that the Crowgard are avoiding unknown humans while the Hunter is here?> Air asked, joining him.

<Even if it doesn't come through the Crowgard, word still travels that he is interested in communicating,> Aiden replied. <Perhaps some other gard will stop by for a visit.>

<Something might stop by.> Air stared at the other occupied cabins. <And *they* are going to visit the Reader soon to exchange books.>

Aiden looked at Air, surprised. <The Five are going to show them-selves?> Uneasiness was an unfamiliar sensation for an Elemental. He didn't like it. <Vicki provides a valuable service to many *terra indigene*, but *they* may not appreciate that. Perhaps one of us should keep watch.>

<Earth is watching tonight. The Five don't want to harm the Reader. They just want new stories.>

The three men from the other cabins came outside and looked around, impatient.

"Hey!" the Roash human shouted. "Can you hear me? I need to ask you a question."

Aiden noticed how Janse froze in place like prey. Then he moved closer to the cabin's porch—and did not ask the shouting Roash any of the questions humans tended to ask, like, what was wrong?

<I think they want to talk to you,> Air said, amused.

<Fools.>

He understood, as well as his kind of *terra indigene* could, why the Sanguinati had rented some of the cabins to the institutions where hu-mans went to learn many things and now wanted to learn about the Oth-ers. Most humans didn't stay longer than the waxing or waning of a moon, but the appearance of the Hunter at the same time *these* males came to Lake Silence was reason enough to distrust these humans, even if they did nothing wrong.

He waited until the humans were looking in the wrong direction, then assumed his human form and pulled on a pair of jeans he'd left in a sack secured to a branch of a tree. No shirt, no shoes. He couldn't dress like this if Vicki was going to see him, because she tried to give him more clothes, convinced that he was going to catch cold.

He was Fire. He didn't catch cold. But he'd helped her light the stove in a cabin when she'd been driven out of The Jumble and stayed here under Ilya's protection, and she associated the human need for warmth with him. In order to talk about something besides sweaters, he dressed in more clothes when he intended to cross paths with her.

Now he stepped out from among the trees and walked toward the cabins.

"Hey!" Roash shouted.

"Hey," Aiden replied. He wasn't surprised that Roash, the trouble-maker, was the shouter, since the man had sent another human to The Jumble pretending to be Crowbones.

"If we're going to be stuck here awhile longer, can we drive into the village and pick up supplies?" Roash asked.

He tried to think like a human, tried to think of how going into the village to purchase food could be turned into something sneaky. When he couldn't think of anything, he said, "How many of you need to go?"

"I'll go." The man called Peter Lynchfield held up a key. "I have a spare key for my car, so I can drive in and pick up some supplies for us."

Since "us" didn't seem to mean "all of us," Aiden looked at the Intuit. "What about you? Do you need supplies?"

"Not tonight," Janse said. "But it's good to know I can drive into the village tomorrow and buy a meal at the diner. And check out the book-store if it's open."

It sounded like he was being asked if those activities were okay, so he nodded.

"When do you think the roads will be open?" Roash asked.

Aiden shrugged. Then he smiled. "When the enemy is dead."

CHAPTER 41

Them

Watersday, Novembros 3

After Roash took a phone call from the informant, he watched the man almost wet himself with excitement. A one-of-a-kind opportunity. Couldn't pass this up. Of course, the Others were watching Roash because of his interest in folklore and urban legends, so *he* couldn't do the deed. No. Better to be one step removed.

It was always better to be one step removed. Wasn't that why he'd chosen Roash to assist him in this part of his project?

And it had taken only a passing comment expressing apologetic doubt about Lynchfield's manliness to have that man fall in with Roash's plan.

With those playing pieces in motion, he looked at the occupant of the other cabin.

Edward Janse wasn't a pansy. Or if he was, that wasn't the reason he came across as sensitive and . . . vulnerable. Janse wasn't one of those Intuits who could tell you about the weather or which horse would run well in tomorrow's race. No, Janse seemed to pick up the undercurrents of people, which made him a potential threat.

Unless that sensitivity, combined with a little feel-good mixed into a mug of tea, could influence Janse's thoughts, encourage him to do something potentially fatal. The drug was harder to come by these days, and he needed to hold back enough to reward his previous helpers, but he thought he could spare enough to find out how an Intuit reacted to a drug made out of blood from the *cassandra sangue*.

CHAPTER 42

Vicki and Aggie

Watersday, Novembros 3

There is something ironic about being afraid to watch horror movies when you live in a place like The Jumble. I was going to have a strong talk with myself about that one of these days.

"This shouldn't take more than an hour," I said for the third time, responding to the third of my four surly guests. This time it was Fred Cornley, who looked like he wanted to try out for the role of ax murderer. I stood my ground—and made sure I was in easy reach of Conan Beargard.

"I don't see why . . . ," Ben Malacki began.

"Because they'll kill you, and Miss Vicki and the rest of us will spend a lot of time cleaning up the mess," Conan rumbled. "And they'll be very unhappy with the rest of you humans if bits of bloody meat end up on their nice books."

No bloody bits of dead human on the nice books. Good to know Julian's customers had priorities.

Breathe, Vicki. Breathe.

"Eat some food," I suggested. "Watch TV." Before there were complaints about the lack of good shows on at that hour, I slipped out of the room.

I wasn't sure if dusk was a particular time for these preferred customers or was just some time between the sun going down and Julian closing the store. Turned out, I didn't need to be sure, because when I walked into the library to check the displays one last time, I found five . . . beings . . . looking around the room and at the books on the tables. And then they looked at me.

They were shorter than me and had the leanness of a girl before puberty gave her breasts and hips. Because of that, it would be easy to mistake them for children if the light was dim and you couldn't really see their faces. But they weren't children, and they weren't young, and I'm sure they would terrify the entire village of Sproing if seen in daylight—and I would bet that any one of them was strong enough to use Conan in his Bear form as a dust mop. My hind brain—the bit that used to tell humans to hide in caves and hope not to be found—recognized that.

"Reader," one said.

No mistaking that voice. *Monkey man.*

Julian wouldn't put me in harm's way. I had to believe that. "Good evening. I set out the books Julian sent over from the store. Hopefully you'll find some you like."

A beat of silence before another one asked, *"Do you like these books, Reader?"* *Moooonkey man.*

"Some of them. I haven't read all of them. I like Alan Wolfgard's stories, even when I'm yelling at the humans in the stories for doing something stupid."

Another beat of silence. Then the first one said, *"But the humans in the stories cannot hear you."*

"I know. I yell at them anyway. Does me as much good as yelling at real humans."

To avoid a discussion of why the anger of a short, plump woman would be ignored, I asked them about the books they liked to read. They showed me the ones they'd brought back to exchange.

I picked up one of their books that I hadn't read. "Is this one scary?" I asked, forgetting who I was talking to. "I like scary if it's not too scary."

"There are bad humans," the second one said.

"That can be the worst kind of scary."

"Yes."

The third one pointed to the new-books display. *"These are different."*

"Those are hardcovers. Humans usually buy them when they intend to keep them. Paperbacks don't cost as much, so people are more willing to trade them for other books."

If they didn't know about the new books, had I just gotten Julian in serious trouble?

"We trade these but can buy those to keep?"

I wasn't sure which one of them asked the question, so I said, "Sure." And I was going to accept whatever currency they wanted to use, be it acorns or pebbles or pieces of string.

They exchanged five paperbacks for five paperbacks. Then each of them selected a hardcover—including Michael Stern's new book.

I wrote down the titles, explaining that Julian needed to keep track of the new books that were sold. When I looked up, I saw one of them remove paper money from a pocket in her slacks. I did not want to know what had made the reddish brown stains on those bills.

They must have seen something in my face, because that one put the money away and another one placed two gold coins on the table. She said, *"Is that enough?"*

"That is plenty for five books." I didn't know that for sure, but I didn't care since I was fairly sure those coins were real gold.

I picked up five of the Lettuce Reed bags that Julian had supplied and that I'd placed under the table. "The bags have handles, so it will be easier to carry the books home." Wherever home was.

"We do not need so many this time."

They watched me divide the books into two bags. "Here you—"

All five of them turned away from the table and stared at the windows. I'd drawn the curtains, so there was nothing to see, but . . .

"Do you hear a rattle?" My heart pounded in my ears, which made it hard for me to hear anything else. "Maybe I should drive you home—or someplace closer to your home. Or you can wait for Julian and he can take you. There's . . ." I was scared, but I held on to common sense enough to realize I didn't want to insult someone whom they might consider a colleague of sorts. "Crowbones might be out there," I finished in a whisper.

They looked at me. I couldn't tell if they were puzzled or amused.

"No," the first one said. *"The Hunter is elsewhere tonight."*

Well, *something* was out there.

They headed for the library door.

"Wait!" I rushed to reach the door before they did. "Let me make sure none of my guests are acting like stupid humans in a story."

I slipped out of the library and looked around. No one in the reception area. The door to the TV room was still closed—and even through the closed door I could hear Wilma Cornley complaining about something.

I looked toward the library and waved a hand. "The coast is clear." I didn't have time to wonder if they knew what that meant. They sort of flowed out of the room and across the reception area's floor. Four of them were unencumbered as they opened the front door and went out. The fifth one carried both bags of books.

She paused at the door and said, *"You should tell the humans to pay attention and be grateful that you yell at them when they are doing something stupid."*

There was a message in those words that I didn't want to translate.

Then she was gone, disappearing into the darkness among the trees.

As I stood in the doorway, letting in the chilly night air and wondering if they had far to walk, I saw a flash . . . a flash . . . a flash . . . and knew what they had sensed.

Someone was out there in the dark with a camera, trying to take pictures of them.

Gods, no.

I froze for a moment, imagining which of the three men I knew would draw the short straw of taking my call for help.

Then . . .

"Monkey man."

"Moooonkey man."

"Broke the promise, monkey man."

Someone out there in the dark screamed. And screamed. And screamed.

Aggie had wanted to stay in the kitchen with Jozi, Eddie, Kira, and Cougar, but Miss Vicki was being so brave dealing with the Five by herself that Aggie felt she needed to be brave too and help Conan keep an eye on the guests.

She wouldn't have thought of this particular bit of human sneakiness if she hadn't seen it on a cop and crime show—who would be sneaky about something like that?—but she had slipped into the TV room before the humans arrived, prepared for the moment when one of them would make the request.

"But I have to *go*," Wilma Cornley whined. *"Right now."*

Aggie picked up the bucket she had tucked behind a chair and set it in front of Wilma. She removed the roll of toilet paper she'd stashed in the bucket and held it out to the human female. "It's the accommodation used in the primitive cabins when humans don't want to go out to the toilets at night. You're responsible for cleaning your pee or poop out of the bucket. If we have to do it, we'll dump your mess in your luggage."

For a moment, she thought the Wilma female was going to slap her—or try to—but a growl from Conan killed that action.

"I'll wait," Wilma said, baring her teeth.

Since Aggie's beak was sharper than those teeth, it wasn't much of a threat. Shrugging, she left the bucket and retreated with the toilet paper. With the roads closed, humans were getting panicky about toilet paper, so it was better not to leave something valuable unattended.

Conan growled again as he turned toward the door. Then his arms became thicker and furrier, and his hands changed to paws with claws. The paws weren't as large as when Conan was in Bear form, but they would "get the job done"—a phrase she particularly liked.

"Sit down," Conan's voice rumbled as he eyed the humans in the room.

Three of Miss Vicki's guests—the cabin people—immediately sat down. The other four began asking questions and wanting to know why they had to sit, why they had to wait, why, why, why.

They might have gone on like that all night if Conan hadn't lost patience and swatted the David Shuman human into a chair. It was a light swat, and Conan barely raked the man with his claws, but Shuman stared at Conan, shocked, while three of the humans began to scream and shout—totally useless—and the cabin people rushed to help Shuman.

Michael Stern yanked off his sweater, then his T-shirt, and pressed the shirt against the wounds. That was good. It wouldn't bother the *terra indigene*, but Miss Vicki wouldn't be happy if bloodstains spoiled the chair's fabric.

Handing the toilet paper to Jenna McKay in case it would be useful,

Aggie dashed behind Conan and put one hand over her eyes before opening the door just enough to shout, "It's okay, Miss Vicki. The situation is under control."

That was another phrase she had heard in one of the cop shows.

She closed the door and leaned against it. Would Miss Vicki be upset with her because she had fibbed? Situations were seldom completely under control in The Jumble. That's what made it so interesting to live here.

Then again, the person who had said that in the story had been fibbing too.

Chief? It's Vicki. I'm really, really sorry, but it's one of those phone calls."

"Crap."

More an exhaled breath than an actual word. Typical Grimshaw.

"What happened?" he asked, sounding cranky.

"I don't know. Someone with a camera, trying to take pictures. I think. And then screaming."

Lots of screaming. Horror movies never quite get that pitch of terror right. Probably for the best.

"Where are you?"

"In the main house. With the doors locked."

"Stay there." A barked order, as if he thought I was going to go outside.

On the other hand, there was some kind of commotion in the TV room, but Aggie said it was under control. I knew she meant the shit had hit the fan, but I was going to pretend to believe her until backup arrived.

I hung up the office phone, then went to the entrance area and sat on the floor in front of the reception desk. You can't fall if you're already on the floor when you faint.

Words to live by.

I just hoped, whatever had happened outside, no bits of dead human had gotten on the nice new books.

CHAPTER 43

Grimshaw

Watersday, Novembros 3

Grimshaw turned on his flashing lights and stepped on the gas.

"Message from Julian Farrow," Ilya said. "Don't come in hot. A car is blocking the access road, and he is backing up to put distance between his vehicle and the other one."

"You get that from one of your boys?"

Ilya nodded. "From Viktor, who also reports that the other car does not have its lights on."

Grimshaw's mobile phone rang. "Answer that."

Ilya picked up the phone. "This is Ilya. Yes, I'll tell him. Are you hurt? That's good. We'll be there soon."

"What?" Grimshaw snapped when Ilya ended the call and didn't say anything.

"Victoria isn't hurt, but she says we should call the EMTs or Dr. Wallace to tend to the guest that Conan Beargard swatted."

Crap. "That's not why she made the first call, and I'm not bringing the EMTs or Doc up here until I know what we're facing."

People were still sitting down to the evening meal, so it wasn't that late despite the darkening sky. Asking the EMTs to make a call wouldn't be as risky now as it would be in a few hours. Still, he didn't want those men walking into a dangerous situation without good reason.

Spotting vehicle flashers at the turnoff for The Jumble, Grimshaw pulled onto the shoulder of the road, leaving The Jumble's access road clear in case Julian needed to make a hasty retreat. Before getting out of the cruiser, he called the EMTs and Doc Wallace to put them on alert so they would be ready to roll the moment they got his second call—if they got a call. Considering what Vicki had said during that first phone call, he expected to be calling Ames Funeral Home and requesting a body pickup.

Grimshaw and Ilya left the cruiser and walked toward Julian's car. Julian looked upset, but he said nothing when he stepped out of his car. Which was understandable. Right now they had no idea who was watching them—and listening.

"The other car is about halfway up the access road," Julian said. "It's facing this way, so I'm guessing the driver backed up that far in order to make a fast getaway after . . . The driver's door is open, but the interior light isn't working, so I couldn't see . . . But I saw enough." He scrubbed his hands over his face. "Gods above and below, Wayne. I didn't think . . ."

Grimshaw held up a hand, stopping his friend. Better for all of them if Julian didn't voice any regrets about his special customers. "Let's find out what's going on first. Then we'll know what comes next."

"Besides the EMTs and the doctor?" Ilya asked dryly.

"What?" Julian yelped.

Seeing Julian's hands shake was confirmation enough that they would need help from the funeral home more than the EMTs or Doc Wallace, but he didn't say that. Instead he said, "What about the boys? Can't leave them in the car on their own." It wasn't that they weren't old enough to be left in the car. It was just too damn dangerous—although maybe not for them.

"They'll come with us," Ilya said.

Car doors opened and closed. Viktor and Karol joined them. Karol held a flashlight and Viktor had the first aid kit that Julian usually carried in the trunk of his car.

"I put it on the back seat before we left the store," Julian said. "Just wanted it within reach."

Grimshaw went back to the cruiser, opened the trunk, and removed his big flashlight, a couple of road flares, the first aid kit he carried, and a roll of yellow crime scene tape.

"Everyone is at the main house, and they're okay except for the guest who got swatted," Viktor said.

"Do you know which guest?" Grimshaw asked.

A moment's silence before Viktor shook his head. "Aggie told Eddie, who told Kira, who told me, but Aggie didn't say which guest—or Eddie didn't tell Kira that part."

Grimshaw gave the Sanguinati teenagers a hard look. He felt the seconds ticking by, but caution was better than dying. "In stories, there's always a baby cop who forgets his training because he wants to be a hero and rushes into danger, ignoring the orders of his commanding officer. Because they're stories, half the time his actions save the day and he gets out of it with just a flesh wound. In the real world, most of the time that baby cop ends up in the morgue. Hear me. I don't care that you're Sanguinati and think you're invincible. You don't go dashing off, no matter what you think you see. You stay with us and you follow orders, or your internship with Julian and me ends tonight. Understood?"

"Yes, sir," Viktor said.

Karol looked at Ilya before saying, "Yes, sir."

We'll have to watch that one, Grimshaw thought. *He's got the vibe that he has something to prove to someone.*

After giving each boy a road flare, Grimshaw took the lead, with Julian a step behind so that their flashlights covered most of the road. The boys walked behind them, and Ilya came last—defense and warning in case something followed them.

As they approached the vehicle, Julian blew out a breath and whispered, "Was that easier than puncturing a couple of tires to make sure he couldn't get away?"

Grimshaw looked at the tires and understood what Julian meant. That car wasn't going anywhere, because the tires were sunk halfway into the road. No possibility of rocking the car out of those tire-size holes.

Car door open. No interior light on. When he shined the flashlight on the driver's side of the car, he expected to find a body. But seeing what the Others could do to a human body was always a mental and emotional blow.

Grimshaw swallowed hard. The boys crowded close to him and Julian, and he wondered if they would be safer in their smoke form or if that wouldn't matter to the *terra indigene* who had savaged that body.

"They were angry," Ilya said quietly.

"Broke the promise," a voice sang out of the dark.

"Vicki wouldn't have—" Julian protested.

"Not the Reader," another voice sang. *"This one did—and someone else."*

"The police and the Sanguinati will find out who broke the promise," Grimshaw said.

"Victoria asked for assistance from other humans to fix a wounded human up at the house," Ilya said. "Will you allow it?"

"The Reader asked?" A third voice.

"Yes," Ilya replied.

A pause. Then: *"Humans should listen when the Reader yells at them."*

Grimshaw didn't know what had prompted that remark, but he heard the threat under the words.

"In The Jumble, the Reader decides," a fourth voice sang.

He didn't hear anything—not the snap of a twig or the rustle of crisp leaves on the ground—but he *felt* the danger move away. That was when he realized he hadn't even considered shining his light toward those voices, that he—and Julian—had known on some instinctive level what would happen to all of them if he had seen the Five in their present form.

"That's Peter Lynchfield in the car," Julian said. "He's one of the professors staying at the Mill Creek Cabins."

"Then what is he doing here tonight?" Ilya asked coldly.

Grimshaw looked at the Sanguinati leader. "And who told him there might be something to see?"

Taking the road flares from the boys, he lit them and placed one in front of and one behind the car. Then he moved on. Nothing he could do for Lynchfield. What he needed was a better idea of what was going on at the main house—and who was Lynchfield's accomplice.

CHAPTER 44

Vicki

Watersday, Novembros 3

Call one man and get all three. How great was that?

Not so great, since there had been screaming before I called. Lots of screaming.

"Hey, Chief." I smiled at Grimshaw. Thought I did, anyway, but the look on his face told me my face hadn't gotten the smile quite right. "Some human was being stoooopid. Did you confiscate his camera?" I frowned and pinched a black fluff feather out of the glass of orange juice I was holding. "Could have been a *her* camera. Stupidity is an equal opportunity, you know."

Julian crouched near my feet and placed a hand on my ankle. "Vicki?" he said gently.

"In shock, I think. I found her sitting here, and Eddie brought her some orange juice." That was Michael Stern's voice.

I looked up. Way up. Why were people so much taller than they'd been that morning?

"Drink the orange juice, Vicki," Julian said. "Did you put anything in it?"

"There was a feather, but I didn't put it there."

"No," Michael said.

My brain, working in slow motion, figured out Julian's question had been directed at Michael, not me.

"Where is everyone?" Grimshaw asked.

"In the TV room," Michael replied.

"Except the cheaters," I said. "Wilma went to the toilet down here to wash her hands and Fred followed her. Either Wilma and her precious sausage are having a doozy of a handwashing session or they're having sex." I drank some orange juice and didn't feel quite as wobbly—and realized people were taller because I was still sitting on the floor. "Gotta find my sand."

"Right now, you've got to sit there and drink your juice until you're steady enough to talk to me," Grimshaw said in his Stern Police Voice.

He was not a happy camper, so I didn't point out that I *had* been talking to him, because I guessed by his voice that he meant official talking.

I drank more juice.

Ilya reappeared, which meant he'd been gone. He looked at Grimshaw. "Call the EMTs or Dr. Wallace. Whoever is available to clean and stitch wounds. Cougar will meet those humans at the end of the access road and escort them here. They will be safe with Cougar guiding them."

"You're sure of that?" Grimshaw asked.

Ilya nodded.

Grimshaw stepped out of easy visual range, so he was out of my mental frame now. Ilya stepped in, standing near my feet. Julian continued to crouch, a hand on my ankle.

"We were having a good time talking about books and looking at what was available on the Mini Munch tables." I looked up at Michael. "They bought your new book."

Seeing him try to smile while he turned pale made me wonder if his new potential fans might find something in the story that would make them feel sharply critical.

I offered him the rest of my orange juice—and he drank it.

"I have something for you," I told Julian. I dug in a pocket of my slacks and pulled out the list of new books and the coins. "They bought five new books and gave me these as payment."

Julian sucked in a breath.

Michael gasped and managed to rattle the juice glass onto the reception desk instead of dropping it on the floor or on me. Then he sank to his knees. "Gods! Are they . . . ? May I . . . ?"

Julian held out one of the coins.

"They look like gold," I said, feeling defensive. Julian was making a slim living from the bookstore as it was. I didn't want him to take a loss on the books I had sold on his behalf.

"They're gold," Julian confirmed.

"I did some research about gold coins for one of my books," Michael said, examining the coin. "This one was cast about a hundred years ago. Equal in size and weight to some of the coins being minted by humans as a standard currency for that time."

Translation: the *terra indigene* had made that coin in order to trade with humans. I wondered if there were newer coins or if trading had lost its appeal—or if paper money taken from humans who broke promises was easier to use because it was lighter to carry, and if it had stains, it was currency and threat rolled into one.

"This one came from the Northeast mint, dated fifty years ago," Julian said, studying the other coin. "I'll have to find out the current price of gold to figure out how much store credit the Five have now."

"The Sanguinati can look that up for you," Ilya said.

Julian nodded. Michael returned the cast coin.

Julian rose and tucked the book list and the coins into the front pocket of his jeans. Then he reached down and hauled me to my feet.

I wasn't the only one who had latched onto the coins as a distraction from whatever was going on in the TV room. Not that there was much going on until the EMTs arrived.

"Victoria, after you informed the guests that they would need to remain in the TV room to accommodate some of Julian Farrow's customers, did you notice anyone making a call from the phone in the kitchen?" Ilya asked.

There were phones in my office and apartment, but they wouldn't be accessible to guests. There wasn't a phone in the TV room, but there was a phone jack in the social room so that guests could connect a portable computer to the secondary phone line and access their e-mail.

"There was no reason for anyone to order out for something to eat," I said. "There are plenty of leftovers. That would be the only reason to use the phone in the kitchen."

"What about you?" Ilya focused on Michael, his voice not as casual or polite now. "Did you notice anyone making a call on their mobile phone after you assembled in the TV room?"

Michael hesitated. I hoped he was smart enough not to lie to Ilya.

"Several people, including me," he finally said. "I called home to reassure my parents that we were fine and the road closures weren't as big a deal as the reporters were making them out to be."

"You fibbed to your parents?" I thought for a moment. "Can Intuits do that?"

"Not if you're in the same room with a parent, and you've just come home from a hot date, and your father asks you where you've been," Julian said dryly. "But over the phone?" He wobbled one hand as if saying *Maybe, maybe not.*

"Besides, I called before things went strange," Michael said, looking at Ilya. "I think Ian made a call to his partner—a 'just in case' call, you know?"

He waited until Ilya nodded, but I wasn't sure if the Sanguinati made that kind of call, since they were one of the reasons those calls were made.

"Umm . . . as I finished up my call, I overheard Jenna McKay asking someone to go to her place and water her plants," Michael continued. "I can't tell you about the others. They may have made a call at the same time I did. I wasn't paying attention, and there was enough understandable tension in that room that I didn't sense anything that might have been cause for alarm."

"Grimshaw will be able to find out the last call made from each phone and the number the person was calling," I said. "So he'll trace the call to the deceased."

"Assuming the communication was of a kind that can be traced," Ilya replied.

I understood what he meant, but I would stake The Jumble that it hadn't been Aggie or Jozi or Eddie who had blabbed. And Conan and Cougar wouldn't be excited about the Five showing up. But they might have warned other *terra indigene* to stay away from the main house and one of those *terra indigene* could have said something that provided a clue as to why everyone should stay away, and somehow that clue reached a human. That information could have been passed out of excitement—or imprudence—opened up the possible sources of leaked information.

Imprudence. Youthful excitement or the need to show off to someone?

Looking at Ilya's grim expression, I realized he had three Sanguinati names at the top of his list of suspects.

CHAPTER 45

Grimshaw

Watersday, Novembros 3

G rimshaw was reaching for the door of the TV room when he heard a piercing scream coming from the downstairs washroom. Before he could take a step in response, the TV room door opened and Ian Stern rammed into him.

"Chief! I heard . . ." Ian stopped and stared as Wilma Cornley rushed toward them trying to straighten her clothes, quickly followed by Fred Cornley, who was also straightening his clothes.

"There's something in the powder room!" she shrieked. "It appeared behind us in the mirror! It . . . it was *watching* . . ." She stopped, as if suddenly realizing that everyone had a good idea of *what* the something was watching.

Vicki, rushing toward the commotion, spun around and ran back to the reception desk. By the time Julian and Michael joined the group to find out what had happened, Vicki had returned and held up the sign that said: IF YOUR BEHAVIOR ATTRACTS ATTENTION, <u>YOU</u> HAVE TO EXPLAIN THAT BEHAVIOR TO SOMEONE WHO MIGHT EAT YOU. GOOD LUCK.

Wilma fell against Fred in a dramatic swoon just as two females drifted toward them from the direction of the washroom. One left drops of water on the floor. The other, more ethereal, Elemental asked in a tone that mimicked a scientist discussing a test subject, "Since they can't see the sex parts, what is the point of humans looking at themselves in a mirror when they are mating?"

Air and Water looked at all the humans present and waited for an answer.

Since it was unlikely that the Cornleys would end up being eaten, Grimshaw chose a strategic retreat. He gave the Elementals a nod and said, "Ladies, if you'll excuse me, I have to check on a wounded man."

He pushed past Ian Stern, went into the TV room, and shut the door. A psychologist and a writer interested in the *terra indigene* should be able to handle the Q&A portion of the evening, and Julian would look after Vicki and make sure she wasn't heading for an anxiety meltdown. She seemed to be holding up well, despite the shock of having someone else die at The Jumble, but if guests started yelling at her, that might tip her over the edge.

Ben Malacki sat on the other side of the room from David Shuman and Jenna McKay, who had bloody hands and a pale face.

"I think the bleeding has stopped," Jenna said. "I don't think any of the wounds are that deep."

"Not deep?" David Shuman said in a voice stripped of vigor. He tried to move, ignoring Jenna telling him to stay still. "That . . . *creature* . . . tried to eviscerate me!"

"If he'd been trying, they'd be shoveling your guts off the floor," Grimshaw replied. He leaned over Shuman and pointed a finger at Jenna. "Let me see the wounds so I can determine who needs to come out here." He'd already called the EMTs and Doc Wallace, and they were on their way, but it seemed better to downplay this conflict if that was possible.

Jenna eased a blood-soaked T-shirt off the wounds. Fresh blood immediately welled up—a sluggish flow but still a concern.

Just as well he'd called Doc along with the EMTs. The EMT vehicle was fitted like a mobile trauma unit, and any of the EMTs probably could stitch up those wounds just fine. But this was one of Vicki's guests, as well as a suspect in the current troubles happening around Sproing. Better to have Doc take care of the stitching and whatever shots might be required.

"I need a hospital," Shuman said.

"There's no way to get you to one, so you're getting the doc and the

EMTs," Grimshaw replied as he headed for the door. He stopped and looked at Shuman. "The doc is also the village's medical examiner. Something to keep in mind before you piss off the Bear again." *Or someone far more dangerous.*

He walked out of the room—and found no one until he reached the reception desk. Ilya sat on the stool behind the desk, reading Vicki's guest register and making notes on a pad of lined paper.

"I gave the Cornleys permission to go up to their suite to finish copulating, although I think their enthusiasm for that activity has waned for the evening," Ilya said. "Viktor and Karol are with Kira and the Crows in the kitchen. Victoria, Julian, and the Sterns are in the library, distracting themselves with books."

"Air and Water?" Grimshaw asked.

"Have left the building. I imagine they've gone to entertain their kin by relating the human behavior they observed."

"And you?" He had to talk to Cougar about bringing Doc and the EMTs up to the main house. But first he needed to confirm that the other people here weren't in immediate danger.

"I'm making a list of all of Victoria's guests for the past month," Ilya replied. He removed a folded sheet of paper from beneath the pad and held it out. "You should add this to the information you collate from police in other parts of the Finger Lakes."

Grimshaw opened the paper. Four Sanguinati names and the names of the towns and villages near the youngsters' home territories. "You think one of them is involved?"

"Until this evening, I didn't have a convincing reason to distrust any of the fosterlings in my care. Now?" A tiny movement of Ilya's shoulder that Grimshaw recognized as a shrug. "Something about Kira's and Viktor's visit to Silence Lodge doesn't ring true, but I have not, as yet, figured out why. And something—or someone—drew Crowbones to Lake Silence. Lastly, someone called Peter Lynchfield and enticed him to come to The Jumble on the night humans were supposed to stay away and stay out of sight. Until we find who is responsible, there are not many people either of us can afford to trust—even among our own."

"I'm going to tape off that vehicle and the body, then help Cougar bring the EMTs and Doc Wallace up here," he said. "Shouldn't be long.

After that, I'll interview the people here and get some answers." One way or another. If he had to march each guest out to the car and have them look at Lynchfield's body, he'd do it. These people were too cavalier about staying in a *terra indigene* settlement. They were treating this whole thing like being in a fun house at a county fair. The scary stuff ended when you walked out the door and nothing could really hurt you.

Here the deadly *began* when a person walked out the door.

Pushing that thought aside, Grimshaw walked out of the main house and felt the dark like a physical weight. He'd never minded the dark when he'd worked highway patrol, the hours of late night. But he'd usually been tucked into his small apartment or driving his cruiser along his designated route, comforted by the illusion that metal and speed could win against whatever might be out there, watching. Waiting.

He called the EMTs and Doc Wallace again, assuring all the men that they would have an escort and no one would think they were trespassing, and confirming that they were en route and would be there as quickly as possible.

He called Officer Osgood, listened to the "nothing happening in the village" report, then asked the rookie to check e-mail before he clocked out, forwarding everything coming in from ITF agents and police captains to Grimshaw's personal e-mail.

"And Osgood?" Grimshaw added. "Check the sent e-mails to confirm that Viktor did e-mail all the ITF agents. Let me know if he missed any."

"He seems to know how to use the computers," Osgood said.

"I know, but he's young. Check it anyway."

"Yes, sir."

Ilya's remark about not trusting anyone scratched at him. Viktor seemed like a solid baby cop in the making, but that didn't mean the youngster wouldn't delete an e-mail that might hold information he wouldn't want the adults to see. And Karol was at an age when impulse control was more of an idea than a reality. Easy enough for him to do something without considering the consequences. Grimshaw hadn't seen enough of Kira to get a feel for the girl, except to recognize she had the looks to be every teenage boy's dream—and every father's nightmare. But Ian's and Michael's concerns about what might be underneath her flirting couldn't be dismissed. Still, she seemed to be doing well with Vicki, so he wasn't going to rock that boat without a reason.

When he reached the car, he taped off the road and the area around the vehicle. He wasn't going to call in a CIU team. No arrests would be made for this death. He closed the driver's-side door to keep smaller predators from making off with bits of Peter Lynchfield, then went around to the other side and looked through the glove box for registration and insurance cards.

Registration and insurance confirmed it was Lynchfield's car.

Glancing into the back seat, Grimshaw frowned at the shopping bags from Pops's general store and the delivery box of wrapped sandwiches that must have come from the diner.

Had Lynchfield been making a supply run and then been lured here for some reason? Or had he picked up the food to have a legitimate reason to be away from the cabins but had intended to come to The Jumble all along?

No answers until Grimshaw could talk to the other men at the Mill Creek Cabins and see if any of them had been aware of Lynchfield's plans—or had overheard a phone call.

A rustle of leaves. A stealthy, barely there sound.

Grimshaw eased out of the car and looked toward the trunk, resisting the urge to reach for his weapon. He didn't shine his flashlight directly at the sound, but he picked up the gleam of eyes and then recognized the Coyote and Bobcat. He didn't think either of them would actively hunt a human, but that didn't mean they wouldn't take advantage of meat when it was easily available—especially when the days were getting shorter and the nights colder.

"I need this body to stay the way it is," he said. "We'll be moving it out in a little while, once we take care of some things up at the house." He waited, certain they had intended to make off with a meaty rib or two. "There's some human food in these bags that will go to waste if someone doesn't eat it. You should take it up to the house and have Miss Vicki and Ilya look it over for anything that might not sit well with you folks."

"Hookay," Bobcat said.

Grimshaw pulled the bags and box out of the car, handed them over, and watched the two *terra indigene* head for the house. Then he closed the car doors and wrapped yellow tape around the vehicle. Wouldn't stop anyone from tearing the tape and taking parts of the body, but he hoped enough of the Others were familiar with police investigating now to respect a taped-off area—or be more curious about what the police would do than about the body inside the car.

As he circled the car a second time, he wondered about the big rock on the road. He didn't remember needing to swerve around it when he'd driven up to the main house on previous visits.

His light reflected off something shiny. More than one bit of shiny.

Examining the ground around the rock, Grimshaw realized the rock hadn't been there even a few hours ago. Someone had picked it up and dropped it on Peter Lynchfield's camera.

CHAPTER 46

Ilya

Watersday, Novembros 3

Why these four youngsters? Why send them here? Why now? How does their presence connect with a being the Elders around Lake Silence refer to as a Hunter?

Thoughts about the fosterlings in his care kept circling as Ilya helped Victoria unpack the shopping bags and box that Coyote and Bobcat had brought up to the house.

"Not even *one* eyeball?" Jozi said plaintively. "The dead human doesn't need it."

"Couldn't have any of the meat either," Coyote growled. "Grimshaw Chief traded bags of food for the meat. Does he always trade food for dead meat?" This was spoken on a hopeful note.

Ilya ignored the question, not wanting to encourage the idea of *terra indigene* dragging dead humans to the police station with the expectation of receiving a bag of groceries. Taking recently dead from the funeral home to trade for other kinds of food would be just as upsetting to Sproing's residents as having someone deliver freshly dead to the police—especially if there had been some nibbling before delivery.

"Dead human doesn't taste as good as rabbit or vole," Bobcat said. "But they are easier to catch."

Seeing the way Victoria's hands trembled and hearing the change in her breathing, Ilya said, <Discussing humans as meat is upsetting Victoria.>

The three shifters looked abashed to have forgotten that Victoria was the same species as the meat under discussion.

"What are those?" Kira asked.

Ilya had the impression the girl would have stood closer to Victoria and asked more questions if he hadn't been in the kitchen with them. With him present, she was trying to balance curiosity with respectful distance from the human to avoid instinctively shifting a hand to partial smoke and doing some unintentional feeding.

If he hadn't been there, would the feeding have been unintentional? Was there something calculated about her interactions with Victoria— and with him—or was he forgetting how females that age presented themselves? *Was* there something about Kira that pricked at his predatory instincts, or was he reacting to the uneasiness about the girl felt by the Sterns? Or was he suspicious and on edge about everything because of the pressure to find answers and end the contamination that had brought a Hunter into his territory?

Victoria held out the container from the diner. "These are deep-fried potato sticks. They're usually served hot, or at least warm, and you can dip them in ketchup or some other condiment."

After Kira took two potato sticks, Victoria offered the food to the shifters in the kitchen, who followed Kira's example and took two sticks. Ilya shook his head when Victoria offered the . . . food . . . to him, but he felt some relief when she ate a couple of pieces before setting the container on the table.

"They are . . . interesting," Kira said.

Victoria smiled. "I don't think they'll be a mainstay of the Sanguinati diet, but humans like to eat them with hamburgers or sandwiches. Helen makes the best potato sticks, and Ineke makes these deep-fried potato rounds that taste amazing."

"Don't need that," Bobcat said, pointing to a bottle of wine. "We just eat the buzzy grapes."

Victoria frowned. "Buzzy grapes?"

"Naturally fermented grapes," Ilya explained.

"So you get buzzed on fermented fruit?" she asked.

Coyote, Bobcat, and Crow smiled at her.

"Our buzzy fruit ends up in a bottle."

The three shifters exchanged a look. Then Bobcat nudged the wine bottle closer to Victoria and said, "You should have the buzzy."

"Thank you." Victoria set the wine bottle in front of her.

While everyone else had been distracted—or were doing their best to distract Victoria from the humans' upsetting behavior—Ilya efficiently divided the sandwiches and other foods that he thought the shifters would actually eat. He set the raw carrot sticks aside and looked at Coyote, who returned his look and nodded to acknowledge that he knew which residents in The Jumble should be offered that treat.

Not knowing what Victoria might have available to eat—and he would ask Dr. Wallace what a human who had had a bad shock should be fed—he kept one of the sandwiches, intending to slip up to Victoria's apartment and place it in her small fridge. Now that she had regular guests spending time at The Jumble, she had purchased a few kitchen appliances for her apartment so that she could eat a solitary meal whenever she needed some peace.

Having four fosterlings in his care, he realized he hadn't appreciated the solitude and peace of Silence Lodge enough when he'd had it.

Coyote and Bobcat headed out with their bags of food, Kira wandered off to join Viktor and Karol in the library, and Jozi let out a big sigh before leaving to find Aggie and Eddie. Maybe she realized that Grimshaw had done them all a favor by protecting the dead body. Three Crows plus two eyeballs equaled a squabble. Better for all of them to avoid more excitement tonight.

"If you would like to go up to your apartment and rest, Mr. Farrow and I can look after things," Ilya said. He preferred to have her out of the way by the time Grimshaw returned and began questioning the humans to find out who had told Lynchfield about the private showing of books.

Victoria shook her head. "My place, my guests."

But that was the answer he expected.

He turned toward the front of the house. "Chief Grimshaw, Dr. Wallace, and the EMTs are here." He glanced at the six-pack of beer that was still on the table unclaimed. "You should put those in the refrigerator for the EMTs."

Victoria sighed. "I liked them. The Five. I don't want to know what they did to the man who tried to take their picture."

He heard the plea in her voice. Because of the position she held as the bridge between *terra indigene* settlement and human village, it was better for all of them if Victoria didn't know some things about the beings she dealt with.

"You don't have to know," Ilya soothed. "I'll make sure of it."

Ilya?>

<Natasha. Is everything all right?>

She hesitated. <I contacted the home shadows of the fosterlings. The shadows that were listed on Lara's and Karol's papers confirmed that those youngsters belong to them and were sent to us.>

Ilya felt chilled. <The other two?>

Natasha sighed. <Everything looked legitimate, but the shadows listed on Kira's and Viktor's papers had never heard of them. The leaders of those shadows wondered if those two ran away, either separately and they just happened to pick Silence Lodge as a place to hide away, or they had planned to come here in order to be together. Either way, they have lied to us.>

<The Five killed a human this evening,> Ilya said. <This is not a good time to confront those two unless you think they are a danger to others.> A danger to Victoria?

Natasha hesitated again. <We only know they are here under false pretenses. We do not know why, so we can't know if they pose a threat.>

<Contact the other shadows in the Finger Lakes region. See if they are missing any youngsters that match Kira's and Viktor's description,> Ilya said.

<All right,> she replied.

He felt a weight in her silence. <Something else?>

<Vlad called with a message from Tolya Sanguinati. About Nicolai.>

Ilya sighed. Nicolai had been terribly wounded in the battle to keep the town of Bennett out of the hands of evil humans. <I had heard that Nicolai is being relocated to Lakeside. The shadow in that Courtyard is larger and Grandfather Erebus lives there. And there is room there for privacy.>

<Yes, that was the plan,> Natasha said. <But Nicolai slipped away from the Sanguinati who were escorting him and has disappeared.>

CHAPTER 47

Vicki

Watersday, Novembros 3

The EMTs and Doc Wallace looked so pale and scared when they arrived, I figured beer wasn't going to be numbing enough and was tempted to raid Grimshaw and Julian's private stash of whiskeys and offer a bottle or two to the men. Then I remembered that someone would need steady hands to stitch up David Shuman, so I kept my thoughts to myself and my hands off the whiskey.

When Conan was asked why he'd swatted Shuman, his only response was to growl at everyone.

Not even Grimshaw asked him for clarification.

I went to the kitchen and made a pot of coffee, not sure who might want to drink it. I put the kettle on to heat up water and set my selection of teas on the kitchen table along with the mugs my guests used at breakfast.

Julian came into the kitchen, placed a bottle of whiskey on the table, smiled at me, and left.

I knew people often added alcohol to coffee to make it a blended drink. I wondered how mint tea would taste with a dollop—or five—of whiskey.

I was willing to play guinea pig and find out.

Intellectually, I recognized that people knowingly took a risk by staying at The Jumble. I recognized that people could get hurt—could get killed—if they misbehaved, because the *terra indigene* put up with only so much nonsense from humans before ending the nonsense, usually in ways that required the police to notify next of kin.

Recognizing those things didn't alleviate the guilt I felt because Conan had swatted a guest and a person who wasn't even staying at The Jumble had been killed because he'd been where he shouldn't have been, doing what he shouldn't have done.

I liked three of my current guests and sincerely hoped they weren't the cause of any of this trouble. The other four people I would have happily kicked to the curb if I had any curbs and if there had been any place for them to go. Until Grimshaw and Ilya figured out who was responsible for killing whom, we were all stuck with one another.

A quick knock on the doorframe before Kira, Viktor, and Karol slipped into the kitchen.

Kira hurried over to the stove and turned off the kettle, which had been boiling away and whistling its head off, unnoticed by me because I'd been lost in thoughts of gore and guilt.

"Can we help?" Viktor asked.

I tried to smile. "I wish I knew."

Not the answer these teens wanted, but it was the best I could do.

CHAPTER 48

Aggie

Watersday, Novembros 3

Aggie fetched the bucket and set it beside the chair so that the Wallace doctor wouldn't drop bloody bits on Miss Vicki's carpet. Eddie slipped into the room with a clean basin and the kettle from the kitchen. Steam rose out of the kettle's spout. He set the kettle on a mat Miss Vicki said was used for hot dishes, handed the basin to one of the EMTs, and slipped out again.

Aggie watched Jenna McKay pour hot water and some drinking water from a pitcher into the basin to wash her hands. She patted her hands dry with some toilet paper, then stood near the wall, watching the EMT humans assist the Wallace doctor while he put stitches into the Shuman guest.

Before all the medical humans arrived, the Shuman guest had bled a lot, and she'd wondered if he was going to die—and how she could snatch any of the best bits with so many humans in the room. Then Chief Grimshaw stepped into the room, and Aggie knew she'd missed her chance, because the Shuman guest hadn't died, and now it looked like he wasn't going to.

The medical humans put proper bandages over the wounds and helped the Shuman guest go up to his room, the Wallace doctor telling

Grimshaw he would remain overnight to keep an eye on the patient and check vital signs.

She could have told the Wallace doctor that the *terra indigene* could check for these vital signs. Breathing, a human was still alive. Not breathing, the human was a snack.

Maybe there were more things to check? Maybe one of the young Sanguinati could shift into smoke form and slip into the room to see what the Wallace doctor considered vital and report back to the rest of them?

Once the medical humans left the room, Chief Grimshaw set the bucket with the bloody T-shirt and wads of toilet paper outside the room. Then he closed the door and stared at the remaining humans—just stared until someone knocked on the door and the other guests returned to the room.

"Peter Lynchfield died tonight," Chief Grimshaw said, "and none of you are leaving this room until I know which one of you called him, because that person is morally responsible for his death."

Aggie sucked in a breath and settled in a spot where she would have the best view to watch all the humans and try to spot clues, just like a civilian helper in the cop and crime shows.

CHAPTER 49

Grimshaw

Watersday, Novembros 3

I want to see your mobile phones," Grimshaw said. "I want to see the log of your recent calls. And may the gods help you if you deleted that log to hide your part in this."

"Even if we made the call, what are you going to do?" Ben Malacki demanded. "Arrest us?"

"I can't arrest you for being an ass and leaking information about a private meeting. But I can say with certainty that if I don't get the information from you now, the next individuals who come to interrogate you will not be the Sanguinati and will not be as understanding of human failings and foibles. Most likely, all of you will die violently and in terror, just as Peter Lynchfield died, and there won't be a thing I can do to help you."

"We're supposed to be safe here!" Malacki shouted.

"You are safe here—until you break their rules."

"When can we go home?" Wilma Cornley whined.

"When the *terra indigene* discover why two of the Crowgard and a student from one of your colleges have been killed." Grimshaw looked at each of them. "None of you are safe until I can tell them who called Peter Lynchfield about the private gathering. This isn't a game, people. If you need reminding of that, I can walk you down to that car and show you what is left of the man. Someone started trouble on Trickster Night. Someone caused more trouble this evening. The Elders will pick you off one by one if that's what it takes. So stop jerking my chain and tell me who made the damn call!"

Michael Stern took out his mobile phone, tapped this and touched that, then held it out. "This is who I've called since arriving at The Jumble."

Two calls made to the same number, one the day of arrival and the other shortly before Lynchfield was killed—and before Julian's special customers arrived. Grimshaw already knew the number of Lynchfield's mobile phone, and it wasn't the number Stern had called. Still, he took out his notebook and wrote down the number. He was fairly sure it belonged to someone in Michael's family, but he'd have Osgood confirm the identity of the person on the receiving end of those calls.

Ian Stern came next. A couple of calls with pretty much the same timing as Michael's calls—arrival and "just in case" calls. There were also calls to local numbers. Grimshaw recognized the phone numbers for Come and Get It and the Pizza Shack. It looked like Ian was either placing an order or asking for business hours to plan ahead. There was also a call to the stables run by Horace and Hector Adams. Maybe Ian had been thinking of doing a trail ride.

Grimshaw looked at Ben Malacki, who crossed his arms, raised his chin, and looked like a belligerent bantam rooster until Conan, still guarding the door, growled at him. Then the man looked like a rooster that knew it was doomed to go into the pot, but Malacki still didn't offer his mobile phone, which made Grimshaw wonder what he was hiding.

Jenna McKay stepped forward. Her hand shook as she gave Grimshaw her phone.

"I didn't call Peter Lynchfield," she whispered as tears ran down her face. "I didn't know this would happen when . . ." She stopped.

Ian Stern put an arm around her shoulders. "When what?" he asked gently. "Who did you call?" He looked at Grimshaw and mouthed, *Sorry.*

Grimshaw didn't care who asked the question as long as he got an answer.

"Professor Roash," Jenna whispered. "I called Roash."

"Why?" Grimshaw asked.

"I didn't know who he was, didn't know he would be here this week-end. My sister works at the same college. She's married and has a couple of kids and she needs the job to help with the bills. I don't know how Roash knew Jill was my sister, but he made a comment on Trickster Night about me being well situated here at The Jumble. I shrugged it off as a weird comment. Then he called earlier today and said I should let him know if anything interesting was happening at The Jumble." Jenna wiped the tears from her face. "He insinuated that if I wasn't helpful, he would get Jill fired for reasons that would make it very hard for her to find an-other job—and I believed he would do it. So I called and told him special customers were coming to look at books around dusk and everyone was supposed to stay away. I didn't know he'd *send* someone."

Roash again. First sending a student to masquerade as the Crowgard bogeyman, then somehow persuading Lynchfield to come to The Jumble and try to photograph the Five. Gods above and below, the man was a slimy piece of work.

"Did you call Roash again?" Grimshaw asked Jenna. No indication that she had, based on her call log, but he wasn't going to assume she didn't use someone else's phone. He turned to Malacki. "What about you?"

"Why aren't you doing something to get the roads open so we can leave instead of persecuting us?" Malacki demanded.

Grimshaw stared at the man. For someone who was supposed to work at a college and had claimed to be interested in observing the *terra indi-gene*, Ben Malacki was a damn fool.

"If I swat him, you can take the phone," Conan rumbled. "Easier than talking to this one."

Malacki paled. He pulled his mobile phone out of his pocket and tossed it at Grimshaw. "Take it, then."

Grimshaw suspected the throw was deliberately short. Clearly, Malacki hoped to damage the phone enough to prevent anyone from seeing his calls, but the man hadn't figured on Crowgard speed and reflexes. Aggie darted between the humans and snatched the phone before it hit the floor.

"Cawt it," she said, grinning. She handed the phone to Grimshaw and darted back to her place near the wall.

No indication that Malacki had called Roash or Lynchfield. Calls couldn't be made outside of a region—the Elders tore down phone lines and cell towers that allowed human communication to cross regional borders—but there was something about the phone numbers that gave him an itch between the shoulder blades. He wrote down the numbers, then tossed the phone back to Malacki.

A quick knock on the door. Conan opened it enough to see who was on the other side, then opened it a little more.

Viktor poked his head into the room. "Chief? The EMTs asked if they could leave now."

Grimshaw looked at Conan. "Can you escort them to their vehicle?"

Conan nodded. Viktor skipped out of the way to let the Bear leave the room, then gave Grimshaw a look he couldn't interpret before closing the door.

That look was another thing that gave him an itch. Nothing wrong with Viktor. The boy was steady, reliable, was everything he would look for in a good baby cop. Just the sort of youngster adults would be inclined to trust. And shouldn't trust?

Crap. Maybe he should have Osgood check the e-mail and let Viktor answer the phones, especially if he started receiving confidential information about killings in other towns. Maybe he should end this internship with the police.

And maybe he should do the job that was right in front of him.

Grimshaw eyed the room's other occupants. "Stay inside tonight. Figure everything you do will be viewed with suspicion, so make sure your actions can't be misinterpreted. You folks staying in the lake cabins? Make sure you have each other's phone numbers and the number for the main house before you go to your cabins. Conan or Cougar will escort you. Take some food back with you, in case you need to shelter in place for a while tomorrow." He eyed all of them again. "A CIU team from Bristol will be here in the morning, so don't figure on getting to the village before they've completed their part of the investigation. Any questions? Good." He walked out of the room before Malacki could take a breath and voice whatever complaint he wanted to voice this time.

Grimshaw found Ilya and Julian standing near the reception desk—a central location and a not-so-subtle statement that they weren't there to keep the humans safe. Not all the humans, anyway.

"Victoria is packing up 'just in case' food for the cabins," Ilya said. "I need to return to Silence Lodge to review the situation with my people and hear their reports, but the youngsters would like to stay and watch the scary movies—something they could not do at the lodge since we have one TV and are trying not to distress our youngest fosterling by letting her view stories that would frighten her unduly."

On another night, Grimshaw would like to discuss what a Sanguinati youngster would consider undue violence or frightening images in stories. He had a feeling that Ilya was no more realistic about such things than any other adult. In a weird way, that gave him some comfort.

"I don't see why not, as long as Vicki doesn't mind," he said. But Ilya had concerns about two of the Sanguinati teens, so was the Sanguinati leader risking Vicki and the humans here in order to protect the youngest Sanguinati fosterling?

Grimshaw looked at Julian, who said, "I'll stay awhile longer."

He'd expected that. "I'll escort the EMTs to the village and check in with Osgood before I head home." *And have a little chat with Professor Roash.*

No one asked if he would be all right walking down the access road on his own. He was the chief of police. He'd spent most of his career as highway patrol, working alone in the wild country. He had to believe he'd earned enough respect from the *terra indigene* living around Lake Silence to do his job or he was no use to anyone.

He walked down the access road, flashlight in his left hand so that he could draw his weapon with his right. Not that he would. It just made him feel a little easier that he *could*, especially once he realized something was keeping pace with him, watching him. No crackle of leaves underfoot or snap of a twig, but something moved silently among the trees nearby— and he realized he was waiting to hear bones rattling in a hollow gourd.

Tempting to whistle in the dark. Foolish to attract more attention.

He caught up to the EMTs, which surprised him. He would have thought they would be moving at top speed to get to the road leading back to the village.

"Chief?" Conan called.

"Here." Grimshaw gave Conan a nod. "I'll escort the men the rest of the way."

Conan turned back to the main house. Grimshaw led the EMTs down the rest of the access road. He walked past a car parked behind Julian's before he realized the EMTs had stopped.

"What is it?" he asked.

"Dr. Wallace didn't park his car there," one man said. "He pulled up on the shoulder, same as we did."

A sour burn filled Grimshaw's belly as he turned his light to see inside.

No bodies. No blood. No vandalism. Nothing to indicate that Doc hadn't parked the car there, except the men saying that he hadn't. Which meant *something*—or more than one something—had picked up the car and placed it on the access road. Something that knew Doc was staying at the main house tonight, and his car, parked on the side of a dark road, might get damaged if another driver didn't see it in time?

"Well, it's here now and out of the way," he said matter-of-factly.

The men hurried past the car and scrambled into their own vehicle. Grimshaw got in the cruiser—after checking the interior for unwanted passengers—and escorted the men back to the village.

He pulled into his parking spot in front of the station and sat for a moment. Long day. He wanted a hot shower and a cold beer. He wanted to eat warmed-up pizza, which he'd forgotten to take with him, and watch a dumb-ass movie with monsters that were nowhere near as scary as the ones he dealt with on a daily basis.

Osgood reported that all was quiet in the village, except for a complaint by Ellen C. Wilson that her neighbor's dog kept barking and barking, and a countercomplaint by the neighbor that her dog barked because Wilson teased him and got him stirred up—*and* Wilson tossed cookies over the fence that the dog gobbled, despite the neighbor having asked Wilson several times not to give the dog treats.

Since Osgood could handle that complaint in the morning, Grimshaw thought he might have an evening at home to regroup and think about what was going on.

Then Julian Farrow called.

CHAPTER 50

Watersday, Novembros 3

Stay,> she said when she returned to the spot where he waited. <Keep watch. I go. Hunt.>

She spoke in the way of someone learning to shape words, and he wondered if Elders spoke a different language or communicated with images—or if she was something so fierce and feral and old, even the other Elders didn't speak to her unless need required it. He didn't know. Didn't even know how to ask the question. Not that it mattered. She understood what he tried to tell her, and that was enough.

After she slipped away to hunt, he looked at the lights shining from the windows of the main house. The Reader was there. Safe? Maybe. But there were other predators besides him out here in the dark.

He moved slowly, quietly, a shadow among the shadows. And he kept watch.

CHAPTER 51

Julian

Watersday, Novembros 3

The Jumble didn't feel right.

Restless and uneasy, Julian went around The Jumble's main house for the second time, checking the windows and the locks on the doors to reassure himself that everything was secure. He knew security was an illusion since so many beings around the place could slip through a crack or knock down a door, but that illusion was all any of them had anywhere. Ever.

Not a baseline change to the place. Whatever didn't feel right was still superficial, but if it took root in The Jumble, it would spread into Sproing, and the village could become a lost place, a toxic ghost town that people abandoned without understanding why they no longer wanted to stay.

He stopped in the doorway of the library, letting the words circle. "Toxic ghost town." He'd been in some places that had become exactly that. He had tried to settle in a few places that had felt all right in the beginning but quickly felt wrong in ways that had him packing and heading out for another town. He'd never been in one of those places right at the start, when he might have witnessed the event that had turned a healthy, prosperous village into an emotional cesspool that eventually drove out everyone who couldn't thrive on the rot.

Was that another factor? Did the arrival of Crowbones start that turn-ing, or did the Crowgard bogeyman arrive *because* a place was beginning to turn?

Julian stood on the wide screened porch that opened off the kitchen and ran the length of the back of the house. The porch door had a lock, such as it was, and the kitchen door had a sturdier lock, but . . .

He heard Michael and Ian Stern's voices before they rounded the cor-ner of the house, the beams from their flashlights illuminating the ground. He held open the porch door.

"We heard the doctor say he was staying overnight," Michael said. "Wasn't sure if there would be a place for him to sleep, so we fetched the air mattress and sleeping bag we had stowed in the car. Better than the floor. You and the doc can flip a coin to see who gets the couch in the TV room."

He hadn't been planning to *stay* since Vicki was full up with guests, but it was hard to argue with Intuits when they had a feeling, and clearly the two men had decided this was necessary.

"Why didn't you knock on the front door?" he asked. "It's closer to the cars, and I could have let you in that way."

Michael hesitated. "It feels safer back here. And we've used this door as a quick route between the main house and the cabins since we arrived."

A recognized scent on an established path. Was that what Michael was trying to tell him?

"Besides," Ian added, "the teens have decided that the boys will spend the night at the Crowgard cabin and all the girls will be spending the night with Vicki in her apartment."

A shiver went down Julian's spine. He shoved his hands in his pockets and resisted the urge to pace. "You staying for the movies?"

"No. Thanks," Ian replied. "The evening has been scary enough, and it feels like we'll be better off if we're where we're supposed to be."

He couldn't disagree with that. "You have everything you need?"

Michael nodded. "Food, drinks, jugs of water, candles, and flashlights in case the power goes out."

"We'll make sure our phones are charged," Ian said. "Just in case. Jenna said she was going to do the same. And Viktor assured us that he can contact the *terra indigene* here at the main house or at Silence Lodge if there is any sign of trouble and human-style communication stops working."

Julian watched the men head to the lake cabins, then locked the porch door before lugging the air mattress and sleeping bag into the main house. He locked the kitchen door before continuing toward the TV room. Then he stopped and headed for the library instead. Plenty of room on the floor there, and the library windows looked out over the front of the house. Wouldn't hurt to have someone there. He'd have to ask if Doc Wallace had a preference as far as sleeping arrangements were concerned since the man was there in an official capacity.

Leaving the air mattress and sleeping bag in the library, Julian crossed the entranceway at the same time Vicki came down the stairs—and something that sounded like a rain of pebbles hit the front door.

"What's that?" Vicki asked, hurrying down the stairs.

Julian held up a hand, palm out, a command to stop. Then he walked to the front door, every step feeling like razors slicing his skin. Delicate slices, not too deep. Just enough to create a shiver of pain. His hands felt numb as he turned the lock, as one hand closed on the knob and turned it.

He flipped the switch for the outside lights, pulled the door open, and looked down.

Small white pebbles scattered just outside the door.

Not pebbles. *Bones.*

He glanced back and saw Vicki—and Kira and Aggie, now standing beside her.

Just like in the Murder game, he thought as a quiet sound coming from somewhere in the dark filled his brain.

Rattle, rattle, rattle. Rattle, rattle, rattle.

Julian slammed the door shut, turned the lock, and rushed toward Vicki.

"Call your guests at the lake cabins. Tell them to stay inside and lock the doors. I'll call Wayne."

"What's out there?" Vicki asked.

"Crowbones," Aggie whispered.

Julian nodded. "The real thing this time."

He watched the color drain from Vicki's face, watched her eyes go blank. Then she blinked, nodded, and hurried to her office with Kira and Aggie following on her heels.

Leaning against the reception desk, his eyes fixed on the front door, Julian took out his mobile phone and made the call.

"Grimshaw."

"Wayne? It's here. Crowbones is here."

"Stay inside. I'm heading back that way and . . . *Crap!*"

"Wayne? Wayne!"

The call was cut off. Then his phone rang.

"Wayne?"

"It's Ilya. You need to stay at The Jumble tonight, Mr. Farrow."

Something strained in the Sanguinati's voice. "Crowbones is here. Right now."

"I know. But you can't reach the village or the Mill Creek Cabins, so staying at The Jumble is your only choice." A pause. "Mr. Farrow?"

"Yes?"

"Crowbones is not the only hunter looking for prey tonight." Ilya ended the call.

Julian closed his eyes and pictured the Murder game board as it had been set up when they were looking for answers the other day. Three teenies together near the entrance of the "house." Natasha placing the crow skull just outside the front door. And him grabbing teeny Vicki and the other two teenies to get them away from the threat.

Human, Crow, Sanguinati. Was that combination the trigger? Or was it those particular individuals?

Vicki hadn't closed her office door. He could hear her talking to someone as he approached. When Aggie spotted him, he put a finger to his lips. No reason to interrupt Vicki. He'd talk to Doc Wallace—and Conan and Cougar. Warn them that the danger was right on the doorstep.

Ilya had said Crowbones wasn't the only hunter out there tonight.

Who would be missing in the morning?

CHAPTER 52

Grimshaw

Watersday, Novembros 3

Grimshaw dropped his mobile phone and slammed on the brakes when the horse and rider suddenly appeared in his headlights. He waited for his heart to resume something close to a regular beat, then put the cruiser in park and stepped out, staying behind the open door.

"Aiden? Is there a problem?"

Fire and Twister approached the cruiser. "The road is closed tonight."

"I was just heading to my cabin."

Aiden shook his head. "Not tonight. Stay in the village, Chief."

Not good. "Can I know why?"

"I am as much in the dark as you are," Aiden replied.

I doubt that.

No point in arguing with an Elemental. A human would never win. "All right. I'll be back in the morning."

Fire watched as he got in the cruiser and drove back to the village.

Someone was going to die tonight, and there wasn't a damn thing he could do about it.

Osgood was just about to bite down on a meat-loaf sandwich when Grimshaw walked into the station. The rookie took one look at him and lowered the sandwich.

"Chief?" Osgood said. "Thought you were heading home."

"Road's closed. The Mill Creek Cabins are out-of-bounds tonight."

"Well . . . You can have my room at Ineke's. I can sleep on the couch. I've done it before when Captain Hargreaves needed a place to stay."

Grimshaw shook his head. "I appreciate the offer, but I can bunk here if there's no one in the cell."

"We don't have company tonight." Osgood made a face. "You sure, Chief?"

"I'm sure."

"There's an extra meal in the fridge if you want it. Helen from Come and Get It called to say she was closing early and asked if we wanted anything, so I picked up a couple of her meat-loaf sandwiches. There's a container of soup too."

"Thanks. I'll heat up something in a bit. You eat."

Grimshaw went into the station's small kitchen, pulled his mobile phone out of the holder on his belt, and called Julian.

"Are you all right?" Julian asked, the question almost a demand. "What happened?"

"Fire happened," he replied quietly. "The road to the cabins is blocked off tonight, so neither of us is getting home. By the way, Doc's car is now parked behind yours, so you can't leave until he does unless you swap vehicles."

"We're sheltering in place for the time being. The guests in the cabins are staying put and checking in. The rest of us . . . Wayne, it was like the Murder board we set up at the bookstore. Vicki, Aggie, and Kira together and then that sound at the door."

"Check in, okay?"

"Will do." A pause. "Where are you staying tonight?"

"I'm going to bunk at the station. Why?"

Another pause. "You have the spare set of keys I gave you for the store?"

"Locked in a safe box in my desk."

"The other keys on that ring are for the space upstairs. It's basic, but there's a bed and a bathroom. Clean towels in the linen closet. Even a spare toothbrush."

Grimshaw could picture Julian's strained smile.

"No food," Julian continued, "but there is a wave-cooker and an electric kettle to heat up water."

"Thanks. I appreciate it. Osgood picked up some supplies from Come and Get It, so I'll be set for tonight."

Strained silence before Julian said, "If you're looking for something to read, the key to the locked filing cabinet is in a small box in the middle drawer of the desk."

Grimshaw said nothing for a moment. "Is there something you think I should see? Something that might relate to what's going on here?"

"Not sure. But maybe something that more than one person should know."

Julian ended the call.

Leaving the food in the fridge, Grimshaw drank a glass of water before returning to the main area.

"We get any response from other police stations?" he asked.

"A few. Some of the ITF agents responded too, although a couple of those e-mails had bounced back—Viktor must have made a typing error in the e-mail addresses. I checked the addresses from the original list and sent those out again. Still waiting to hear back from them."

Typing errors or a deliberate delay?

Osgood picked up a pad of lined paper off his desk and held it out. "From the responses we've received so far, I made a list of the places where there were similar . . . occurrences . . . in the past two years."

Grimshaw looked over the list. Osgood had indicated the ITF agent who had sent the e-mail, the location of the trouble, and the highlights of what had happened. The deaths seemed to end as suddenly as they began, which made him think the predator had moved on.

Why move on when there was still prey in the area? Or was the predator following someone who also looked for prey?

Grimshaw reviewed the e-mails, reading all the details that had been sent by the ITF agents. When Osgood finished eating, he turned to the rookie. "You head out and keep an eye on things at the boardinghouse. I'll stay here in case someone needs help." He wrestled with loyalties for a moment before adding, "I might be over at the bookstore. I've got keys to the place, and Julian won't object to me browsing."

He didn't mention that he wasn't planning to browse through the books.

Once Osgood had driven away, Grimshaw put an In Case of Emergency sign on the door with the number of his mobile phone. Complainers tended to call Osgood. People who really needed a cop tended to call him if there was no one at the station.

He found a container in the kitchen and took half the soup and the other meat-loaf sandwich, then packed the Come and Get It delivery bag with the food, a copy of Osgood's listings, and a folded regional map of the Northeast. Then he locked the station and walked across the street to Lettuce Reed.

As he walked around the building to the doors in the back, Grimshaw wondered if anyone would call the cops if they saw a light on the second floor. Or would Sproing's residents just think that Julian had finally rented out the space?

Looked like he was about to find out.

A plain metal door with a high-end dead bolt. Could have led to a utility room or storage space or even a basement if the store had one, but it opened to a wide flight of stairs heading up. Grimshaw found the light switch. Two bare bulbs, one at the top and one at the bottom of the stairs.

Grimshaw locked the door and headed upstairs. He stopped at the top of the stairs and looked around. Heavy shades and blackout curtains on the windows confirmed that no one was going to notice a light, so he stepped into the front room and turned on a lamp.

As Julian had said, the place was basic. There was a comfortable reading corner with chair, hassock, and lamp. Even a crocheted afghan, which made Grimshaw wonder if Farrow had purchased it or if there had been someone in Julian's life at one time who had made it for him. The rest of the room held a wooden rolltop desk with pigeonholes and plenty of drawers, another desk with a computer and printer, a big worktable filling up the center of the room, a couple of filing cabinets, and several bookcases.

The furnished bedroom had a single bed, a night table, a bookcase, and a dresser that held a spare set of sheets and pillowcases in the bottom drawer. The other two bedrooms held packing boxes of books.

Basic. A bolt-hole. Or a place to keep the secrets that had come from working with the *terra indigene*?

He laid out the regional map and the information from the ITF agents on one end of the big worktable, then heated up the soup and half of the meat-loaf sandwich. He didn't find any coffee, but there were bottles of beer in the fridge. He opened a bottle and took his meal to the table. He ate standing, looking from Osgood's list to the map and back again. Finishing off the last bite of the sandwich, he rummaged in the desk drawers, stumped for a moment when he found the middle drawer was locked—and then thought to try one of the keys on Julian's key ring. He found a package of removable color-coded labels, the small dots in various colors that women used on family calendars to keep track of appointments—and cops sometimes used on maps when they were keeping track of a suspect's movements or searching for a pattern to a series of deaths.

Grimshaw took the labels and returned to the map, applying dots to each town or village that had had an incident resulting in what the police had identified as a ritualized killing.

We're not the first, he thought as he studied the map. *Not even close to the first. But what do those places have in common?*

He rummaged in the desk again and found a legal pad and a pen. He wrote the names of the guests staying at The Jumble and at the Mill Creek Cabins. Under those names, he wrote *Ineke* as a reminder to find out where her guests were from. Then he began to fill in what he could remember about everyone's current place of residence and put a different colored dot next to each name that matched a trouble spot.

Grimshaw took the dishes back to the kitchen and washed them before taking another beer out of the fridge and returning to the table.

He stared at the map. Stared and stared. Then he set the beer down, fetched the key from the middle drawer of the desk, and opened the file cabinet to find out some of Julian Farrow's secrets.

CHAPTER 53

Vicki

Watersday, Novembros 3

It was a dark and stormy night.

Okay, it wasn't stormy—unless you counted Ben Malacki's sulky hissy fit—but it was definitely dark. But saying it was dark and stormy sounded appropriately atmospheric since we were trapped inside The Jumble's lake cabins or the main house, and something that scared the feathers off the Crows was wandering around outside waiting for someone to be foolishly inquisitive.

Who would survive? Who would be eaten? Who would end up squashed under a large Elder's foot like a crunchy-shelled bug with a squishy middle?

I so did not want to be the bug with a squishy middle.

Maybe I should do more exercises for my core, because squishy is as squishy does?

Focus, Vicki.

"Officer Osgood has advised my guests to remain indoors this evening," Ineke said after I called and gave her the latest warning about things that go bump in the night. "He suggested putting Maxwell on a leash and taking him out close to the house to do his business, but that won't work. Maxwell might water the plants near the house, but he has his potty spots at the back of the property for other business and he won't go anywhere else unless he's having tummy troubles."

"He's smart enough not to linger if he senses something out there." I tried to sound encouraging. Being a border collie, Maxwell was smarter than a lot of Ineke's guests, but that might not be enough if something caught him with his pants down, so to speak.

I took a deep breath and finally said the words that were the real reason for the phone call. "Julian is here. For the night."

"Oh?" A noncommittal sound brimming with undercurrents of interest.

"What should I do? What would you do?"

"Two entirely different questions," Ineke replied.

"If you had three teenage . . . females . . . spending the night in the room next to your bedroom?"

"Under the circumstances, offering a good friend half of your bed because it's that or the floor isn't the same as offering to have wild, naughty sex with him."

"What if *he* thinks one offer means the other?" This had been worrying me for an hour and had me dithering. The girls were going to be in my sitting room sharing the air mattress donated by the Sterns. Or maybe Aggie and Jozi were taking the love seat after shifting to Crow form and Kira had the mattress. I didn't know what they had decided, but I did know even I wasn't short enough to comfortably nap on the love seat. Anyway, Doc Wallace was probably going to be on the couch in the TV room downstairs. And that left Julian sleeping in a chair or on the floor somewhere.

I wasn't an Intuit, but I had a feeling that if he wasn't inside my apartment, Julian would be sleeping in front of the door so he would be nearby in case . . . well, in case whatever had spooked him started to happen. And I kind of wanted another grown-up to be around if the spookies started, especially if Julian was the grown-up.

"It's Julian," Ineke said. "He knows you. He will take the offer at face value." A beat of silence. "Besides, you can find out if he has a tolerance for cold feet."

"My feet aren't that cold," I muttered. "At least not before winter."

She laughed in a way that made me wonder if she was talking about body parts or a different kind of cold feet.

We talked for another minute, promising to check in with each other in the morning. Then I went to find Julian to make an offer, not quite knowing if I wanted him to accept or refuse.

I found Julian all right, having a heated discussion with Ben Malacki.

"Is there a problem?" I asked. Of course there was, and it would be more of a problem the moment Cougar or Conan joined the discussion.

"You can sleep on the sofa bed in your suite, or you can sleep down here on the couch in the TV room," Julian said, his voice tight with anger. "Doc Wallace said he will take whichever one you don't choose."

"Let a stranger rummage around in my things? Go through my work?" Malacki puffed out his chest. "I don't think so."

"Fine. Then you stay in your suite."

"With Shuman? In his condition?"

"Conan and Cougar will be sleeping downstairs," I said, giving Malacki a big, big smile and wishing I could borrow Natasha Sanguinati's fangs for a minute. "So you'll have company if you stay down here."

"How dare—" Malacki stared past me.

Cougar, in his furry form, stepped up beside me. In a contest of claws, I really didn't want to know who could do more damage to a human— Cat or Bear. I suspected motivation could be a factor, so I, for one, wasn't going to place a bet since I had the impression that Cougar was feeling pretty motivated about swatting my annoying guest right out the door.

"I'll stay in my suite," Malacki grumbled. "But I want something to eat first, and I'm not eating *up there*."

I'd like to believe it was consideration for his colleague, since I didn't know what David Shuman could eat right now, but it was more likely that Ben Malacki didn't want to be put off his own meal.

"Julian?" I jumped in before the two men could find another thing to discuss. "If I could have a word?"

He followed me to my office. "Problem?" He gave me a tired smile. "Besides the obvious ones?"

It is rude to feed the guests to the wildlife. It is rude to feed the guests to the wildlife.

"Rude to the guests or the wildlife?" Julian asked.

Darn it! I must have said that out loud. "Both."

Julian's smile became warmer and less strained.

"Look, we're both adults, and you need a good night's sleep, which you probably won't get anyway, but there's half a double bed that most of me doesn't use . . ."

"Most of you?"

"My feet tend to wander, but that's beside the point." I was nervous and feeling a little testy. And scared. And wondering when I'd take a spin on the anxiety wheel. "The *point* is you could sleep in my room. With me. If you wanted to *sleep.*"

I looked in Julian's direction, but I couldn't quite look at *him*. Probably too much emphasis on the "sleeping" part, but I really didn't want to find out that I needed a sedative to quiet the anxiety and Doc didn't have any in his medical bag.

"Okay," Julian said. "Thanks."

My jittery nerves jittered a little less. *Okay. Thanks?* Was it really that simple?

"All things considered," he continued, "maybe we should skip the scary movies and set up one or two of the jigsaw puzzles in the social room."

"Good plan." Ben Malacki probably would watch a scary movie or two just to be annoying and interfere with Doc Wallace getting some sleep, but Cougar or Conan could sort out any difficult guests.

We found Doc Wallace in the library reading one of the Wolf Team books. He wasn't interested in watching movies, but he agreed to join us for a while to work on the puzzles since he could dip in and out of the activity when he needed to check on his patient.

Now that I'd made the decision and Julian had accepted, I did my best not to think about the retiring-for-the-evening part of the evening. Since Ben Malacki and the Cornleys stayed away from the rest of us, we almost had an enjoyable night.

For a while, anyway.

CHAPTER 54

Grimshaw

Watersday, Novembros 3

Grimshaw removed his duty belt and laid it on the rolltop desk's chair, but he took his service weapon and set it on the table where it would be close at hand. Then he double-checked that the safety was on and tucked the weapon into his waistband at the small of his back. He was alone. The doors and windows were closed and locked. No one knew he was in the apartment above Julian's store. He still wanted his weapon where he could reach it.

He opened the filing cabinet. Knowing Julian, he started with the bottom drawer and removed a stack of hanging files that had odd designations. A code of some kind?

Some of the files had a single sheet of paper, typed. Others had several sheets. Each sheet had a heading that began *CS* and a number.

After reading a couple of the files, and chilled by the realization of what the headings meant, he looked at the folder name, then at the regional map, and followed the location markers. *J7. M12.*

Something was wrong with the locations, since they weren't indicating towns or villages the way they should. At least, they weren't indicating any towns or villages that would show up on a *human* map. In fact, the first location would put someone in Lake Tahki, and he was pretty sure you wouldn't find an island at that spot.

CS. Cassandra sangue. Blood prophets who saw the future—or at least a possible future—when their skin was cut.

The files were confirmation that Julian had been involved in transporting some of those girls to safe, and secret, places. The files would be worth a fortune to someone who wanted to get his hands on even one of those girls. Would be worth torturing a person to get the locations where those girls could be found.

Remembering some of the scars he'd seen on Julian's body, Grimshaw didn't think Julian had ever been caught—the man was too canny and skilled for that. But wounded while getting a girl to safety? Grimshaw could imagine that easily.

He glanced at the computer, then shook his head. There might be a memory stick hidden somewhere, but Julian would have scrubbed the information from his computer—if he'd saved the files to begin with. More likely, the information was being stored somewhere else, *with* someone else.

More than that . . . Advance and retreat. One letter forward and two numbers back? Or two letters forward and one number back? Maybe. Getting to the correct reference points might even require using a specific map. Trust Julian to be so cautious.

Grimshaw returned those files to the filing cabinet and checked the next drawer. Nothing cryptic about the labels on these files. Towns. Villages. Cities. All in the Northeast Region, which made sense, and not all that many.

He took everything in that drawer, spreading out the files to keep them from spilling off the table. Then he picked up his beer, opened a file, and began to read.

Places where Julian had lived—or at least stayed, although sometimes the stay wasn't more than a few days. Healthy towns, decaying villages. The first hint of rot under a pristine surface, a rot that pushed Julian away, had him moving on.

Choosing differently colored dots, Grimshaw had marked a handful of towns on the regional map when he felt the hair on the back of his neck stand on end.

Casually, he set the bottle of beer on the table. Casually, he began to reach behind him for the weapon secured at the small of his back.

Black smoke curled around his wrist. Became a strong hand . . . that was attached to an arm covered in the black sleeve of what looked like a very expensive suit.

"If I wanted you dead, you would be dead." The voice was educated, calm, polite. Chilling.

He felt another hand at his back remove his service weapon before the Sanguinati released his wrist and stepped away.

Grimshaw didn't know all the Sanguinati who lived at Silence Lodge, but he was certain he would have heard about this one, because all his instincts told him this one didn't take orders.

Suddenly he wondered if Ilya was still alive.

"Does Ilya know you're here?" Grimshaw asked.

"He's the only one who knows I'm here. The only one who *can* know I'm here." The Sanguinati smiled, carefully not showing any fang. "But he didn't know this place would be occupied, or he wouldn't have suggested I stay here."

"If you're supposed to be a secret, where does that leave me?"

"That depends, Chief Grimshaw, on whether or not you can be trusted."

So. This stranger knew who he was—and didn't care. "I've held a secret or two. Whether I hold this one depends on if the people I swore to protect would be at risk if I kept this secret."

"Not all of them would be at risk." The Sanguinati set the service weapon on the table, out of reach. "I am Stavros Sanguinati. I'm currently the leader of the Talulah Falls Courtyard. Previously I was the Toland Courtyard's problem solver."

Problem solver. A specialist in killing? He wouldn't have thought any kind of *terra indigene* needed such a being, but that was before Crowbones had come to Lake Silence.

"Someone thinks Ilya can't handle this?" Grimshaw asked.

"Oh, Ilya could handle this," Stavros replied. "He wouldn't be the leader of Silence Lodge if he couldn't. But Grandfather Erebus felt it was better to have someone . . . transient . . . deal with the problem. Whatever happens, I will return to Talulah Falls, and you can continue to pretend that the Sanguinati you deal with are . . . tamer."

Gods above and below.

"Besides," Stavros continued, "Grandfather doesn't want The Jumble's caretaker to develop a fear of the Sanguinati living around here, so it is best if she doesn't appreciate the depth of what Ilya is."

"Why not stay at Silence Lodge? Why hide out here?"

"As I said, no one but Ilya can know that I'm here—including the rest of the Sanguinati."

Grimshaw nodded as pieces started coming together. "You're another hunter. Crowbones for the Crowgard. You for the Sanguinati." Another piece fell into place as he thought about the Murder game. "Who's the other hunter? Me? Or Julian Farrow?"

A beat of silence. Then Stavros gave him a slow smile. "You're human, but you have a bit of wild country in here." He tapped his chest. "You, I think, although Ilya is of the opinion that Mr. Farrow can be quite dangerous if provoked."

Stavros took a step closer to Grimshaw, then looked at the map. "Your thoughts?"

"Connected killings." Grimshaw pointed to the dots on the map. "Crow's feet tied to one victim like a signature—or a warning. At least two bodies in each place, one of those bodies being a crow or Crowgard. I'm guessing that someone who is involved with all those killings has ended up around Lake Silence and is trapped."

"And these?" Stavros picked up a file.

"I wanted to see if the places Julian felt had become unhealthy matched up with any of the killings, whether those killings were before or after he was there."

"Then let us begin."

As Grimshaw added colored dots to the map, Stavros read Julian's notes out loud—and a grim pattern began to take shape.

CHAPTER 55

Vicki

Watersday, Novembros 3

In the dream, I was in bed, surrounded by something warm that wasn't soft but still felt comfy. Felt comforting. Then I was in the kitchen, wearing bunny slippers made out of real bunnies harnessed to my feet, and we hopped around the kitchen while I tried to start the coffee and put some bread in the toaster. In the center of the table was a round tray filled with pieces of wood that looked like swollen clothespins.

Then something big smacked one of the windows and made the clothespins rattle, rattle . . .

Rattle, rattle, rattle.

Awake now and frightened, I tried to sit up but a weight held me down. I tried to scream but a hand clamped over my mouth.

"Shh," Julian whispered in my ear. "Shh."

Julian. Yes.

I nodded to let him know I was aware.

"Stay here," he whispered. "I'm going to check it out."

Bad idea. Bad! People who did this in the movies ended up being buried in the cellar or tossed in the wood chipper.

Apparently Julian was going to ignore all the lessons one could learn from the movies. He slipped out of bed and pulled on the jeans he'd folded within easy reach. I'd thought it odd he'd left his shirt and sweater on a low chest I used as a window seat, and he'd put his shoes and socks next to it, but he'd wanted the jeans right beside the bed. Because the mobile phone was in a pocket?

Not a phone. I hadn't closed the heavier winter drapes, and enough moonlight came through the sheer curtains that I saw the gun in Julian's hand as he silently crossed the bedroom and eased open the door to my sitting room.

Wishing I'd taken to keeping a baseball bat or a frying pan under the bed in case I had reason to whack someone, I eased out of bed and crept toward the bedroom door.

"Stay here" meant stay in the room, not in the bed. That would be my reasoning if Julian or Ilya or, gods help me, Grimshaw demanded to know what I was thinking.

As soon as I reached the doorway, I felt cold air around my legs. Who had opened a window?

Julian studied the window and said softly, "Turn on a light. Low."

I felt my way to a two-shelf bookcase. It held a decorative lamp that provided soft light when I watched TV or just wanted the friendliness of a lighted room when I returned to my own apartment. I turned on the light, expecting the girls to be instantly awake. They weren't. Kira blinked a couple of times, rubbed her eyes, stared at me, and said, "Wha . . . ?" Aggie, perched on one arm of the love seat, barely stirred at all, and that was wrong enough to be frightening.

Julian pushed the open window up all the way, removed a small, high-powered flashlight from his pocket, and shone the light on the ground below. He stared at something. Stared and stared. Then he closed the window and locked it.

That's when I looked around the room and said to the two bleary-eyed adolescents, "Where's Jozi?"

Julian Farrow braced one hand on the window frame and closed his eyes—and I didn't ask again.

CHAPTER 56

Watersday, Novembros 3

His brain . . . blinked . . . and he wasn't sure what he had seen, wasn't sure what had been done. Except . . .

There was death. He had given the warning; the Reader was safe. But there was death.

He wasn't sure what he had seen—the pattern shifted and re-formed, shifted and re-formed. But he knew the taste of it, the feel of it enough to give it a name.

Betrayal.

CHAPTER 57

Grimshaw

Earthday, Novembros 4

When he got up the next morning, Grimshaw saw no sign that Stavros Sanguinati had been in the apartment—except for a message pad that had been left on the worktable. A phone number had been written on the top sheet with the words *If you need to call*.

Grimshaw tore off the sheet, folded it, and tucked it in his wallet. He looked around. He and Stavros had cleaned up last night, putting the files away and making sure everything was as tidy as it could be. He wasn't sure what Julian wanted him to do about the towels and toothbrush he'd used, but he'd ask about that later. He didn't want his friend to check on the apartment and run afoul of Stavros.

He went downstairs and checked the delivery bag before he locked the door. Helen from Come and Get It would expect the bag and food containers to be returned the next time he or Osgood stopped by the diner. If something was missing, she would want to know why, and he didn't want Helen asking about much of anything since the gossip was going to be flying about the additional road closure.

Satisfied that he had everything he needed to return to Helen, as well as the other half of the meat-loaf sandwich, the regional map, and the e-mails from the ITF agents, Grimshaw walked up the driveway that accessed the bookstore's small parking lot and aimed for the police station.

His mobile phone buzzed as he crossed the street. He didn't need to look at the display since he could see the agitated man who held a phone and stared at the sign on the station's locked door.

"Mayor Roundtree. I'm surprised to see you here on Earthday. Problem?"

Roundtree spun, still listening to the ringing of an unanswered phone. Then he ended the call and shouted, "Yes, there's a problem! Someone called my home phone this morning—*my home phone*—and told me to come here and . . . Look!" He pointed toward the government building next door.

Figuring that Roundtree would have a coronary if he took a minute to open the station and set the delivery bag on his desk, Grimshaw followed the mayor to the government building and sighed as he took in the grisly message written on the steps:

BEE HEPFLUL.

"Look at that!" Roundtree pointed. "The nincompoops can't even spell."

"That a message aimed at you was written in cat's blood is a little more important than the spelling, don't you think?" Grimshaw asked.

"Blood?" Roundtree blanched. "Aimed at me?" More blanching. "Cat?"

Grimshaw pointed to what looked like a discarded calico scarf—except the scarf had what was left of a head partially tucked into the open belly.

"Matilda!" Roundtree wailed. "That's my cat!"

Grimshaw let out a slow breath and resisted the urge to tell the mayor to be grateful it was his cat and not one of his children. Then again, maybe the mayor liked his cat more than his children.

"I think you should do everything you can to deliver the information Ilya Sanguinati asked for about our new residents, Mayor Roundtree," he said quietly. "You really should do that because I don't think the next message will be as restrained."

"It's those damn vampires." Roundtree's venom was sincere, but he had sense enough to keep his voice down.

"No, it's not. They all know how to spell." *And they wouldn't have wasted the blood.* "Call whoever you need to call to come in and get me that information. *Today*, Mayor."

Grimshaw unlocked the police station's door. He started the coffee and warmed the meat-loaf sandwich in the wave-cooker. He didn't have much appetite after seeing the cat, but he ate. By the time he poured his first cup of coffee, he had the computer on and had checked the latest e-mails—a wave of reports from other police stations in the Northeast Region, mostly in the area between Hubbney and Lake Silence. In other words, the Finger Lakes.

The station phone rang and rang as he forwarded all the new e-mails to his personal account before Viktor Sanguinati arrived to help. *If* Viktor arrived.

Then his mobile phone buzzed.

"Grimshaw."

"Wayne." Julian, sounding tired. "Come to The Jumble as soon as you can. I've already called Ilya. He's on his way." A hesitation. "You'll also need to stop at the Mill Creek Cabins. One of the professors is missing."

CHAPTER 58

Ilya

Earthday, Novembros 4

In his smoke form, Ilya traveled close to the surface of Lake Silence, aware of the shadows that swam beneath him. The lake's Elders. There were ways to harm—or kill—one of the Sanguinati. He couldn't say if these Elders knew how it was done. The residents of Silence Lodge had taken care to work with, and accommodate, the more dangerous *terra indigene* who lived around the lake. He did know that these Elders, along with the Elemental known as the Lady of the Lake, had saved Victoria last summer, had brought her to him so that he could summon the human doctor and look after her while her wounds mended.

He didn't think they followed him for any malicious intent. Like him, these Elders took an active interest in The Jumble and its caretaker. Unlike him and the rest of the Sanguinati, they could offer protection only when Victoria was in or on the lake.

He aimed for the sandy beach that was part of The Jumble's property, intending to remain in smoke form until he reached the lake cabins. He'd check on Viktor and Karol—and Victoria's guests—before going up to the house to meet Julian Farrow and examine the . . . remains.

One of the shadows in the water veered away, moving swiftly toward

The Jumble's dock. Then more of them veered away, and one said, <Follow us, bloodhunter.>

<I am expected—>

A delicate dorsal fin broke the surface of the lake, almost close enough to brush against smoke. A tail slapped the water in warning. <Follow us.>

Ilya followed.

When he neared the dock, voices sang out from the nearby trees.

"*Ilya,*" the first voice sang.

"*Illllyaaa,*" the second voice sang.

"*This way, bloodhunter,*" the third sang. "*This way.*"

The Elders in the lake turned away but circled nearby. Ilya reached the dock, reluctant to shift into a human—and much more tangible—form.

Then he heard a flutter, a weak caw.

Moving to the far side of the dock, he saw a Crow hanging upside down, secured to the dock by string tied around its feet.

"*Freshly found,*" a fourth voice sang.

That explained why the Five hadn't helped the Crow. It was one explanation, anyway. He chose not to consider any others.

Another flutter and a fading word. <Help.>

<Jozi?>

Ilya flowed to the top of the dock, then shifted to human form as he knelt and reached for the Crow. Time enough to find out how she'd ended up there.

Panicked flapping of wings that set her swinging. <No!>

<Jozi, it's Ilya.>

<No!>

"*Bloodhunter?*" No singsong teasing in the fifth voice. Just deadly suspicion.

Ilya didn't turn around, didn't look. He lifted Jozi by the legs with one hand and snapped the string with the other, leaving a couple of inches dangling from the dock. The moment Jozi stopped flapping and fluttering, he wrapped both hands around her.

"She's confused," he said.

He didn't hear them retreat to the shadows among the trees, but he felt their absence. Hurrying off the dock, he headed for The Jumble's main house.

"Is she confused?" the fifth voice asked. *"Is she really?"*

He hoped so. For the sake of every Sanguinati living around Lake Silence, he hoped so.

CHAPTER 59

Grimshaw

Earthday, Novembros 4

Grimshaw called Osgood, then sat in his cruiser to wait for the rookie to show up for work before he headed out to the Mill Creek Cabins to find out about the missing professor.

The cat bothered him. It bothered him enough that he pulled out his wallet, stared at the paper with the phone number, then made another call.

"Yes?"

He wondered if Stavros Sanguinati was watching him from some dark corner. "Would an Elder kill a cat? Would any form of *terra in-digene*?"

"Was the cat threatening one of its young?" Stavros asked.

"Doubtful. It was a small domestic cat."

"Was the Elder hungry?"

"A cat that size wouldn't even make an appetizer. But the cat's blood was used to write a message on the steps of the government building."

"Are you sure?"

Grimshaw stared at the government building. He didn't doubt for a moment that the message was written in blood, but something about the way the cat's head had been shoved into the hollowed-out belly bothered him. And now that he thought about it, the way the words had been misspelled bothered him too.

Getting out of the cruiser, he walked over to the corpse. As it was Earthday, none of the government offices were open. Employees usually used the back entrance anyway since there was a parking lot behind the building, so they might not notice the "encouragement" that had been left out front. Would Roundtree call someone to remove the carcass and wash off the steps before the offices opened for business tomorrow?

Or was the mayor foolish enough to think he'd take care of that?

He crouched, reached—hesitated. Then he pinched the cat's neck with two fingers to pull the head up and . . .

"Crap." He released the neck and stepped back. "It's a fake," he told Stavros. "Some Trickster Night prank using a hollowed-out toy." But a high-quality toy with realistic faux fur that could fool a person at first glance—especially if that person was more concerned about the rest of the tableau.

"Ah," Stavros said. "That is good news for the cat. But it leaves you with a problem."

"Yeah, I know." Grimshaw ended the call and returned to his cruiser.

He had a problem, all right, because *something* had been bled to leave that message for Mayor Roundtree—and as he considered the way the words had been misspelled, he wondered if a human was, or humans were, trying to implicate the Others in order to cause more trouble in Sproing.

CHAPTER 60

Julian

Earthday, Novembros 4

Julian stood inside the main house's screened porch, drinking coffee while he waited for Ilya Sanguinati.

Michael Stern had called a few minutes ago to check in. Nothing around the cabins last night to cause alarm. They had food, but could he come up and fill a thermos with coffee to share with Ian and Jenna?

Julian felt a little guilty about saying no since he was on his second mug of caffeine, but he wanted Ilya to see everything before anyone else came up to the house. And it bothered him that whatever happened last night had occurred while he'd been sleeping in the next room. It bothered him that something had left Kira groggy and Aggie so disoriented and weakened that she couldn't shift to her human form to tell them what, if anything, she knew.

The quick thump on the bedroom window that woke him up, followed by that warning rattle, bothered him most of all. Would something or someone have tried to harm Vicki if he hadn't been there? Had she been the target all along?

He spotted Ilya hurrying toward the house from the direction of the lake. Not unexpected. The access road was still blocked by cars, so Boris couldn't have driven the sedan up to the house to drop off the Sanguinati's leader.

Then he noticed the black bundle Ilya carried. Setting his mug on the nearest table, he rushed out to meet the vampire.

"What . . . ?" Julian pivoted to open the porch door.

"It's Jozi," Ilya said.

Still alive, Julian thought, feeling a moment's relief. *But if this is Jozi, then who . . . ?*

"I found her at the dock, tied upside down." Ilya laid her on one of the porch chairs. "I think she was there for a while, and she's very upset." He glanced around the porch, as if making sure she couldn't get out.

There was a local veterinary practice that took care of the animals on the nearby farms as well as people's pets, but Julian didn't know the office's phone number offhand and didn't know how much the vet might know about *terra indigene* forms.

"Should I call Michael Stern and ask him to deliver a message to Eddie?" he asked. "Do the Crowgard have their own healer?"

"All the gards have healers for their own kind of *terra indigene,*" Ilya replied. "But there is no physical injury that I can detect."

"What about anemia?" The words were out as soon as the thought formed.

Ilya gave him a cold stare. "Is that an accusation, Mr. Farrow?"

"That's a question, Mr. Sanguinati. Jozi was taken and didn't struggle or sound an alarm. Kira was groggy when we woke her. Aggie is still disoriented to the point she can't shift to human form. *Something* entered Vicki's apartment through an open window on the second floor without *anyone* waking up and realizing we had an intruder." He paused. They needed to work together, so arguing with Ilya was pointless. "You should see the body before we discuss this further."

Ilya glanced at Jozi, who didn't seem to be paying attention to them. "If Victoria has some available, perhaps she could offer a small amount of orange juice to Jozi and Aggie—and a little food."

"I'll ask her. The body is around the side of the house." He waited until Ilya headed in that direction before he went inside to find Vicki and tell her about giving the Crows some juice. It's what humans were given when they donated blood at a hospital.

He wished Ilya hadn't suggested the juice, since it confirmed his suspicion about blood loss causing disorientation.

CHAPTER 61

Vicki

Earthday, Novembros 4

I think there was a poem about fog coming in on little cat feet, but I'm here to tell you it doesn't. Fog comes in on clompy pony hooves, looking for a carrot in payment for hiding a crime scene until the authorities—meaning Grimshaw—need to see the body and collect evidence.

I don't know how the pony got into the kitchen without Julian noticing him, but I figured Fog could go wherever he wanted, being about as stoppable as the Sanguinati, who could slip through any kind of crack when they were in their smoke form.

Not something I wanted to think about right now, what with Doc Wallace suggesting that I give the girls some juice to see if low blood sugar might be causing Kira's grogginess and Aggie's disorientation. So I concentrated on cutting up a carrot and telling Fog he'd been very clever to create a unique crime scene tent, and how I'd be sure to tell Chief Grimshaw when I saw him.

Fog seemed pleased with his payment, and I hoped on hope that Grimshaw wouldn't give me his patented grim look because I'd unintentionally encouraged one of the Elemental's steeds to become an assistant to the local police.

Julian walked into the kitchen and frowned at Fog's tail.

Fog, focused on the last chunk of carrot but perhaps picking up a bit of tension in the human, flicked his tail at Julian.

"There, now," I said brightly, because a positive attitude helped keep one's toes out from under clompy hooves. "You've had your carrot, so I need to get started on feeding the humans."

I wasn't sure what I expected—I hadn't known Fog was there until my elbow bumped his nose, which just showed that things like doors and walls weren't much of an impediment for Elementals or their steeds—but I hadn't expected the pony to make a tight turn, give Julian another tail flick when the man opened the kitchen door as a clear exit route, and then head for the front of the house.

"Did you do something to annoy him?" I asked.

"How could I? I didn't know he was here," Julian replied.

I hurried to the front of the house and walked into the dense fog that covered the large entrance hall and reception area. I found the reception desk by bumping into it, and it gave me a reference point for finding the front door. I'd heard of people walking in circles during a snowstorm and freezing just a couple of feet from shelter. Would Julian eventually find me sitting on the floor, lost and disoriented, just inches from the door?

I found the door. I unlocked and opened the door.

The fog stayed put.

I sighed. "I can't play now. I really have to feed my guests."

The fog thinned enough for me to find my way back to the kitchen. When Eddie showed up for work—*if* Eddie showed up for work—I'd ask him to close the front door. That had nothing to do with safety and everything to do with keeping heat in the building.

"Ilya found Jozi at the dock," Julian said when I returned to the kitchen.

"But you found—"

He shook his head. "She's alive but has been through an ordeal and is very frightened. Ilya suggested a little orange juice might help."

"That's what Doc Wallace said to give Kira and Aggie." I pulled the bottle out of the fridge. Then I turned and stared at Julian. "If Jozi is alive, who did you see last night?"

"I need to talk to Ilya about that. Grimshaw will be here after he answers a call at the Mill Creek Cabins."

If he had to deal with one body before coming to see us, Grimshaw was going to be cranky by the time he got here to talk to me about *another* dead body at The Jumble. Maybe it would be better that the body was a crow? At least Cougar thought it was a crow and not Crowgard when he gave the body a sniff. But a body was a body was a body, and unless Grimshaw was here for pizza and a game of pool, it seemed he was here staring at me and looking all large and official because, hey, we found a body! And while I *knew* that he didn't mean to do it, Official Grimshaw often put Anxiety in the starting gate for the Meltdown Derby.

Why could I never channel the bit of Grimshaw I got through the blood transfusion when I had to *deal* with Grimshaw?

While my brain was distracted by that conundrum, Julian slipped out of the kitchen.

CHAPTER 62

Ilya

Earthday, Novembros 4

Ilya stared at the remains of a crow. Had Jozi been taken to make everyone think she'd been killed? Or had there been a change of plans because Victoria's unexpected invitation to Julian Farrow had complicated someone's intentions and Crowbones's warning rattle made killing Jozi too risky? Or had this crow been killed before the intruder invaded Victoria's apartment?

"That's not good," Julian said when he reached the area where the fog was rapidly dissipating.

"Better than it being one of the Crows who work for Victoria, but, no, it's not good."

"I heard the warning rattle. Did Crowbones do this?"

Ilya crouched and gently examined the carcass. "The kill? I don't think so. What could an ordinary crow do to earn such a savage killing?" He pointed to the wing that was missing three feathers. "Feathers of the fallen. From what we've learned about Crowbones, that is an indication that the crow was an innocent killed by someone other than the Crowgard bogeyman."

"And the lower legs and feet?" Julian asked. "Did the killer or Crowbones take those?"

Ilya rose. "We'll know that if or when they show up at a crime scene."

CHAPTER 63

Grimshaw

Earthday, Novembros 4

No Elementals blocked the road leading to the Mill Creek Cabins. No Elementals—or Others of any kind that Grimshaw could see—were waiting to be helpful. He had a bad feeling their absence was telling.

He drove down the lane and pulled onto the patch of gravel that served as the driveway for his cabin. By the time he got out of the cruiser, Roash and Cardosa, looking haunted and hollow-eyed, had come out of their cabin to meet him, more or less. He noticed they didn't leave the dubious safety of their cabin's enclosed front yard.

"Edward Janse said he had an odd feeling and went out to check on something last night," Richard Cardosa said when Grimshaw reached the gate in that cabin's low stone wall. "He didn't come back. That's why I called."

"Peter Lynchfield went out for food yesterday and didn't come back," Rodney Roash grumbled. "We all pitched in for supplies, and he never came back."

Gods above and below, was it only last night that the Five had gone to The Jumble for books, which had led to all the rest?

"He could have run into some trouble and stayed in the village," Richard Cardosa said, his voice sounding weary and strained, as if he'd been saying the same thing for hours.

Grimshaw studied each man in turn. "Lynchfield is dead. And that, Professor Roash, is something you and I need to talk about, since you're the one who sent him to his death."

Blustering and denials from Roash, which he expected.

"Peter is dead?" Cardosa looked sick. "I should have gone with him. I offered to go with him, but . . ."

"There's nothing you could have done." Grimshaw wasn't sure about that. It was possible Cardosa could have convinced the other man to stay away from The Jumble, but he doubted it.

"Chief?" Cardosa raised his voice to be heard over Roash's continued protests of innocence. "I'm sorry Lynchfield is dead, but Edward Janse might not be. Shouldn't we look for him?"

Grimshaw spotted a hawk flying just above the cabins' rooflines, heading toward the woods. Could be a regular hawk, but he doubted it, so it looked like he had a helper after all.

"I'll look," he said. "You stay here."

He headed in the same direction as the Hawk. By all the gods, what had Edward Janse been thinking to go out after dark? The man was an Intuit. He should have sensed something that told him he was in danger—unless his particular Intuit sensitivity was tuned to something like weather.

But if, as Cardosa claimed, Janse *had* sensed something and that was the reason he'd left the safety of his cabin? Had he found an answer or just an enemy?

Grimshaw spotted the Hawk perched on a branch, watching him. When it didn't fly away, he figured the body would be nearby—and he was right.

The killing was as savage as, or worse than, the way Adam Fewks had died—as if something hated humans or, at the very least, the human form. But Grimshaw didn't think he was looking at the work of the same killer.

Janse wore a sportsman's all-weather coat, olive green in color. Would a Crow identify that color as a muddy green? *Could* Janse have been the man who had met with Civil and Serious Crowgard? Why? Or had someone—some*thing*—seen the coat and killed the wrong man?

Someone had cut open the body from breastbone to groin and scooped out the intestines and other internal organs, which lay in a pile at Janse's feet. It reminded him of the faux cat's hollowed-out body, and he wondered if there was a connection.

The worst part was the way the man had been secured to the tree. His mouth had been opened and a wooden stake had been driven through the mouth and the back of the head, impaling Janse to the tree trunk.

Grimshaw pulled his small, high-powered flashlight from his belt and shone it into the mouth. Then he swore softly.

No tongue.

He didn't see it among the organs on the ground, and he wasn't about to dig around to locate it. Besides . . .

He studied the body and the ground again. The kill had the look of something frenzied and brutal. The stake driven through the mouth and back of the skull produced a bone-deep terror that whatever had done the staking had no care for anything human. But the more he looked at the body and the ground, the more convinced he was that these were two separate events.

What if something *did* care about this man's death but didn't understand how another human would react to seeing the body displayed this way? What if this had been the most expedient way to get the body off the ground—or warn other predators to stay away? Or make the body easy to find?

What if leaving the body like this was an attempt to assist in the investigation?

He'd bet Doc Wallace would tell him pinning the body to the tree was done postmortem. He'd also bet Doc would tell him that Janse's tongue had been cut out while the man was on the ground, grievously wounded and dying but still alive.

Grimshaw stepped back, pulled out his mobile phone, and placed another call to Captain Walter Hargreaves at the Bristol Police Station, requesting further assistance from Detective Kipp and his CIU team. Based on what Julian had told him that morning about the dead crow, he was sure that Janse's death was connected with whatever happened at The Jumble last night, because dangling from some black thread tied to Janse's bottom front teeth were the lower legs and feet of a crow.

* * *

Edward Janse had been a few yards into the trees when he'd been attacked. Almost within sight of the cabins. The man must have thought he was safe enough, or why go out at all? What had compelled an Intuit to go out last night?

Grimshaw stopped at the edge of the trees and called Julian.

"Who's with you?" He was asking a friend who was an ex-cop. He didn't need to specify that he was asking about individuals who could fight.

"Ilya. He found Jozi tied up at the dock. The body I saw is an ordinary crow."

"It's going to take me a while to get there. Edward Janse is dead. It was savage."

"Were any bones taken?"

"No. At least nothing obvious. But a pair of crow's feet were left at the scene."

Julian swore softly.

A thought occurred to him. "Hold on a minute." Thinking about the Crowgard and how they often revealed themselves even when they could otherwise pass for human, Grimshaw went back to the body and studied the head. "I can't be sure, but it looks like someone cut off three locks of hair."

"Feathers of the fallen?" Julian said.

"Could be." Which would mean Janse had been considered an innocent who had been wrongfully killed.

"Can I tell the guests staying at the lake cabins that they can come up to the main house? They're all looking for coffee and company."

"Tell them to stay on the path leading up to the house. Then ask someone with a good sense of smell to sniff around the crime scene and tell you if there were any strangers around last night."

"Let's hope they find a scent," Julian said. "If they don't, Vicki's guests could be in a lot of trouble."

Not just the guests, Grimshaw thought as he ended the call and made one more.

"Yes?" Stavros said.

"Julian Farrow should be included on the need-to-know list, and I think the four of us should meet tonight," Grimshaw said.

"You found whose blood was used to write the warning?"

"Not sure, but we have found two more bodies, one human, one crow."

Silence. Then: "Very well. Bring Mr. Farrow with you tonight."

Grimshaw returned the mobile phone to its place on his belt and took a minute to consider what had to be done.

Detective Kipp and his CIU team would be driving up to The Jumble by now to examine the crime scene and remove Peter Lynchfield's body and take it to Ames Funeral Home for examination. Would Kipp recommend the remains go to Bristol where they could do a full autopsy, or would the CIU team's leader realize learning too much could be dangerous to his team? Same thing with Edward Janse's body, although Grimshaw wasn't sure Janse had been killed by any form of *terra indigene*, so a full autopsy could be useful.

It suddenly occurred to him that there was one possible reason why Janse would have ignored any warnings from his Intuit sensibilities. Drugs. Two drugs—gone over wolf and feel-good—had caused all kinds of trouble last year. Gone over wolf made a person off-the-charts aggressive, and feel-good made a person so passive they had no sense of self-preservation. This killing could be the result of someone—or more than one person—taking gone over wolf. Had someone managed to dose Janse with feel-good in order to persuade him to go out last night? Who?

Well, if it wasn't one of the *terra indigene*, which was likely since they hated both drugs for no other reason than both were made from the blood of *cassandra sangue*, then his pool of suspects was down to the other two men staying in the cabins.

He'd think about that later. Right now he needed to get the blood on the steps of the government building analyzed to see if it was human or animal, and he still needed to locate Tom Saulner, the missing teenager he'd dubbed Hatchet Head.

More than anything, he needed to figure out who was behind what was happening before he ended up investigating another body.

CHAPTER 64

Vicki

Earthday, Novembros 4

Viktor, Karol, and Eddie walked into the kitchen with Michael, Ian, and Jenna McKay. The humans were looking for coffee. The boys were looking for . . . something . . . that required opening all the cupboard doors and checking the pantry and ended with the three of them staring into the refrigerator.

"You do that much longer, you'll get frostbite on your nethers," I said.

Michael Stern almost snorted hot coffee out of his nose and he grabbed at the napkin Jenna McKay held out.

Karol jackknifed his hips away from the cold wafting into the warm kitchen. Viktor studied me and eased back a step.

Eddie rolled his eyes and said, "That's Miss Vicki's way of saying, pick something and close the refrigerator door." He pulled out leftover pizza and closed the door.

The kitchen wall phone rang.

I grabbed the phone on the second ring. "Vicki's Asylum. Vicki speaking."

Okay, I was a wee bit stressed-out by the parade of corpses and let Inner Vicki answer the phone, which is never a good idea from a business point of view. Tomorrow I would go back to being the responsible care-taker / innkeeper / whoever I usually try to be. Really.

"Ms. DeVine? This is Detective Kipp. Bristol CIU?"

Oh, crappity crap crap. "Good morning, Detective," I said brightly. Too brightly? Maybe he would decide The Jumble *had* become an asylum since his last visit, and he would go away and find Grimshaw.

Who would give me his patented grim look.

"Sorry, Detective. It's been a rough night."

"That's what I've been hearing." Kipp paused, and his voice sounded stressed-out and yet relieved when he added, "We made it through the tunnel."

Tunnel? What tunnel?

"We need to get closer to the crime scene that is located on your access road," Kipp said, "but there are two cars blocking the way. Is anyone able to move those vehicles?"

The phrasing had me looking around the kitchen as if it were full of blood spatter and body parts. Everyone looked intact and functional, although I wasn't quite sure about me.

When Doc Wallace walked into the kitchen, I began to connect the dots. "Yes, Detective. Julian Farrow and Doc Wallace will move their cars so you can bring up your official vehicles."

"Appreciate it."

I hung up, then smiled at Doc Wallace. "Coffee first; then move your car." He probably was more alert than I would have been, he being a doctor and all, but it was going to be a rough day for the doc as well as everyone else. "Grab anything you want for breakfast. I'll find Julian."

Julian and Ilya weren't hard to locate. I just went around the house until I reached the lingering patch of fog.

"Detective Kipp got through the tunnel and he and his team are here," I told Julian. "You need to move your car."

"Tunnel?" Julian said. He exchanged a look with Ilya, and I realized they understood something I didn't. After another silent communication, Ilya nodded and Julian walked away.

Goody. Tag team protection. Which made me wonder why I needed protection during the day, when just about everyone currently in The Jumble would be in the kitchen stress eating.

"Is there something I should know?" I asked Ilya once Julian had hurried off to move his car and, most likely, have a private ex-cop–to–cop discussion with Kipp about what was going on around Lake Silence.

Ilya hesitated. "Edward Janse, one of the professors staying at the Mill Creek Cabins, was killed last night."

Thank goodness Julian and Grimshaw didn't make it home last night.

Not that I didn't feel bad about Edward Janse, but if Julian and Grimshaw had gone home, they would have been out there, in the dark, trying to help—and maybe getting killed themselves.

"Is this my fault?" I asked before I had a chance to shush Inner Vicki, who was currently playing the "It's Always Your Fault" song I had learned during my marriage to Yorick Dane. "Did this happen because I told the Crows about Trickster Night?"

My heart felt heavier and heavier when Ilya didn't answer.

Finally he said, "No, it's not your fault, at least not that I can see. But the trouble seems to circle around you and The Jumble, and we need to figure out why."

Well, that sure made me feel better.

"I would like a list of all the places you've lived," Ilya said. "Where you went to school. That would be helpful."

"All right." That wouldn't be hard. It was a really short list. "Is this where you promise to keep me safe?"

Another silence. "There are powerful unknown beings around Lake Silence right now, and I don't know why they are fixated on you and The Jumble. I am your attorney, and I hope you consider me a friend. I will do my best to protect you, Victoria, but I can't promise that I'll succeed."

"Okay. I appreciate the honesty."

Ilya gave me a tight smile. "No, you don't."

"I don't—and I do." That much honesty required an intervention, so I headed back to the kitchen to do my share of stress eating.

CHAPTER 65

Grimshaw

Earthday, Novembros 4

Problem, Chief Grimshaw?"

Grimshaw looked over his shoulder and watched Aiden approach. How long had Fire been there, watching him?

"I've got plenty of problems," he replied, "but my immediate one is how to keep this crime scene secured while I take care of other police business."

"You are concerned about humans . . . tampering . . . with evidence?"

Gods above and below. Did the Elementals watch the cop and crime shows too?

Grimshaw stepped back from Janse's body and looked toward the cabins. "I don't think Roash or Cardosa will have the nerve to come out here." He stopped. Thought. "But someone had the nerve to come out last night and do this to another human. Did that person get away?"

"I wasn't here last night, so I can't say," Aiden replied. "You could ask the Owlgard. They might have seen something."

"But they wouldn't interfere?"

"Human and human doing whatever humans do? Why would the Owlgard interfere? Human and Elder?" Aiden shook his head. "None of the gards would interfere with an Elder."

Grimshaw blew out a breath. It looked like he would have to call Osgood to come here and secure the scene—and then remain here. Alone.

"You don't need to worry about *terra indigene* taking away evidence." Aiden pointed. "Because of that."

That was the crow's feet tied to Janse's lower front teeth.

"The Hawk will keep watch for any sneaky humans, and I will stay nearby to deal with them until your police people come to retrieve the body." Aiden smiled. "Will that be satisfactory?"

Since he heated his cabin with a woodstove, he had no desire to upset Fire in any way. "That will be satisfactory. Thank you."

Grimshaw headed for the cabins, trusting a crime scene to an Elemental and a Hawk. Then he stopped and turned back. "Are any of the Elementals keeping watch over Vicki DeVine today?"

"Should we be?" Aiden asked.

"Might set folks' minds at ease if someone was there, quietly keeping watch."

"I will pass along the suggestion."

He had to be satisfied with that.

He was certain this next bit of business would feel a lot more satisfying.

You're *arresting* me?" Roash shouted from his side of the gate.

"I'm not arresting you. You're coming with me to assist the police with their inquiries," Grimshaw said. "Since you're indirectly responsible for the deaths of one student and two academic colleagues, you have some questions to answer." Not to mention the two Crows and a crow that had died.

"You don't know that!" Roash's face was turning purple. "You can't prove that!"

"Do you have any idea how much trouble you're in?" Grimshaw asked quietly. "Not with the police. With the *terra indigene*. Bodies are piling up, Roash, and everything is pointing at you being the cause."

Roash crossed his arms over his chest. "What if I don't want to go with you? Are you going to *shoot* me in front of a witness?"

At this point, Grimshaw wasn't sure Cardosa wouldn't look the other way. If he'd been stuck in a cabin with Roash, he'd have been tempted to smother the man in his sleep.

Movement near one of the vehicles. For a moment, just long enough to draw the humans' attention, a chubby brown pony with a storm gray mane and tail stood next to the minivan. The next moment, the minivan was spinning across the lane and heading for the creek.

"Twister?" he called over the exclamations of the academics. "I don't think Water will be happy with you if you dump that vehicle in her nice creek. You just bring it back here, okay?"

The spinning slowed a little before curving away from the creek and returning to the cabins, picking up speed again.

While the other men watched the spinning minivan head toward the space between two of the cabins, Grimshaw pulled out his handcuffs, grabbed Roash, and had the man cuffed and stumbling toward his cruiser before Cardosa shook off . . . Fascination? Horror? Grimshaw had seen what Twister and Fire had done to rigs hauling backhoes and other large pieces of equipment. This was just play for the pony. But the underlying message was it could be more . . . and worse . . . if humans didn't play nice.

With Roash in the back seat of the cruiser and the minivan parked in its space, more or less, Grimshaw drove up the lane and headed back to the village.

CHAPTER 66

Julian

Earthday, Novembros 4

Peter Lynchfield looked a lot worse in daylight.

Julian had waited for Doc Wallace to check on David Shuman again and confirm that the wounds from Conan's claws were healing and showed no sign of infection. After Wallace reassured Vicki that her guest would survive, the two men headed down the access road. The doc didn't look toward the body inside the car as they walked past the crime scene; he simply said that he wasn't sure what help he could offer as medical examiner, but he would be available later in the day for anything Chief Grimshaw needed from him.

For people like Doc Wallace, life had been so much easier when they'd been able to believe the Others were Out There instead of Right Here.

When they reached their cars, Doc drove home for a shower and a fresh set of clothes. Julian parked his car on the shoulder of the road and waited until Detective Kipp and his CIU team cautiously backed their vehicles up the access road. He gave them a few minutes to view everything on their own. Then he walked to the crime scene.

The smell of fresh vomit. Not surprising. Even seasoned professionals would have difficulty with the amount of trauma that had been done to Lynchfield's body, especially when there was no way to know if the beings who had done that trauma were out there watching the team—and deciding if these humans should remain among the living or die the same way.

Kipp looked at him and wagged a finger—a request to join him at the car.

"This is as bad as it gets," Kipp said quietly.

"No," Julian replied. "It isn't." He'd seen worse during the years between leaving the police force and settling here in Sproing.

"Do you know what did this?"

"I do. They come into Lettuce Reed once a week to exchange books. I see what they allow me to see. They were very clear that the only person allowed to see them last night when they came to The Jumble for a book exchange was Vicki DeVine because she holds the esteemed position of being the Reader for this *terra indigene* settlement, as well as being the place's caretaker. Lynchfield tried to take photographs of them as they were leaving."

Kipp gestured toward a rock and the shiny bits surrounding it. "I'm guessing the camera is under that?"

Julian leaned closer to Kipp and lowered his voice. "If there is anything left that might contain an image or might give you a way to access an image—"

"We should see what we can get?"

"No, you should destroy it before there is any possibility of you or your team seeing anything you weren't invited to see."

"Destroying possible evidence . . ."

"Saving your team."

They studied each other. Then Kipp nodded.

"Sir?" someone called. "The hearse is here for the body."

"Tell them to come up," Kipp said. "They can take the remains to Ames Funeral Home. The local medical examiner can examine the body there, sign the death certificate, and fill in cause of death." He looked at Julian and lowered his voice. "And say whatever is usually said in cases like this."

"There's another body," Julian said. "At the Mill Creek Cabins. Chief Grimshaw suspects a human killer. Possibly more than one killer."

"I'll wait until I see it before deciding if we need to take that one to Bristol for a thorough autopsy," Kipp replied. "For now, let's deal with the one in front of us."

There was nothing for Julian to do, but no one wanted him to leave, because he was known to the *terra indigene* who lived in The Jumble and the surrounding area. Besides, the CIU team startled at every snapped twig and would lose their nerve if they were alone—a hard truth since this team had dealt with last summer's grisly remains and stayed solid.

"I thought someone said these tires were sunk into the road so deep the car couldn't be moved," Kipp said once the body had been removed and the team started examining the car. "Even a couple of humans pushing at the back would be enough to help a driver rock the car out of these ruts."

"They were deeper last night." Julian smelled rich, sun-warmed earth after a rain before he saw the female who stepped out of the trees and stood beside him.

"Was that not helpful?" Earth asked. "Was the tunnel you traveled through to reach The Jumble not helpful?"

All the men stared.

A human shape, but no one would mistake an Elemental female for human.

A shiver ran down Julian's back. *All* the roads leading out of Sproing and the Lake Silence area were blocked by mounds of earth—except the road heading east, which was currently under a small glacier. Coming up from Bristol, Kipp and his team shouldn't have been able to reach The Jumble—unless someone had overheard Grimshaw's request for the CIU team and a particular Elemental had formed a tunnel through one of the earth mounds to be helpful.

Gods above and below.

"Yes, that was very helpful," Julian replied. "And appreciated." He hoped the tunnel was still there when Kipp and his team tried to leave.

"We will watch Vicki today so that you and Ilya can deal with the humans," Earth said.

"Also appreciated."

She stepped off the road and disappeared.

No one spoke. No one moved.

Julian heard all the men suck in a breath—and then didn't hear anyone exhale.

The resident Bobcat—at least the one who gave guests a donkey-cart tour of The Jumble—stepped out of the trees along with a Coyote who was in a between form that allowed him to walk upright but didn't change much of anything else.

"You're observing?" Julian asked, since no one else did.

Bobcat pointed to the car. "Food in box. In bags. In back. Grimshaw gave. Ilya divided."

Julian nodded. "No point wasting food."

The two *terra indigene* looked at the front seat. Bobcat said, "A trade."

He heard someone gag when the humans realized what Bobcat meant.

While Bobcat and Coyote observed—and thankfully didn't ask questions the way the Crows would have—Kipp and his team went about their business. There was a brief discussion about whether to call a tow truck to haul away the car or have one of the team put down a sheet and drive the vehicle to . . .

Another sticking point. Considering what the inside of the car looked like, where could they put it? Sproing didn't have an evidence garage where large pieces from a crime scene could be stored. Such things were usually taken to Bristol or Crystalton.

After checking the glove box for the car's registration, Kipp confirmed that the vehicle did belong to Peter Lynchfield.

Julian called Ilya Sanguinati.

"Humans would not have access to the vehicle while it is at Silence Lodge, but we do have a building where it could be stored temporarily," Ilya said after listening to Julian's request.

Hearing the emphasis on "temporarily," Julian made arrangements for Boris Sanguinati to pick up the car and drive it to Silence Lodge. Kipp wasn't easy about releasing the car but agreed there wasn't another place in the village where some curious resident couldn't go poking around and get scared into a heart attack.

Finally, as the last piece of evidence to be collected, Julian helped Kipp lift the rock off of Lynchfield's camera. What should have been Lynchfield's camera. All that remained were the broken bits and pieces that had been around the rock. The rest of the camera, including any part that might have held an image of the Five, was gone—and the freshly churned earth explained why.

Kipp put all the broken bits into an evidence bag. Boris Sanguinati arrived, walking down from the direction of the main house.

Julian waited until Kipp and his team drove away to deal with the crime scene at the Mill Creek Cabins and Boris drove off with Lynchfield's car. Then he retrieved his own car and drove up to The Jumble's main house to check on Vicki and collect Karol and Viktor before he headed to the village to open his store for a few hours.

Buried treasure. Easy enough for Earth to do—bury something or bring it back to the surface.

How deep had she buried that camera to make sure whatever was left of what had been seen would not be found?

CHAPTER 67

Grimshaw

Earthday, Novembros 4

Rodney Roash kept up his belligerent whining all the way to the station. But Grimshaw heard the fear underneath the words. The man knew he was in trouble, but he didn't yet understand that having the chief of police demonstrate human law at work was the only thing keeping Roash safe from a different kind of justice.

Once they were inside the station, he patted Roash down, having Osgood stand nearby as a witness. He took Roash's wallet and mobile phone before he removed the handcuffs and ordered the man to put everything else in the tray Osgood set on the desk.

"I'm entitled to a phone call," Roash said.

"You certainly are," Grimshaw agreed, while Osgood made a list of Roash's property.

"I need to call my college and let them know about this mistreatment. And I need to call my attorney."

"You get one phone call."

"Then I'll take my mobile phone back and—"

"No." Grimshaw sat behind his desk. "There is a human attorney in the village. It's Earthday, so he won't be in his office, but I can call and ask him to be present during your questioning if you'd feel more comfortable with that."

"I want *my* attorney!"

"Then you'd better tell him that this village is closed off until the killer is found, and if he makes it past the barriers and reaches Sproing, he won't be able to leave. Since you'll be staying here for the time being, I guess he could use a bed at one of the Mill Creek Cabins, because there is no other place for him to stay. You be sure to tell him that. You should also tell him the reason you're sitting here, about to be questioned, is that you have a direct connection with the deaths of three humans and two *terra indigene*." Grimshaw smiled. "Professor Roash, if I was your attorney, I wouldn't return your calls in the foreseeable future—assuming you have a future."

"Then I'll talk to the attorney who's here."

"I'll give Mr. Diamante a call and arrange a time for all of us to sit down and talk. Officer Osgood, take the professor back to the cell and make sure he gives you his belt and shoelaces."

"Yes, sir," Osgood said.

Roash huffed. "You think I'm going to use a belt or shoelaces to harm myself over this?"

"We're not worried about *you* using those things," Grimshaw replied.

It took Roash a moment to catch on. Then he paled. "I need protection!"

"Yes, you do. That is one of the reasons you're here."

As Osgood led Roash to the station's cell, Grimshaw called Paulo Diamante to see if the village's human attorney was willing to advise the man currently assisting in a police inquiry.

Then he swore. He'd been so focused on the bodies, he hadn't connected the dots when he'd made the call to Bristol this morning, hadn't considered the large obstacle that stood in the way of his getting any help.

Blowing out a breath, he called Samuel Kipp to find out if the CIU team had managed to reach The Jumble.

CHAPTER 68

Vicki

Earthday, Novembros 4

Earthday morning felt like it was three days long and wasn't over yet, but the guests were fed and the dishes were washed. Julian had looked in just long enough to assure himself that nothing disastrous had happened in the time he'd been assisting the CIU team with previous disasters and to collect Karol and Viktor, who would report to their assignments in the bookstore and police station. Natasha called to check in and see how everyone was doing on this side of the lake. That she called me and not Ilya made me wonder if Sanguinati had spousal spats like humans did, or if this was her way of letting Ilya know that his wanting her to stay at Silence Lodge felt oppressive rather than protective.

I ended up in the social room because no one else was in there. I tidied the stack of magazines, going so far as to group them by title and then by date. People—meaning humans—used to throw out magazines once they'd looked through them. That changed after the Great Predation because all kinds of supplies were harder to come by, including paper for printing newspapers, magazines, and books. When I took over The Jumble last winter and began the hard job of renovating and upgrading and bringing the main house and one set of cabins up to standards that would let me have paying guests, Ineke Xavier had suggested that I start a collection of magazines that guests could browse, pointing out that not everyone wanted to settle in and read a novel during a weekend away, and photographs of places or events or even wildlife could entertain for an hour. The two most popular magazines were *Nature!* and *Urban Life.*

Guests oohed and cooed over pictures of big-eyed baby owls. Pictures of Mama staring at the photographer as if telling him he'll lose a finger if he gets any closer to her hooty bits of fluff? Not much cooing over Mama—who, according to a reliable source, had been an Owlgard mama capable of nipping off more than a finger.

I did not ask for details.

Urban Life was published quarterly now instead of monthly. The newer issues were filled with articles about surviving the rationing of goods, surviving the fear of leaving one's home and the illusion of safety it provided, surviving in a social desert. Basically, the new issues were about surviving truths about the world that humans had ignored for too long. Older issues of the magazine—meaning a couple of years ago— were now viewed as some yesteryear fantasy of a kind of glamorous life that had been and would never be again. Guests talked about the houses and parties and things they had never actually done as if a couple of generations had passed between Then and Now, when the truth was, we were barely a year past the war that showed humans how little significance they had in the world's scheme of things.

Small places like Sproing had a chance to flourish, if we could just stop people from doing things that ended with them being eaten. But there were sections of the bigger cities in Thaisia that would always be a scar on the landscape—a forever reminder of what the Humans First and Last movement had cost all of us.

I tucked the issues of *Urban Life* beneath the issues of *Nature!* and continued with the tidying.

Since my guests were trapped at Lake Silence and sufficiently terrified of being thrown out of their rooms for bad behavior, they were making an effort to be tidy, so there wasn't a lot for me to do, despite not having any helpers. Which is why I ended up staring at one of the jigsaw puzzles. We had started two at different tables. All the outer pieces had been found and fitted in on both. One group of puzzlers had separated pieces according to color. The other table had grouped pieces according to shape. The thing is, you can have two shapes that fit together but the colors don't match, don't make a visually correct part of the picture.

I moved some pieces around on one table, not really thinking about anything anymore. Then I picked up a few pieces from the other puzzle—the ones separated by color, which you would think would make it easier. But each puzzle had a blue sky. Not quite the same color blue, but . . .

Pieces from one puzzle fit with pieces of the other puzzle. Not surprising. I imagine there were only so many shapes that were used for all puzzles. It was the picture that made each puzzle different.

"Victoria?"

Ilya stepped up beside me. I had no idea how long he'd been watching me.

"The pieces don't fit together. Physically they do, but that's a deceit."

"More like a confusion since you took pieces from one puzzle and fit them into another puzzle," he said. "People will expect one thing only to discover too many pieces in one puzzle and not enough in the other."

"And eventually they'll realize that things don't really fit because they didn't recognize that they're working on two puzzles instead of one and they've mixed up the pieces." I shook my head, undid the pieces I'd put together, and returned the bits of blue sky to the other puzzle—and hoped I'd put the correct pieces back. "I'm trying to understand how a simple event like Trickster Night has turned into all of this. I keep moving around everything that happened like each death was a puzzle piece and trying to fit them together in a way that produces that aha moment. It just seems like some of the pieces don't look like you'd expect them to look—out of context they look too big or the wrong color—but then that one piece slips into place and suddenly things make sense. Which I'm not making."

Ilya stared at the puzzle. Finally he said, "Unfortunately, Victoria, you are making a great deal of sense."

CHAPTER 69

Them

Earthday, Novembros 4

He'd wondered if he could influence a human like Edward Janse, and now he knew that he could. Supposedly, Intuits had an extra bit of intuition or sense of their surroundings. Supposedly, they weren't as susceptible to doing things outside their normal behavior or being provoked into irrational behavior, but Janse's impulse to help other people was a weakness easily exploited—especially after Janse had ingested a hefty dose of feel-good that had been mixed in a mug of tea.

How else could he have convinced the Intuit that someone needed help that required walking into the woods last night?

He wished he had dared to go out and see the body for himself. Had the *terra indigene* killed Janse? Or had his rival's former subjects—her little monstrosities, as she liked to call them—been given extra treats filled with gone over wolf before being aimed toward the cabins, toward *him*?

He wished he could interview them and find out how they had managed to elude the Others in order to reach the cabins, but all her subjects became unmanageable after a certain age—although a combination of fear and reward seemed to keep them sufficiently subservient to *her*.

Was this about rivalry? Had Edward Janse been killed by the Others because he'd been at the edge of the woods and was easy prey? Or had he been killed because his rival's little monstrosities had been pointed toward someone wearing a certain color coat?

Picking up his olive green coat from where he'd dropped it last night, Richard Cardosa hung it in the closet out of sight.

CHAPTER 70

Grimshaw

Earthday, Novembros 4

What made it abundantly clear that this police station was considered an auxiliary station in an insignificant human village was the lack of a private office for the person in charge. That wasn't a problem for weeks at a time. Grimshaw preferred not having a place where people could have a private chat with him. The possibility of someone walking in and overhearing something intended only for police ears encouraged residents to get to the point faster. Besides, if he needed a private place, he could ask Ilya for the use of the outer room in the Sanguinati's office upstairs.

But this needed some privacy, which was why he sat in the station's break room looking over the reports and e-mails that had come in from ITF agents and from various police stations in the Northeast.

Incidents. Deaths, both human and Crowgard. Investigators had noted the removal of the lower legs and feet of the dead Crowgard—and noted that those feet showed up tied to the bodies of some human victims—but they hadn't known about Crowbones, hadn't understood the significance of two victims being connected in that way.

Then there were reports of minor conflicts between *terra indigene* and humans. Usually adolescents of both species, if he was reading between the lines correctly. The police could confirm the ages of the humans but had no measuring stick for the Crows or other small *terra indigene* who had been caught up in a conflict.

Not all the police stations had answered his query, but based on the ones that had, the boundaries for these conflicts were Hubb NE to the east, the Addirondak Mountains to the north, towns a couple of hours' drive south from the Finger Lakes—and Lake Silence to the west.

No indication that the city of Lakeside or the other towns around Lake Etu had seen this particular kind of killing. Because this—whatever this was—hadn't reached them yet or because . . . ?

Grimshaw opened the map of the Northeast Region. All the Crows who lived around Lake Silence were born around here or, at least, in the Northeast. Was Crowbones a regional bit of folklore? Would Crowgard in the Southeast Region have heard of this Hunter? What about in the western regions? Elementals had territories. There wasn't just one Elemental named Winter or Fire or Earth. Elders also usually kept to a territory. Why not one of these Elders who had a designated role as a Hunter? Maybe this Crowbones wasn't the *only* Crowbones in existence. Maybe they all used the same signature pieces—the cape made of feathers, the hollow gourd filled with bones, and tying the lower legs and feet of a crow or Crow to a corpse to indicate who had been innocent and who had done the killing.

Aggie seemed to think that Crowbones had appeared because they had given some offense, had done something to warrant that harsh attention. Something he needed to talk over tonight with Julian and Ilya—and Stavros Sanguinati.

Osgood stepped into the break room's doorway. "Chief? Paige and Dominique Xavier need to see you."

"About?"

"The storefront that is supposed to be a flea market? They went in to look around, and they think something is wrong over there."

He'd meant to give them some petty cash and ask them to look inside that store but hadn't had the time. Sounded like the place was bumped up to a priority.

Grimshaw folded the map and put all the e-mails and reports into a file folder before taking them back to his desk and tucking them in a drawer. Then he smiled at the two young women. His smile faded when they didn't smile back. For a Xavier not to respond was cause for concern. "Something you want to tell me?"

Paige looked at Dominique, who nodded.

"Our guests are getting a little stir-crazy because they're *bored* and have no appreciation that being bored is better than being eaten," Paige said.

"And they're making us feel a little crazy too," Dominique added.

Not what he wanted to hear. The only thing worse than hearing a Xavier say she felt a little crazy was hearing Vicki DeVine say those words.

"So, you went to the new flea market?" he prompted.

"Ineke asked us to check it out before she suggested it to our guests as something to do," Paige said. "We think it's a front for something. For one thing, it's too dirty to attract customers."

Dominique gave a dramatic little shudder. "The place smells *ripe*."

"That was three of the guys who were hanging out there. I don't think they understand that body odor is not a natural cologne," Paige said.

"What did they look like?" he asked.

The descriptions matched three of the teenagers who had strutted up to The Jumble on Trickster Night. He glanced at Osgood and received a nod. His officer recognized those boys too. Which meant Tom Saulner, the one he'd dubbed Hatchet Head because of the Trickster Night costume, was still missing.

"The fourth one, the one who seems to be working there . . . We think he's a Crow," Paige said.

"Dark eyes, black hair—he kept trying to smooth the hair over a couple of feathers—and delicate build," Dominique added. "Like Eddie Crowgard."

Grimshaw nodded. The Crows working for Vicki all had that delicate build, unlike lean and sturdy Cougar or big-boned, and hairy, Conan. "Anything else?"

Paige and Dominique looked at each other, then nodded. Paige said, "Under the body odor, the place smelled like something had died in it."

Newspapers call that burying the lede, Grimshaw thought as he quietly unlocked the drawer where he stored his service weapon and duty belt. "Did anyone pay attention to you when you left? Could they know you stopped into the station?"

Dominique nodded. "One of the smelly boys came outside and watched us, but we went further up the street and then doubled back after he went inside the store."

Grimshaw looked at Osgood. "Call Julian. Tell him to come over."

While Osgood made the call to Lettuce Reed, Grimshaw made his own call. "Ilya? We may have a situation. I need you as fast as you can get here." He ended the call and looked at the Xaviers. "You need to stay here. Call Ineke and tell her you'll be delayed getting back to the boardinghouse."

"Wouldn't it be better if—," Paige began.

"No." He turned to Viktor, who had remained at the computer desk, watching and listening. "When Osgood and I leave, you lock the door and don't let anyone in until we get back. *Anyone.* And if anything comes in that can't be stopped by a locked door, all three of you get out and holler for help. You understand?"

"What about Professor Roash?" Viktor asked. "Should I open the cell door if we have to escape?"

If something was coming for Roash, Viktor couldn't do anything to stop it. "If there is trouble and you three need to leave, sounding the alarm is the best way to protect Roash."

"If Ilya is with you, who's going to answer?" Viktor asked, sounding like a scared young cop who had been left to guard the station and the civilians inside. Which, essentially, was what he was.

"Someone will answer," Grimshaw replied. He just wasn't sure who it would be.

CHAPTER 71

Earthday, Novembros 4

Did she track by scent or some special sense? He didn't know, but he followed her down the lane that ran between the backs of business buildings with their parking lots on one side and resident garages on the other. He followed her, except . . .

It was daylight, and daylight meant he was easily seen. He didn't like being seen. He didn't like seeing how others reacted to what he was now. So much easier to hide in the dark.

But she had followed the tracks of an enemy to this place, so he was here too.

She studied the back of a building. A wide strip of grass separated the parking lot of that building from its neighboring lot. The next lot was behind a chest-high wooden fence.

<Foulness inside,> she said. <Wrongness.> Her hand brushed against his arm, the merest touch. <Stay here.>

She moved away, not toward the building with the foulness but toward the lot that had the wooden fence.

He lost sight of her. His brain . . . blinked . . . and for a moment he panicked, not sure where he was—or why.

Then he heard quiet footsteps, saw men coming up the lane. Saw them step into the parking lot behind the building with the wrongness.

And he recognized one of them. Remembered one of them.

It was daylight. He would be seen, maybe captured. And yet . . .

Had to give a warning. Because he remembered one of them, he had to give a warning.

CHAPTER 72

Ilya

Earthday, Novembros 4

Ilya got out of the black luxury sedan and looked across the street. A Closed sign on Lettuce Reed's door.

"Looks like you're not the only one Grimshaw called," Boris said.

Ilya resisted looking at the windows of the bookstore's second story. The drapes were closed, as they always were, but even a look at a place that was supposed to be empty might give Boris a reason to ask questions.

"Go into the bookstore," Ilya said. "You'll be able to see this part of Main Street from the windows without being in the open."

"That leaves the car vulnerable to sabotage," Boris protested.

Ilya looked at his friend. "The car can be replaced. Besides," he continued after a moment, "you would see anyone who got near the vehicle and did something that looked sneaky."

Humans glanced at the two Sanguinati and hurried past. A few women offered a smile aimed more at Boris than at him.

"Be careful," Boris said quietly.

Ilya smiled. "Worried about me?"

"I don't want to be the one who has to explain to Natasha that you acted like a human and did something stupid."

Picturing Natasha's reaction all too easily, Ilya nodded and went inside the police station.

"Possible situation," Grimshaw said as soon as Ilya walked into the station. "I don't like having you and Julian come with me and Osgood, but considering the viciousness of the kills that have occurred around here, I need your experience and skills."

The last part of that speech seemed aimed more at Julian Farrow than at him—although *he* was the most dangerous predator among them and his skills might be needed.

"There is a lane that runs behind all the buildings on this side of Main Street," Grimshaw continued. "We'll go that way and approach the flea market building from the back. Paige and Dominique confirmed that there wasn't much out front beyond a couple of long folding tables piled with a dubious selection of goods—some of which were probably stolen. So anything of value would be in the back, and I don't want to give one of them time to destroy it if we walk in the front door."

Grimshaw looked at Viktor, then walked over to the front door and locked it. "Remember what I said. You lock the back door behind us and keep it locked. No heroics. That goes for all three of you. Your job is to stay safe and stay alive. Got it?"

"Yes, sir," Viktor replied.

Paige and Dominique nodded.

"Where is Karol?" Ilya asked.

"I flipped the Closed sign on the door and told Karol to stay there and lock up behind me," Julian replied.

<Boris?> Ilya said. <Is Karol in the bookstore with you?>

<No.>

Not the answer he wanted, but it was the answer he'd half expected.

<Karol?> he called. <Karol!>

No answer, which wasn't surprising since the youth wasn't where he was supposed to be. Viktor would follow orders, but Karol had some driving need that made him act rashly sometimes. Unfortunately, Ilya didn't have time to round up a foolish youth—which was fortunate for Karol.

Grimshaw led, striding down the parking area that was used by employees in the government building, until he reached the lane. Young trees grew on either side of the lane. The side opposite the businesses was mostly garages with short driveways that belonged to houses that must have faced the next street. That meant there were very few people who would have a view of whatever went on behind Sproing's primary business area.

They fanned out, Grimshaw and Osgood taking the lead until Julian Farrow let out a low, quick whistle. Grimshaw signaled Osgood to fall back, and Julian took the lead alongside Grimshaw as they reached the paved area behind the flea market.

Ilya stayed alert, ready to shift to his smoke form in an instant. An instant could be an instant too late, but he wouldn't be able to communicate with the other males if he wasn't in human form.

Trees on either side of the entrance to the paved area. Grimshaw darted behind one while Julian took up position behind the other.

And they waited. Ilya wasn't sure what they waited for, but they waited. Then Julian breathed in and out—and shook his head.

Grimshaw looked at Ilya and Osgood and said quietly, "Julian isn't sensing anything yet, so he and I are moving closer. Wait until we're halfway to the building before you move forward."

Grimshaw and Julian drew their weapons and moved forward quickly. Quietly.

They were halfway to the building and Ilya had taken the first step to follow them when he caught a movement near the edge of the pavement. Out of the corner of his eye, he saw Grimshaw turn and raise his service weapon. He saw Julian maintain watch on the building. And he saw . . .

<Karol! Get away from here!> Anger flooded him.

<I want to help. I *can* help.> Defiance.

A sharp look from Grimshaw, aimed at Osgood. Osgood nodded and turned his attention to the young Sanguinati.

Ilya moved closer to Julian and Grimshaw, angling his body to keep an eye on Karol.

"I wasn't sure when we were farther away," Julian whispered, "but something's wrong with this place. It feels wrong."

<What are you waiting for?> Karol asked. <I can see one of the windows is broken in the corner. I could slip inside that hole in the glass and take a look around.>

<No,> Ilya said sharply. He'd been thinking of doing the same thing

himself, but the way Grimshaw and Julian held themselves, the way they watched the building, had stopped him. Cops. Warriors who had survived situations in their youth by depending on Julian's instincts about the feel of a place.

Julian took one more step forward—and stopped. Shook his head. This time the movement was decisively negative.

Grimshaw took one step back, always watching the building.

If they all stood there much longer, wouldn't someone in the building see them?

Ilya moved closer to the two men and . . .

Rattle, rattle, rattle.

The men froze. Ilya shifted to smoke, leaving his arms, chest, and head in human form as he turned toward the sound and saw . . .

The cape made of black feathers. The hollowed gourd filled with bones. A malformed body with a head that still looked misshapen despite what the Sanguinati bodywalker had been able to mend.

Couldn't be. *Couldn't be.* Nicolai Sanguinati had been on his way to Lakeside when he'd slipped away from his handlers and disappeared. What was he doing in *Sproing*? And what was he doing wearing . . . <Nicolai?>

Before anyone had time to ask a question, they heard a shrill scream.

"Help me! Ilya! Help me!"

Kira? She was supposed to be with Victoria.

"Something's wrong," Julian said, not bothering to lower his voice.

Ilya surged forward, then snarled when Julian grabbed one of his arms. Before he could lash out at the man or shift to smoke completely . . .

Rattle, rattle, rattle. Louder. More insistent. Perhaps the only warning Nicolai could give.

Ilya hesitated.

"Help me! Ilya! Help me!"

"I'll save her!" Karol shouted, shifting to smoke and racing to the building and through the hole in the broken window.

"No!" Grimshaw shouted.

One hand still gripping Ilya's arm, Julian rammed into Grimshaw, sending the three of them to the ground a moment before the building exploded.

CHAPTER 73

Grimshaw

Earthday, Novembros 4

Grimshaw gave himself a moment to catch his breath and take stock, decided a visit to Doc Wallace was needed but could wait, and rolled away from Julian and Ilya before trying to stand up.

Ilya was on his feet—if you could say that about someone who was mostly a column of smoke. The grief was expected. So was the rage. But Grimshaw didn't think the Sanguinati leader had taken it all in yet.

Checking that the safety was still on, he holstered his service weapon before holding out a hand to Julian, who seemed to need help getting to his feet.

"I could have saved him," Ilya snarled at Julian.

"No," Julian replied. "As soon as Karol entered that building, you couldn't save him. You weren't meant to save anyone."

"Chief!" Osgood shouted as he ran toward them. "Chief, are you . . . ? Gods, you're bleeding!"

Grimshaw checked his hands, relieved that he hadn't ripped them up when he fell. Then he looked down and saw the right pant leg turning wet and red around the knee. "It'll keep." But not for long. That much blood meant it wasn't a minor scrape.

Sirens. Volunteer Fire Department and EMTs responding.

"Osgood, get around to Main Street and stop anyone from going into that building. And call the utilities. We have to get those shut off ASAP." Grimshaw turned to Ilya, who was pointedly not looking at his knee—or the rhythmic gush of blood that the trousers couldn't hide. "Would it be safe for someone like Air or Earth to check out that building? Could they be harmed if there is another explosion?"

"It will take too long for Officer Osgood to get back to Main Street," Ilya said. "I've contacted Boris. He will convey your order to stay out of the building while Officer Osgood makes the telephone calls. I will ask the Elementals if any of them are willing to assist."

Grimshaw nodded. "Thank you."

Multiple screams followed by an anguished cry that turned into a terrified caw.

A swath of grass divided the paved lot where they stood from the lot next door, but a chest-high wooden fence formed the boundary for the lot beyond that. The screams and cry had come from behind that fence.

Ignoring his knee since he hadn't lost any mobility—at least none that he felt at the moment—Grimshaw ran to the lane and turned left, sensing Osgood and Julian behind him. He wasn't sure where Ilya was until the Sanguinati shouted, "Here!"

He ran into the parking area of another supposedly reclaimed store a couple of doors away from the explosion and stumbled to a halt.

Gods above and below.

He recognized the faces. They were three of the boys who had come to The Jumble on Trickster Night. They were the boys Paige and Dominique had told him were in the flea market storefront just minutes ago.

Maybe all of them had snuck out of the store minutes after the Xaviers came to the station and had waited in that other parking area for him to come over and check out the store. But he didn't think so. Because of the fence, the boys couldn't have seen the area behind their store any better than he could have seen them. Not without being visible. At least one of them would have needed to know who had taken the bait before bolting out of the store just ahead of the explosion and then hiding with his friends to watch the success of their plan.

But something else had been hiding behind that fence. Waiting.

Between their screams and his running down the lane to reach them . . .

Something incredibly strong and incredibly fast had done this—as fast as the kill on Trickster Night at The Jumble. All three teenage boys were gutted, their torsos hollowed out. And the Crow . . . The lower legs and feet were almost human size but looked like a Crow—and they had been severed and dropped on the pile of organs that had been scooped out of the human bodies.

"They're each missing a finger," Ilya said. "Including the Crow."

Grimshaw wasn't sure if the Sanguinati's eerie calm indicated genuine control or shock. He knew what he'd call it if Ilya were human.

"Air doesn't think there is another exploding device," Ilya reported. "But she doesn't know what such a thing would look like if it's mixed with the debris. She thinks it is safe in a dangerous way for humans to enter the building."

"In other words, there aren't more bombs, but the building could collapse," Grimshaw said.

Ilya nodded. "Air informed Boris, and he has conveyed that information to Officer Osgood and the emergency people." He looked pointedly at the ground near Grimshaw's feet. "You need to see the human bodywalker."

Grimshaw looked down and watched blood drip from his pant leg onto the ground.

Crap.

The adrenaline rush faded, leaving him shaky and cold. He couldn't afford to go down. For one thing, Osgood didn't have enough experience to handle all of this alone. For another, he wasn't putting the rookie in the position of facing off with whatever had killed those three teens and the Crow.

"I'd better see Doc Wallace." Grimshaw looked at Julian. "You should too." He focused on Ilya. "And you should get checked out by whoever looks after your people."

Ilya nodded, then said, "Air wants your people to know that there are two bodies in the wreckage. Only one is Sanguinati."

*   *   *

Do yourself and whoever does your laundry a favor and stay off that leg until those gouges in your knee have a chance to start clotting. Otherwise you'll be walking around the village looking like a horror movie extra.

Doc Wallace hadn't minced words when he'd arrived at the station with his medical bag. He'd been efficient about cleaning out the wounds, muttering that, considering the impact of knee on pavement, Grimshaw was lucky that no bones were broken and nothing inside the knee was torn. As Doc put away his supplies, he said he'd be back in a couple of hours to replace the bandages since they would need replacing by then—a not-so-subtle message that Grimshaw shouldn't shrug off the injury just because it looked small and dealing with it would be inconvenient.

Julian was banged up and had inflamed tendons or some such thing and should use cold packs on his shoulders. Doc recommended taking it easy but said it was okay for Julian to open the bookstore.

Ilya and Boris had retreated to the Sanguinati office above the police station after checking on Viktor, who asked to remain at the station and help out.

Paige and Dominique returned to the boardinghouse, shaken.

As Grimshaw drank coffee and waited for the over-the-counter painkiller to kick in, he thought about Sproing and The Jumble and killings that produced a gut-deep fear in him and everyone else who had seen the bodies. If this was the work of Crowbones—and he believed it was—he could understand why even the Elders who were a human's nightmare wouldn't want to tangle with this particular Hunter.

He understood why Aggie and Jozi had freaked when they thought they saw the Crowgard bogeyman on Trickster Night.

But how to reconcile the savagery of the kills with the warning rattle that had stopped them just beyond the blast radius and saved their lives?

And what would Stavros Sanguinati have to say about all of this?

Samuel Kipp walked into the station, gave Grimshaw a sour look, then settled in the visitor's chair.

"By all the dark gods, you're making my team earn their pay," Kipp growled.

"I wish it wasn't necessary," Grimshaw replied. The past couple of days were catching up to him and he suspected he'd lost more blood than he wanted to admit. And he hadn't needed Doc to point out that not moving his right knee meant not driving—and that was a damn inconvenience right now. "Want some coffee?"

Kipp shook his head. "We got coffee and sandwiches from the diner. Told them to put the bill on the station's tab."

"Good."

Kipp rubbed at a spot on his pant leg. Grimshaw waited.

"The body at the Mill Creek Cabins. You guessed right about Edward Janse being killed by a human. Big hunting knife from the looks of it, and maybe more than one killer, but the ME will have to say officially. We saw a bit of that kind of crazy last year in Bristol when human males in their late teens or early twenties were using gone over wolf. You need that kind of pumped-up aggression to be that savage when you're killing another person. As for the other kills . . ." Kipp scrubbed a hand over his face. "I'd guess sickle or a scythe blade combined with a short handle. Probably the scythe, going by the look of the wounds. This is one pissed-off *terra indigene*, but why use a human tool? Why not use fangs or claws?"

"Not how this particular Elder operates," Grimshaw replied.

"You sure it's an Elder?"

"Pretty sure."

"Then you're in deep shit."

"Yeah, I know. What about the bodies found in the building?"

"The Sanguinati boy . . ." Kipp shook his head. "He must have been shifting back to human form when he got caught in the blast. We gathered what we could recognize. I handled that part personally. Figured that was another case of making sure the team doesn't know more than it's safe for them to know. An ME would have to confirm, but that other body didn't die in the blast."

"Dead before? That makes sense. Paige and Dominique Xavier commented on the store smelling like something had died in it."

"Dead before," Kipp agreed. "Killed by a hatchet embedded in his head. He looks to be the right age to be your missing teen. I think I should take this teen, along with Edward Janse's body, back to Bristol for a full autopsy. Maybe something will be found that will help you identify who provided the provocation behind all these killings."

Grimshaw felt relieved that Kipp had phrased it that way—especially when there was no way of knowing if an Elemental was listening in. "Be sure to have them tested for drugs, especially Edward Janse."

"Will do." Kipp pushed out of the chair. "We're about done here, and my men would like to go home—*if* we can get home." He paused before adding, "Try not to get blown up. You're the ringmaster trying to control a circus of crazy, and the humans in this village would have a much harder time if you weren't here."

"I'm not the only ringmaster," Grimshaw said.

"That's true—you're not. But you and Ilya Sanguinati were both out there today, and I don't know if it's sunk in yet just how close you were to getting caught by the blast."

"It's sunk in." A lot of things were sinking in. "Thanks for the help."

"Stop the killing, Wayne. Stop it while there is still a chance that people like you and me *can* stop it."

"I'll do my best. Let me know if you have trouble getting back to Bristol. If you're stuck, I'll talk to Vicki DeVine about having you and your team stay at The Jumble. She's full up with guests, but . . ."

"Sleeping bags and travel kits are standard equipment these days when we get a call from Lake Silence." Kipp gave Grimshaw a half wave and walked out.

It wasn't until Grimshaw got up to relieve himself that he realized he hadn't seen Viktor in a while.

He called Ineke Xavier and emphasized that Paige and Dominique weren't to blame for the explosion. If they hadn't come in to tell him about that flea market, which he was sure was a front for something else, someone else would have. Or he would have received an anonymous tip that would have brought him and Ilya to that store to investigate. It was a trap, and nothing that happened was the Xavier women's fault.

He called Vicki DeVine to get a tally on her guests and helpers.

He called Captain Hargreaves to give the Bristol captain a rundown of what was happening—and to confirm that Kipp and the CIU team were still in one piece.

Then he called Stavros Sanguinati to confirm they would be meeting tonight.

By the time he ended that call, Viktor had returned to the front room of the station and sat on the chair at the computer desk.

"You okay?" Grimshaw asked. The boy wasn't okay, but he was alive and unhurt, and that was a place to start.

"You told us the teaching story about what can happen when young police don't follow orders," Viktor said. "You *told* us, and Julian told Karol to stay in the bookstore. Why didn't he stay?"

That was one of the questions he wanted answered, but not by this youngster.

"And Kira . . ."

"Is fine. She's fine, Viktor. She's at The Jumble with Vicki."

"But someone said she was in that building, calling for help."

"A recording," Grimshaw said. "Bait for a trap. Not the real girl." He waited a moment for that to sink in. "Who told you Kira was in the building? Another *terra indigene* using that silent communication you all can do?"

Viktor shook his head and pointed to the phone on Grimshaw's desk. "Phone call. Male voice. Didn't recognize it, but I wouldn't recognize human voices but yours, Officer Osgood's, and Julian Farrow's." He paused. "And Miss Vicki's, of course, but the voice was definitely male."

Just because Viktor hadn't recognized the voice didn't mean he hadn't *heard* the voice before. Which didn't eliminate any of Vicki's guests or the remaining professor staying at the Mill Creek Cabins. "What did you say in response to that information?"

"I said I would give you the message, that I was manning the phones and couldn't leave the station. But he kept insisting that I had to help Kira. He sounded . . . distraught. When *I* insisted that I couldn't leave, he hung up."

"Anything else? Did you hear any sounds in the background? Cars going by, or music playing, people talking?" He waited a beat. "Bobcat singing?"

"Caterwauling, you mean?"

Grimshaw smiled at the boy's effort to make a joke. "Yeah, that."

Viktor shook his head. "I told Paige and Dominique what the man said and was about to contact Ilya—I figured it would be faster and you might turn off your mobile phone so you wouldn't give away your location—when Paige saw Karol run out of the bookstore and head in the direction of the flea market building. So I contacted Karol instead, told him we were supposed to stay put. He said Kira was in trouble and needed him to save her, and he knew where she was."

"Do you think there was enough time in between your hanging up and Karol running out for him to receive a similar call? Something that might have provoked him into acting?"

"Maybe. I'm not sure."

If whoever had made those calls wanted a Sanguinati in that building at the time of the explosion, would the second call have been made if the first call had produced the desired response? He'd had the impression that Karol was the more impulsive of the two males. Would the boy have hesitated, thought things through long enough for the person to make another call and try to lure Viktor to the scene? Why involve either boy? The cry for help was aimed at Ilya, by name.

The timing was off in Viktor's account of what had happened. If Karol had left the bookstore when he and Ilya and the other two men had been in the lane moving toward the storefront, why hadn't he been in the store when Boris entered? Why was Paige the only one to see Karol when Boris had been watching the street by then? Of course, he had only Viktor's word that Paige had seen anything.

Had there been a phone call to the station? Or had luring Karol into that building been part of someone's plan all along?

He put those questions aside for a time when a predator wasn't paying close attention to his heartbeat and breathing.

"Did Karol have . . . romantic . . . feelings for Kira?" That would explain some of the hasty decision to rush in, regardless of when the phone call had been made. Would Ilya have allowed himself to be delayed by the human caution of a police officer and Julian's Intuit gift if Natasha's voice was on the recording?

What was the difference between Natasha and Kira? Age? Access? Location? Even if she'd been in serious danger, he couldn't see Natasha making that damsel-in-distress cry for help, and maybe that had been the deciding factor. Had someone convinced Kira to make that recording as another prank? If that was the case, who had done it—and when?

"We don't have those kinds of feelings for one of our own until we're mature enough to be a mate," Viktor said.

He doubted that. "It's my understanding that adult Sanguinati are very good at kissing, so you all must practice with someone," he said, making sure his voice conveyed that he was teasing.

Viktor eyed him warily. "You should talk to Ilya about that."

"Fair enough."

"Should I check e-mails now?"

"Sure. Do that." Grimshaw knew it was an excuse to retreat from the conversation. That was fine with him. He was going to have to listen to plenty of people before the day ended.

CHAPTER 74

Ilya

Earthday, Novembros 4

Ilya arrived early for this secret meeting between humans and Sanguinati, slipping through the narrow space at the bottom of the outside door before flowing up the stairs to the unoccupied apartment above Lettuce Reed. Once inside the main room, he shifted from smoke to his human form.

"I know you're here," he snarled. At this time of night, the heavy drapes Julian Farrow had over all the windows kept out every sliver of outside light—and made sure that no one outside would notice lamplight and wonder who might be up there above the bookstore and what they might be doing.

He didn't think Farrow intended it as a bolt-hole. The human would have a better chance of escaping an enemy if he stayed on the ground floor of the building. But the couple of times Ilya had come up here to look around when Farrow was occupied elsewhere, he'd had the impression of a fiercely private place, as full of lies as secrets.

Julian Farrow wasn't a fool, which was why Ilya had made it easy for him to purchase the bookstore in return for being the Sanguinati's informant.

The quiet click of a lamp being turned on. Then Stavros Sanguinati stepped from behind the reading chair in one corner of the room.

"You knew." Ilya spit the words. "You knew and didn't tell me?"

"I told you why Grandfather Erebus sent me here," Stavros replied.

"Not about that. About Nicolai being here."

He saw the surprise on Stavros's face.

"Nicolai is *here*?" Stavros stared at him. "Are you sure?"

"I saw him." Ilya smiled bitterly. "He was wearing a cape made of black feathers and carried a hollow gourd full of bones. The warning rattle made us hesitate when Grimshaw, Farrow, and I went to investigate that flea market storefront. Probably saved us from being caught in the explosion." He tried to push down the anger—and the feeling of betrayal—he felt for Erebus Sanguinati, who was the leader of the Sanguinati throughout the continent of Thaisia, and for the problem solver standing in front of him. "Nicolai has taken on the mantle of this Crowbones, hunting here, *killing* here, and *you didn't tell me!*"

"He isn't Crowbones," Stavros snapped. "He isn't the Hunter, and he wasn't supposed to be here. When Tolya acknowledged that Nicolai would never fully recover from the injuries he received during the fight to hold on to Bennett, he told Grandfather that the shadow of Sanguinati in that town was too small and too exposed to properly take care of someone that damaged. Nicolai was supposed to be taken to Lakeside, but he slipped away from the Sanguinati who were sent to escort him to the Courtyard there. He just . . . disappeared. This is the first sighting any of us have had."

The anger drained out of Ilya as he absorbed Stavros's relief—and remembered that Stavros and Nicolai had lived in the Toland Courtyard for many years as friends and comrades before the *terra indigene* abandoned that city just ahead of the Elementals' and Elders' wrath and destruction.

"Did he know you were sending him to Lakeside?" Ilya asked.

Stavros nodded. "He enjoyed the stories about Broomstick Girl. More so after he was injured. Grandfather thought being in the same Courtyard might help him mentally. Emotionally. But . . . Tolya thinks Nicolai may have been shown a vision drawing done by Hope Wolfsong and that's why he slipped away from his escorts. There's no proof, and Tolya said his source of information, an Intuit woman who had seen the drawing, insisted that she didn't recognize the woman in the drawing and can't guess where the woman is located. But she said the woman in the drawing had curly brown hair and was holding a book."

Ilya released a long breath. "Victoria is The Jumble's Reader." Was Nicolai here to find Victoria—or harm Victoria?

"Another human whose stories are entertainment and lesson," Stavros said. "I don't think your Victoria's adventures have traveled as far west as the stories about Broomstick Girl, but they have reached Lakeside, Talulah Falls, and Great Island. She sounds . . . interesting. Definitely not a run-of-the-mill human."

"She is an unintentional trouble magnet," Ilya replied. "But the Elders and Elementals are curious enough about her to interact with her and a few other humans, so Victoria is a vital link between the human village and the *terra indigene* settlement."

The two Sanguinati studied each other.

Finally Stavros asked, "How vital?"

CHAPTER 75

Grimshaw

Earthday, Novembros 4

Grimshaw opened the map that had the colored dots indicating the possible attacks by Crowbones, based on police reports of humans savagely killed who had a couple of small bones removed and had the signature crow's feet attached to some part of what remained. Some police stations had also mentioned Crowgard dying in the same area—and how several times it looked like they had been killed by other Crows.

"Perhaps these . . . collisions . . . between Crowgard and humans is an experiment," Ilya said. "Like that professor having a student dress up like Crowbones so that he could observe Aggie, Jozi, and Eddie's reaction."

"Maybe it's an experiment," Julian said, "but I would lean toward brainwashing—and the use of mind-altering drugs as a way to reward and control. Look at the police reports. Most of the humans who were victims of Crowbones's alleged attacks and were somehow connected with Crowgard being killed were in their late teens and male. An ideal age for this kind of work if you know how to manipulate someone."

Crap. Grimshaw had hoped nobody else had been thinking along those lines. Especially because the Crowgard weren't the only form of *terra indigene* who routinely brushed against humans.

He didn't like the way Ilya and Stavros stared at him and Julian now that Julian had brought up a possibility that could trigger another purge of humans if a human was behind the killing of *terra indigene*.

"You're not fools," Julian said. "You must have considered it. But things spun out of human control when the Elders and Elementals closed off any way to escape Lake Silence and Sproing after the first killing—spun out of control enough to have the Sanguinati's problem solver show up, in secret, to help hunt down whoever is responsible."

"How were the Sanguinati youngsters chosen for this opportunity to interact with humans—or at least a select handful of humans?" Grimshaw asked. "I imagine there were plenty of youngsters who might like the adventure. Did you pull names from a hat? Or was there something about at least some of them that made the Sanguinati uneasy, that made you all want to observe these youngsters in a different, more contained setting?"

"Or get them away from a bad influence?" Julian suggested.

"Take Lara out of the mix," Grimshaw said. "She's a kid and doesn't fit the profile. I think having Lara stay with a different . . . shadow? . . . and exposing her to Vicki and The Jumble's residents is like sending a human child to a summer camp experience of working on a farm, for example. It's an adventure and a chance to meet different individuals. Select individuals."

"The profile of what?" Ilya asked in a voice that held a cold warning.

Grimshaw ignored the question and the warning since he was certain that Ilya Sanguinati, canny attorney and leader of Silence Lodge, knew perfectly well what he meant. "The boy who dressed up as Crowbones. The boys who blew up the store, intending to kill some of us. The two Crows who were connected with those human boys. Three of the Sanguinati fosterlings. Humans, Crows, Sanguinati. I think what they all have in common is that they're teenagers."

Stavros nodded. "And adolescents that age are more vulnerable to influence."

"And peer pressure," Grimshaw said. He looked at Ilya. "And wanting to impress someone."

"That's true of humans at that age," Julian said. "Maybe someone is trying to find out if that's true of other species. Maybe someone is conducting experiments to manipulate behavior."

Ilya brushed his fingers lightly over the dots on the map and said quietly, "If that's true, then The Jumble wasn't the first place where those experiments were conducted."

Stavros added just as quietly, "But it will be the last."

CHAPTER 76

Vicki

Moonsday, Novembros 5

I was at my desk, busily organizing the bills to be paid so that I could tell myself I'd done something toward paying them without actually doing anything that required too many brain cells. After putting the bills in the Bills to Pay folder, I was debating if I should organize my one sheet of postage stamps when I was saved from that intellectual gymnastic by the phone ringing.

"Good morning. The Jumble. Vicki speaking."

"This is Meg."

I couldn't tell if the woman was usually quiet or trying not to be overheard. "Meg?" Something about the name made my stomach flutter. Who did I know named Meg?

"From the Lakeside Courtyard."

Oh golly. *Now* I knew why I knew that name.

"There isn't much time," Meg said. "You have to listen and write it down."

Oh gosh golly. "Did you see something in your prophecy cards?" She was the one who read cards, wasn't she?

"The cards said I need to do this. I won't remember what I've said, so you have to listen and write it down."

Gosh golly with whiskers. I grabbed a pad of paper and a pen, took a deep breath, and said, "I'm ready."

Ready? Really? Not a chance.

I heard her let out a shuddering breath, and then she spoke. Her voice changed, sounded dreamy, like some part of her wasn't really there anymore, was someplace else.

Word images. Phrases. I could feel her effort to tell me something vital in the only way she could.

Then she made a sound I could imagine a woman made after a very intense orgasm.

"Meg?" I asked, unsure what I should do now.

"Meg!" The word was a roar, a snarl, a violence of sound that made me bobble the phone. Then that voice was right in my ear, saying, *"Who is this?"*

Couldn't let him find me. Couldn't let him know . . .

My stomach got that awful foamy-milk feeling, and I knew I was about to have a full-blown panic attack and throw up. I dropped the receiver back in the cradle, shaking so hard I was close to having convulsions. Bad panic attack starting. Bad, bad, bad. Had to get over it, had to tell someone that Meg needed help, needed to be rescued from that roaring, snarling voice.

COPS. FANGS. BETRAYAL.

PROBLEM SOLVER. ALLY.

FEATHERS AND BONES.

A NO SIGN OVER PITY.

LAKESIDE. PEACE.

I pushed myself to my feet and stared at the words written on the paper—and realized that, because of the first warning, I didn't know who I could trust with this information if I couldn't tell a cop or someone with fangs. Had to think. Had to throw up first—and get to a toilet really fast before I inconvenienced everyone—then had to think.

I saw the last line of the prophecy or vision or message or whatever this was.

RUBBINGS. PENCIL ON PAPER, REVEALING SECRETS.

I remembered a cop in a show lightly rubbing the side of a pencil over what looked like a blank sheet of paper, revealing an address that was an important clue. I looked at the pad of paper in front of me.

I tore off the top sheet of paper, folded it, and stuffed it in my pocket. Then I tore off several more sheets and shoved those in the Bills to Pay folder, which I put back in the drawer with the other hanging files. Then I wrote a list, pressing a little harder on the paper than I usually did.

Peanut butter. Jelly. Crackers. Cheese. Milk.

I tore off that page, left the pad on the desk, and was about to drop the pen into the cup that served as a holder for writing implements when I thought of one more thing.

On the back of the next piece of paper on the pad—a piece that carried a faint impression of words—I made a small mark in one corner.

Then I dropped the pen and ran for the downstairs powder room, reaching it moments before my stomach gave its last blurp of warning and I donated my breakfast to the porcelain bowl.

An hour later, after a meal of ginger ale and crackers—and not answering questions lobbed at me by Julian, Grimshaw, and Ilya because Michael Stern had called Julian and blabbed about seeing me run to the powder room, obviously ill, and each male had called to find out *why*—I returned to my office.

Hoping that I was alone, I took the prophecy message out of my pocket and stared at the words, trying to make sense of them.

A no sign over pity. What did that mean? The only sign I could think of that meant "no" was a circle with a diagonal line through the center. On the pad of paper, I wrote the word "pity," then around it drew a circle with a diagonal line through it.

Oh. No pity.

I was sure that Meg from Lakeside had done more than read a few cards in order to tell me these things, so I couldn't dismiss a single word even if I didn't understand most of what she'd said. Maybe I just needed to remember so that I *would* understand at the right time.

I read the last line. RUBBINGS. PENCIL ON PAPER, REVEALING SECRETS. Then I studied my desk and the pad of paper.

Nothing looked like it had been touched. But someone had been in my office, because the piece of paper that had the slight impression of my shopping list on the front and the mark on the back was gone.

CHAPTER 77

Julian

Moonsday, Novembros 5

With Grimshaw in the passenger seat and both of them in need of coffee and breakfast, Julian drove away from the Mill Creek Cabins and Richard Cardosa, the remaining academic, who looked more like a sheep penned for slaughter than an educated man.

Considering everything that had happened lately, it wasn't a harsh comparison.

When he reached the intersection that would take him to The Jumble if he turned right or Sproing if he kept going straight, Julian pulled onto the shoulder of the road and put the car in park.

"You forget something?" Grimshaw asked.

"No."

"You want to check on Vicki before driving me to the station?"

He did, but he wasn't sure it would do any good. After Michael's call to tell him something had produced a reaction in Vicki that was violent enough to make her ill, he'd called and tried to talk to her, but all she'd given him were evasions and nonsense. He'd thought they were getting closer. Now he wasn't sure.

The back door opened. Ilya slid in, closed the door, and looked at both of them. "Victoria was not forthcoming about the cause of her distress."

"Yeah, we got put off too," Grimshaw said.

"However, she called Natasha, asking her to tell me to call the Lakeside Courtyard."

Julian twisted in his seat in order to see Ilya better. So did Grimshaw.

"I spoke to Vlad," Ilya continued. "Apparently, Meg Corbyn called Victoria just before the blood prophet made a cut. Only Victoria knows the words of prophecy that were spoken."

"And whatever was said is the reason Vicki wouldn't say anything to any of us?" Grimshaw asked. "Because there was something in the prophecy about us?"

Ilya ignored the question. "Apparently Simon Wolfgard's reaction to finding Meg is the reason for Victoria's panic attack."

"I can imagine how he'd react," Julian said softly. He could easily imagine how Vicki had reacted to that male anger and distress if any of it was directed at her, even over the phone.

Ilya hesitated, then seemed to gather himself. "Nicolai Sanguinati is here."

Grimshaw frowned. "You have a friend staying at Silence Lodge?"

"Not exactly. Nicolai was living in Bennett, a town near the Elder Hills, and was supposed to go to Lakeside. He ended up here. There is some speculation that he was directed here by a vision drawing."

"Crap."

Meg Corbyn was using cards for prophecy, at least most of the time. That meant . . . "Another blood prophet aimed this Nicolai toward Lake Silence?" Julian asked.

"Yes," Ilya said. "A girl whose visions are quite accurate, regardless of how she reveals them."

"Gods above and below," Grimshaw muttered. "What is going on?"

"I don't know." Ilya opened the back door and stepped out. "But we need some answers soon."

Yeah, they did need that.

When Julian and Grimshaw were once more heading for Sproing, Grimshaw said, "Did you notice how our Sanguinati friend didn't confirm or deny that we were mentioned in that prophecy?"

"I noticed." For him the real question was this: Was Vicki's evasion about the prophecy because she was afraid *of* the men she had called friends a day ago, or was she afraid *for* them?

CHAPTER 78

Grimshaw

Moonsday, Novembros 5

B rainwashing," Grimshaw said, thinking things through while Julian drove to Sproing.

"What if Civil and Serious Crowgard were playing mind games with Clara Crowgard, claiming that they wanted to recruit her for their cause but needed to be sure of her loyalty before they told her anything of significance?" Julian said in turn. "Based on what Aggie, Jozi, and Eddie told us, Civil and Serious were isolating Clara from her friends, making it sound like working for Vicki was a bad thing while *they* were, in fact, working with a human—or at least having conversations with one or more humans. Except things started to go wrong, and either Civil or Serious was killed on Trickster Night, and the Crow's feet ended up tied to Adam Fewks's rib cage, connecting those two deaths."

"And then the Others barricaded the roads, and we've been assuming that whoever is behind all this is trapped in the area."

"Safe assumption." Julian seemed to be debating with himself. "I've been wondering if the Others would have reacted as fast if Adam Fewks had knocked on the door of Xavier's boardinghouse instead of showing up at The Jumble. Did someone miscalculate the degree of interest that *terra indigene* like the Elders and Elementals have for Vicki and expect to be dealing with just Crows and Sanguinati because those are the *terra indigene* most in sight these days?"

"Ian Stern is a psychologist—and an Intuit." Grimshaw let the statement hang.

Julian's hands tightened on the steering wheel. "You're thinking he knows how to brainwash people? That he would use his extra sense of people to find their pressure points and make them susceptible to being controlled? Convincing them to murder other humans for some cause or for some fucking science project?"

"Humans murder other humans for all kinds of reasons—including a warped ideology. The Humans First and Last movement proved that much." Grimshaw paused. "You're friends with Ian. You may not see him clearly. Not all Intuits are good people, Julian."

"I would trust Ian Stern with my life. Michael too," Julian snapped.

"Would you trust them with Vicki's life?"

Julian swung into a parking space and braked so hard, Grimshaw was glad to be stopped by the seat belt and not by having his face meet the windshield.

Julian shut off the car and stared at Grimshaw. "I hadn't seen Michael or Ian for several years, but there is nothing about the feel of them that is different, that makes me uneasy being around them."

"Your strength and gift is feeling a place, not individual people," Grimshaw said quietly. "I'm asking you to keep an open mind."

"I suggest you do the same." Julian started the car. "If you don't mind, I need to open my store."

Grimshaw got out. Julian pulled out of the parking space and drove to the small lot behind Lettuce Reed.

Maybe he was too focused on a university degree that implied knowledge about how to control a person. The gods knew there were plenty of people who could manipulate and exploit people without having a degree in psychology. Look at Ellen Wilson. She was a walking vessel of ill will and soured everyone around her to the point that some merchants gave in to her demands just to get her to leave their other customers in peace.

Come to think of it, he didn't know if Mrs. Wilson had a degree of some kind. Something else to check.

"Open mind," he muttered as he walked into the station. Then he stopped just inside the door when he heard the whining pleas coming from the direction of the cell.

Crap! With the explosion and everything else yesterday, he'd forgotten the day had started with him bringing Rodney Roash in to assist the police with their inquiry. Had Osgood stayed at the station, or had they left Roash here alone?

"Help! Is anyone there? Tell her to go away!"

Her?

This morning he couldn't ignore that he'd been on, the edge of an explosion yesterday and his knee was a mess, but he moved as quickly as he could to reach the station's single cell.

The cell door was open. Was that Osgood's decision or that of the female who turned her head and smiled at him before fixing her gaze on Roash again.

Not Air. Had he seen this one at The Jumble the other day?

"Ma'am," he said. "You are . . . ?"

"Water."

That's what he thought.

Grimshaw took a step closer in order to look inside the cell. "Professor Roash? Do you need to use the facilities?"

"Do you promise she'll stay right there?" Roash whimpered.

Water laughed.

"Yes, she'll stay here." Which didn't mean a thing if any of the Elemental's kin were in the building.

Roash eased out of the cell and scampered to the station's bathroom.

Grimshaw took another step closer to the cell, wondering if Osgood was going to have to swab it out. He forgot all about that possibility when he saw the shoes encased in ice.

"Officer Osgood had to respond to a call," Water said. "Winter and I came in to keep watch. The little human was not . . . respectful . . . of females until we provided incentive for him to be polite and stop making noise."

"You formed a block of ice around his shoes."

"This time we gave him the opportunity to take his feet out of the shoes before the ice hardened. The next time we will not—and the ice will cover more than his feet. We explained this to him." Water smiled.

"I appreciate the help, but I can take over now if there's someplace else you need to be," Grimshaw said, but he thought, *Winter and Water, working together. Gods above and below.* He was *not* going to think about Constance Dane. When her husband and his pals tried to take The Jumble away from Vicki, the woman had been choked by a hand made of ice coming out of a bathroom sink.

No, he wasn't going to think about Constance Dane. But he would, if he had to, tell Rodney Roash just how close the man had come to wearing an ice shroud.

"Officer Osgood is bringing food from the diner on his way back from his task," Water said. "He'll return soon."

"Ma'am." Grimshaw stepped out of the way.

The bathroom door opened. Roash stuck his head out, spotted Water, then ducked back inside.

Not the best choice of rooms to hide in if Water was annoyed with you.

Grimshaw didn't actually see her leave. As she moved past him, she just wasn't there anymore.

He hoped that was true.

He coaxed Roash out of the bathroom, located a couple of ratty towels he and Osgood used to wipe their shoes if they'd been out in the wet or in mud, and gave them to Roash to put under the shoes so his socks wouldn't get wet when the shoes started to thaw.

Osgood returned, looking like a man who had slept at his desk. He took a travel mug of coffee and one of Helen Hearse's breakfast specials to Roash, then divided the rest of the food he dug out of the delivery box.

"Do you need to go back to the boardinghouse for a couple of hours and get some sleep?" Grimshaw asked.

"No, sir. I'm all right."

What else would a rookie say? Then again, Osgood was young enough that it might be true.

"Is Viktor coming in?" Osgood asked after they'd been eating in silence for a couple of minutes.

"Don't know. Yesterday was hard on him, losing a friend that way," Grimshaw replied. "Harder still because he didn't respond to the bait and Karol did." The timing of that was still something he needed to piece together.

Osgood looked up. "Someone tried for both of them?"

He nodded. "And used a recording of Kira calling for help to lure them into the building."

"Huh. If someone was aiming for Viktor, they used the wrong lure."

Grimshaw swallowed his coffee and kept his tone casual. "Viktor doesn't get along with Kira?"

"Oh, they get along fine, but . . ." Osgood took a bite of toast and chewed slowly. "It's like . . . if someone called and said Pops Davies was trapped in a building, I wouldn't forget procedure, wouldn't stop thinking like a cop. Not the way I might if someone told me Paige was trapped in a building. Karol seemed more keen to show his devotion to Kira, and Viktor wasn't interested. That's all." The rookie shrugged and went back to the serious business of eating.

Interesting, Grimshaw thought.

When they'd all finished the meal, Osgood collected the dishes and took them and the delivery box back to Come and Get It.

Accepting that his knee required at least another day to heal before he could pretend it was back to normal, Grimshaw settled in to answer phones and read through the information the mayor's office had provided about Sproing's new residents.

It didn't surprise him that a number of newcomers had lived in other towns in the Finger Lakes area. He made note of anyone who had come to Sproing from any of the places that had killings similar to the ones here.

Then he came across one name. He looked at it for a long time.

Ellen C. Wilson. He hadn't known what the *C* stood for—until now. And until now, he hadn't had any reason to think she had some connection with the academics who had come to Sproing to observe Trickster Night.

Observe? Or do something more?

He looked at the list of Ellen Wilson's previous residences and considered how they tallied with some of the killings in other towns. Nothing in the information compiled by the mayor's office to indicate if she'd ever taken courses at a college, but that didn't mean anything. People were self-taught in any number of subjects, and it would be easy enough to do if a relative actually was enrolled at a college and taking courses that could become the twisted foundation for experimenting with other people's minds.

Was all the whining and complaining and the particular way she pitched her voice simply the woman? Or was it all calculated to achieve a specific result?

Maybe she was behind some of what was happening in and around Sproing, but not all of it. He didn't think she was the one who had persuaded Adam Fewks to put on a costume and pretend to be the Crowgard bogeyman.

But she might have a partner. Or a competitor?

Were all these deaths being tallied on some kind of scorecard?

Grimshaw carefully closed the folder and made sure all the papers inside were aligned so that no one would realize he'd found a possible connection between Ellen C. Wilson and at least one of the academics who had come to Lake Silence for Trickster Night.

Then he went back to the cell and said, "Professor Roash? Tell me again how you ended up coming to The Jumble for Trickster Night."

CHAPTER 79

Vicki

Moonsday, Novembros 5

was going to have to do something about food. Like, buy some, unless I was willing to talk to Bobcat and Cougar about letting my guests share whatever was left of the dead donkey. Which by now might be only a hoof and part of an ear. Since *I* wouldn't be convinced that some butter and strawberry jam would turn those bits into a tasty, or even tolerable, meal, I doubted I could convince anyone else.

I pulled out a jar of peanut butter and a sleeve of crackers. Add a bit of jam to that and you had breakfast. Or lunch. Maybe not dinner since I was feeding adults, but I could tout PB and J as a valid choice for the other two meals—especially if the alternative was donkey bits and butter.

Really needed to drive to Sproing and buy whatever food Pops Davies might have left on the shelves. Or I could ignore token good nutrition and buy pizzas so we could all eat ourselves into a carb coma.

Ian Stern walked into the kitchen, saw me, and hesitated. He looked around, as if making sure we were alone.

My heart began to beat a little harder. I hoped he wouldn't notice, but a psych doctor *would* notice things like that. Wouldn't he? Maybe not. A Sanguinati psych doctor would—if there was such a thing—since *all* Sanguinati noticed little things like heartbeats.

Focus, Vicki.

"How are you feeling today?" Ian asked.

"Okay. Fine. How are you?"

He came closer. And closer. My heart beat harder.

"I'm concerned. You've been nervous since the phone call yesterday that made you ill."

"I'm fine now. All okeydokey." Yep, the phone call had made me nervous. Plus there was that tiny bit of excitement when a couple of my friends almost got blown up, and one of the Sanguinati youngsters *did* get blown up.

He shook his head. "I have a feeling that you're suddenly uncomfortable around all of us, human and *terra indigene*, rather than just wanting to see the backs of some of your guests."

Darn Intuit with a psych degree. "I . . ."

"I think you're right to be uncomfortable," Ian continued. "I don't think it started out that way, but you're now at the center of whatever is going on—and I have the uneasy feeling that someone wants to . . . disrupt . . . the center."

"Is 'disrupt' a fancy way of saying 'kill me'?" I hadn't had enough coffee yet to have this kind of discussion. Not when mulling over breakfast was a challenge.

He seemed about to answer, then looked thoughtful. "Maybe not deliberately, but . . ." Hesitation. "Has there been a drug problem in Sproing? There always seems to be a little of this and that around the colleges, but I wouldn't think the sale and use of substances could stay hidden long in a small village."

"Why are you asking?" Doc Wallace had given me some pills for the times when an anxiety attack couldn't be blunted any other way, but he gave me only a few pills at a time—partly to assure himself that I wouldn't overuse them and partly because the medical practice in Sproing had to order supplies from Bristol or Crystalton pharmacies and shipments arrived when they arrived, so Doc divided the contents of one bottle of pills among the patients who needed them. But Ian wasn't referring to the drugs you got from a doctor, who wrote that information in your medical chart.

"The way Aggie and Kira acted," Ian replied. "Might have been blood loss. Might have been their reaction to a human sedative—or some other kind of drug." He took a breath and let it out slowly, as if our chat had been the buildup toward what he really wanted to say. "I'm worried about Jenna McKay. She's very groggy this morning, slurring her words. Similar to the way Aggie and Kira acted the other day. I actually came up here to see if you had any orange juice left."

Caffeine wakes up a groggy brain. Orange juice is a staple for someone who has lost more blood than you'd lose from a cut on your finger.

"There's some orange juice in the fridge, unless someone already drank it."

Ian opened the fridge and pulled out the bottle. I took a water glass from the cupboard and set it on the table so our hands wouldn't touch, accidentally or on purpose. He filled the glass, put the rest of the juice back in the fridge, and looked at me.

"I remember hearing about some substances that affected the *terra indigene* as much as, if not more than, the humans who used them," Ian said quietly. "There are circumstances when a friend might not be a friend because they've been influenced by something—or someone. If you have a friend who can't be compromised by . . . substances, tell that individual what you know. Just in case you find yourself with a friend who is no longer a friend." He picked up the glass. "Thanks for the juice. I'll take it to Jenna."

He left the kitchen and went out the porch door, taking the path back to the lake cabins.

I thought about all the bits of information casually dropped into conversations over the past several days, things I might have revealed about myself or the Others. I thought about all the things that had happened since Trickster Night. I thought about what Ian Stern was telling me without quite telling me: *Don't trust anyone whose body or behavior might be altered by a drug.*

But there was another way to alter behavior, another way to shape someone until they believed what you wanted them to believe.

Words.

Behavior modification achieved by verbal punishment or praise.

Who would know that better than someone who studied the mind and had a facility with words?

Aggie and Eddie found me in my office when I went in for my purse and car keys. "I'm going to Sproing to pick up some food. I'll be back as soon as I can. The guests will have to cobble together breakfast from what's available or wait until I get back."

"Should you go alone?" Eddie asked.

I couldn't say I didn't want anyone with me because I didn't trust anyone, even the Crows who worked for me, so I said, "Why not?"

"Crowbones," Aggie whispered.

She still didn't look well. "I'll be fine." I had to believe that, so I promised myself I could have a mini anxiety attack when I returned.

I tried to look casual while I checked the back seat and the front seat before getting into the car. Of course, if someone had tampered with it, I'd find out too late, so there was no point in worrying about that.

I drove down the access road. Only the flutter of yellow crime scene tape indicated where Peter Lynchfield had died. I wondered why Conan or Cougar hadn't removed it. Then I wondered if some of the *terra indigene*, especially the ones who were not familiar with written human words, would like the color and take some of the tape to decorate whatever they called home.

I drove until I was in sight of the road. Then I stopped and rolled down a window.

"I have to run some errands in Sproing," I said. "When I get back, I really need to talk to Aiden. Could someone tell him that?" I started to roll up the window, then stopped and added, "Thank you."

I drove to the village without knowing if anyone had heard me—and wondering if anything that had heard me was an ally or enemy.

CHAPTER 80

Aiden

Moonsday, Novembros 5

Aiden watched the remaining human who was staying in the Mill Creek Cabins. More truthfully, he watched the cabin and the little flicks of the curtains as the survivor tried to see what might be out there, too afraid now to even venture out on his porch to look around.

Definitely too afraid to get into one of the metal boxes and go out foraging for food.

Then again, those metal boxes were no protection against Fire.

An odd beat of silence pulled his attention away from the cabins and had him focusing on the surrounding trees. Nothing close to him.

He almost returned his attention to the cabins when that odd beat of silence came again. Closer now. Very close.

If he had been any other form of *terra indigene*—except an Elder—he would have been alarmed by the sudden appearance of a column of smoke. The Sanguinati he had observed had stealth, but this one was a predator of predators.

Aiden waited, curious what the being would do. His own human form wasn't a shape that could be harmed. He was Fire—and even the Sanguinati could burn.

The smoke took a human shape.

"You are not part of the shadow at Silence Lodge," Aiden said.

"I am not," the Sanguinati replied. "I am a problem solver who was sent to deal with the trouble here."

A wisp of smoke drifted away from the bark of the tree Aiden leaned against. He stepped away before the wisp became more and damaged the tree. Then he focused on this intruder. "The Reader . . ."

"Is not a problem," the Sanguinati said smoothly. "But she is the reason I am here, talking to you."

Aiden's focus sharpened. Humans were too alien for him—for any Elemental—to befriend, but that didn't mean the Elementals who resided around Lake Silence didn't feel friendly toward Vicki DeVine. His kind might not need The Jumble to be a thriving *terra indigene* settlement, but they could see how it mattered to the shifters.

Besides, spending time around The Jumble often included assisting the police, and that was quite entertaining.

Fire found nothing entertaining about this problem solver.

"Victoria has gone to Sproing," the Sanguinati said. "When she returns, she needs to talk to you."

"Why were you in The Jumble?" Aiden asked.

"Hunting." The Sanguinati smiled, showing a hint of fang.

The look in those dark eyes made Aiden wonder if he was as invulnerable in this form as he believed.

"A young deer," the Sanguinati added. "I took enough for sustenance but not enough to kill." A pause. "And I am searching for another Sanguinati. A damaged one. I think he is spending time in The Jumble." Another pause. "Have you seen him?"

Oh, he'd seen the damaged one. They had all seen him. "Leave him be."

The words startled the Sanguinati. "We only want to help him."

The words sounded truthful, which was the only reason Aiden decided to give a warning. "For now, leave him be."

They studied each other. Then the Sanguinati nodded.

"If you see him, tell him Stavros is here to help him—and to help the Reader."

He didn't promise to tell anyone anything.

A human form changed to a column of black smoke that moved low to the ground with a speed that no prey animal could outrun—not even prey trying to escape in one of those metal boxes.

Aiden stared at the cabins for a few more minutes, thinking about why a predator of predators would be sent to Lake Silence.

Then he headed for The Jumble to see Vicki.

*F*ire," the first voice sang.

"*Fiiiirrre,*" the second voice sang.

"*Is something going to burn?*" the third and fourth voices sang.

Aiden wasn't surprised by the appearance of the Five. He'd already had Crows and a Coyote come to this spot to see what he was doing and report back to the rest of the *terra indigene* who lived in The Jumble. Seeing Earth, Air, or Water was a reason for mild curiosity since the appearance of an Elemental could mean that something interesting was happening. But Fire on wooded land? The Others didn't come because they were curious; they came to find out if their homes would burn. Not that they said that, exactly. No one *asked* him why he was standing to one side of the access road.

Until now.

"I am waiting for Vicki," Aiden said. "She asked to see me."

Nothing. Not even the rustle of a leaf. Then one of the Five stepped up to the road and stood almost within reach.

"*She is our friend too,*" the fifth one said.

Hearing the warning, he nodded. "Vicki has many friends. She also has enemies."

"*Humans.*" She made the word sound like something cursed.

Aiden nodded. "Humans, yes. But there might be enemies among the *terra indigene* too. It would be good if Vicki's many friends remain close enough to hear a call for help."

She stepped away from the road, gone.

He wondered how long it would take the Five to tell the rest of the Elders that there were humans, and possibly some *terra indigene*, who posed a risk to the Reader. He wasn't sure what the Elders would do to any *terra indigene* involved in this trouble, but he didn't wonder what would happen to any human in The Jumble whose actions weren't easily understood. Not when the Five were among the Elders keeping watch.

When he heard the car, he stepped into the road far enough for Vicki to see him.

She stopped the car. He opened the passenger door and got in.

"I know we aren't exactly friends, but we are friendly," Vicki said.

"That is true," Aiden agreed.

"It was suggested that I share some information with someone whose form could not be compromised by substances that might alter their behavior."

"This is a trusting?"

Vicki nodded. She turned off the car, undid her seat belt, unbuttoned her coat, and then turned her body this way and that until she finally removed a piece of paper from her pocket. She handed him the paper and looked . . . flustered . . . and he wasn't sure why. She did not have the sinuous grace that was common in so many *terra indigene* forms, but she was human, so no one expected it.

Perhaps not expecting it was considered rude among her kind?

Aiden opened the paper and read the list of words and phrases. Some meant nothing. Others . . . "Where did you get this?"

"Meg from Lakeside called me. She spoke. I listened and wrote down the words."

He studied this human female who thought she was ordinary and didn't understand how many things she did weren't ordinary at all.

"Someone came into my office when I was unwell and tried to find out what I'd written down," Vicki said. "They didn't find out, but the fact that someone tried means I can't trust anyone staying in the house or the cabins. But someone else needed to know about this in case . . ."

"Julian Farrow?"

"Human body. He would help me, but he could be hurt. Or compromised."

COPS. FANGS. BETRAYAL.

Her hesitation to show this list to Chief Grimshaw or Ilya Sanguinati made sense now. He didn't think Ilya would betray Vicki, but there was that predator of predators staying in the area, and that suggested a fight among the Sanguinati. And this warning *had* come from Broomstick Girl.

Aiden pointed to the line that read, PROBLEM SOLVER. ALLY. "His name is Stavros. He will help you."

"How do you know?"

"I met him. He said he was a problem solver and that he would help you."

She nodded. "I'd better get these groceries up to the house before my guests start thinking nibbling on dead donkey is a good idea."

Even for a human, she said the most peculiar things. That's why he found her appealing.

Aiden returned the list and got out of the car. Vicki did her gyration to shove the paper back in her pocket before she put on the seat belt and started the car.

He watched her drive away.

There were things he could have explained about other parts of that prophecy, but he thought the outcome, good or bad, would depend on Vicki's ability to understand Broomstick Girl's message on her own.

CHAPTER 81

Grimshaw

Moonsday, Novembros 5

Using pliers to pull out his own toenails wouldn't be as painful as listening to this college admin's evasions and justifications and blah blah freaking blah as the woman tried to deny that his query was legitimate and she should give him the information he'd asked for, which should have been public information that could be found in the college's catalog if he had time to request one and wait for it to be mailed.

But he didn't have time and he lost his last shred of patience, so Grimshaw said, "Ma'am, I will say this once more. This is a murder investigation, and Richard Cardosa is a person of interest. I want to know what he teaches at your college, or what his field of study is if he doesn't actually teach. Either you provide me with this information in the next five minutes or I'm going to hang up the phone, and the next people who are going to ask you for that information will be standing in your office, will have Sanguinati as their last name, and will be much less polite. Do you understand me now?"

Bleating and tears. And an odd refusal to believe.

He wondered if this was an example of brainwashing.

Grimshaw looked up as Ilya walked into the station. He waved the vampire over to his desk, then held out the phone. "Tell her who you are and that you'll bite off her face if she doesn't give me the information I asked for."

Even with the receiver held between them, they heard the woman shriek before she started to babble.

Ilya took the phone. "This is Ilya Sanguinati. I will not bite your face off, no matter what Chief Grimshaw says. The Sanguinati have specialists who take care of things like that. Now, don't hang up or we will be very unhappy with you. Simply scream for your superior and put him on the phone. The clock is ticking. Tick. Tick."

Fortunately for both their eardrums, Ilya was in the process of handing him the phone when the woman screamed for help.

"Tick, tick?" Grimshaw said.

The next voice was male. Not calm but not in a complete state of panic.

Grimshaw repeated his request and emphasized that this information was part of a murder investigation.

"I see," he said as he wrote down what he was told. "No, there's no reason to acknowledge where I came by this information. I appreciate your assistance."

He hung up the phone, sat back, and stared at Ilya. "Richard Cardosa's contract with the college was not renewed because of some questionable behavior that might have been connected to the emotional deterioration of several students in his classes, including two whose deaths are still under investigation even though the official verdict was 'death by *terra indigene*.'" He continued to stare. "The woman on the phone. Did she remind you of anyone?"

Ilya shook his head. "But I'd have to be starving to spend more than a minute in the same room with her." He paused. Considered. "Of course, if I was starving, I wouldn't need much more than that before she lost enough blood to make her quiet."

Grimshaw filed that bit of information away with the other things he'd rather not know about the Others but needed to know to do his job—and stay alive.

No reason for any of the Sanguinati to have encountered the village troublemaker. In fact, Grimshaw would bet Ellen C. Wilson made every effort to avoid being noticed by the residents of Silence Lodge while she manipulated her way through Sproing's businesses.

Picking up the phone again, Grimshaw called Lettuce Reed. "Julian? I need you at the station right now. Make sure you're carrying." He hung up.

"Am I supposed to understand this?" Ilya asked.

"You will." Grimshaw waited until Osgood walked into the station, quickly followed by Julian. "Officer Osgood, you and our deputized citizen are going to the home of Ellen C. Wilson to arrest her. You will also bring her son, Theodore, in for questioning."

Osgood bounced as if he'd been stabbed in the ass. "Chief? Shouldn't you do that?"

"No, you should do that because I told you to."

"I'm not a cop," Julian said.

"You're a deputized citizen. Osgood needs backup who can move if he needs to move. My knee won't hold up to that today, so you're it."

"I have a business to run," Julian argued.

"Boris is sitting outside in the sedan. He can watch the store and answer the phone." Grimshaw looked at Ilya. "Right?"

"Right," Ilya replied. "Boris could even make up a new window display. Books about body trauma, perhaps. That would go over well when one of the Sanguinati is standing behind the counter."

Grimshaw ignored the snarky tone, mostly because he was tired enough and hurting enough that the proposed window display held a lot of appeal—especially if it encouraged Sproing's residents to behave.

"What am I supposed to tell Mrs. Wilson?" Osgood asked.

"Yes, Chief," Ilya said. "What is Officer Osgood supposed to tell her that you haven't shared with us?"

Grimshaw looked at the leader of the Sanguinati, then at the other two men. "You can tell Ellen Cardosa Wilson that she's being brought in as an accessory to murder."

CHAPTER 82

Julian

Moonsday, Novembros 5

Do you think Ellen Wilson is related to that professor staying at the Mill Creek Cabins?" Osgood asked as he drove to the woman's house. "I mean, Cardosa isn't that common a name. Maybe in Hubbney or Toland, but not around here. Do you think she's really involved in those killings?"

"I'm not thinking," Julian said. *Not about anything I'm willing to discuss right now,* he added silently. What he was thinking about circled around one word: brainwashing.

Humans couldn't fight the *terra indigene* and survive. The Great Predation last year proved that. But what if you could find individuals among the *terra indigene* who were malleable and rebellious enough that they could be turned against their own kind? What if you discovered a talent for manipulation and control, perhaps had an Intuit ancestor and had inherited just enough of that ability to sense what other humans couldn't see, and used it to exploit other beings?

Cardosa and Roash had worked at the same college. That's why they were sharing the cabin leased to that college. On Trickster Night, Roash had told Julian how he'd convinced Cardosa to come with him to observe the Others. Had Roash really done any convincing, or had Cardosa deftly inserted himself into Roash's plans in order to use the man's interest in the Crowbones folklore as a way to study fear that could be generated in the Others? If everything had gone as planned, Adam Fewks would have played his role as Crowbones and disappeared, all the academics would have left last Firesday, and the police, having no leads except the intensity of Roash's interest in the subject matter, would have put it down as a prank.

Maybe the other things that had happened since Trickster Night had been intentional. Maybe they had been nothing more than someone taking the opportunity to cause more mischief. But when the Elders and Elementals closed off the area in order to hunt down a contamination, the mischief makers had escalated their efforts, trying to create sufficient turmoil so that they could escape.

And what better place to create turmoil than at The Jumble, which was its own kind of experiment of humans and *terra indigene* working together?

Then again, Julian still wondered if things would have escalated so fast and with such ferocity if the trouble *hadn't* started at The Jumble.

Osgood pulled up at the Wilsons' house, blocking the driveway. Two people—one from across the street and the other next door—rushed toward the police car the moment Julian and Osgood stepped out.

"I just called the station," the man said, holding up his mobile phone.

"I was about to call," the woman said, also holding up her phone.

"Lots of shouting," the man said. "More than usual. But just Mrs. Wilson. Haven't heard Theodore."

"I think he's in the house," the woman said. "But he's a quiet boy. Never has much to say for himself when he's outside."

Julian felt the hair rise on the back of his neck and fought the urge to look around. Something out there, watching them. Something powerful—and silent. By all the gods, had Ilya contacted one of the Elders, or was this one here for its own reasons?

Or was he jumping at shadows?

No. He was an Intuit. He didn't jump at shadows unless the shadows hid something. Something dangerous.

"Did you hear the shouting from the front of the house or the back?" he asked.

"Back," the woman said. "And Mrs. Wilson—you *never* call her Ellen—was louder than usual. I couldn't make out what she was saying because my dog goes nuts when he hears her voice, so all I heard was the angry tone."

The man nodded agreement. "I was at the curb, putting some bottles in the recycling bin, and I could hear the shouting. And then the dog."

And yet neither of these neighbors had approached the house to find out what was going on. They had called the police rather than check on Ellen Wilson on their own.

"Go inside your houses and stay there," Julian said quietly, trying to remain in the here and now and not slip back into the memory of an alley where he was badly wounded and bleeding—and had felt the presence of . . . something . . . that slaughtered the men who had been trying to kill him. "Walk calmly. Do it now."

The two neighbors jerked, had that look of panic when they realized what he was saying.

"Calmly," he said again. "You helped the police by providing information and now you should go back inside your houses." He looked at the woman. "And get your dog inside."

Osgood stared at him, all the color leaching from his brown skin.

"You good?" Julian studied the rookie once the neighbors had headed back to their houses.

"Is one of . . . them . . . here?" Osgood asked.

"Maybe. That's not our concern." Until it *was* their concern—or until one of them was dying because he had miscalculated the reason for *terra indigene* presence.

Julian started up the driveway, then stopped, looked toward the corner of the house where he sensed that presence, and said quietly, "We're going to enter the house by the back door. It would help the police—and Miss Vicki—if anyone who tried to escape out the front door was contained so that Chief Grimshaw and Ilya Sanguinati can question them."

No answer. He didn't expect one. But his sense of place gave him strong feelings that within the boundaries of this house and yard, any and every human was on dangerous ground. He just hoped whatever watched them understood about containing in a way that meant *still alive*. And he hoped no one thought to ask him how Vicki figured into apprehending

this woman. He just used her name in the hopes of getting interested assistance instead of a violent response.

With Osgood beside him, Julian headed around the house to the back
door. He hadn't heard Ellen Wilson since they'd pulled up to the house.
Now the ranting began again.

"You stupid boy! You stupid, stupid boy! I *told* you. Didn't I tell you?
And now look what you've done, after all the years I invested in you!"

The glass storm door was closed but the kitchen windows and the
wooden door that provided entry into the kitchen were open despite the
brisk temperature. Julian drew his weapon, quietly opened the storm
door, and rushed inside. Then he froze for a moment as he took it all in.

Theodore, on the kitchen floor, eyes staring, flecks of foam around his
mouth. A broken cookie jar on the floor next to him, cookies broken or
crushed around him.

"Osgood, call the EMTs," Julian said as he went down on one knee to
see if he could find a pulse—although the smell of voided bladder and
bowels was evidence enough that he wouldn't find one—his eyes never
leaving the red-faced, wild-eyed woman. "What happened?"

"I told him I made those cookies for the neighbor's nasty little dog,"
Ellen Wilson shrieked. "I told him he wasn't allowed to eat any of them.
I *told* him! But he snuck in the kitchen and gobbled some, the greedy pig.
And now look. *Look!* Years of effort *ruined.* Now I'll have to find another
one and spend all those years training it until it's old enough to be useful."

Find another one? Julian stared at the woman and thought, *Oh gods.
What has she done? How many children has she "found" over the years? And
where are they?*

"EMTs are on their way," Osgood said.

Julian nodded. "Read Mrs. Wilson her rights and handcuff her."

"You have no right!" Ellen Wilson shrieked. "Get out of my house—
and take *that* with you!"

Out of the corner of his eye, Julian saw Osgood stare at the woman,
then at the dead boy. And he saw the rookie harden just a little more as
her words sank in and he realized why this woman was treating the boy
who was supposed to be her son like a broken tool that was easily disposed
of and replaced.

"It's your fault, you know," Ellen Wilson snarled, spitting the words at

Julian while Osgood put the cuffs on her. "If all the visitors had been allowed to leave, none of this would have happened. But you just had to go and muck up everything because you're just so stupid." She looked at Theodore and started laughing. "Yeah. This one was stupid too. Stupid and too *willful* to live. All those little acts of defiance. Like eating cookies when I told him not to. Not like my other boys, my lovely monstrosities." Her eyes fixed on Julian, full of hate. "But I lost them too—because of you."

Monstrosities.

Julian thought about the four teenagers who had come to The Jumble looking to cause trouble. "Your . . . experiments . . . were killed when they tried to blow up Chief Grimshaw and Ilya Sanguinati?" He wondered if three of those boys had killed the fourth. Because they wanted to? Or because she had told them to?

"Dead now." She looked irritated. "Then again, when I sent them to the cabins, they had a fifty-fifty chance of getting it right, and they *still* killed the wrong man, so they weren't that useful anyway."

She blinked, looked at Julian—and started raving again about Theodore being a greedy boy.

Julian holstered his weapon and pulled out his mobile phone as he followed Osgood and Ellen Wilson to the patrol car. The presence, whatever it had been, had left. Thank the gods for that.

Seeing the EMTs arrive, he waved them toward the back of the house. "Wayne? We've got a problem."

CHAPTER 83

Vicki

Moonsday, Novembros 5

Victoria?" Natasha sounded furious. "Viktor just attacked Lara. I stopped him before he did much harm, but I had to stay with her, and he got away. I think he's heading for your side of the lake. You have to be careful."

My brain stuttered for a moment. "Viktor? But he's . . ." So solid. So polite. So helpful. So dependable.

Aren't those all the things an enemy intent on infiltrating a protected place would try to be?

"Are you hurt?" I asked, since that was the important question. "Have you told Ilya?" Next important question.

"Ilya needs to find the traitor and protect our allies," she snarled. "I and the other Sanguinati will defend Silence Lodge." She hung up.

Okeydokey. I put the receiver back in the cradle.

Natasha didn't say she *wasn't* hurt, but she wasn't going to tell Ilya about the attack, because he would go rushing back to Silence Lodge to protect his mate—which sounded reasonable and romantic, except Natasha was one ticked-off vampire right now and probably would bite him for showing up, and that bite wouldn't be one he enjoyed.

But she didn't actually say *I* couldn't tell Ilya. On the other hand, she might think telling her mate was a betrayal of girl friendship or something.

So I called Grimshaw. "Hey, Chief."

"Vicki, this isn't a good . . . ," Grimshaw began. A pause before he continued in Wary Official Police Voice. "What can I do for you?"

"Is Ilya with you?" I figured the faster I said it, the more I could say before I lost his attention. Assuming I had his attention. But . . . trouble magnet, so I probably had more of his attention now than I wanted. "Tell Ilya he really, really shouldn't go tearing home, because Natasha has already handled the trouble at Silence Lodge, and if he goes tearing home to rescue her, he's going to end up bunking with you until she gets over being mad at him, because *he's* supposed to find the traitor and protect the Sanguinati's allies." Which, come to think of it, could be Grimshaw since he and Ilya were definitely allies.

A beat of silence. A deep breath in, a deep breath out. "Vicki." Stern Police Voice. "Are you talking about Richard Cardosa?"

"The professor? No, it was Viktor who attacked Lara. Natasha said he was headed for this side of the lake, so I guess he's on the run and Ilya needs to find him."

"Where are you? Specifically."

"The main house."

"Stay there. Do you understand me? Tell Cougar and Conan that you're in danger, and they need to stay close."

"But I'm not—"

"If Viktor is heading for The Jumble, he's coming to attack you. You got that? Right now you are nothing but prey."

Well, that made me feel special. "Okay, Chief. We'll batten down the hatches. Full speed ahead." Why did I say that? Who knows? It made sense to Anxiety Brain.

"Just be careful. I'll send what help I can." Grimshaw sounded sterner. I hadn't thought that was possible. Silly me.

I hung up and realized he didn't tell me to lock the doors and windows. I guess we both knew that wasn't going to do any good against a Sanguinati in smoke form. Then I wondered why Grimshaw thought I was the only one Viktor would attack. There were other humans at The Jumble. Maybe the rest of us could throw the Cornleys at Viktor when he arrived and then ask him if adultery had a taste. Sweet and spicy? Tart with an aftertaste of bitter?

Focus, Vicki.

I was about to go in search of Conan and Cougar when Eddie appeared in the doorway and said, "Have you seen Aggie and Kira?"

CHAPTER 84

Aggie

Moonsday, Novembros 5

"Where are we going?" Aggie asked, stumbling despite Kira's grip on her arm. "We shouldn't be out here."

Gonna gitcha.

"We're helping Vicki," Kira replied.

How were they helping Miss Vicki by walking toward the Mill Creek Cabins? And why did she feel so woozy and odd? She'd been feeling that way on and off since the night when they had stayed in Miss Vicki's apartment. Something had happened after she and Jozi and Kira had drunk some of the special juice that Viktor had brought for Kira before Miss Vicki and Julian Farrow came upstairs. Something that she couldn't remember. She couldn't shift quickly or properly into her Crow form. She knew that was very, very bad, but somehow she just couldn't seem to care about the bad.

And she couldn't understand why she felt odd and woozy but Kira looked glittery-eyed and excited.

"No offense to your kind, but those Crows the professor chose as his new helpers just weren't up to the job," Kira said. "The *only* thing they managed to do was get killed. Well, one of them *did* kill your friend, but that's not much of a thing, is it? Viktor and I helped *lots* of humans around the colleges die. The professor said we were his *best* students. Then he got annoyed with us. He said we'd done too much, drawn too much attention from the authorities, and they were asking questions about his experiments that he didn't want to answer.

"He left," Kira continued. "Left the college, left the town. Left us. That was a couple of years ago. We continued hunting for a while, but the leader of our shadow started asking questions too, became *concerned* that we'd been sneaking off to hunt on the college grounds. Then we heard the whispers about possible contamination from exposure to the wrong kind of humans." She scoffed. "The professor isn't the *wrong* kind of human. He's brilliant, and he showed us that hunting could be fun and feel *so* good when your prey feels too good to care what happens. Just like you and Jozi the other night."

Something in the flask that Viktor had given Kira? Something that made it hard for her to shift her form even now?

"I wanted to taste Vicki, but Julian Farrow got in the way of that. Julian and . . ." Kira shrugged, but she didn't seem as excited anymore. She kept looking around.

Waiting to hear the *rattle, rattle, rattle?*

Kira wasn't a friend. Not to Crows, not to Miss Vicki.

Had to warn Miss Vicki.

<Eddie? Jozi?>

"No!" Kira said sharply, giving Aggie a hard shake that knocked the thoughts right out of her head.

"Where are we going?" Aggie asked again.

"We're almost there," Kira said just before Aggie felt fangs tearing at her throat.

CHAPTER 85

Ilya

Moonsday, Novembros 5

Ilya stared at Grimshaw. "Viktor?"

"That's what Natasha told Vicki," Grimshaw replied.

But didn't tell me? <Natasha!>

<There is a reason you are the leader of Silence Lodge,> she said in response to his call. <Be the leader.>

Be the dominant predator among the terra indigene *forms who were not Elders or Elementals.* That's what she meant. That's why she had accepted him as her mate. The strongest. The most lethal among the Sanguinati living around Lake Silence.

If he failed, she might break with him and choose another as her mate.

Someone like Stavros, who wasn't mated yet.

Ilya shook off those thoughts. There was work—and death—to be done.

"As soon as Osgood returns, we'll pick up Richard Cardosa," Grimshaw said.

"You have no evidence that Cardosa killed Edward Janse," Ilya pointed out.

"I don't think he held the knife, but I believe he is involved in some kind of brainwashing or psychological manipulation and was the human

Eddie Crowgard saw talking with Civil and Serious Crowgard," Grimshaw argued.

"Circumstantial."

"Let's just bring him in. Then we'll worry about that."

Ilya sighed. "Unfortunately, Chief, I'm required . . ."

Julian walked into the station, followed by Osgood and a raving Ellen Wilson.

"You can't blame me," she shouted. "You *can't*. I *told* him not to eat those cookies. I told him!"

Grimshaw hurried to the cell in the back of the station and returned with Rodney Roash.

"You!" Ellen Wilson spit when she saw Roash. "You couldn't even do one little thing, could you?"

Roash looked confused. "I don't . . ."

"Put her in the cell," Grimshaw said.

"You can't!" Ellen Wilson yelled. "I have to make sure that stupid boy eats his macaroni and cheese."

Ilya started to step back. He was needed for a hunt.

Julian looked at Ilya and said quietly, "Ask your secret friend to go to The Jumble and keep an eye on things. And tell your people to keep an eye on your fosterlings."

"Natasha is already taking care of Lara," Ilya replied. But what about Kira? Would she be another casualty, or was she Viktor's ally? If she was . . .

<Stavros,> he called. <You're needed at The Jumble.>

<Already on my way there,> Stavros replied. <Hunters are gathering around the lake.>

Not good.

"Julian?" Grimshaw said as he returned to the front room.

Ilya turned his attention back to the trouble right in front of him.

"The Wilson boy was dead when we arrived," Julian replied. "Some kind of poison from the look of things, mixed into the cookies. They were intended for the neighbor's dog." He closed his eyes for a moment. "You should inquire about missing children near the towns where Ellen or Richard Cardosa lived. You should also ask about runaways in those towns because I don't think Theodore was Ellen Wilson's biological son. She said she *acquired* him."

Ilya stiffened as Julian's comment about keeping an eye on the Sanguinati fosterlings made a different kind of sense. "She *stole* that human boy?"

Julian nodded. "That's my guess. And he wasn't the first. She admitted that she had sent her 'monstrosities' to the cabins, and they killed the wrong man. I think she sent those boys out there to kill Richard Cardosa, her perceived rival." His mobile phone buzzed. He pulled it out of his jacket pocket and answered. "Hello?"

Ilya couldn't hear what was said, but the thin white scar on Farrow's left cheek faded as his face lost all color.

Julian ended the call. "That was Michael Stern. Vicki got a call from Kira saying Aggie was hurt and needed help. She went tearing out to find them and only told Michael where she was going because she literally ran into him when she dashed out the door."

"Crap!" Grimshaw said. "I told her to stay put."

"Someone used a friend to bait the trap. Did you really expect Vicki to sit still and wait for you?"

<Stavros,> Ilya called. <Have you reached The Jumble? Victoria is in danger.>

For a moment, there was no answer. Then the problem solver said, <I know.>

CHAPTER 86

Vicki

Moonsday, Novembros 5

I didn't run into the lake, and I wasn't standing on the road. Hopefully that meant I was dashing in the right direction to find Aggie and Kira before something else found the two of them. How we were supposed to get back to safety before that something found the three of us was anyone's guess, because I had no clue.

But I had sand. I surely did. And that's what I would tell Grimshaw when he started yelling at me for not following orders and staying inside. I would not have an anxiety meltdown because a large man with official cop doodads on his belt was yelling at me. I would tell him I had sand and went out to save my friends.

Would Ilya represent me if Grimshaw arrested me for not obeying orders? Which I wasn't required to do because I didn't work for him, so phooey on orders. Wayne Grimshaw was not the boss of me!

I stopped walking and wondered how long I'd been having this argument with myself, because now that I looked around, I had to admit that running off to find Aggie and Kira by myself had been foolish, especially since I'd left my mobile phone on my desk and couldn't call for help. And I had to admit that I really was in trouble, starting with being lost on my own property. Again.

CHAPTER 87

Aggie

Moonsday, Novembros 5

Hard to think. Hard to move. But she could listen, and that's what she would do. She would listen—and she would stay alive long enough to tell someone what she'd heard.

"Where is she?" Viktor's voice. Angry.

"I don't know!" Kira, the traitor, sounding upset. "I told her where to find us. She should be here!"

"He'll be disappointed in you." Viktor sounded pleased about that.

Who would be disappointed? Was there another traitor?

Sound. Someone walking through leaves.

Aggie turned her head just enough to look, to see, to remember.

Walking boots. Jeans. Muddy green coat.

This was the enemy the traitors obeyed. What had Kira called him? Professor.

Aggie couldn't attack and kill the enemy, but she hoped she lived long enough to peck out one of his eyes.

CHAPTER 88

Ilya

Moonsday, Novembros 5

Bloodhunter.>

Now it comes, Ilya thought as he and Grimshaw sped toward The Jumble. <Fire?>

<The last human who is staying in your cabins is missing. Twister and I are heading toward The Jumble from the direction of the cabins. Air and Fog are riding up from the main house after a human told Cougar that Vicki ran off to find Kira and Aggie.>

Kira. A willing betrayer of her own kind? Or a puppet that a human had used?

<We are not the only ones looking for Vicki,> Fire said. <There are many hunters in the woods today.>

<Understood.> Ilya didn't ask for details. He would be told soon enough.

"We're going to get there too late," Grimshaw said. "That's why you insisted that Julian stay in the village."

"Yes," Ilya said. "Whatever is going to happen will be done before we arrive, and he doesn't need to see . . ." Then he considered what Fire had said. <Aiden? Why is everyone looking for Victoria?>

When Fire told him, relief flooded through him. He smiled and turned to Grimshaw. "We may not be too late after all."

"Why is that?" Grimshaw said, spraying gravel as he turned into the access road for The Jumble.

"Because Victoria must have followed the directions she was given and gotten lost."

CHAPTER 89

Vicki

Moonsday, Novembros 5

Crap. Crappity crap crap.

Well, I did find a clearing, but I think I also found the septic tank for the main house and the lake cabins.

If I headed north from here, I should be heading for the Mill Creek Cabins and should reach the clearing where Kira said she and Aggie would be waiting.

Okeydokey.

Which way was north?

Finally!

I saw Aggie on the ground and ran to her.

"What happened?" I asked as Kira rushed toward me and grabbed my wrist, burrowing under sweater and coat sleeves to touch bare skin.

"I did like you, but you kept getting in the way," Kira said.

Natasha told me Sanguinati were often in their smoke form when they extracted blood from prey. Biting someone was more personal, more intimate. She also said the advantage of feeding in their smoke form was that the prey didn't notice the loss of blood.

She was soooo wrong.

Or maybe Kira was still too young to have sufficient skill, because I sure noticed the sudden drop in blood pressure as she fed off me.

I staggered. She released my wrist and grabbed my hair as she tried to pour the contents of a small bottle into my mouth.

Being Sanguinati, she was strong. But I had sand. I surely did.

I also had a healthy fear that if I was injured and survived, I would be given another transfusion of Grimshaw blood. Who knew what traits I would acquire from another dose of Grimshaw?

I knocked the bottle out of Kira's hand. Some of the liquid went down my throat as I choked and coughed and shoved her away from me. I fell on my hands and knees, too dizzy to stand. I was in trouble. So was Aggie, who looked terribly hurt, with her neck all bloody. But I started to feel good and just didn't care what was going to happen next, except to think it would be pretty interesting.

I didn't think blood loss would make you feel good, so my vote was drugs. Yep, probably drugs, since I swallowed some of the stuff in that small bottle.

"Adequate, Kira, but not stellar work," a male voice said.

I looked up and saw the muddy green coat first. Crappity crap crap. Then I looked at the face.

"Richard Cardosa," he said pleasantly. "Not that you'll remember."

Why not? Oh. I was going to be the next dead donkey. Phooey.

Just a point of information? A drug that is supposed to make you feel good cannot compete with terror. Terror will sober you right up. Or leave you gibbering. It's pretty much fifty-fifty.

For me, there was a moment of clarity as I stared at this man with the cruel smile and the eager look in his eyes—as I stared at Viktor, who stepped up beside him and looked just as cruel, just as eager. I had no chance of getting away from them, let alone getting Aggie somewhere safe. But I could give these killers and deceivers a moment of uneasiness. Maybe even a lifetime of looking over their shoulders.

I got to my feet and was proud that I didn't just fall over and land on Aggie. Then I said in my best "I got sand" voice, "Crowbones is gonna gitcha."

That's when things got weird.

CHAPTER 90

Moonsday, Novembros 5

She followed the scent of contamination or the whispers of other hunters or whatever it was that only she could sense—and he followed her until she touched his arm.

<You go. Protect,> she said, pointing in one direction. Then she pointed in a slightly different direction. <Contamination. I hunt.>

She simply disappeared into the woods, became a dreaded silence.

As he moved in the direction she'd pointed out, he heard voices, caught a glimpse of someone who was also moving toward a particular spot. Another Sanguinati?

His brain . . . blinked . . . and he forgot about the battle in the town of Bennett, the battle that had cost him so much. Forgot that he wasn't whole in so many ways.

He was a hunter again. A fighter again.

Protect is what she'd said. *Protect the Reader* is what she meant.

The Reader was just up ahead. In danger.

Then he saw them. All of them. And he heard the Reader say, "Crow-bones is gonna gitcha."

He heard the words—and he knew.

Gonna gitcha.

Enemy. Found.

CHAPTER 91

Them

Moonsday, Novembros 5

Richard Cardosa wanted to sneer at this last bit of bravado from a creature whose spirit had already been broken by an expert in gaslighting and mental abuse. He used those same techniques often enough, so he recognized the signs in someone who had been exposed to that kind of psychological alteration. Did she really think she was healing, that she was ever going to be able to cope with the world when it took so little to push her to the edge of panic and being unable to function? He couldn't figure out why this fat bit of nothing was so intriguing to the Others. She was *prey*, a broken thing he hadn't considered interesting enough to even toy with. And yet, because of her, he'd been trapped in this place with that idiot Roash—and with Ellen, who had decided to end their sibling rivalry by trying to kill off her rival.

Time to go. With the chaos his two bloodsucking helpers were about to create, it would be easy for him to slip away. He'd have to walk out in order to get past the barricades, but he was fit. He could do it. All the attention would be on his twisted, fanged darlings, who had been willing to be led and had been ripe for everything he could teach them. For a moment, he regretted their loss, but their enthusiasm had made them a liability a couple of years ago, and they were a liability now. He couldn't afford to let the cops or the bloodsuckers make a connection between him and Kira and Viktor.

But that fat bit of nothing said, "Crowbones is gonna gitcha," as she swayed from blood loss and the effects of the feel-good drug, and he, Richard Cardosa, felt cold sweat pool in his armpits, felt . . .

Rattle, rattle, rattle.

"*Monkey man,*" a voice sang from somewhere nearby.

"*Moooonkey man,*" another voice sang.

Rattle, rattle, rattle.

A snarl, and a sense of something moving toward him too fast.

Then thick fog covered the small clearing and he couldn't see anything.

"Deal with them," he told Viktor.

He turned and headed back the way he'd come, a straight line that would get him out of the fog.

Sounds of vicious fighting. Screams that might have been delicious if he'd still been the one controlling this project. But he had to get away now, had to . . .

The fog suddenly thinned, and the woman . . .

A face too symmetrical, too perfect, too *human* to be human. Then he saw the feathers entwined in the long black hair, and when her lips pulled back in a snarl . . .

CHAPTER 92

Vicki

Moonsday, Novembros 5

*R*attle, rattle, rattle.
  "*Monkey man,*" a voice sang from somewhere nearby.
"*Moooonkey man,*" another voice sang.
Rattle, rattle, rattle.

Fog so thick I couldn't see my hand—which meant, thankfully, I couldn't see anything else. Didn't interfere with my hearing, though.

I heard Cardosa give the order to deal with us. I think Viktor sprang at me, but something attacked him with a speed that gave him no chance to shift to his smoke form. So I heard him scream as squishy bits plopped on the ground and bones broke and broke and broke. It took only moments.

Kira grabbed at me, probably intending to drain me past saving, but something slammed into her and tossed her aside. That same something knocked me off my feet but caught one arm and eased me to the ground.

I didn't hear Richard Cardosa shout, so I figured he got away.

The fog thinned. I was sitting on the ground, partially hidden by a pair of legs in black trousers made from a fabric that probably cost as much as the entire population of Sproing made in a year. Okay, exaggerating a bit, but not the sort of fabric used for an off-the-rack suit. I looked up, confirming that the rest of the clothes were just as fine. Up a little higher to the dark hair and olive skin.

Sanguinati. Definitely.

"Can you stand?" he asked, his eyes fixed on something slowly coming toward us.

I thought about Aiden pointing out one line in a list of words and phrases. PROBLEM SOLVER. ALLY. "Are you Stavros?"

"I am."

He held out his hand. I took it and let him pull me to my feet.

"Vicki!" Grimshaw's voice, a ways away but coming nearer.

"Victoria!" Ilya, also a ways away.

But right in front of us . . .

"Hello, Nicolai," Stavros said gently.

Whatever had happened to this Sanguinati had been horrific, and the damage that I could see, especially to one side of his face and skull, made me think he would never fully recover. But he looked at me and made an attempt to smile as he held up a gourd and . . .

Rattle, rattle, rattle.

Not a threat. A warning to be alert, to be careful.

The female who came toward us . . .

It was possible for a being to be too beautiful. Her face, so painfully perfect, would give humans nightmares for generations. The rest of her . . .

I didn't need to see the short-handled scythe dripping blood from its tip or the feathers woven into her black hair to know I was looking at Crowbones. Predator. Elder. Destroyer. Protector?

FEATHERS AND BONES.
A NO SIGN OVER PITY.
LAKESIDE. PEACE.

When I saw Crowbones gently adjust the cape made of black feathers that Nicolai wore to hide whatever else was wrong with his body, I suddenly understood the message from Meg.

"She . . . cannot speak . . . human words," Nicolai said as if he had to struggle to find each word. "I speak . . . for us."

I saw Grimshaw enter the clearing—and I saw Ilya grab him to hold him back.

"I have a message from Broomstick Girl." I wrapped both hands around Stavros's arm so that I could say this before I fell down. "She said you should go to Lakeside. Both of you. You should stay in Lakeside over the winter and return to your work in the spring."

Crowbones might be an Elder who had lived a solitary existence as protector and predator, delivering her own kind of justice to *terra indigene* and humans alike, but she wasn't alone anymore. And neither was Nicolai, who would never be normal but had a purpose again. Had friendship. Had a partnership without pity.

"It would be my pleasure to drive you both to Lakeside and speak to Grandfather Erebus on your behalf," Ilya said.

"Nicolai?" Stavros said, his voice still gentle. "Is that acceptable to you?"

Nicolai looked at Crowbones. Then he looked at Ilya and Stavros. "It is . . . acceptable . . . to us." And then he looked at me and smiled. "We . . . will have . . . a new story . . . to share."

Okey . . . Oooh, no.

As Stavros lowered me to the ground, I realized Ilya, Stavros, and Nicolai were looking at me with various expressions of amusement and concern while Grimshaw stood a little apart telling the EMTs that I needed medical attention pronto.

"No Grimshaw blood," I pleaded. "I will drink orange juice until I turn orange, but I've got enough sand, so I don't need more Grimshaw blood." I explained this to Stavros since I was still clutching his sleeve. I might have been petting the fabric because it really did feel good, but I would deny that, I surely would.

"Ilya?" Stavros said, clearly looking to someone else for an explanation.

"When Victoria was badly injured this past summer and needed a transfusion, Chief Grimshaw donated the blood," Ilya explained. "Depending on how much blood she has lost now, she may need another transfusion."

The donor stepped up and stared at me.

I narrowed my eyes and stared back. Maybe. I was feeling a bit loopy at that point.

"What are you doing?" Stavros asked.

"I'm channeling my Grimshaw."

Grimshaw shook his head. "She's too out of it to understand a thing I say."

But still not so out of it to misinterpret the patented grim look that told me clear as clear that I was still in trouble. So I focused on Ilya. Both of him. "If Grimshaw arrests me for ignoring orders, will you still be my attorney?"

"If Ilya can't because of a conflict of interests, then I will be your attorney," Stavros said.

Ilya hissed, a sound of annoyance. Or warning. What happened to someone who tried to poach a client from a Sanguinati attorney?

I smiled at Stavros and said, "That is so nice of you to offer."

A lot of things happened after that, but I don't remember any of them because I sort of passed out at that point.

CHAPTER 93

Vicki

Windsday, Novembros 7

I woke up and found Ineke Xavier sitting in a chair beside the bed.

"What are you doing here?" I asked, trying to get my blurry vision to unblurry. "And where is here? Who's looking after your guests?"

"*Here* is your bedroom in your apartment at The Jumble," Ineke replied, marking her place in the book she'd been reading.

I blinked a couple of times and looked around. Yep. My place. My room. My bed. Yippee.

"My guests scurried off within ten minutes of being told the roads had reopened," Ineke continued. "So did your guests, except for Ian and Michael Stern. Ian's been offering free counseling to the Crows, as well as Lara Sanguinati, and Michael has been helping out around The Jumble, answering phones since Cougar snarled someone on the line into hysterics and Conan crushed one of the phones because it kept ringing. Julian purchased a new phone for your office. The receipt is on your desk."

"Okay, but what are you doing here?"

"I'm doing my turn at Vicki watching," Ineke replied. Her smile faded. "Kira almost drained you to the point of no return. You've been out of it for a couple of days. There has been someone here every hour since you were brought home. And Cougar has shown up every morning to stare at you and determine that you were not on the menu for breakfast."

Good old Cougar.

I sighed as what Ineke said sank in. "More Grimshaw blood."

She leaned forward and touched my arm as she grinned. "Xavier blood this time. Doc Wallace said Grimshaw was still recovering from his own blood loss and couldn't be a donor. And I pulled up just as the EMTs carried you out of the woods to their vehicle. Turns out I was an acceptable donor, so they hooked us up, and here you are."

"But . . . why were you there?"

"Someone named Aiden—scary guy but great hair—came to the boardinghouse and told me you needed blood or you would die, and the Elders and Elementals would be very unhappy with humans if that happened. I knew many humans in the village, so maybe I knew who had the kind of blood that would keep you alive. I remembered talking to you about this when you were recovering from your summer adventures and said I was a suitable donor. I got in my car and several *terra indigene* stood on the side of the road along the way and pointed me in the right direction. So there I was and there you were, and here we are now."

"Oh." I peeked under the covers, but someone had put me in a long nightgown and I couldn't see my legs.

"What are you doing?" Ineke asked.

"Looking to see if I acquired any tattoos with my Ineke blood."

"You don't get tattoos from a transfusion." She gave me a thoughtful look. "But if you're interested, there is a tattoo artist in Crystalton who has a gift for creating tattoos that are perfect for each customer."

"Oh, I don't know. Maybe." Hmm. "Has Grimshaw been here? Am I under arrest?"

"He's looked in and called a couple of times a day for status reports. Didn't say anything about you being under arrest. He grumbled something about fitting you with a tracking device, but your attorneys—both of them—went into full-fang mode and opposed that idea before they headed to Lakeside with some friends of yours."

Ineke didn't quite make it a question. She'd lived in Sproing long enough to know it was better not to talk about some kinds of friends who might have been staying in The Jumble.

"Natasha has checked in to see how you're doing, but she's been dealing with Lara's trauma of being attacked by one of their own kind," Ineke continued. "Boris has taken a turn at bedside vigil. And I was told there were five . . . beings . . . who kept watch for several hours the first night. No one but Julian actually saw them, but he stayed on guard in your sitting room to make sure no one disturbed them."

Wow. The Five had come to check on me.

That was more than I needed to know right now.

"You probably don't remember, but Julian kissed you," Ineke said oh so casually.

"What?" I yelped. He kissed me while I had unconscious breath?

"Mm. Just a touch of his lips to yours. Very sweet and romantic. You might let him try it again sometime when you're awake."

Having delivered her opinion about kisses, Ineke started telling me the village gossip, but I fell asleep and didn't hear most of it.

CHAPTER 94

Ilya

Windsday, Novembros 7

Ilya drove through the night, heading into the Addirondak Mountains. There were a few small shadows of Sanguinati tucked away in the wild country. Not an ideal situation for urban hunters, but the Sanguinati's presence was necessary because human prisons were built far away from human communities, and some form of *terra indigene* was needed to act as liaison between the prisoners and the people who drove the supply trucks.

Besides, the inmates provided sufficient sustenance.

"It wasn't my fault," Kira said, sounding young and bewildered. "Viktor f-forced me to do those things."

It wasn't easy to restrain or confine a being who could shift into smoke, but the Sanguinati had learned to do such things out of necessity. Sometimes evil found fertile ground, regardless of species.

Evil sat beside him as he drove to the place that Stavros had confirmed was still used for private discussions. He would never know if she had been corrupted by Richard Cardosa or if the human had simply found her a willing acolyte who helped him conduct various experiments in manipulating behavior and feelings because that had been her nature all along.

It no longer mattered. For the sake of the rest of the Sanguinati in the Northeast Region of Thaisia, he couldn't allow it to matter.

"And that professor . . . ," Kira began.

"Best not to talk about him," Ilya said, not interested in what lies she would tell about Richard Cardosa—or what truths she might tell.

He and Stavros, along with Natasha, Boris, Grimshaw, and Julian Farrow, had collected and pooled information from their various sources to create a kind of map of the destruction caused by Richard Cardosa's experiments in manipulation and control of other beings. In other words, brainwashing humans and *terra indigene* alike.

Cardosa was not alone in his interests, but it was impossible to say if Ellen Cardosa Wilson had developed a taste for such things on her own or if she was her brother's first experiment. Either way, she had left behind a trail of broken families, and several young boys who had been hastily buried each time she acquired a new test subject and left town.

Ilya wasn't concerned about Ellen Wilson. That was Grimshaw's territory and decision. But Kira . . .

He listened to her excuses and justifications and lies, saying little as he drove to the spot where he would finally say what had to be said.

So young to be so corrupt. He might have understood Kira targeting a human, even if that human was Victoria and the death of the Reader would have torn up more than Lake Silence. After all, humans were the Sanguinati's natural prey. He might have understood, to some degree, going after the Crowgard in The Jumble because they were too present and too curious and could easily reveal secrets. But Kira had tangled up Karol, using the methods she had learned from Richard Cardosa, as well as her own female attraction, to manipulate the Sanguinati adolescent and ultimately set Karol up to die in that explosion. Well, *he* was the primary target, but Karol had been positioned as the second choice.

Luck of the draw, Vlad had said when Ilya, Stavros, Nyx, Vlad, and Grandfather Erebus had met in Lakeside to discuss what had happened around Lake Silence. Some odd things had been happening to some of the Sanguinati young around the Feather Lakes—things the adults couldn't explain. There was concern that human contact prior to adulthood led to subsequent contamination that the Elders would not tolerate much longer—especially since the Sanguinati weren't the only form whose young had contact with humans and were exhibiting strange behavior. Sanguinati leaders decided to send a few youngsters to places that had the right blend of containment and human contact to find out if this change in behavior was specific to a place or if it was something that now threatened the Sanguinati as a whole. Lara and Karol had been sent to Silence Lodge as a kind of blind test since neither of them had shown signs of this strange behavior but some youngsters in neighboring shadows *had* been contaminated. Subtle changes, but changes nonetheless.

Ilya had not been informed that the fostering was more than it appeared on the surface, a fact he didn't appreciate—and a decision that, in hindsight, Grandfather Erebus admitted had been a mistake. If Ilya had known about the contamination sooner and the real reason Lara and Karol were at Silence Lodge, he would have viewed Kira and Viktor's unexpected arrival with justified suspicion—and Karol might still be alive.

As for Kira and Viktor . . .

Realizing that the Sanguinati leaders were getting too close to learning about their part in the suspicious deaths that were being investigated in towns around the Feather Lakes, Kira and Viktor chose Lake Silence as a destination because they thought it was small and dull and no one would look for them there. Their letters of introduction were full of false information that would make it difficult to trace them back to their home shadows if anyone tried to confirm they'd been chosen for this fostering.

If Adam Fewks hadn't dressed up as Crowbones and riled all the Elders, Kira and Viktor's plan to hide out at Silence Lodge might have worked.

Maybe they could have resisted their own natures for a while and continued the pretense of being courteous youngsters, but Richard Cardosa's coming to Lake Silence had put Kira and Viktor within reach of the mentor they felt had abandoned them, and that had overwhelmed caution—especially when Cardosa offered them doses of the feel-good drug in exchange for their assistance.

When Grimshaw and Julian Farrow searched the suitcases Cardosa left at the cabin, they found notebooks that contained records of Cardosa's experiments, written in code. They also found written instructions to Professor Roash on where to deliver the suitcases as a favor to a colleague.

Farrow was able to unravel enough about the manipulation of Sanguinati and Crowgard youngsters to give everyone who enforced the law around Lake Silence a good idea of what the "professor" had encouraged his subjects to do.

Ilya listened to Kira telling him how sorry she was, how it wasn't her fault.

Wasn't it? It no longer mattered if Cardosa had seduced a young Sanguinati female into playing these mind games just to see if he could, or if Kira, in the first flush of female seductive power, put herself in the path of this predator, choosing to join forces with him for the fun of harming others. What mattered was simple: Kira and Viktor had used Karol's feelings for Kira to maneuver the youth into rushing to Kira's "rescue" and ending up being killed when the flea market storefront exploded.

They had killed one of their own. For fun.

Viktor had attacked Lara to distract the Sanguinati adults in order to meet up with Kira and Cardosa—and kill Victoria.

Ilya turned off the paved road and drove to the end of a narrow gravel lane that ended at a tiny cabin. No smoke rising from the chimney. No lamps or flicker of candlelight.

Empty. But not abandoned. Arrangements had been made for privacy.

Ilya shut off the car and removed the key, dropping it on the mat between his feet.

"What are we doing here?" Kira asked, sounding young in a way he understood she hadn't been in a long time. Then her voice changed, her manner changed, and the look in her eyes held seduction as well as malice. "What do you want to do here?"

He looked straight ahead, but he was aware of her. Very aware of her.

"I have been the leader of Silence Lodge for several years now," he said quietly. "The shadow of Sanguinati who live there is small, of necessity, to maintain a balance with the available prey, and until a year ago, keeping watch over Sproing was, I admit, a boring assignment."

Kira smiled and leaned a little closer to him.

"But, you see, leadership of even a small shadow that keeps watch over a boring little village is a reward Grandfather Erebus gives for a specific kind of service rendered."

She leaned a little closer and stared at his neck. "What kind of service?"

"Until I became the leader of Silence Lodge, I was one of Grandfather's problem solvers." Ilya turned his head and looked into her eyes. "And you, Kira, have become a problem."

CHAPTER 95

Julian

Thaisday, Novembros 8

Julian stopped arranging a display of new books when Michael Stern walked in. "Want to sign a few copies of your latest?"

"Sure," Michael replied.

He studied the man who had been a friend in his youth. "But you didn't come in to browse."

"No. Well, that wasn't the only reason." Michael looked around. "Mostly used paperbacks?"

"This part of the store is more of a used-book exchange. Most of the new books are in the back."

"That doesn't make good business sense."

"It does if you notice the names of the authors. Although I think it's time to bring those books to the front." Julian removed a dozen copies of Michael's newest book and brought them over to the island.

"I'm not poaching," Michael said.

"Since books aren't rabbits, taking one is called theft, not poaching," Julian replied. But Michael didn't seem in the mood for teasing.

"I'm not sure if it's clear to Vicki yet, but I can see how you feel about her. I don't intend to be competition. It's just . . . It's time to leave Ravendell, and as a writer, I can live anywhere."

"And you're thinking of relocating here." Now this conversation was starting to make sense. "And you're thinking of staying at The Jumble."

Julian felt a twinge. Not jealousy, exactly, but he carried scars and a lot of emotional baggage. Michael carried neither. A steady, stable man who should be a better fit for helping Vicki with her own baggage.

Should be. But wasn't.

"You do realize Vicki only provides breakfast?" Julian said.

Michael grinned. "I got that part. And pizza and salad on cop and crime nights. I also got that the kitchen is a communal space and guests are free to make their own meals as long as they clean up after themselves." His grin faded. "I'm not sure I'm cut out to be a long-term resident of The Jumble—or this village, for that matter. But there's a good energy here, and some fresh inspiration. That's why I came in the first place, to have a chance to observe the Others up close."

"Got more than you bargained for." Julian opened the books in preparation for Michael signing them.

"I did. We did."

Julian thought about that for a moment. "Is Ian thinking of relocating too?"

Michael shook his head. "He's more rooted because of his existing commitments, but he would like to spend some time in Sproing. There's a need here, Julian, and Ian has a feeling he can help a few people."

A bitter smile. "Like me?"

"Maybe. Mostly he'd like to continue helping the Sanguinati and the Crows who were traumatized by what happened here." Michael hesitated. "You wouldn't fit in Ravendell anymore. I wondered why you didn't come back after you left the police force, but seeing you in this village, among these people? I don't wonder anymore. We were friends once. I'd like to think we still are. But the close friends you have now aren't people who write about characters who make brutal choices and carry them out. Your close friends *are* the people who make brutal choices and carry them out. And you're like them. That's why I wanted to know if you'd have a problem with me staying here over the winter, maybe longer."

"No, I don't have a problem with that," Julian said as Michael signed the books. "If you and Vicki can't come to an arrangement for renting one of her cabins, you can check with Ineke Xavier. You'll get meals at her boardinghouse. And there may be an opening at the Mill Creek Cabins. I heard the Sanguinati are implementing new rules for the universities that are renting their cabins."

"A lot of things to think about," Michael said, signing the last book.

Yes, Julian thought as Michael walked to the back of the store to look at the new books. *A lot to think about.*

CHAPTER 96

Grimshaw

Earthday, Novembros 11

Grimshaw met Captain Walter Hargreaves at a truck stop located between Sproing and Bristol. As usual, Hargreaves had arrived ahead of him.

Not many customers at this time of the morning, which was what he'd expected—and the reason he'd asked Hargreaves to meet him on an Earthday.

"I ordered the breakfast special for you," Hargreaves said.

"Thanks." He slid into one side of the booth moments before the food arrived.

The waitress distributed the plates and poured coffee before hustling to check on the customers in the other occupied booth.

"Read your report," Hargreaves said, applying butter and syrup to his pancakes. "You going to stand by it?"

"I am," Grimshaw replied.

Hargreaves nodded and focused on his meal for a minute. Then he drank his coffee, waited for the waitress to come by with a refill, and said, "Now tell me what really happened."

Two days earlier.

Fear was a powerful motivator, especially when Sanguinati paid a call on government officials and police chiefs received phone calls from sources who didn't supply any names, just a list of catastrophic consequences that would happen in the Northeast Region of Thaisia if police in other towns didn't help the police in Sproing find out about two humans named Richard Cardosa and Ellen Cardosa Wilson.

The information supplied wasn't new, but it was confirmation of what Grimshaw and Julian and Ilya had already put together.

Richard and Ellen Cardosa were siblings as well as sophisticated predators who had a taste and talent for psychological brutality and emotional torture that sometimes included physical abuse. Children went missing. Children were found in shallow graves in another part of the Northeast. And some survived Ellen's form of maternal care to become her "monstrosities" and carry out their own forms of brutality—brutality enhanced by drugs Ellen provided as rewards.

Richard didn't want the messiness of living with his subjects, but working at colleges gave him access to youngsters who were the right age for his experiments—and gave him access to the *terra indigene* youth who were drawn by curiosity or hunger to that herd of malleable humans. That was where the contamination of Crowgard and Sanguinati started, but Cardosa always moved to another college in another town before a connection was made between him and the violence and suicides taking place among students.

Grimshaw's insistence on knowing where new residents had lived before coming to Sproing put pressure on Ellen Cardosa Wilson, especially after the Elementals locked down the entire area to prevent the Trickster Night visitors from leaving. Suddenly her "monstrosities," whom she had summoned to Sproing, were trapped and were not only colliding with some of Richard's subjects—they were *colluding* with them. That had infuriated her enough to give her boys a hefty dose of gone over wolf and send them out to eliminate her rival.

Richard Cardosa was Deceased, Location Unknown, and that DLU form was sent to the last college where Cardosa had worked, as well as to the authorities in that town who would have the futile task of finding and informing next of kin.

Ilya pointed out that they had circumstantial evidence that supported what they believed about Ellen Cardosa Wilson, but where could she stand trial, and for what specific crime? Since Ellen often claimed Theodore became ill after eating something from the diner or the Pizza Shack, she could say that her ravings when Julian entered her house were due to distress that her son had eaten cookies and had an allergic reaction. They couldn't find a convenient box of poison to prove she'd intended to kill the neighbor's dog.

They couldn't prove she had snatched children and disappeared with them over and over, always moving to set up in a small village and play her manipulation games with business owners and neighbors. They couldn't prove Tom Saulner and his friends had been youngsters that Ellen had released from her care because they were damaged enough, and still dependent enough, to commit atrocities to please her.

They couldn't *prove* anything. They'd even asked Paulo Diamante, the village's human attorney, to review the material. He was appalled by what they had found, but he agreed that it was all circumstantial, and he couldn't see Ellen Wilson successfully being convicted of any crime in a human court, especially if she went into court sounding like an emotionally unhinged woman with a tenuous grasp on reality.

They couldn't keep her in the cell in Sproing, and the other towns where she had lived vehemently refused to keep her in their jails, not with the lockdown of Sproing being fresh in the mind of every human official.

Nothing they could do but let her go and watch her move on.

That was what Grimshaw, Julian, and Ilya believed.

That was when the phone in the police station rang and Grimshaw answered it.

He knew those voices. They crept into his dreams some nights.

"*Grimshaw.*"

"*Griiiimshaw.*"

He wrote down the instructions—the roads, the route, the place where he was supposed to leave Ellen Wilson. The place where she would receive a different kind of justice.

Saying nothing to Julian and Ilya, he left Osgood in charge, put Ellen Wilson in the back of his police cruiser, and drove away from Sproing.

He followed the roads, the route, recognizing where it would lead. He was complicit in what was about to happen, but he couldn't see a way around it. Human law had checks and balances, and that was right and necessary. But sometimes it failed when viewed through the eyes of the *terra indigene*. One or many? Not the first time he'd made a choice, and it wouldn't be the last. But it was the first time he'd made such a choice about someone he knew by name, even if he didn't like her.

As he drove, she talked and talked and talked, her voice finding the crack in his resolve and working it open, working it open, telling him what he already knew—that delivering her to the Others wasn't a human, or humane, thing to do. She should be punished for not taking better care of Theodore. She should go to prison.

Talking and talking and talking, and he couldn't keep that voice out of his head. It drilled into his brain until he finally saw reason. She needed to go to a human prison and be punished in a human way.

When he was within sight of one of the prisons, he put on the flashers and turned off the cruiser, resisting the urge to drive right up to the gates. While Ellen Wilson demanded to know what was going on, Grimshaw opened the back door and said, "End of the line."

She got out, a look of triumph in her eyes.

Uneasy, he got back in the cruiser, locked the doors, and turned back the way he'd come, leaving her standing in the middle of the road.

Something wrong. That look of triumph in her eyes.

He wasn't supposed to leave Ellen C. Wilson within sight of a human place. He was supposed to take her on a long ride into the wild country. This wasn't the bargain he had made with the Five.

Talking and talking and talking, her voice like a drill piercing his brain and changing his intentions, leaving him to explain why he had defied the instructions he'd received from Elders.

He was a strong-willed man, but she'd gotten to him, had found that tiny chink of doubt that he was doing the right thing by handing her over to a brutal justice.

If she could wear him down enough for him to alter his intentions in just the time it had taken to drive to this place, what could she do with all those prisoners in a few weeks' time? And how many people would die because of what she might do here?

He stopped the cruiser and watched her in the rearview mirror. Watched her marching up the road toward a place that was considered neutral ground.

Grimshaw opened his door, stepped out of the vehicle, and shouted, "That female stole human children and killed them."

He got back in the cruiser and let the vehicle roll forward as he kept his eyes on the rearview mirror.

He never saw what snatched Ellen Wilson off the road and took her into the trees. All he saw was her dress and coat as a blur of color before she disappeared.

The *terra indigene* didn't kill their young unless a youngster became warped in a way that threatened the rest of their kind. For them, what Ellen Wilson had done made her the very worst kind of human, and the Elders who guarded this road and kept watch on the humans had done what human justice couldn't do.

And in the end, he had done what the Five had told him to do in order to protect the people in Sproing.

Present, Earthday

Grimshaw drank coffee turned cold.

"Hard decisions," Hargreaves said quietly.

"Yeah. But easier to live with than doing nothing and having a hundred other people die," Grimshaw replied. "Possible contamination brought in by these newcomers. A threat to the *terra indigene* settlement at Lake Silence."

"Some of those newcomers are going to run back to wherever they came from."

He nodded. "I imagine some are already packing up after seeing how fast a place like Sproing can be cut off from everything human."

Hargreaves studied him. "It was easier for you being on highway patrol."

"In a lot of ways. But the hardest thing about all this will be calling Theodore's family. Julian Farrow, Ilya Sanguinati, and Paulo Diamante are going through the information other police stations have sent, and they'll find the boy's parents. Then I'll have to call those people and tell them we found their son, but not in time."

Grimshaw took some cash out of his wallet and set it at the end of the booth to pay the bill. "Those people will grieve again for what they lost, but if they understand what a DLU form is and what it means, I think they'll take some comfort in that."

EPILOGUE

Vicki

Michael and Ian Stern, Ineke Xavier, and I reached an agreement. Ineke pointed out that winter around Lake Silence wasn't prime tourist season—yet—and she'd be willing to rent her best en suite room to Michael at a reduced rate if he committed to renting the room for the whole season. Which he did.

Then she encouraged Michael to rent one of the lake cabins from me as his writing room for the same amount of time. Michael agreed to do that if he could share the cabin with Ian, who had rearranged his prior commitments so that he could be in The Jumble a couple of days each week to offer counseling to the *terra indigene*—or any human brave enough to come to The Jumble to talk about their fear of things that would eat them.

As part of his rent for the lake cabin, Michael offered to help with phone calls, reservations, and guests at The Jumble—when and if we had any. I offered to drop his rent a little more if I could read the chapters of his new book as he wrote them.

He said no.

Aggie would recover, but it would take a while. We weren't sure why, but she wasn't able to fully shift from human form to Crow or from Crow back to human, which meant her human form didn't look all that human, and she didn't want to be around strangers. That was one reason Michael had offered to help out at the reception desk, since Eddie was my only functioning, non-scary employee at the moment.

Aggie, even more than Jozi, needed time to recover.

I didn't ask what had happened to Kira. Ilya had a look in his eyes that matched the look in Grimshaw's, and they—and Julian—played more pool together than their usual weekly gathering. More like a survivors' club where they chalked cues instead of talking about . . . anything.

To help with her recovery, Lara Sanguinati came to The Jumble once a week with Ilya or Natasha for our young-readers book club, which consisted of Lara, my employees, various residents of The Jumble, and Michael or Julian, who, along with me, provided the human element. Sometimes Dominique Xavier joined us to talk about a Wolf Team story, but I noticed she came only when it was Michael's turn to be the human male in the group, so I think she was more interested in the writer than in the stories.

Michael reworked my brochure for a winter package, pointing out that the bridle paths through The Jumble would also be great for cross-country skiing. I'm not sure if we'll get any bookings, but it's worth a try—as long as the *terra indigene* don't see humans on skis as a new toy to chase and nibble.

Julian found a couple of snow gliders—round thingies that were smaller and more lightweight than wooden sleds and could be used for sliding down a hill. The first day we got a few inches of snow, Lara and the Crows were out on the slope that ended at the beach, sliding and laughing until the adults standing watch got cold and made them all come inside.

Sproing and all the residents who lived around Lake Silence would recover, but I don't think anyone will forget again how fast the *terra indigene* react to a threat—or who comes calling when humans don't behave.

Two weeks after I was "almost dead donkey"—a phrase I'm sure will never be forgotten—two boxes arrived from the Lakeside Courtyard. One was filled with baked goods from a place called Nadine's Bakery. The other was filled with new books. I'd heard of some of the authors but hadn't purchased their newest titles because I didn't want Julian to feel obliged to underwrite my book-buying habit more than he already did. And there were some authors I'd never heard of and wasn't sure Julian had either, because the publishers were located in other parts of Thaisia.

When it came to books, someone in Lakeside had a very good pipeline. Inside the box with the books was a note. An apology of sorts that read:

Ilya told Vlad that I scared you so much I made you sick, and Meg says I should tell you I'm sorry.

Meg was bleeding, so I'm not sorry I snarled.

Now that Nicolai has told us the story about how you helped him and the Hunter even though you were almost dead donkey, I am a little sorry I snarled at you. (Since everyone agrees that you're human, we don't understand about the donkey. Must be a human thing.)

Vlad and I are sending you these books as a way to say sorry for snarling at you and making you sick. I will try not to snarl next time, if there is a next time.

—Simon Wolfgard

P.S. Meg said I need to work on how humans say sorry. I said giving you books is better.

As I tucked in on cold nights with a cup of hot chocolate and a book—and sometimes with Julian as well—I decided I liked Simon Wolfgard's way of apologizing just fine.

GEOGRAPHY
AND OTHER INFORMATION

NAMID—THE WORLD

CONTINENTS/LANDMASSES

Afrikah
Australis
Brittania / Wild Brittania
Cel-Romano / Cel-Romano Alliance of Nations
Felidae
Fingerbone Islands
Storm Islands
Thaisia
Tokhar-Chin
Zelande

LAKES AND RIVERS IN THAISIA

Great Lakes—Superior, Tala, Honon, Etu, and Tahki
Feather Lakes / Finger Lakes (not all of them are named in this story)—
    Silence, Crystal, Prong, Senneca
River—Talulah / Talulah Falls

MOUNTAINS

Addirondak
Rocky

CITIES AND VILLAGES MENTIONED IN THE STORY

Bennett—western town near the Elder Hills
Bristol—human town located on Crystal Lake

Crystalton—Intuit town located on Crystal Lake

Ferryman's Landing—Intuit village located on Great Island

Hubb NE (aka Hubbney)—human-controlled city; the government for the Northeast Region is located there

Lakeside—human-controlled city on the northeastern end of Lake Etu

Putney—human town located on Prong Lake

Ravendell—human/Intuit town located on Senneca Lake

Sproing—human village located near Lake Silence

Talulah Falls—human city

Toland—human-controlled city on the East Coast

CALENDAR

DAYS OF THE WEEK

Earthday (a spiritual day and a day of rest)

Moonsday

Sunsday

Windsday

Thaisday

Firesday

Watersday

MONTHS OF THE YEAR

Janius

Febros

Viridus

Aprillis

Maius

Juin

Sumor

Messis

Frais

Grau

Novembros

Dormente

CAST OF CHARACTERS

HUMANS IN THE STORY

RESIDENTS OF SPROING

Horace and Hector Adams—owners of the stables

Sheridan Ames—owner of Ames Funeral Home, along with her brother Samuel

Jane Argyle—postmistress

Pops Davies—owner of the general store

Victoria "Vicki" DeVine—owner/caretaker of The Jumble and the Reader for the *terra indigene* settlement

Paulo Diamante—attorney

Julian Farrow—owner of Lettuce Reed

Fred and Larry—owners of the bait-and-tackle shop

Helen Hearse—manager of Come and Get It, the village diner

Gershwin Jones—owner of Grace Notes

Silas and Ethel Milford—fruit growers

Bertram Roundtree—mayor of Sproing

Dr. Steven Wallace—junior partner at the medical office; medical examiner

Ellen C. Wilson and her son, Theodore

Dominique Xavier—works for Ineke

Ineke Xavier—runs the boardinghouse

Paige Xavier—works for Ineke

Maxwell—Ineke's border collie (no one told him he isn't human)

POLICE

Captain Douglas Burke—patrol captain in Lakeside

Wayne Grimshaw—Sproing's chief of police

Captain Walter Hargreaves—patrol captain, Bristol Police Station
Detective Samuel Kipp—leader of the Bristol Criminal Investigation Unit (CIU)
Officer David Osgood—works with Grimshaw

GUESTS AT THE JUMBLE AND THE MILL CREEK CABINS

Richard Cardosa
Fred and Wilma Cornley
Edward Janse
Peter Lynchfield
Ben Malacki
Jenna McKay
Rodney Roash
David Shuman
Ian Stern
Michael Stern

THE REST OF THE HUMANS IN THE STORY

Meg Corbyn—blood prophet, Lakeside Courtyard
Constance Dane—Yorick Dane's second wife
Yorick Dane—Vicki DeVine's ex-husband
Adam Fewks—student
Greg O'Sullivan—agent in the Investigative Task Force
Tom Saulner—teenage boy; aka Hatchet Head
Jesse Walker—Intuit, Prairie Gold
Hope Wolfsong—blood prophet, Sweetwater

THE OTHERS (AKA *TERRA INDIGENE*)

Aiden—a Fire Elemental
Air—an Elemental
Bobcat—Lynxgard
Conan Beargard—Black Bear
Coyote—Coyotegard
Crowbones—Elder and Hunter
Agatha Crowgard (aka Aggie Crowe)

Civil Crowgard
Clara Crowgard
Eddie Crowgard
Jozi Crowgard
Serious Crowgard
Earth—an Elemental
Elders—old, powerful forms; are called Namid's teeth and claws
The Five—Elders
The Lady of the Lake—a Water Elemental
Robert "Cougar" Panthera—Panthergard
The Ponies: Fog, Twister, and Whirlpool
Boris Sanguinati—Ilya's driver
Erebus Sanguinati—leader of all the Sanguinati in the Northeast
    Region of Thaisia
Ilya Sanguinati—attorney; leader of the Sanguinati around Lake Silence
Karol Sanguinati—fosterling
Kira Sanguinati—fosterling
Lara Sanguinati—fosterling
Natasha Sanguinati—CPA; Ilya's mate
Nicolai Sanguinati—lived in Bennett
Nyx Sanguinati—lives in the Lakeside Courtyard
Stavros Sanguinati—leader of the Sanguinati in Talulah Falls; a
    problem solver
Tolya Sanguinati—leader of the Sanguinati in Bennett
Viktor Sanguinati—fosterling
Vladimir Sanguinati—lives in the Lakeside Courtyard; runs the
    bookstore with Simon Wolfgard
Sproingers
Water—an Elemental
Winter—an Elemental
Simon Wolfgard—leader of the Lakeside Courtyard; runs the bookstore
    with Vlad Sanguinati

ACKNOWLEDGMENTS

My thanks to Blair Boone for continuing to be my first reader and for providing encouragement and feedback in the story's roughest stage; to Debra Dixon for being second reader; to Doranna Durgin for maintaining the Web site; to Adrienne Roehrich for running the official fan page and Ashley Laxton for running the Anne Bishop Fans and Anne Bishop Fans—Spoiler Group pages on Facebook; to Jennifer Crow for luring me into the nonfiction section of bookstores and showing me all sorts of other possibilities to explore; to Anne Sowards and Jennifer Jackson for the feedback that helps me write a better story; to all the publicity and marketing folks at PRH who help get the book into readers' hands; and to Pat Feidner for always being supportive and encouraging.

A special thanks to all the friends who offered to let me use their names for characters in the Others' world. You know who you are.